PRAISE FOR THE NOVELS OF MARY BALOGH

SIMPLY MAGIC

"Absorbing and appealing. This is an unusually subtle approach in a romance, and it works to great effect."
—*Publishers Weekly*

SIMPLY UNFORGETTABLE

"When an author has created a series as beloved to readers as Balogh's Bedwyn saga, it is hard to believe that she can surpass the delights with the first installment in a new quartet. But Balogh has done just that." —*Booklist*

"A memorable cast . . . refresh[es] a classic Regency plot with humor, wit, and the sizzling romantic chemistry that one expects from Balogh. Well-written and emotionally complex." —*Library Journal*

SIMPLY LOVE

"One of the things that make Ms. Balogh's books so memorable is the emotion she pours into her stories. The writing is superb, with realistic dialogue, sexual tension, and a wonderful heart-wrenching story. *Simply Love* is a book to savor, and to read again. It is a Perfect 10. Romance doesn't get any better than this."
—*Romance Reviews Today*

"Balogh is a gifted writer. . . . *Slightly Tempted* invites reflection, a fine quality in romance, and Morgan and Gervase are memorable characters." —*Contra Costa Times*

SLIGHTLY SCANDALOUS

"With its impeccable plotting and memorable characters, Balogh's book raises the bar for Regency romances." —*Publishers Weekly* (starred review)

"The sexual tension fairly crackles between this pair of beautifully matched protagonists. . . . This delightful and exceptionally well-done title nicely demonstrates [Balogh's] matchless style." —*Library Journal*

"This third book in the Bedwyn series is . . . highly enjoyable as part of the series or on its own merits." —*Old Book Barn Gazette*

SLIGHTLY WICKED

"Sympathetic characters and scalding sexual tension make the second installment in [the Slightly series] a truly engrossing read. . . . Balogh's sure-footed story possesses an abundance of character and class." —*Publishers Weekly*

SLIGHTLY MARRIED

"[A Perfect Ten] . . . *Slightly Married* is a masterpiece! Mary Balogh has an unparalleled gift for creating complex, compelling characters who come alive on the pages." —*Romance Reviews Today*

A SUMMER TO REMEMBER

Web
of
Love

MARY BALOGH

A DELL BOOK

WEB OF LOVE
A Dell Book

PUBLISHING HISTORY
Signet mass market edition published April 1990
Dell mass market edition / July 2007

Published by Bantam Dell
A Division of Random House, Inc.
New York, New York

This is a work of fiction. Names, characters, places, and incidents either
are the product of the author's imagination or are used fictitiously. Any
resemblance to actual persons, living or dead, events, or locales is entirely
coincidental.

Dell is a registered trademark of Random House, Inc., and the
colophon is a trademark of Random House, Inc.

ISBN 978-0-440-24305-2

Printed in the United States of America
Published simultaneously in Canada

www.bantamdell.com

OPM   10   9   8   7   6   5   4   3   2   1

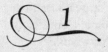

1

"WILL WE REACH BRUSSELS SOON, ELLEN? I must say, Belgium is a disappointment so far. It is so flat and uninteresting. Will Brussels be more exciting? I have dreamed about it all through the dreary winter at school. Is it as magical a place as they say?" Miss Jennifer Simpson sat with her nose almost touching the glass of the carriage in which she traveled with her stepmother. She was clearly not intent on waiting for answers to her questions. She had asked the same ones a dozen times since they had left Antwerp.

"It is just an ordinary city," Ellen Simpson said, "made extraordinary by the presence of so many allied troops at present and so many different uniforms. We will be there soon enough. You will feel better once you have seen your papa again. I know he can scarce wait to see you."

"Oh," Jennifer said, withdrawing her gaze for a moment from the passing scenery, "I still cannot quite believe that I am finished with school forever and ever, Ellen. I am eighteen years old, and this time I will stay with you and Papa, not be packed off back to school almost before I have started to enjoy myself."

Ellen smiled. "I know your papa is rather concerned about bringing you here," she said. "It was really too bad that Bonaparte was allowed to escape from Elba and that the King of France has fled to Ghent. I had hoped that the wars were over. But it appears that they are not. You may not be here for long after all, Jennifer. But I know your papa wanted you with him for a while."

"Oh, but the Duke of Wellington is here now," Jennifer said. "You told me so, and Helen West's sister wrote her that all would be safe once the duke arrived. And she also wrote that there are so many entertainments in Brussels that it is sometimes hard to choose among them. That is true, is it not, Ellen? And you helped me buy all those gorgeous clothes. And the city is full of officers and scarlet uniforms. It is a pity that Papa's uniform is green. It is not near as dashing as the Guards' uniforms."

"I am quite sure you will be here quite long enough to enjoy yourself," Ellen said. "I hope so. I know your papa wants to spend some time with you before he has to go into battle again."

"I suppose he thinks he might die," the girl said indignantly. "He should not be so gloomy. Papa has always come through safely."

"But there is always a grave danger that he might not," Ellen said quietly. "You do not know, Jennifer. Your papa always kept you away from the army, which was as well. You were never in Spain and did not see the battlefields after battles." She shuddered. "If you had seen, you would have marveled that anyone survived at all. Your papa has lived through so many battles. It does not seem fair that he must face yet another."

"I forgot." Jennifer laid a hand on her stepmother's arm, her pretty face contrite. "Your own papa was killed in one of those battles. And you were there with him. It must have been dreadful."

"Yes." Ellen patted the girl's hand. "It was. But at least he was killed instantly. That is a blessing one learns to be thankful for when one has lived close to battle."

Jennifer squeezed her stepmother's arm before removing her hand. "And you and Papa married," she said. "He is fond of you, is he not? I used to be jealous for a while. I think I even hated you until I met you. Do you think I will find a husband here, Ellen? Am I pretty enough, do you think?"

Ellen smiled into the anxious face turned to her own. "You know you are," she said. "But I would not be in too much of a hurry to fix your choice if I were you, Jennifer. Not with the times so uncertain. There is no point in inviting heartache."

They lapsed into silence while Jennifer gazed with renewed eagerness and impatience from the window. Indeed, the girl was very pretty, Ellen thought. She was small and shapely, with masses of shining dark ringlets peeping from beneath her bonnet, and an eager, dark-eyed, rosy-cheeked face. She would doubtless be a great favorite with the officers who thronged the drawing rooms and ballrooms of Brussels. And she would have all the entertainments and activities she dreamed of. Even before Ellen had left for England three weeks before, there had been an almost desperate gaiety about social life in Brussels. There was a great battle looming. She could feel it in her bones.

And though she looked with amused indulgence at the openly impatient girl turned to the window beside her, she found herself too looking eagerly from the window, trying to recognize landmarks, hoping to see one that would indicate they were close to Brussels at last. Close to home.

Not that Brussels was home, of course. But then, nowhere else was home either. She had not had a static home for ten years. Home was Charlie. And Charlie was in Brussels. She would see him soon. Three weeks she had been away from him. An eternity! She had never been away from him for so long, not since their marriage five years before. She felt tears prick at her eyelids as she gazed from the window.

Charlie was fifteen years her senior, forty to her five-and-twenty years. He was not at all the sort of man she would have expected to love, but she did love him with a fierceness that was almost a pain. He looked perhaps even older than his years. He was balding and portly, though not with soft living. He had been a soldier since he was sixteen, and had been hardened by rough living conditions, especially the almost indescribably harsh conditions of life in Spain during the Peninsular wars.

She had met him in Spain when she had gone there with her father, and he had always been kind to her. She had been fifteen years old at the time, and she had been bewildered, distraught over the events that had taken her there with a father who was a stranger to her, and unable for a long time to adjust to life lived in the tail of a vast army.

When her father had been killed in battle, Charlie had been the one to break the news to her, the one to comfort her, though by that time she had made a wide circle of friends. And they had married soon after. Perhaps it had seemed to some that it was a marriage of convenience on her part. And perhaps it was in a way. She certainly had not seemed to have anywhere else to go. But she had loved him even then, and her love had grown daily since. There was not a kinder man in the world than Charlie Simpson.

He treated her always as if she were a precious and treasured possession.

Ellen closed her eyes. She would not get there sooner by willing the miles to pass. Soon now she would see him again. She would feel his arms around her again. She would be safe again.

And once more she would begin the wait for yet another battle. Another battle that might take him away from her forever. They had talked of a home in the country in England when Napoleon had been finally defeated and exiled to the island of Elba. She might finally have had a life free of anxiety. It did not seem fair. Oh, it was *not* fair!

But for all that, life lived with an army was something that somehow got into one's blood. Charlie had not wanted her to come to Brussels with him. He had wanted her to stay in England. But how could she have done that? She would have been away from the only person in the world who really mattered to her. And she would have been away from her friends—Charlie's friends, and a few of their wives.

She liked to bring some of the comforts of home to those men who did not have wives. She was particularly fond of Lord Eden—Lieutenant Lord Eden—her husband's closest friend, and as different from him as night is from day. Lord Eden was her age; he was a baron, the younger brother of the Earl of Amberley; he was very handsome. He was tall, broad-shouldered, well-muscled, agile; and he had fair, wavy hair, distinctive green eyes, and a laughing, handsome face. He was wealthy, well-educated, and charming. So different from Charlie, whose father was titled, it was true—he was Sir Jasper Simpson—but who had been estranged from his family nineteen years before and had known nothing in his life beyond the army.

Lord Eden had spent a great deal of his time with them since his arrival in Spain three years before. Many was the time he had sat in their tent or in their rooms, talking with Charlie, often about army matters that were of no great interest to her, while she quietly sewed or made them tea. She had always enjoyed those times.

She looked forward to seeing all her friends again. She looked forward to seeing Lord Eden and to entertaining him again, just as she and Charlie had always done. And perhaps—who knew?—he would take a fancy to Jennifer.

She could hardly wait.

Would they never be home?

Had Charlie missed her as much as she had missed him?

"Will we be there soon?" Jennifer asked, turning from the window, a frown of impatience between her brows.

"Not long now," Ellen said with a smile. "Oh, Jennifer, I can scarce sit still here. I am so longing to see your papa again."

CAPTAIN CHARLES SIMPSON was on his way home through the park in Brussels with his friend Lieutenant Lord Eden after a tiring day of work.

"They do have a distinct advantage over us poor riflemen, don't they?" Captain Simpson said, nodding in the direction of a cluster of scarlet-coated officers gathered around two young ladies who were feeding the swans on the lake. "Why did you choose the green, Eden? You have the rank and wealth. Why did you not choose one of the more glamorous cavalry regiments?"

Lord Eden smiled. "I did not join the army for the glamour of it," he said. "I joined because I had to, Charlie. I would sooner not have done so, you know. I fair broke my mother's heart, and my twin sister threw every cushion in the house at me when I broke the news to her, and refused to speak to me for a whole day afterward. But I had to join. And finally, at the advanced age of two-and-twenty, I did. I wanted to fight where the main action always is. With the infantry."

"Well," the captain said with a hearty laugh as one of the young ladies caught sight of Lord Eden and looked a second time, blushing, "it is doubtless just as well you are in green rather than scarlet, lad, or you would be so busy fighting duels with all the other young officers that you would have no time for old Boney. You're a handsome devil, and no denying the fact. You will stop in for tea?"

"I am quite sure it would not be at all the thing," Lord Eden said. "If Mrs. Simpson has arrived with your daughter, none of you will want the added presence of a stranger. Some other time, Charlie."

"A stranger!" Captain Simpson looked quite offended for a moment. "You? Ellen will scold me all evening if I fail to bring you with me. Besides, I want to show off my Jennifer. A fetching little thing, Eden, even if I do say so myself. You would not think to look at me, would you, that I have a pretty little thing for a daughter?" He roared with laughter, turning not a few heads in their direction. "She favors her mother, fortunately for her."

"I will look in for a few minutes, then," his friend said. "But only for a few minutes if they have arrived, mind. They will be tired from the journey. If they haven't come yet, I'll share some brandy with you, Charlie, and put my feet up for a while. You have been like a coiled spring all day."

"One thing is for sure," the captain said. "I'm not letting Ellen go away from me again. We haven't been apart in five years, you know, since our marriage. You get used to having a woman around. You should try it sometime, Eden."

His friend grinned. "I would have to be awfully fond of her," he said. "I have a habit of falling out of love as fast as I fall in. You are fortunate in Mrs. Simpson, Charlie. A nice quiet, loyal wife."

The captain laughed again. "Your tone of voice says that you would be bored silly with such a wife in a fortnight, Eden," he said. "You wait, my boy. You will fall in love to stay one of these days. And you couldn't do better than someone like Ellen. She's a treasure. Here we are."

He had stopped outside the house on the Rue de la Montagne where he was billeted. And his beaming face grew even brighter after he had climbed the stairs to his rooms to discover that his wife and daughter were indeed home before him. Though only just. Both still wore traveling dress, and one trunk with a hat box perched precariously on top still stood in the middle of the living room. His wife's maid whisked the latter into a bedchamber as his daughter came rushing across the room shrieking and hurled herself into his arms.

"Papa!" she cried. "Oh, Papa. I thought the journey would take forever. And I was dreadfully sick on the boat. And Ellen says that there is bound to be a great battle soon, but it is not so, is it? Not now that the duke is here. Oh, Papa, I am so happy to be free of school at last. You cannot imagine!"

Her father held her at arm's length and chuckled. "Hello, puss," he said. "You are looking as fine as fivepence. Can this really be my little girl all grown up so soon? Welcome home, sweetheart." He hugged her to him.

Ellen curtsied to Lord Eden and held out a hand to him. He took it in both of his and raised it to his lips.

"I am pleased to see you safe at home, ma'am," he said, smiling warmly down at her. "Charlie has been like a fish out of water, and it has not been the same here in your rooms without you. Have you had a tedious journey? You look tired."

"I am a little," she said. "But only because I could not wait to be home. It is so good to be back again." She withdrew her hand after he had squeezed it between both his own.

And he watched as she turned from him, and as Charlie turned from his daughter. And he felt as he felt frequently in the presence of these two friends—an amused sort of affection as it became obvious that if he fell through a hole in the ground and disappeared forever, they would not even notice.

"Ellen," Charlie said, opening up his arms to her, "you are home."

"Yes, Charlie," she said. "At last."

She did hesitate a moment, feeling the presence of the other two, but the pull of those extended arms was obviously too strong for her. She went into them and hid her face against her husband's shoulder as he hugged her close and rocked her.

Lord Eden wondered as he had done a hundred times before at the deep affection that bound the two of them together. It was clear why Charlie doted on her. She was always quiet and cheerful and dignified. And she was rather lovely, with her slim, graceful figure, her shining fair hair drawn back into a knot at her neck, and her oval face with the large expressive eyes and straight nose and pretty mouth. One would not expect such a woman to be devoted to a man like Charlie, who was neither young nor handsome nor adept at the social graces.

It was good to see her back again. It was true that Charlie's home had not seemed quite as comfortable a place without Mrs. Simpson in it, though when she was there she never made her presence obtrusive.

Lord Eden waited to be presented to the little beauty, who was eyeing him in some embarrassment and blushing most becomingly. Charlie had said, of course, that his daughter was pretty, but fond papas could frequently be unreliable when extolling the charms of their own daughters. On this occasion, though, the girl's beauty had been underestimated, if anything. She was quite exquisite and quite the kind of woman who had always taken his fancy— small, well-endowed with curves, with a lovely eager face and a look of innocent timidity that called out for the protection of some male.

Perhaps he was destined to fall in love again, he thought as Charlie put an arm about the girl's waist and presented her to him, fairly bursting with paternal pride. The girl blushed an even deeper shade and swept into a low curtsy. Dark eyelashes fanned her flaming cheeks. He had not been in love for a long time. Not since Susan, in fact—three years before. He had flirted since with almost every unattached lady he had met, and had possessed more than he could remember of a different class of female. But he would not be able to flirt with this girl. Not Charlie's daughter. And of course she was not at all the kind of female whom he would try to possess. Perhaps he was due to fall in love again.

He smiled with appreciation at the girl and turned back to Mrs. Simpson. "I stepped inside to keep Charlie company if you had not yet arrived, ma'am," he said, "and to welcome you home if you had. I will not stay. You are travel-weary, I can see."

"Will you not take tea with us, my lord?" she asked, smiling at him. "It will be no trouble at all. You are no stranger."

"You see?" the captain said. "I told you she would be offended, did I not, Eden?"

But Lord Eden looked into her tired eyes and smiled. "My own family has arrived since you left, ma'am," he said. "Amberley, my brother, with his wife and children. And my twin sister. They were convinced that I needed fussing over, and came. I told my sister-in-law that I would probably be home for tea. And my nephew is planning to share his bread and jam with me, I was warned. He is going to feed me."

"Then you must certainly make yourself available for target practice," Ellen said. "Perhaps some other time, my lord. Tomorrow?"

"Tomorrow it is," he said. "I would like to make you known to my sister and my sister-in-law sometime, ma'am. They have heard a great deal about Mrs. Simpson, who spoils me with cups of tea and who does not object to my sitting for hours on end in her living room, droning on to her husband about topics that are not designed for a lady's amusement." He grinned at her and took her hand again.

"I shall look forward to meeting them," she said, and turned to smile at her husband with that warmth that always made Lord Eden vaguely envious.

"Lady Madeline Raine has the same green eyes as Eden," the captain said. "She is far prettier than he is, though."

They both laughed.

Lord Eden took one more appreciative glance at Miss Simpson before bowing and taking his leave. Yes, she was very pretty indeed. And very much his type.

• • •

THE EARL AND COUNTESS of Amberley and Lady Madeline Raine were gathered in the drawing room of the house they had rented in Brussels, waiting for Lord Eden's arrival for tea. The earl's infant son and daughter were with them, Lady Caroline Raine in her aunt's arms, staring unblinkingly up at her, Viscount Cleeves crawling under chairs and tables, intent on some quiet game of his own.

"How can such tiny fingers be so perfect?" Madeline said, spreading the baby's fingers over one of her own. "Oh, Alexandra, I am so envious of you at times."

The Earl of Amberley lowered his paper and looked over the top of it at his sister. "You have no need to be, Madeline," he said. "You could have a nursery full of your own children by now. The Duke of Wellington could make up a separate regiment of all the suitors you have had and rejected in the last seven or eight years. You could have been married twenty times over."

"I know," she said. "I suppose I am just not the marrying kind, Edmund. Perhaps there will be someone quite irresistible at the duke's ball, and I shall live happily ever after with him."

"I thought you were already interested in Colonel Huxtable," the countess said.

"I am," Madeline said. "At least I am interested in his uniform. I am quite in love with it, in fact." She laughed and returned her attention to the baby.

The earl put down his papers when he felt his son tug at the leg of his breeches. "Are you getting impatient for your tea, tiger?" he asked, scooping the child up into his arms and getting to his feet. "And that wicked Uncle Dominic is late. I think perhaps I hear him coming, though."

The child shrieked with laughter as he was tossed toward the ceiling and caught again.

"You had better go and meet him," the earl said, setting his son down again and watching as he scurried across the room to meet Lord Eden.

The child was soon being tossed in the air again.

"I should have asked before I did that if you have had your tea yet," Lord Eden said. "You aren't about to toss bread and jam all over my uniform, are you, old pal?"

"No, old pal," the child said, laughing merrily.

"Any news?" Lord Amberley asked.

"More troops and artillery arriving daily," Lord Eden said. "And the duke apparently bellowing for more. The usual."

"Will it really come to war, Dominic?" the countess asked. "Surely Bonaparte could not be that foolhardy. The British are here, the Dutch and Belgians, the Prussians. And more arriving daily. And promise of troops from Austria and Russia."

"I wouldn't count on those last," Lord Eden said, "and there aren't enough of the former. And those soldiers we have are Johnny Raws, half of them. It's a pity most of the veterans were sent off to America. It will be touch and go whether they will be back in time."

Madeline surged to her feet, the baby held to her shoulder, contentedly sucking on the muslin of her day dress. "I hate all this talk of war," she said. "Can we talk of nothing else here?"

"You should not have left England," her twin said unsympathetically. "You have done nothing but grumble ever since you arrived, Mad. You should have stayed in London with Mama as she wanted you to do. And with Uncle William and Aunt Viola. Anna is making her come-out this spring, is she not?"

"And bemoaning the fact that you are not there to see

her," she said. "But you know I could not have stayed. Not with you here, Dom. Why did you not sell out when you came home from Spain, as I begged you to do? I think you enjoy all the killing and all the danger to your own life."

"If you really think that, you must be stupid," he said. "No one willingly puts himself into a position to stare death in the face. There is such a thing as loyalty to one's country and belief in certain principles."

"I just think you have done enough," Madeline said. "It should be someone else's turn now, Dom. And you don't have to bring talk of war into the house, anyway."

"I have come from Charlie Simpson's house," he said. "Mrs. Simpson has just come back from England with Charlie's young daughter. You should be more like her, Mad. Charlie and I sometimes sit and talk for hours about military matters, and I have never heard one word of complaint from her or one hint that perhaps her husband should sell out. And he has been in for longer than twenty years."

"Then she must be a very foolish woman," Madeline said. "Perhaps she does not care for him a great deal."

"Don't argue in front of the children," Lord Amberley said in the quiet tones that had always quelled the twins' frequent differences of opinion.

The countess spoke almost simultaneously. "Captain Simpson must be very glad to have his daughter safely here," she said. "And how reassuring it must have been for the girl to have an older woman with whom to travel."

Lord Eden laughed. "I don't think Mrs. Simpson is any older than Mad and I, Alexandra," he said. "She must have been little more than a girl when Charlie married her five years ago. I am glad to see her home again. I will be taking tea there tomorrow, by the way. And I have told her that I want to present her to you and Mad. I hope you will not mind."

"Of course not," the countess said. "I will be delighted to meet the captain's wife. I like him, Dominic."

"I take it I am to learn from her how to be docile," Madeline said, "and how to accept male stupidity. I heartily dislike her already, Dom. She must be totally lacking in spirit."

Lord Eden raised his eyebrows. "If you had seen her in Spain," he said, "living in a tent, tramping through mud, fording swollen rivers on horseback, saying good-bye to Charlie every day, never knowing if she would see him again, you would not say anything so foolish, Mad."

"The children will be back in the nursery after tea," the earl said with quiet authority. "The two of you may go at it then, if you wish. You may even come to blows. Alex and I will be obliging enough to remove ourselves beyond earshot. But for now you will be civil. And I see the tea tray has arrived."

"With bread and jam included for Christopher," the countess said. "If I were you, Dominic, I should make a quick trip upstairs to change out of your uniform. I believe my son still has his heart set on feeding you."

"Do you, old pal?" Lord Eden asked, grinning down at his nephew. "Here you go, then, to Papa while I go and dress appropriately."

Madeline set the baby in the countess's arms. "I'll pour," she said, seating herself behind the teapot. "Edmund, is there really going to be a battle? It is not just a show of strength to discourage Bonaparte? There is really going to be fighting?"

"It is hard to say with any certainty," her brother said

gently. "We will just have to wait and hope, dear. And trust the Duke of Wellington, of course."

"Oh," she said, putting down the teapot with only one cup poured, "how childish of me to ask you such a question, Edmund. Of course there will be another battle. You know it and I know it. One more battle for Dom."

"He has escaped well so far," the countess said. "Flesh wounds only."

"If he dies," Madeline said, jumping to her feet, "I shall die too. I can't live without Dom, Edmund, I can't live without him."

Lord Amberley rose hastily to his feet and crossed the room to take her into his arms. "In all probability you will not be asked to," he said. "But we both know—and Alex too—why we came out here this spring when we would far prefer to be in London for the Season or at home in Amberley. We came to be with Dominic. We must make the best of the time we have with him, Madeline. It is always so with loved ones. Any of us could die at any moment. We must be sure to enjoy one another's love while we have it."

"Sometimes I hate you, Edmund," she said, putting her arms up around his neck and her cheek against his. "You can be so damnably wise. Now, where is that teapot?"

She was pouring tea with a determinedly steady hand when her twin returned to the drawing room.

ELLEN SANK DOWN onto the sofa beside her husband and snuggled her head against his shoulder as his arm came around her. She had just seen Jennifer to her room for the night.

"She is very tired," she said. "The journey was exhausting for her, Charlie, and she was dreadfully sick on the boat. An early night will do her good."

"I still find it hard to believe that such a pretty little thing can be my own daughter," he said. "Imagine, Ellen."

"I am happy for you," she said. "She is truly delightful."

He looked down at her and kissed her forehead. "I'm sorry, lass," he said. "Boasting about my daughter and all that. Have I caught you on the raw?"

"No," she said hastily. "No, you must not be forever thinking that, Charlie. It does not matter. It really does not. I have you, and you are all I need. And I have Jennifer too. She is fond of me, I believe. You must not always think I mind."

"It must have been that injury I had the year before I married you," he said. "That is what the old sawbones said anyway, Ellen. I can't think why else. I'm sorry about it, though. For your sake. I would have liked . . ."

She lifted her head and kissed his cheek. "Charlie," she said, "if I had a child, I would not be able to travel about with you so easily. I could not bear to be separated from you. You know that. I am not unhappy. I am not. And maybe the fault is in me, anyway. We do not know for sure."

"I missed you," he said, rubbing his cheek against the top of her head.

"And I you," she said. "And I missed everyone else too. I am looking forward to seeing everyone. Is Mrs. Byng feeling better? I must call on her tomorrow. It was good to see Lord Eden. He is quite like one of our family, is he not?"

"Do you think he fancies Jennifer?" he asked. "I think she fancies him."

"That would be hardly surprising," she said. "And I think it is very likely that he will be taken with her too. He will come to tea tomorrow? He will not feel that he is unwelcome now that we are no longer alone?"

"He'll come," he said.

Ellen put one arm about his waist. "I don't ever want to go away from you again," she said. "I don't mind too much this time because it was for Jennifer. But there cannot be another reason good enough to separate us, can there, Charlie?"

"No, lass," he said. "We won't be apart again."

"There is going to be fighting, isn't there?" she said.

"I don't know," he said. "We will have to wait and see."

"That means there is going to be fighting," she said. "Oh, I hoped so very hard that it was finally over."

"It is, almost," he said. "One more defeat, and no one will be hearing any more from old Boney."

"One more," she said with a sigh. "One too many."

"Just one more," he said, putting one hand beneath her chin and lifting her face to his. "And it won't be just yet, lass. We have time. Shall we go to bed early too?"

She smiled at him. "Yes," she said. "I am tired. And I shall be able to sleep well for the first time in three weeks. The bed has felt dreadfully empty without you."

"Mine too," he said. "Come on, then, lass, we'll put each other to sleep, shall we?"

"Yes," she said. "Charlie, I love you so very much."

"Double that for me, my treasure," he said, kissing her on the lips.

C APTAIN AND MRS. SIMPSON HAD BEEN INVITED
to the concert, ball, and supper to be given at the Salle
du Grand Concert by the Duke of Wellington the following
week. And they had procured an invitation for Jennifer,
too. They accepted the invitations, though the captain usually avoided as many formal social engagements as he possibly could. As he told Ellen, when one had a grown-up
daughter's happiness to see to, one occasionally had to
make a few sacrifices.

The ball would be Jennifer's introduction to society,
Ellen thought. She was somewhat surprised, then, to find
that the week leading up to the ball soon became crammed
with activity. And only some of it was of her own making.
She took Jennifer with her the day after their arrival in
Brussels to visit her friend Mrs. Byng and a few other wives
of officers in her husband's regiment. And she was pleased
to see Jennifer making friends with Mrs. Cleary, a young
ensign's wife fresh from England, and with the two young
daughters of Mrs. Slattery.

Lord Eden came to tea, as promised, and brought with

him an invitation from his sister-in-law to take tea with her and Lady Madeline Raine the following afternoon.

"I shall be off-duty early tomorrow," Lord Eden said. "I shall escort you and Miss Simpson there myself if I may, ma'am. I don't suppose you would care to come along too, would you, Charlie?" His eyes twinkled as he asked the question. He knew his friend as well as Ellen did.

"I think I can entrust my ladies to your care, Eden," Captain Simpson said with a drowning look that had both his wife and his friend laughing.

"You don't mind, lass?" he asked Ellen later when they were alone.

"I don't mind, Charlie," she said, laughing and wrapping her arms about his neck. "Actually, it gives me a warm feeling to know that you trust me to take your daughter about. Almost as if I really am her mother."

Jennifer, who was not at all shy by nature, was definitely shy with Lord Eden, Ellen discovered. She blushed and talked very little. It was doubtless because he was so very handsome and splendid and self-assured. But he did fancy the girl. He looked at her with open appreciation and made every effort to converse with her and set her at her ease.

Nevertheless, as they walked through the streets of Brussels on their way to the Earl of Amberley's house, Ellen on Lord Eden's left arm, Jennifer on his right, it was with Ellen that he conversed most of the time. They talked about Spain, and told Jennifer some of the funnier anecdotes they remembered. And they talked about Brussels, and pointed out to Jennifer some of the uniforms and the regiments to which their wearers belonged.

Ellen had never talked with Lord Eden a great deal. She had almost always been a quiet audience to the conversations he held with Charlie. But he was a pleasant and a charming companion, she found. So very suitable for Jennifer. And it was no wonder that Jennifer blushed and was tongue-tied. He was very splendidly tall, and his arm beneath her hand was firm and well-muscled. Ellen felt an impish sort of amusement at witnessing more than one female head turn in their direction and gaze wistfully at Lord Eden and enviously at her and Jennifer.

Lady Amberley and Lady Madeline Raine were not to entertain them alone, Ellen was surprised to find when they arrived. The Earl of Amberley was in the drawing room too, as were his two children.

"I hope you do not mind the children being present, Mrs. Simpson," the countess said after Lord Eden had made the introductions. "My husband has one eccentricity that I fully endorse. It is that when we are at home to tea, our children join us in the drawing room, even if the Queen of England is our guest."

"Of course I do not mind," Ellen said. "Oh, what a beautiful little girl you have. She is like you." She glanced at the dark-haired, dark-eyed beauty of the countess. "May I hold her?"

Lady Amberley sat down beside her, smiling, while Ellen held the baby. Jennifer was chattering eagerly with Lady Madeline and the Earl of Amberley, who must have seemed far less threatening to her than his more splendid brother, though he was almost equally handsome. He also had a very kindly face and a quiet manner.

There was a special feeling about a baby—a softness, a living warmth—and a special smell, of powder and milk. Lady Caroline Raine regarded Ellen from wide, unblinking dark eyes. Ellen felt a little like crying.

"You are so very fortunate," she said quietly, looking up at the countess.

"Yes." Lady Amberley regarded her curiously before smiling and talking of other matters.

The half-hour of their visit seemed to fly by. Ellen liked Lord Eden's family, all of whom had made an effort to be friendly, though Lady Madeline had spoken more with Jennifer than with herself. When Lord Eden rose to escort them back home again—though Ellen protested that he had no need to do so, as she was there to chaperone Jennifer—the Earl of Amberley also got to his feet and extended a hand to her.

"We would be honored if you and the captain and Miss Simpson would join us at the opera tomorrow evening, ma'am," he said.

Ellen's eyes met Lord Eden's, and he grinned.

"Poor Charlie!" he said. "It would almost serve him right for not coming this afternoon if you accepted for him, ma'am. I am afraid that Charlie Simpson marches into battle with far greater eagerness than he attends any social function, Edmund. But I hope Mrs. and Miss Simpson will accept."

"We would be delighted, my lord," Ellen said, glancing at the flushed and eager face of Jennifer.

"Colonel Huxtable is also to be our guest," the earl said. "I shall invite young Lieutenant Penworth as well, perhaps, to make up numbers."

Ellen smiled her agreement.

And so, she found, the arrival of Jennifer was having an immediate effect upon her own life. For the previous five years she had lived as quiet and domesticated a life as her husband's. And she had never had a complaint. She was never happier, she had always felt, than when she was at home alone with Charlie, his arm about her shoulders, talking about the day's events, or sometimes reading a book.

But there was something exhilarating about being included in an evening party. The opera with the Earl and Countess of Amberley! And with Lord Eden and Lady Madeline. And the colonel and the lieutenant, who were unknown to her. It all sounded very grand.

"You don't mind, Charlie?" she asked him that night when she lay beside him in bed, her head resting on his arm. "There will be four ladies and four gentlemen. You could have been one of them, but Lord Eden refused for you. And I thought you would be relieved. You don't mind?"

"Four ladies and four gentlemen, eh?" He chuckled and kissed the top of her head. "Should I be jealous, lass? Are you going to run off with one of them?"

"Only if I cannot persuade two of them to run off with me," she said.

He chuckled again. "You go and enjoy yourself, Ellen," he said. "I am the one who should be asking you if you mind. After all, Jennifer is my daughter, and she needs to be taken about. But you are a good mother to her, even if you are young enough to be her sister. And a good wife to me. Lift your face to me, sweetheart."

She lifted it. "I would far prefer to stay home with you tomorrow night," she said. "You know that, Charlie. I am happiest when I am with you. Things will not change between us with Jennifer here? We will not grow apart?"

He looked at her in the darkness of the room and smoothed one large hand over the side of her head. "I have room for the both of you in my heart, lass," he said. "I don't love you one whit less because there is Jennifer. Is that what you are afraid of? You know that you are my treasure, my very greatest treasure. You are the one who gives me my reason for living."

"I wasn't questioning your love," she said. "Oh, I wasn't doing that, Charlie. I have never done that. I am just very selfish. I don't want things to change. And they are changing. But I don't resent Jennifer, either. I don't want you to think that. I love her dearly, and I am very happy for the both of you that you are together at last." She laughed suddenly and leaned forward to kiss him on his bare chest. "I don't know what I mean. I am talking a lot of nonsense. I am very happy, Charlie. Happy to be home again. Happy to see you happy."

He raised himself on one elbow and leaned over her, smiling warmly down into her shadowed eyes. "I love you, lass," he said. "That is not ever going to change. Not ever, do you hear me? And these arms are always here for you. And I'm always here for you."

"Charlie." She reached up and touched his cheek with her fingertips. "Kiss me. Make love to me." She opened her arms to him.

"WELL, I LIKE THEM," Madeline told her brother that same evening. "Mrs. Simpson is very lovely, is she not? I was surprised. And I suppose you are quite in love with Miss Simpson already."

He grinned. "Why do you suppose that?" he asked.

"Because she is just your type," she said. "She is small and has those large eyes and blushes easily. Though I believe she has more sense and more spirit than your usual flirts, Dom. I approve."

"Ah," he said. "That is something, at least. You actually approve of something in my life."

"You are in love with her, then?" she asked.

"Let me put it this way," he said. "I am thinking about it. What surprised you about Mrs. Simpson?"

"I expected a pale, wilting creature," she said, "or else a manly, insensitive Amazon. She seems sensible. Edmund and Alexandra were much impressed. What on earth is she doing married to Captain Simpson?"

He grinned again. "Loving him and caring for him, apparently," he said. "He is one of the happiest men of my acquaintance."

"Well," she said, "I have to admire women like Mrs. Simpson. I'm afraid I am swayed a great deal by what a man looks like. Do you think that is one reason why I am an old maid, Dom?"

"You?" he said. "An old maid? Hardly, Mad. You have half the officers in Brussels sighing over you. Don't you fancy any of them?"

She shrugged. "I fancy a large number of them," she said. "That is the whole trouble. It used to be different, Dom, didn't it? For both of us. We always used to be deeply and painfully in love with someone. That does not seem to happen any longer."

"Because we are older and a little wiser," he said. "Do you ever think of Purnell? Was he the last one you were in love with like that?"

"I scarce remember him," she said. And then, after twisting and turning her teacup on its saucer, "Sometimes I wish I did not have a twin. There is no lying to you, is there, Dom? Of course I think of him. And I always feel a little sick every time Alexandra has a letter from him. He has been gone three years and is making a life for himself in Canada, by the sound of it. Well, good luck to him. I just wish I had never met him. I wish he were not Alexandra's brother. I wish he had not spoiled my life."

"Those are strong words," he said. "Did he really do that?"

"I have never been able to fall in love since," she said. "Although I constantly try, Dom."

"You don't still love Purnell, do you?" he asked curiously.

"I don't believe I ever did," she said. "I disliked him intensely. I was a little afraid of him. And I was obsessed by him. I really never knew him at all. That is not love. There was nothing about him that was lovable. Only the mystery of what it was that made him so morose, so untouchable. No, I don't love him or pine for him, Dom. Of course I don't. So you are to escort Miss Simpson to the opera tomorrow. And are to dance with her at the duke's ball next week, I would wager. Do you feel any of that old magic, Dom?"

She leaned her chin on her hand and gazed at her brother. She looked remarkably like him except that all the attributes that made him a handsome male made her a lovely female. She was tall and slender with short fair curls and a face that was made beautiful by the glow of life that animated it.

Was he feeling any of that old magic? It was a question that Lord Eden had asked himself from the moment of his first meeting with Jennifer Simpson, and a question that he was to ask several times in the coming days. He saw a great deal of her. He went home with Charlie almost as often as he had always used to do. And apart from the visit to Alexandra and Madeline, and the evening at the opera, he took her walking twice, once in the park and once in the botanic gardens. Always with Mrs. Simpson as chaperone.

He enjoyed the outings. Very much. The girl was pretty,

becomingly modest, and shy. And yet, as Madeline had observed, she had sense and character. If he could be alone with her for a short while—even alone in a crowd—perhaps he would find her an intriguing companion.

Perhaps he would fall in love with her. He did not know.

As it was, he seemed to spend more time talking with Mrs. Simpson than with her stepdaughter. He would have thought that after five years of meeting her so frequently at Charlie's, he knew her well. He had always thought of her as a quiet, serene, dutiful woman. He had always liked her, admired her, respected her.

But he did not know her, he was discovering. She was an interesting conversationalist. She had a lively sense of humor. They laughed a great deal over memories of Spain. And she did not dwell on the horrors of life there, he found. She had a gift for recalling the small, absurd incidents that he had forgotten all about. The incidents that helped him to remember his years there with some pleasure, horrifying as they had been in the main.

The evening at the opera was amusing. A little annoying too, perhaps, but basically amusing. Lieutenant Penworth, it seemed, had a passion for Madeline, and monopolized her company, completely cutting out Colonel Huxtable, who did not look at all pleased at being bettered by an inferior officer. He turned in some pique to Miss Simpson.

And so Lord Eden was left to amuse himself with Mrs. Simpson. Very good thing that he liked her, he thought, and found her an easy companion. And it was a pleasant surprise to see her dressed in an elegant silk gown with her hair dressed more softly than usual about her face. She really was a strikingly lovely woman.

"Do you think the tenor has to stand so close to her," he whispered in her ear at a most serious point in the opera, nodding in the direction of the leading soprano, "in order to stick a pin in her so that she can reach the high notes?"

"Oh." She slapped a hand to her mouth and looked at him with eyes that held a horrified sort of amusement, and her shoulders shook. "Oh, don't," she said with something of a squeal when she had herself a little under control. "I shall disgrace myself by laughing aloud. And just at a time when everyone is dying so tragically all over the stage."

"It will be her turn soon," Lord Eden whispered. "I have seen this opera before. Then the tenor will be able to put his pin away and concentrate on his singing until his turn to expire comes. It is all most tragic, is it not? Would you like to borrow my handkerchief, ma'am? It is large, I do assure you."

"To wipe away the tears of laughter?" she said. "You have quite ruined an affecting drama, my lord. I would have expected such unappreciative comments of Charlie. I did not expect them from you." But her eyes brimmed with suppressed laughter as she scolded.

Lord Eden grinned and winked at her.

"You are quite right," she said when the performance had finished and the singers were taking their bows. "The singing was inferior."

It was pleasant at times, Lord Eden consoled himself after an evening in which he had hoped to sit beside Miss Simpson, to have a companion with whom he could relax, someone with whom he could share a joke, someone who knew how to laugh. If he really had sat beside Miss Simpson, he would probably have had to pretend raptures for very inferior vocalists. And perhaps he really would have had to lend that handkerchief.

Charlie was a fortunate man. To have such a wife. And— of course—to have such a daughter.

• • •

"I DO LIKE Mrs. Simpson a great deal," the Countess of Amberley said to her husband later that night. "She is very sensible and very charming, is she not, Edmund?"

"Mm," he said. He was lying in bed, his hands clasped behind his head, watching her brush her long dark hair, though her maid had already done it for her in her dressing room.

"I wonder why she is married to Captain Simpson," she said.

"I suppose because he asked her and she said yes," he said.

The brush paused in her hair and she smiled at him. "You know what I mean," she said. "It is rather a case of Beauty and the Beast, is it not?"

"Ooh," he said. "Cruel, love. He is older than she is, yes."

"Dominic has always been very fond of both of them," she said. "I suppose they must be contented together if he enjoys their company."

"I would be a great deal more contented with you if you did not feel obliged to stand there brushing your hair," he said. "A great deal more contented, Alex."

"Silly," she said, putting down the brush and slipping beneath the blankets, which he held back for her. "Do you think Dominic is in love with Miss Simpson? She is a delight, is she not?"

"Mm," he said. "But I have given up waiting for Dominic and Madeline to fall in love to stay. They don't have my good sense."

"But you were nine-and-twenty when you married me," she said. "Only three years ago, love."

"Was I?" he said. "It must have been because you did not have the sense to meet me sooner, Alex."

"Captain Simpson must be shy," she said. "It was a pity he did not come tonight. Do you think Mrs. Simpson minded not having his company, Edmund?"

"No idea," he said. "I would mind not having your company, but I can't speak for anyone else."

"Lieutenant Penworth is taken with Madeline," she said. "But I think he is too young to interest her. What do you think?"

"I think that I might wait all night for you to be finished with your mouth if I don't take drastic measures," he said. "Hush, love. I have better use for it."

"Do you?" she said. She smiled at him as he raised himself above her. "What?"

He leaned right across her in order to blow out the candle on the table beside the bed. "This," he said.

"Oh, Charlie, you do look splendid!" Ellen set her hands on the captain's shoulders and stood back to look at him in his dress uniform, her eyes dancing with merriment. "And you do look as if you are about to face a firing squad."

He grinned sheepishly. "But you won't expect me to dance, will you, Ellen?" he asked. "I will if you want me to, you know, and I'll be there so that you can take my arm whenever you don't have a partner. But I can't dance, lass. My legs seem to turn into two stiff poles when I try."

"Of course you don't have to dance," she said, kissing him on the cheek. "We decided that yesterday when Lord Eden was here and teased you so mercilessly. And he has already reserved two sets with me, and Lord Amberley one, as well as Captain Norton and Lieutenant Byng and Mr. Chambers. Goodness, Charlie, my card is half-full and we haven't even arrived at the ball yet."

"And so it should be, lass," he said. "You will be easily the loveliest lady there."

"Oh," she said, "you had better not let Jennifer hear you say that."

"She will be the loveliest girl there," he said. "But you are a lady, lass, and the handsomest one I have ever laid eyes on. Especially tonight. So this is the gown you bought in London and have been keeping a secret, is it? It's beautiful, sweetheart. Green is your color."

"I remember your saying that in Spain when I had that riding habit I was wearing when I fell off my horse into the mud one day. Do you remember?"

"I remember thinking you must be dead," he said. "I didn't think it was possible to gallop through mud until that day. But both Eden and I did it, only to find you lying there cursing in most unladylike fashion."

She laughed. "But I remembered that you liked me in green when I was having this gown made," she said. "You know, Charlie, tonight will not be so very bad. We are not nearly important enough to have been invited to dinner at the Hôtel de Belle Vue. That would be an ordeal, I grant you, with the King and Queen of the Netherlands as guests of honor. Lady Amberley says that the earl dreads the thought of going. I think he is something of a hermit too. And the evening is to start with a concert. Madame Catalani, no less. All you will have to do is sit and listen. And when the dancing begins, there will be no lack of men who will feel as you do and be quite content to stand in a corner talking politics or horses or women or whatever it is you men like to talk about when there are no women present."

He smiled and kissed her. "Thank you, lass," he said. "Thank you for understanding me and accepting me as I am. But I am going, you see. I want to watch you and

Jennifer dancing and enjoying yourselves. You have been enjoying yourself since she has been here, haven't you? I'm glad for that. I know I am sometimes dull company."

She shook her head. "Do I look like a woman who is dissatisfied with her lot?" she asked. "Do I, Charlie?"

He looked into her eyes. "You are smiling," he said.

"All the way inside me," she said. "Right down to my toes. Because I am the happiest woman alive. I love you and I am married to you. And Jennifer will be tearing her room apart with impatience if we don't go and fetch her soon. Oh, wait until you see her gown, Charlie. She looks quite like an angel in it. You will be proud enough to burst."

"I already am that," he said, taking the hand she held out for his.

And she really was happy, Ellen thought. She was going out for the evening with the husband she loved and with the stepdaughter she had grown to love. And her mirror had just told her that she was looking her very best. And she was going to dance for most if not all of the evening. Even one of the waltzes on her card had been taken already, and she loved to waltz. Lord Eden had signed his name next to it the day before when Charlie had finally admitted that he would not dance, even with his own wife.

"Which set did you dream of dancing with Charlie, ma'am?" Lord Eden had asked when they were still laughing over his quite untrue comment that Charlie's two left feet sometimes led him to march off in a different direction from the rest of the company on the parade ground. "A waltz, certainly. And after supper, during the romantic hours of the ball. Now, where are my country dances? Ah, yes, the third set of the evening, I see. I shall sign myself for this waltz as well, then, and we will make Charlie sorry he lost the chance, shall we? I shall twirl you and spin you and make him purple with jealousy." He had laughed at Charlie and winked at her. He had already written his name twice in Jennifer's card.

She was going to enjoy the evening, Ellen thought as her husband exclaimed over a radiant and excited Jennifer. It was going to be quite, quite splendid. They had been to dances in Spain, but it was a long time since she had attended a ball quite as grand as this one promised to be.

3

$\mathcal{A}$FTER DINNER AT THE HÔTEL DE BELLE VUE with the more elite of his guests, the Duke of Wellington arrived with the Dutch royal family at the Salle du Grand Concert in the Rue Ducale when all the rest of his guests were present and seated. There was a great stir as everyone rose. Jennifer, standing beside Ellen, followed her lead and swept into a deep curtsy as the King and Queen of the Netherlands were led to their seats.

"The duke looks more like a king than that other man," she confided in a whisper. "I am glad he is not the King of England, Ellen."

"Sh," her stepmother said with a smile as they resumed their seats and settled for the beginning of the concert. But all the performers were merely tolerated, she felt, sensing the buzz of anticipation as the audience waited for the performance of Madame Catalani, the famous soprano, who had just recently arrived in Brussels.

The singer favored her audience with only two songs, and no amount of enthusiastic applause and calls for an encore could persuade her to sing more.

"She is very lovely," Jennifer said.

"And has the most glorious voice I have ever heard," Ellen said.

Her husband leaned toward her at that moment and spoke in a whisper. "I have been gazing about me ever since we came, Ellen," he said, "and I don't see any lady that looks lovelier than you. Or any girl that looks prettier than Jennifer."

"Not even Madame Catalani?" she asked with a twinkle in her eye.

"Madame who?" he asked.

"Charlie!" Ellen giggled and linked her arm through his.

Lord Eden joined them before the dancing began. "Ma'am?" he said, bowing to Ellen. "Miss Simpson? Charlie, it is positively not fair that you should have two such lovely ladies in your charge. Especially when you have no intention of dancing with either of them. I am going to take them away from you." He grinned at Ellen and Jennifer, and extended an arm to each, favoring them with an exaggerated bow. "Will you join my sister and me at the other side of the ballroom, ladies? I am afraid she is rather tied up with prospective partners at the moment."

"Do you mind, Charlie?" Ellen laid a hand lightly on his arm.

"Go and enjoy yourself, lass," he said, patting her hand. "And Jennifer too. I see Fairway and Hendon over there. I'll go and have a word with them."

"Are Lord and Lady Amberley here too?" Ellen asked as Lord Eden led her and Jennifer away.

"They have gone home for a while for Alexandra to, er, put the baby to bed, I believe," he said. "They will be here later. I'm afraid Alexandra has rather vehement views on the question of wet nurses. Indeed, my brother and his wife are somewhat eccentric in several ways."

"Oh, but I agree with the countess," Ellen said.

He smiled at her before turning to Jennifer in order to point out to her the rather unimpressive figure of the Prince of Orange and the more gorgeous one of the Earl of Uxbridge, leader of the allied cavalry.

Lady Madeline greeted them both with a friendly smile. She drew Jennifer's arm through her own and presented her to a large group of admirers. How she had succeeded in gathering such a court about her when she had been in Brussels for less than a month, Ellen did not know, but she was undoubtedly a very lovely and a very vivacious lady. Several of the gentlemen were signing their names in Jennifer's card, Ellen was pleased to see. Her stepdaughter was looking exceptionally lovely in her gown of delicate pink silk overlaid with white lace.

Colonel Huxtable bowed and asked Ellen if he might sign her card.

Lord Eden had turned away to talk with a pretty little auburn-haired lady who had tapped him on the sleeve. Lady Madeline turned from her group of followers and smiled at Ellen.

"You are such a surprise," she said. "Dom has mentioned both you and the captain in several of his letters home. I pictured you as a dumpy, comfortable-looking lady of middle years. You must be no older than I. And that is a glorious shade of green you are wearing."

"Thank you." Ellen smiled. "You, on the other hand, look very much as I expected. You are like your brother."

"Have you been with the army ever since your marriage?" Madeline asked. "You must be very brave."

"I joined my father in Spain when I was fifteen," Ellen said. "But there is no courage involved in staying with one's husband, you know. I think it would take a great deal more to stay in England and wait for news. I could not bear that. Charlie might be hurt or worse, and I not know about it perhaps for weeks."

"I know." Madeline's eyes looked tormented for a moment. "I do not have a husband, Mrs. Simpson, but I do have Dom. And I have lived through three years of being separated from him. But not again. I am going to stay here until this is all over."

"We have this evening," Ellen said. "This evening, at least, there is no danger. Only lights and music and laughter. When you have become a part of army life, you learn to accept each day and each evening as a precious gift."

Madeline looked as gay as she had appeared a few minutes before. "Of course," she said. "Perhaps after all, we are more fortunate than other generations, Mrs. Simpson. We have learned to live and to love for the moment instead of wasting time planning for an elusive future. Here is a gentleman wanting to dance with you, I believe."

Ellen turned to find Captain Norton, an officer of the Ninety-fifth Rifles, smiling at her and bowing. "My set, I believe, Mrs. Simpson," he said. "I suppose Charlie won't dance tonight, as usual?"

"Oh, he would make the supreme sacrifice if there were any danger of my being a wallflower," Ellen said, placing a hand on his sleeve. "But you and several other gentlemen have kindly reprieved him, you see."

LADY MAISIE HARDCASTLE joined Madeline at the end of the first set. They were old acquaintances from London, though Madeline would not have attached the label "friend" to their relationship. She disliked Maisie's constantly barbed tongue.

"My dear Madeline," she said now, tittering and tapping Madeline on the arm. Ever since the former Maisie Baines had married Sir Humphrey Hardcastle two years before, she had affected a condescending air with her old acquaintance. "I saw you talking with Mrs. Simpson earlier. Do you know who she is? I did not know myself, actually, but I was just talking with Lady Lawrence, who arrived from London only last week."

"Mrs. Simpson is the wife of Captain Simpson of the Ninety-fifth," Madeline said, fanning herself and hoping that the orchestra would not delay much longer before striking up for the second set so that Lieutenant Penworth might come to her rescue.

Maisie tittered again. "I thought you could not know," she said. She looked dramatically about her as if she expected to see all the hundreds of guests leaning her way, ears extended for her news. She lowered her voice. "She is the Countess of Harrowby's daughter."

"Indeed?" Madeline said, her foot tapping with some impatience. "Then it is surprising that she does not attach the title 'Lady' to her name."

"Oh." Maisie smirked. "I did not say that she was the *Earl* of Harrowby's daughter, my dear."

Madeline turned her head to stare at her, her eyes hostile. "Indeed?" was all she said.

"You do not know the story?" Maisie asked. "I did not know myself until Lady Lawrence told me."

"No," Madeline said, "and I am not excessively interested in gossip, Maisie."

"Oh, this is not gossip," the other said, two spots of color appearing high on her cheekbones. "I would not indulge in gossip. You should know me better than that, Madeline dear. This is quite true, and such an old story that everyone knows it anyway. So one cannot be accused of being malicious. But I thought you would want to be warned, my dear. In a place like this, one does not always know quite with whom one is cultivating an acquaintance, does one? It is an act of simple friendship to warn someone when one is privy to some unsavory story."

Madeline looked at her coldly. "I see Lieutenant Penworth approaching," she said. "I have promised him the next set. I thought the music would never resume, didn't you?"

"How inopportune!" Maisie said. "I will call one afternoon if I may, my dear, and give you the full details. Lady Amberley would doubtless be grateful to know too."

"We both plan to be out that afternoon," Madeline said with a smile before turning with a far more sparkling one for the lieutenant.

That dazzled officer would not have known from her manner during the following twenty minutes that she was seething with indignation. Maisie had always specialized in character assassination, and yet no amount of pointed insult seemed to penetrate her armor of self-righteousness. One could probably tell Maisie with one's mouth six inches from her ear that she was an ass and she would still simper and call one her "dear."

LORD EDEN DANCED the opening set with Jennifer. She was looking extremely lovely, he thought, and sparkled with an excitement that many very young ladies tried to hide behind a pretense of sophisticated boredom. Although she still blushed every time she looked into his eyes, she seemed to have recovered the use of her tongue in his presence.

When the pattern of the dance allowed conversation, he questioned her about her years at school, and delighted in the humor with which she recalled several incidents there. She had spent her holidays in London with Charlie's sister, Lady Habersham, the only member of his family, it seemed, from whom he was not estranged. But of course she had always been too young to participate in any adult entertainments.

The world was new to her, Lord Eden realized, and thought how long ago it seemed since he had looked on life with such fresh eyes. And yet he was only five-and-twenty even now. He had done a lot of growing up during the past several years, especially during the three since he had bought his commission.

He felt a tenderness for the girl. It would feel good to be in love with her. To be in love again with youth and innocence. It would be good to marry such a girl, and to spend his life protecting her from the rougher side of life. It would be good to marry Charlie's daughter.

Charlie would be his father-in-law. Now, there was a thought!

He smiled in some amusement at Jennifer as the pattern of the dance brought them together again, and drew another blush from her.

Perhaps he would let himself fall in love with her. After this battle. Not before. He did not want any emotional entanglements before the battle. He might not survive it.

He returned Jennifer to Ellen's side at the end of the set and went in search of Susan Jennings, who had stopped to talk with him earlier, and whose card he had signed for the next set. Susan. The same Susan he had loved and almost married three years before. She had married Lieutenant Jennings soon after and had been with him and the army ever since. But three years of rough living had done nothing to destroy her look of fragile innocence and youth. He had seen her occasionally during those years.

"It is exceeding kind of you to dance with me, my lord," she said as he led her onto the floor for the beginning of the set. She looked up at him with large hazel eyes. "I did not think you would sign my card when there are so many grand ladies present."

"Ah, but how could I resist dancing a set with you, Susan?" he said. "You are easily as lovely as the grandest lady here."

"Oh," she said, blushing and lowering her eyelashes, "you are just saying that to tease me, my lord."

"Not at all," he said. "And how is life treating you, Susan? I have not talked with you in an age."

"We spent the winter with Lord Renfrew," she said. "My husband's brother, you know. He is still unmarried. And Dennis—he was the middle brother—died two summers ago of the typhoid. He was in Italy. My husband is now Lord Renfrew's heir."

"Is he indeed?" Lord Eden said with a smile. "So one of these days I may be able to address you as 'my lady,' Susan."

"Oh," she said, looking up at him with wide and stricken eyes, "you must not think such a thing, my lord. I do not let it enter my mind, I am sure. I am excessively fond of his lordship."

"Quite so," he said. "It was a bad joke, Susan. Forgive me?"

"There is nothing to forgive," she said.

He might have married her, Lord Eden thought. He had almost done so, except that he had finally made the choice between her and buying his commission. And the very evening on which he had renounced her and watched her run away in tears after declaring her love for him, she had announced her betrothal to Lieutenant Jennings. And had entered the very life into which he had thought it impossible to bring her. She seemed not to have suffered.

"Have you heard from your family recently?" he asked.

"Colin has married Hetty Morton," she said. "Did you know that? Howard is still unmarried. Mama and Papa are well."

The Courtneys were prosperous tenants of Amberley. Lord Eden had known Susan all her life, from the time when she was a tiny, worshipful little girl who seemed always to be crying over a kitten in trouble.

"I am glad to hear it," he said.

"We were at home last summer for a while," she said, "for Colin's wedding. The rector's wife had another daughter, you know. And did you know that Lady Grace Lampman has a son? I was never more surprised in my life. She is so very old. Mama said she almost died three years ago when their daughter was born. And Mama said that Sir Perry was almost beside himself when he knew she was in a delicate way again."

Lord Eden listened in some amusement as she prattled on. Obviously as a married lady she felt it quite unexceptionable to assail his ears with such talk. The Susan he had known would have swooned quite away if someone had so much as whispered the word "pregnancy" a hundred yards from her.

"Yes, I did know about that," he said. "Edmund told me. Perry is a particular friend of his, you know. And he declares that Lady Lampman is so very proud and happy that she looks a full ten years younger."

"She should be happy," Susan said. "Sir Perry is a handsome and amiable gentleman."

Would he have continued to love her if he had married her? Lord Eden wondered. She was a quite delightful mixture of artifice and innocence, of girlish timidity and matronly assurance. He had a sudden image of being alone with her in her boudoir undressing her while she regaled him with all the latest *on-dits*. He did not believe he would find the experience wildly arousing.

But had he married her, their love would have had a chance to grow and develop. She might have adjusted to him and he to her. They might have been happy. Might have been! And might not have been. But he did not want his nostalgic dream of the past to die entirely. If his love for Susan could die a natural death, then perhaps there was no such thing as love. Or not for him, anyway. Alexandra and Edmund had it, of course. Sometimes it was painful to live in the same house as those two. Not that they ever embarrassed him and Madeline by so much as touching in public, of course. But they did not need to touch. Their every glance was a caress and a communication.

Well, he thought, glancing across the room to where Miss Jennifer Simpson was dancing with some fresh-faced youth, her face aglow, perhaps he would be able to love again. With a love that would last for a lifetime.

ELLEN WAS TALKING with Lady Amberley when Lord Eden came to claim his waltz with her after supper. She was looking forward to it immensely. She had waltzed once before that evening, with Lieutenant Byng, the flame-haired husband of her particular friend, but he did not dance the steps with anything more than competence. Lord Eden waltzed well. Ellen had seen him perform the dance before. And of all other dances, she loved the waltz.

She had enjoyed herself this evening. She had been without a partner for only one set, the one before supper, but she had been happy rather than disappointed about that, since Charlie had come to take her on his arm, and she had been able to relax and catch her breath and go in to supper with him. And they had sat with the Byngs and the Clearys and the Slatterys, and she had had to make no effort at all to make polite conversation. There had been a great deal of laughter at their table.

She had danced every other set and enjoyed lively conversations with her husband's friends, with Colonel Huxtable, and with the handsome, kindly Earl of Amberley. And with Lord Eden, of course, during the first set they had danced together.

But now it was time to waltz. She smiled and placed her hand in Lord Eden's as he exchanged a few words with his sister-in-law.

"Has Madeline invited you to the picnic tomorrow?" he asked as he led her toward the floor.

"No," she said.

"She doubtless has asked Miss Simpson already," he said. "We are getting together a group to go out into the Forest of Soignes. It is beautiful out there. Have you been? We are hoping that you will be willing to act as chaperone, yet again. I hope it is not becoming tedious to you to do so, ma'am. And I hope Charlie is not getting cross at your frequent absences. But if he is, it is entirely his own fault, as I shall tell him." He grinned. "He can come too, if he wishes."

"It would be cruel," she said, her eyes sparkling back at him. "And on his day off duty, too."

"We shall leave him at home, then, shall we?" he said. "And steal away into the forest to enjoy ourselves."

"Just like children escaping their parents' supervision,"

she said with a laugh. "But I do thank you, my lord, and Lady Madeline. I hoped when we brought Jennifer out here that she would have plenty of entertainment, but I did not dream that there would be quite so much. I know she is enjoying herself enormously. And who knows when it will all come to an end?"

He set his hand at her waist and took her hand in his. "You must not even hint at such things during a ball, ma'am," he said with a smile. "You know army etiquette."

"I'm sorry," she said. And resolutely shut her mind to the certain knowledge that all these splendidly uniformed officers would be engaged in perhaps the deadliest battle of their lives before too many more weeks had passed. The last battle of their lives for many of them. She smiled brightly.

And soon she was smiling in earnest. She had never waltzed with Lord Eden before. He was a superb dancer. He held her firmly and moved in such a way that she followed his lead without thought. And he spun and twirled her about the floor, so that she had to look up into his face to prevent herself from becoming dizzy. He was so very tall and strong.

He smiled back. "You waltz very well, ma'am," he said. "You are not afraid to follow a lead. You feel like a feather in my arms. Charlie does not know what he is missing."

"Oh, yes, he does," she said, "and that is why he is missing it."

He laughed and his teeth showed very white. His green eyes crinkled at the corners. He was quite startlingly attractive, Ellen thought. Was it possible that he would single Jennifer out for more and more marked attention? They had looked very handsome together as they had danced earlier.

He had always noticed that she was a lovely woman, Lord Eden thought. But it was only recently—since her return from England—that he had realized that she could sparkle with a truly vibrant beauty. She was sparkling tonight. She looked like a girl.

"Do I detect a touch of London fashion?" he asked. "That is a very becoming gown."

He was interested to see her blush. "I bought it as a surprise for Charlie," she said. "He thinks green is my color."

"It is," he said. "He is quite right."

He had never danced with her like this before. Never held her. Her slim body was warm and supple beneath his hand. Charlie was a fortunate man.

He recalled his first meeting with Mrs. Simpson in Spain, and his surprise at her youth and beauty and elegance. She was not at all the type of woman he would have expected to be married to the rough-mannered and big-hearted Charlie Simpson.

And yet there could be no doubt about the fact that her world revolved about her husband. His respect for her had grown with the years. He would never forget coming upon her after one vicious skirmish in Spain when all was still confusion on the battlefield. He had suffered a flesh wound in the arm and must have looked unusually pale as he staggered back from the front toward her tent, the first familiar landmark he had seen. Her hands had gone to her mouth, her eyes had grown round with horror, and she had begun to wail so that he had forgotten his own pain for a moment.

As it turned out, she had noticed only the paleness of his set face and had assumed that he was bringing her bad news. Her manner had changed instantly when she realized her mistake, and calm, steady hands had soon been easing his coat from him and cutting away his blood-soaked shirtsleeve and cleansing and dressing his wound. But she had cried again an hour later when Charlie had appeared, tattered and incredibly dirty, but miraculously unhurt. And she had hurled herself against him and wrapped her arms around his neck and murmured his name at least a dozen times.

He could feel envious of his married friend at such moments.

"Do you think Charlie is watching and wishing he were in my place?" he asked her, looking down into her eyes and grinning. He spun her around a corner of the floor until she laughed up at him with delight.

And then another twirling couple collided with her from behind and sent her careering against him. His arms came tightly about her to steady her. Her face was still turned up to his.

Probably no more than a second passed while he became aware of her slim and shapely feminine form pressed to him, and found himself looking directly into her wide gray eyes and down to her parted lips. He was surrounded by the fragrance of her hair, of which he had been vaguely aware since they had started dancing.

She felt him with every part of her, from her shoulders to her knees. All hard masculine muscularity. She felt suffocated by his cologne, mesmerized by his green eyes, only inches from her own.

She felt herself blush hotly.

"So sorry. Clumsy of me!" a genial giant called over his shoulder as he maneuvered his partner into the throng of dancers again.

Lord Eden set firm hands on her shoulders as he stepped back from her. "How careless of me not to foresee that," he said. "Are you hurt, ma'am?"

"Not at all," she said, brushing her hands over her skirt and smiling at his chin. "Please forgive me."

"For allowing yourself to be tossed by an ox?" he said. "I would be tempted to slap my glove in his face if he did not look as if he were enjoying himself so vastly. Oh, dear, it has happened again to another unfortunate couple. I shall be sure to keep half a ballroom between him and us for the rest of the set, ma'am, I do assure you."

She laughed and placed her left hand on his shoulder again. "Perhaps instead of challenging him to a duel, you should hang bells around his neck, my lord," she said, "so that everyone will know that he is coming."

He felt uncomfortable. How unforgivably clumsy of him to have allowed her such embarrassment. He forced himself to laugh back. "And I thought you did not have a malicious bone in your body, Mrs. Simpson," he said. "For shame, ma'am."

She found it very hard to look up into his eyes. He suddenly seemed very large indeed, and very close to her. She felt more breathless than the exercise of dancing would account for. How unspeakably embarrassing!

Would the music never end?

They smiled and talked on.

THE COUNTESS OF AMBERLEY was drawing a brush absently through her hair and regarding her husband in the mirror. He was standing beside her stool, his arms folded.

"Do you think Madeline will marry Colonel Huxtable?" she asked. "He seems a very pleasant man, don't you think, although she has known him for only a few weeks."

"I suppose he will have to make her an offer before the

question becomes relevant," the earl said, taking one of her curls between his finger and thumb.

"Of course he will make her an offer," she said, smiling at him. "Doesn't everyone?"

"Then I would have to guess that she will say no," he said. "Doesn't she say that to everyone?"

She sighed. "Perhaps she is looking too hard for love," she said. "Perhaps she would grow into love if she would only give herself a chance to get to know some eligible gentleman."

"Like we did?" he said.

"Yes," she agreed, "like we did. We had no thought of loving each other when we became betrothed, did we?"

"Oh," he said, "I had every thought of loving you, Alex. The betrothal might have been largely forced upon me, but I had every intention when I contracted it of coming to love you. And it did not take long."

She reached back and touched his hand with her free one. "Dominic likes Miss Simpson," she said. "She is very sweet. I like her. But is she a little young for him, Edmund?"

"There are eight years between you and me," he said. "Are you too young for me?"

"No," she said. "I did not mean just in years. Oh, never mind. They have only recently met. Edmund, do you know what that horrid Maisie Hardcastle told me?"

"Can't imagine," he said, lowering his head and nuzzling her earlobe. "Some shocking scandal, doubtless."

"I gave her no encouragement whatsoever," she said, "and tried my best not even to listen. But she would insist that it was her duty to tell me so that I might protect Madeline's reputation."

The earl snorted. "Did she, indeed?" he said. "Are you

ready for bed, Alex? If we don't go there soon, Caroline is going to be up, hungry as a bear, ready to start the day."

She got to her feet and turned into his arms. "She said that Mrs. Simpson is the daughter of the Countess of Harrowby," she said. "Do you know her?"

"I know of her," he said, undoing the top button of her nightgown and moving his hands across her shoulders beneath it. "I know poor old Harrowby, of course. An alcoholic wreck, I'm afraid."

"Maisie made a point of saying that she did not say that Mrs. Simpson was the daughter of the Earl of Harrowby," she said.

"Quite likely, I'm afraid," the earl said, undoing the second and third buttons of her nightgown so that he could open it back over her shoulders. "The lady has something of a spicy reputation."

"Poor Mrs. Simpson," she said. "Maisie will slaughter her character if she can, you know."

"I believe she tried with you once, my love," he said. "But I thwarted her by marrying you."

"Thank you," she said crossly. "We all know that without your generosity my reputation would have been in shreds forevermore. And do take that grin off your face."

"I love you when you are prickly," he said. "And you know very well that you married me eventually quite of your own free will. Though Christopher might have found himself in a nasty situation if you had not."

"Edmund," she said, catching at his wrists, "don't do that until we are lying down, please. You know it always makes me weak at the knees."

"Easily remedied, my love," he said, stooping down and swinging her up into his arms.

ELLEN WAS LYING beside her husband, his arm beneath her head, as usual.

"You would not like to come?" she asked. "Tomorrow is a free day for you, Charlie, and the forest is said to be a beautiful place."

"I would as soon stay at home, lass," he said, "unless you really want me to come. Is it asking too much to expect you to go about everywhere with Jennifer? I am very selfish, aren't I? I'll come, then. I'll come with you, Ellen."

"No." She sighed and kissed his cheek. "You would hate every minute of it, and I would not enjoy myself at all. But it would have been pleasant, would it not, to have been at home together tomorrow? We could have taken a stroll in the park in the afternoon. But never mind. We will have the evening. The Slatterys have invited Jennifer to the theater, remember?"

"Mm," he said. "That will be nice, sweetheart. Would you prefer that I took you out somewhere?"

"No," she said. "I want one of our quiet evenings at home together, Charlie. Just you and me. Just like old times."

They lapsed into silence, and she was back in the ballroom, the music swirling in her head, the room spinning wildly about her. Noise and laughter, color and movement. The smell of a man's cologne. She turned restlessly onto her side.

"I'm cold," she said when her husband opened his eyes and turned his head.

"On a warm night like this, lass?" he said. "Hey, you are shivering." He rubbed his large hands over her back and pulled the blankets close about her. "Cuddle close, sweetheart. I'll warm you up."

"I love you, Charlie," she said, burrowing her head

beneath his chin and closing her eyes tightly. She spread her hands on his broad and warm chest. "I love you so very much. You do believe that, don't you?"

"Of course I believe it, lass," he said, smoothing one hand over her hair. "And you know you are my treasure and always will be. Are you feeling warmer? Lift your face to me and let me kiss you."

She tipped back her head with an almost desperate eagerness and slid one arm up about his neck.

4

THE SUN SHONE FROM A CLOUDLESS BLUE sky as two open barouches made their way along the Rue de la Pépinière, out through the Namur Gate at the south end of Brussels, and on their way to the Forest of Soignes. It was a perfect day for a picnic.

Lady Madeline Raine rode in the first carriage with her friends Miss Frances Summers and Lady Anne Drummond. Ellen and Jennifer Simpson rode in the other, the picnic hamper on the seat opposite them. Colonel Huxtable, Lieutenant Penworth, Lord Eden, Captain Norton, and Sir Harding Whitworth rode beside the carriages.

Madeline twirled a yellow parasol about her head and felt determinedly happy. It was possible to feel so if one concentrated only on the warm sunshine and the beauty of the forest that was approaching, and if one looked only at the splendor of the uniforms of four of their escorts and forgot about the significance of those uniforms.

"I have never been out to the forest before," Lady Anne said, "though I have heard that it is lovely. I did not expect the trees to be quite so large."

The three ladies gazed about them at the beechwood trees, their trunks tall and massive, smooth and silvery.

"I always feel as if I should whisper when I am here," Madeline said. "It is almost like being in a cathedral."

"I believe this is where we should turn off the main road," Colonel Huxtable said, turning back to see Lord Eden's affirming nod, "before we reach the village of Waterloo."

"Is this the way the French will try to come?" Lady Anne asked of no one in particular as horses and carriages turned from the wide Charleroi Chaussée and into the forest with its widely spaced trees.

"Oh, no," Miss Summers said quite firmly. "Ferdie says that they will come from the west to try to cut off our supply lines with Ostend. That will be the best tactical move, he says."

"I think that for the rest of today we should declare military talk strictly forbidden," Madeline said gaily.

"I could not agree more," Colonel Huxtable said, "for everyone knows that the French are not going to come from any direction at all. Trust his grace and the allied armies to ensure that, ladies."

"I would regret not having had one chance to take a good poke at old Boney's men, though," Lieutenant Penworth added.

"Yes, a captured Eagle would be a splendid souvenir to keep in one's ancestral castle for the rest of one's life, would it not?" Sir Harding said in his somewhat bored voice. "Your youthful eagerness is quite exhausting, Penworth, and is boring the ladies." He bowed from the saddle to Madeline with exaggerated courtesy.

Madeline twirled her parasol and bit back the retort that it was all very well to affect world-weariness when one was a civilian and ran no danger of ever seeing an Eagle waving menacingly in one's face from the clasp of a French hand. She smiled at a flushing Lieutenant Penworth.

The colonel handed her from the barouche when a suitable picnic site had been chosen, and asked her to take a walk with him, since it was too early to eat. Lady Anne and Frances were already settling themselves on blankets that Captain Norton had spread on the ground. Sir Harding joined them there. Lieutenant Penworth was bowing over Jennifer Simpson's hand.

It was perhaps not quite proper to agree to walk alone in the forest with a gentleman, Madeline thought as she took the colonel's arm and allowed him to lead her away. But she was past the age of chaperones and all that faradiddle. It felt good sometimes to be five-and-twenty and as free as a bird.

"Now I know why you wore a dress of such a bright yellow," the colonel said. "It was so that we would have sunshine even in the middle of the forest."

"Ah, my secret is exposed," she said gaily, twirling the parasol even as she realized that its use was quite redundant with the trees acting as an effective shade.

They settled into their usual conversation of light banter. It was the way she talked with almost all men these days. Never anything deeper. Was she afraid to get to know any man too closely? Was she afraid to allow any man to know her? But she shook her head and smiled. This was not a day for introspection.

"You know . . ." the colonel said, and Madeline was instantly alert. The tone of his voice had changed. "Despite your very sensible ban on a certain topic for today, I will say that it is highly probable that I will have to leave Brussels at a moment's notice."

"You did so today," she said, smiling up at him, "to attend a picnic."

But she could not control this part of the conversation. His eyes were grave as he smiled back.

"I may not be able to return immediately," he said. "Perhaps you will be gone back to England before I do so."

"I shall stay," she said. "Until Dominic is ready to go back, that is."

"If you have returned to England before I see you again," he said, "may I find you out there?"

"But of course," she said gaily. "I always enjoy finding absent friends again, sir."

"Do you comprehend my meaning?" he asked, looking searchingly into her eyes.

She gave up her pretense of gaiety. "Yes," she said hesitantly. "Yes, I do, sir. And I wish you would not. Let us not spoil a day of pleasure."

He smiled ruefully. "You do not care for me?" he asked.

"Oh, yes, I do," she said hastily. "I do."

"But you are afraid of what might happen?"

She drew in a deep breath. "I do not think of it," she said. "It is not that at all."

"Ah," he said. "There is someone else, then?"

She looked sadly into his eyes. "Yes," she said. "I'm sorry."

He smiled slowly. "And so am I," he said. They walked on in silence for a while. "I do hope you are unrolling a ball of string behind our backs. Do you have any idea how to get back to the carriages? We might be doomed to wander here forever and ever, you know."

"What a dreadful fate!" she said. "But I am sure that after a few days, sir, when I am about to die of starvation, you will be gentleman enough to climb a tree to see if you can see the spires of Brussels or some other sign of civilization."

He laughed. "But these are not exactly a schoolboy's dream of trees for climbing, are they?" he said.

She had said yes, Madeline was thinking. She had said that yes, there was someone else. Why had she said that? Had she lied because it was an easy way to put an end to an uncomfortable conversation? And yet she had not felt as if she were lying. Was there someone else? Was that her problem?

But she did not either like him or love him. She had not seen him for three years and was unlikely ever to see him again. He had settled in Canada. He had gone beyond Canada into the vast inland wilderness, working in the fur trade. She very rarely thought of him consciously except when Alexandra had a letter from him. But she had said yes. She had agreed that there was someone else.

It was a long time since she had loved and hated James Purnell. A long time since that strange night at Amberley when he had danced with her in Edmund's formal gardens to the faint sounds of music coming from the ballroom. When he had kissed her with a tenderness she had not known him capable of and with a passion that had had her expecting that she would be taken there in the garden, and wanting to be taken. When he had told her that she should leave him if she knew what was good for her, that he did not love her, that he felt only lust for her. When he had left in the middle of the night, even before the ball was over, and taken ship for Canada.

It was all a long, long time ago. Like something from another lifetime. Yet she had just told Colonel Huxtable that there was someone else. James with his severe, handsome face and lean, restless body. James with his very dark hair and the lock that fell constantly over his forehead, no matter how often he pushed it back.

Yes, she had loved him. Against all reason. A long, long time ago.

LIEUTENANT PENWORTH BOWED to Jennifer. "Would you care to walk a little way, Miss Simpson?" he asked. "Perhaps you feel like some exercise after sitting for such a long time."

Well, the devil! Lord Eden thought. He was losing her to a scarlet cavalryman's coat, to a young and eager boy. If he was not careful, he was going to find himself paired with Miss Frances Summers, who had been signaling her availability to him for all of the past month. But Miss Simpson would need a chaperone if she intended to walk out of sight, a strong possibility when they were in the middle of a forest.

"Shall we stroll along too, Mrs. Simpson?" he asked. "I confess to a need to work up more of an appetite for tea."

"Thank you," she said, taking his offered arm.

And they settled into a silence that he found difficult to break. It was strange—he had never felt awkward in her presence before. But he had noticed during the ride from Brussels that she had not once looked into his eyes. Damn him for a careless dancer. Their collision of the previous evening had been a small matter, but it had embarrassed her dreadfully.

And he had woken in a sweat during the night with the fragrance of her hair in his nostrils.

She was Ellen Simpson. Charlie's wife. The quiet woman whose presence had always made Charlie's tent a haven of peace and comfort. The woman in whose presence he had always been able to relax fully. The woman whose presence he had often been unaware of, though he had always noticed when she was not there for some reason.

She was just Ellen Simpson.

"Do you ever miss England?" he asked. "This is a very lovely spot, I must confess, but it is not home, is it?"

"Home!" she said softly. "Home is not a place to me, my lord. Home is my husband. And he has a habit of moving about with the army." She smiled.

He looked down at her in some curiosity. He had never asked her about herself. He knew very little about her, in fact.

"Were you with your father from infancy?" he asked. "When did your mother die?"

"I went to Spain with my father when I was fifteen," she said, "and lived with him until he was killed. And then I married Charlie. Ten years altogether. Ten years of wandering."

She had not answered the second of his questions. Had her mother died when she was fifteen? Was there no other family to whom she could have gone?

"Which part of England are you from?" he asked.

"London mostly," she said. "My father . . . That is, we had a home in Leicestershire, but we rarely went there. I grew up in London."

"Do you not dream of going back?" he asked. "Of finally having a home of your own again? A place where you belong?"

"Yes, sometimes," she said. "In the countryside. With no troubles and no dangers. So that I would not always have to live in terror that something was going to happen to Charlie. It must be heaven to live with one's husband in peace. And in one place. A place that is one's own. Oh, yes, I do wish for that."

"The time will come soon enough," he said, touching the hand that rested on his arm and withdrawing his fingers hastily. He did not want to make her uncomfortable again. "Charlie is talking of selling out once this business with Bonaparte is finally finished with."

"Yes," she said. "But I have learned in the past ten years not to look too far ahead and not to dream too much. I have my husband today. We will spend this evening together. That I can look forward to with some certainty and some eagerness. But not the home in the country. I will not think about that yet."

"Charlie is a fortunate man," he said.

She looked up at him, startled. "Oh, no," she said. "I am the fortunate one. If you only knew! Charlie is the kindest and the most wonderful man in the whole world. He gave me a reason for living when I had none, you know. He is everything to me. My world would collapse if I did not have him."

He had learned in the previous few weeks that there was more to Ellen Simpson than just the quiet strength of character that he had been long familiar with. He had learned that she could be gay and humorous and vitally beautiful. And now he was seeing that there was passion in her. He looked down at her, intrigued.

"I know something of Charlie's kindness," he said. "I am not sure that I would not have bolted from the terror of my first experience with battle if your husband had not been there to encourage me. It must have been a comfort to have him for a friend when your father died. Were you very fond of him?"

"He was good to me," she said. "But I never knew him

well. I had terrible problems adjusting to army life when I first went to Spain." She smiled. "Charlie found me crying outside my tent one day because I had just brushed my hair and found the brush to be gray with dust, and there was nowhere to wash my hair. Or my clothes. I had never really experienced dirt before. He put his arm around my shoulders and sat on the ground with me and told me stories, just as if I were a child." She laughed. "He was wholly paternal, you must realize. I was fifteen, and he thirty. And he told me of his little girl, whom he missed. Jennifer. After that, he used to seek me out often to see that I was not unhappy. And he used to bring me presents whenever he had been into a town. A fan. A mantilla. A clean comb."

It was hard to imagine Mrs. Simpson as a bewildered girl, crying in the dust. He knew her as a woman who endured the worst of hardships with quiet cheerfulness. The only time he had seen her react to discomfort was when she had fallen from her horse into the mud one day and had been cursing like one of the men when he and Charlie had come up to her.

"I made friends among the women quite fast," she said. "And I got used to the life. But you cannot imagine how having just a glimpse of Charlie came to light up my days. Sometimes he would wink at me from a distance. I suppose he was like the father I . . . He was like a father to me. Or an older brother."

Like the father she had never had? Lord Eden completed in his mind. There was something fascinating about discovering what two of his friends had been like before he had met them.

"I asked him to marry me," she said, and she flushed when he looked down at her with a grin. "It is shocking, is it not? After my father died, he wanted to send me to his sister in London. Lady Habersham, with whom Jennifer always stayed when not at school. He was willing to do that for me. But I asked him to marry me. I even begged him. He did not think it fitting. He said he was too old for me and not right for me."

Lord Eden laughed aloud. "I shall have to tease him," he said, "about being led squealing to the altar."

"Oh," she said, and she was laughing too. "Please don't do that. Please don't. I was very selfish. I did not even consider that perhaps he did not want to marry me. But I loved him so dearly. I could not bear the thought of being parted from him. Life would have had no more meaning. But I don't think he has been sorry. I think I have brought him happiness, too."

"If you had had to spend your days with him as I did when you were gone to England, ma'am," he said, "you would be in no doubt about that. He was like a bear in a cage."

She smiled brightly at him. "I am sorry," she said. "I must have been boring you terribly, telling you these things."

"On the contrary," he said. "I have been fascinated." And that was certainly no lie. He was totally surprised. He had always assumed that Mrs. Simpson had been persuaded into a marriage of convenience after the death of her father, though he had never been in any doubt of her devotion to Charlie. But of course, when he thought about it, he had to admit that her story made sense. Charlie was not at all the type of man to take advantage of an unhappy and bewildered girl.

"It seems that Lieutenant Penworth would make a good reconnaissance officer," he said. "I am afraid I would be hopelessly lost in this forest by now. But you see? He has brought us full circle, and there is the picnic party."

She seemed to have run out of confidences and conversation. It was something of a relief to be back with the others again and to be able to arrange matters so that he sat down on the blanket beside Jennifer. She was glowing with high spirits, as usual, and looking particularly fetching in a blue muslin dress and straw bonnet trimmed with blue flowers.

Lord Eden did not know why he could not shake from his mind the memory of Mrs. Simpson pressed to his body the night before, her face turned up to his. Surely such a thing must have happened to him before. If she had been a stranger or a passing acquaintance, doubtless he would have forgotten all about the incident by now. It was just that he was unaccustomed to thinking of her as a woman. She was Charlie's wife, someone he liked and respected a great deal. But still, just Charlie's wife.

It was foolish to feel this embarrassment, this awareness, in her presence. And to know that she shared the feeling. He did not like it at all. He set himself to charm Miss Simpson.

CAPTAIN SIMPSON TURNED to Ellen and blew out his breath from puffed cheeks. He laughed.

"Have you ever seen such a little whirlwind?" he asked. "If her mouth could move any faster, Ellen, she would make it do so."

Ellen too laughed. "But she is enjoying herself so much," she said. "And she has made so many friends, and amassed so many admirers, Charlie. You must be very proud of her."

"I am," he said. He walked away from the door through which his daughter had just whisked herself on her way to the theater with the Slatterys. "Sometimes I have to pinch myself, Ellen, just to believe she is my daughter. Can you imagine me being father to such a pretty little creature?"

"I can," she said.

He smiled and sat down beside her on the sofa. "So this afternoon it was all Lieutenant Penworth, was it?" he said. "Can't say I know the puppy, except that he's a Guardsman. From Devon, she says, with a parcel of younger brothers and sisters and a love of riding and sailing and playing cricket. Do you fancy visiting our grandchildren in Devon, lass?"

"Oh, Charlie," she said, laughing at him. "Jennifer is not ready to fix her choice yet. She very much has eyes for Lord Eden, but I think she is shy of talking to you about him because he is your friend."

"Well," he said, "I don't want her married yet. She should have time to enjoy herself, shouldn't she? Did you have a good time, lass?"

"Yes, I did." She reached up a hand and smoothed it over the thinning hair at the side of his head. "But I would have preferred to be at home with you. Did you miss me?"

"I went to the shops," he said.

She laughed. "You, Charlie?" she said. "To the shops?"

"How else could I buy you a present?" he said, grinning at her.

"A present? You bought me a present?" He had not done that for a long time, not since they were in Spain. Oh, he had given her money when she went to England, with strict orders to spend it on herself. But it was the little, often absurd presents that she had always valued most. "Where is it?"

"In my pocket," he said. But he clasped a hand over the pocket as her hand went toward it. "What do I get first?"

She knelt on the sofa beside him and wrapped her arms

about his neck. "What do you want?" she asked, and kissed him lightly on both cheeks.

"The lips," he said. "Nothing less than the lips."

"Oh," she said, "it must be a very valuable present, then. All right, the lips it is."

They were both chuckling after she had finished kissing him lingeringly.

"Maybe we should forget the present," he said.

"Not a chance!" She reached into his pocket. Her fingers closed around a package wrapped in soft paper that rustled.

"Perhaps you will not like it," he said, sitting quite still.

"I will," she said, drawing it out. "I don't care what it is. What is it?"

He laughed. "Open it and see, lass," he said.

It was a pair of earbobs, tiny, delicately made, each set with an emerald.

"To wear with your new evening gown," he said. "The one you wore last night."

"Oh, Charlie," she said, "they are lovely. And must have cost you the earth. You shouldn't have. You don't need to buy me expensive gifts."

"Yes, I do," he said. "Oh, yes I do, sweetheart. And they were the very smallest jewels in the shop."

They both laughed as she wrapped her arms about his neck again. "Thank you," she said. "But I don't have a present for you."

"Yes, you do," he said, closing his arms about her. "You are a whole treasure, remember? My treasure."

She rested her cheek against the bald top of his head as he hugged her. Then she sat back on her heels and looked at him, the earbobs in her hand.

"Tears?" he said softly, reaching out and wiping away

one tear from her cheek with his thumb. "What is it, sweetheart?"

She shook her head. "Nothing," she said. "Oh, Charlie, nothing. And everything." The muscles of her face worked against her will, and more tears followed the first as his arms came firmly about her. She slid her legs from under her and hid her face against his shoulder.

"What is it, sweetheart?" He was kissing the side of her face.

"Everything is changing," she said when she could. "It is all different this time. I'm frightened, Charlie. Time is running out for us, isn't it?"

He forced her chin up and dried her eyes with a large handkerchief. "Nothing has changed," he said firmly. "We are still here together, lass, and we still love each other. And it is unlike you to talk this way. You never did before. I have always come back to you, haven't I?"

"Yes," she whispered.

"Well, then," he said. "I'll come back this time too. And this will be the last time. I promise. We'll go back to England and buy that cottage at last, and you shall have your own garden and dogs and cats and chickens and anything else you like. We'll be there by this time next year."

"I don't care about the dogs and the cats," she said, "or about the cottage or the garden. I only want you, Charlie. Tell me you will be there. Promise me you will. I can't live without you. I wouldn't want to live without you."

"Sweetheart!" His voice held surprise as he caught her to him again. "Sweetheart, what has brought on this mood? It is most unlike you. Have I been neglecting you? Is that it? I have been, haven't I? I'm so selfish. I thought you were enjoying yourself with Jennifer and with Lady Madeline and Eden and Mrs. Byng and Mrs. Slattery and all the rest. I'm sorry, lass. I've been neglecting you. But I love you, Ellen. You know I love you."

She pushed away from him suddenly, grabbed the handkerchief from his hand, and dried her eyes with it. She smiled a red-faced and watery-eyed smile. "How foolish I am!" she said. "What a goose! And all over a pair of earrings. They are more precious to me than the costliest of diamonds, Charlie. Shall I put them on? Though they will look quite dreadful with this pink dress. But you must kiss me anyway and tell me how beautiful I look. And then I want you to tell me all those old stories about your childhood. The fishing stories, and the Christmas stories. Will you?"

"What a silly lass you are," he said, taking her free hand as she rose to her feet to find a mirror, and lifting it to his lips. "You have heard those stories a hundred times. Go and put the earrings on, then, sweetheart, and come for your kiss."

She sat curled in to his body for the rest of the evening, his arm about her shoulders. And she played absently with the buttons on his waistcoat, and laughed at his stories, and kissed his chin while determinedly shutting from her mind unwilling memories of a strongly muscled arm and a broad shoulder well above the level of her own, and of laughing green eyes and fair wavy hair. And of that cologne that he had worn also the night before.

5

THROUGH MAY AND THE EARLY PART OF JUNE in that fateful year of 1815, it might have seemed that the predictions made by sons to anxious mothers, and husbands to wives, and brothers to sisters, that nothing would come of Napoleon's escape from Elba and the King of France's flight to Ghent, were quite right. All would pass over peacefully, they said. Old Boney would never be able to gather together a large enough army to threaten the one the Duke of Wellington was amassing in Belgium and the Prussian one that Marshal Blücher was bringing to his assistance. And even if he could, he would think twice about attacking the forces led by two such formidable generals.

And yet rumors persisted that the French army led by their emperor himself was larger than ever and that it was marching on Belgium. Some rumors even developed into scares and panics. The French were over the border already and marching on Brussels, Napoleon at their head. No one ever believed the rumors, of course, and scoffed at those who did. But still, one never knew. One never knew quite where the Corsican monster might rear his head. If he could escape from confinement on Elba—and had not

British soldiers been his guards?—he could also march an army on Brussels and arrive before anyone was ready for him.

But despite everything, and despite the persistent gaiety of Brussels and of the Duke of Wellington himself, the preparations went on. Those battalions and brigades already in Belgium drilled and readied themselves for what they knew might well be the battle of their lives. Other battalions poured into the country almost every day, some of them made up almost entirely of raw troops, and took up their billets at Liedekerke or Schendelbeke or Enghien or Grammont or wherever else in the vicinity of Brussels they could be squeezed in. And the Peninsular veterans who had gone to America and whom the duke needed so badly were on their way back.

And always, it seemed, artillery poured across the English Channel and rumbled ominously over the countryside to remind those who denied the fact that war was indeed imminent. Wellington complained constantly to London that the amount of artillery he was receiving was woefully inadequate, but there was quite enough to dampen the spirits of all those who witnessed its arrival.

And still the entertainments went on: balls, theater parties, court parties, reviews of the troops, excursions to places of interest, afternoon picnics, moonlight picnics. Young men who knew that their days might be numbered danced and flirted with determined gaiety. Young ladies who refused to believe that war was coming but who secretly could not believe their own self-deception gave themselves up to the pleasure of being feted by so many attentive and splendidly uniformed gentlemen.

Everyone knew what was coming. Most refused to believe it or to admit that they believed it.

The Earl of Amberley waited for his wife to finish nursing their daughter and set her down, sleeping, in her crib one afternoon after they had been out walking in the park. He laid down their son, who had fallen asleep against his shoulder after protesting that he was not tired and did not want to go to bed. He took his wife's hand and led her from the nursery to her sitting room.

"Poor Christopher," she said, laughing. "He would be so cross to know that he had fallen asleep even without his tea. He worked too hard this afternoon feeding the swans and running back and forth on the bank when they swam away. Are we going to have ours here, Edmund, instead of in the drawing room? How cozy!"

"I want to talk to you," he said, tugging on the tasseled bell-pull to summon the tea tray.

"That sounds ominous." She smiled at him and reached out a hand for his so that he would sit beside her on the love seat.

"I think we may have to go home soon," he said, taking her hand in both of his and seating himself.

"To Amberley?" Her face paled. "Is it coming soon, then?"

"It is coming closer," he said, attempting to smile.

"But we cannot leave Dominic," she said. "He is why we came, Edmund. And we cannot force Madeline to leave. She would have the hysterics. Besides, we will be quite safe here, will we not?"

"I have great faith in the duke," he said. "But I cannot take the risk of placing the lives of my wife and children in his hands, Alex. We must leave. Not immediately. But soon, I think. I want you to be ready."

"No," she said. "No, I won't leave. It would be cowardly, Edmund. And how could we be back in England, not knowing what is happening here? It would be Spain all over again."

"I cannot put you in unnecessary danger, Alex," he said. "And more especially the children. I will not. And I am sorry, but the matter is not open for discussion. I have decided."

"Have you?" she said. "And what has happened to your promise that I might always argue with you, that I need never feel that I must obey you just because you are my husband? I want to argue now."

But she had to wait for a few minutes while a footman and a maid brought in the tea tray and cakes.

Lord Amberley smiled at her when they were alone again. "You may argue, my love," he said. "You may fight me if you like. But I will not let you win. And don't cry unfair, Alex. Sometimes one feels too strongly about something to be willing to change one's mind. As you did about our coming here. You insisted on having your way then because you knew how worried I was about Dominic. Remember?"

"I hate you," she said.

He grinned. "Would it be safer to change the subject now that that unpleasantness is behind us?" he asked.

"No," she said. "You have said that I may argue. Let us compromise, then, Edmund. I will take the children home. You stay here. Dominic needs you."

"No." He cupped her face in his hands. "Dominic does not need us, love. We need him. He has a job to do. Perhaps he would do it better without having our feelings to worry about. Certainly he is going to be too busy soon to spare us a thought. He has the training and the welfare of many men to concern himself with. We are the ones who need to cling to him because we love him and know we may lose him."

"No," she said. "Dominic has always survived."

"Yes," he said. "And we will pray that he will survive one more battle. But we will not keep him alive by staying here. I must come with you. When all is said and done, my first duty is to you, Alex, and to our children. You three are my life. I cannot be separated from you."

"How will you break the news to Madeline?" she asked.

"Very carefully," he said with a rueful grin. "I expected worse explosions from you. I am quite sure I will have them from my sister."

"Will it be very soon?" she asked.

He shook his head. "It is impossible to say," he said. "But when it finally comes, Alex, there is going to be a rush to leave Brussels and reach the ports. I don't want to wait that long."

She nodded. "I hate you when you are so wise and right," she said.

"Kiss me," he said. "I have been dreading this interview and am feeling in need of some reassurance."

"The tea will get cold," she said.

"At the risk of shocking your delicate ears, my love," he said, "to hell with the tea. Kiss me."

"I shouldn't," she said, wrapping her arms around his neck. "I hate you."

"I know," he said. "Kiss me, Alex. Don't tease me. I need you."

MADELINE HAD GONE to the park with her brother and sister-in-law and the children. They had met Ellen and Jennifer Simpson there, and she had stayed to stroll with them after the baby had begun to fuss and show signs of hunger and had been taken home.

Madeline had grown fond of both ladies. Jennifer reminded her of herself at the same age. She seemed to have an endless capacity to enjoy herself and a quite genuine exuberance for life. And men were attracted to her like bees to flowers, especially the very young officers.

The girl favored Dominic, Madeline thought sometimes. Certainly she blushed whenever he came into her sight, and gazed upward at him almost worshipfully. But was she in love with him? Or was it a hero worship she felt? Equally uncertain were Dominic's feelings for her. He certainly favored her, dancing with her at every ball, escorting her to the theater, taking her for walks in the park and rides in the Allée Verte beyond the walls of the city, calling almost daily at her father's rooms. And he had a way of looking at the girl, with a type of gentle affection, that was different from the way he usually looked at his flirts.

But was it love? He did not confide his feelings to his sister, as he always had. And that in itself was perhaps significant. Madeline was not sure how she would feel about having Miss Jennifer Simpson as a sister-in-law. She liked the girl. But she did not seem right for Dom, somehow. But then, Madeline thought, and turned weak at the knees with horror at the thought, perhaps the question of approving a bride for her brother would not be relevant at all by the end of the summer.

"Can you quite believe that the weather can be so lovely day after day?" she asked the two ladies. "I wonder if they are having an unusually fine spring in England, too."

"It is lovely," Ellen Simpson said. "You would appreciate it even more if you had spent several years in Spain, Lady Madeline. There is nothing there but searing heat and dust, or rain in torrents when it comes."

"Dominic wrote to us about it," Madeline said. "It must

have been dreadful. I used to cry over his letters when they came."

"There were compensations," Ellen said. "Living like that sometimes destroys people. I have seen men go mad. But much more often it brings people closer together. There was a wonderful camaraderie among the men in Spain, and examples of great kindness and heroic self-denial. It is a strange irony that soldiers whose business it is to kill can often be the kindest and most generous of men. A life like that builds character in a man. And those are not empty words spoken by a recruiting officer," she added with a laugh. "They come from my experience."

That life built character not only in men, Madeline thought, as two young ensigns appeared on the path before them, their faces wreathed in smiles when they saw Jennifer. Bows and curtsies and bright pleasantries had to be exchanged with these acquaintances. The life she had lived had built character in Mrs. Simpson too. Madeline had grown to admire her, though she had been prepared at first to find her spineless.

Lady Lawrence and Maisie Hardcastle had done their best in the previous few weeks to raise a scandal over the fact that Mrs. Simpson, who was received at all the best homes in Brussels as the wife of Captain Simpson, was the daughter of the Countess of Harrowby. Madeline did not know the significance of the fact since she scorned to listen to the explanation that Maisie burned to give her, and Alexandra and Edmund knew no more than that the countess had a reputation for loose living and indeed lived separate from her husband the earl.

She had not asked Dominic what he knew. Dom was very friendly with the captain, and she was shy of asking him anything quite so personal about his friend's wife, and something that smacked so much of malicious gossip. She guessed that Mrs. Simpson must be an illegitimate daughter of the countess.

And Mrs. Simpson must know of the gossip herself. Fortunately most people did not seem to feel that it was of any great significance. And the Simpsons did not go out into society a great deal and had their own circle of friends, who would not be affected by society scandal. But there were those, mostly matrons who felt they were better than the general run of mortals, who took every opportunity to snub her. And yet that lady was as dignified, as warmly friendly and charming, as she had ever been.

"Here comes Papa!" Jennifer cried as they were walking beside the lake. "And Lord Eden."

"They are finished early today," Ellen said. "They both look tired."

Both men were smiling, but, yes, Madeline thought, there was that set quality to Dom's smile that usually denoted tiredness.

The captain winked at his daughter and bowed to Madeline before smiling at his wife in that way that had begun to make Madeline envious.

"Charlie," Ellen said, "you are on your way home? You are tired."

"Not too tired to accompany you on your walk," he said, offering her his arm.

Madeline heard no more as she was caught up in an exchange of words with her brother and Jennifer. But it was soon clear that Mrs. Simpson had insisted that her husband go home with her.

"We must have Lady Madeline and Eden come home to tea with us, Ellen," the captain said.

"They will be very welcome," she said. "But I would not

wish them to feel obliged to come, Charlie. Lord Eden is tired."

Who else would have noticed? Madeline wondered. Dominic's eyes were twinkling from some teasing remark he had just made to Jennifer. Living close to an army had made Mrs. Simpson sensitive to such things, it seemed.

"I am going to take Dominic home," she said. "But thank you, sir, for your invitation. Some other time we will be glad to accept."

"I suppose you really are going to march me home too and tuck me up in bed," Lord Eden said with some amusement after they had taken leave of the Simpsons.

"Yes," she said. "Mrs. Simpson was right. You are tired, Dom. You have been working too hard."

"I am not used to having a female to fuss over me," he said. "In the old days I would have gone back to tea with Charlie and droned on talking to him until we were both asleep. And Mrs. Simpson would have removed the tea tray quietly so that we would not kick it over in our sleep."

"Poor lady," Madeline said with a laugh. "She must be very long-suffering. I would kick you both awake and demand to be entertained."

He chuckled. "You would, too, Mad," he said. "She loves him, though, you know. I would have married years ago if I could have found someone to love me like that."

"What is it?" she said with a sigh. "What is it between those two, Dom? If you think about it, they seem so very unsuited in every imaginable way. But they light up in each other's presence. It should not be allowed, should it?"

"No," he said with a grin. "There should be a law. And I say, before I lose my nerve, I have to tell you this. You are going to have to go home, you know."

She stiffened immediately. "You mean to England, don't you?" she said. "I'm not going."

"Yes, you are," he said, his voice unusually grim. "Things are going to get pretty hot here soon, Mad, and I won't have you caught up in it. Edmund will be taking Alexandra and the children home within the next week or so—I mentioned the matter to him yesterday. And I have promised Charlie that I will try to arrange for Miss Simpson to travel with them—and you."

"I'm not going." Madeline's voice was shaking.

"I knew you would be difficult," he said. "But you will have to go, Mad. You can't stay here without Edmund. And it wouldn't be right anyway. Do you know what happens to women when a city is sacked?"

"Brussels is not going to be sacked," she said. "I have faith in our army if you do not."

"Of course I have faith in it," he said. "I am part of it. But I am not playing any games with my sister's life. Or her virtue. You are going, I'm afraid, even if I have to carry you kicking and screaming all the way to Antwerp."

"I would come right back again," she said. "And I am not being difficult or childish or anything else you are about to accuse me of. You are here and you are going into battle. And you are the half of my life, Dom. I won't leave you. I can't. You will kill me if you send me away. I don't care that Edmund is going. It is right that he should, for his life is centered on Alexandra and the children. But mine is centered on you, Dom. There will be any number of people staying. I will stay with one of them. Lady Andrea Potts, perhaps. She is my friend, and she will be staying, since her husband is a colonel. I won't go. Don't try to make me." Her voice was shaking almost beyond her control.

"What a goose you are, Mad," he said. "As if you can do

me any good by staying here. And I will have you to worry about."

"Then maybe it is time you did a little worrying," she said. "I have lived with far worse than worries for three years, Dom."

"Hey," he said. "You aren't crying, are you, Mad? And we have three people to pass before we reach Edmund's door. Deuce take it, you never cry."

"Well, I am crying now," she said crossly, sobbing and hiccuping all at the same time and lowering her head until her chin rested against her chest so that the couple they were passing would not see her shame. "You can't send me away, Dom. You might need me. You might be hurt. You might . . . Oh, Dom, you might *need* me!"

"Silly goose!" he said. "We will have to see what Edmund has to say. He won't like it by half if you insist on being difficult, you know."

"Edmund won't be any problem," she said. "Edmund never treats women as weak females who must be protected at all costs. At least he has not since he married Alexandra. He will understand and allow me to make my own decision."

"Silly goose!" he said.

It was Captain Simpson's day off duty again. He was strolling with Ellen along the Allée Verte, a long stately avenue lined with two rows of lime trees, with a canal flowing along one side of it. It was a peaceful place, deceptively peaceful when one considered the fact that most of the gentlemen walking there wore military uniform, and when one remembered that the troops quartered in Brussels had been reviewed there a few days before, including the men of the Ninety-fifth Rifles and indeed the whole of the Fifth Division to which they belonged.

Ellen was feeling happy. It was a beautiful day, she had the whole of it to spend with her husband, and what was in the future was in the future. She could control it no more than she could control the past. The very best course was not to think about it.

She smiled up at the captain.

"Happy, lass?" he asked, laying one hand over hers on his arm.

She nodded. "Happy."

He had come everywhere with her in the past few days. When he was off duty, that was. She had still gone shopping with Mrs. Byng and to take tea with Lady Amberley and some of her more personal friends with only Jennifer for company. But he had accompanied them to the theater, to a soirée at Mrs. Hendon's, and to a ball at Lady Trent's.

Poor Charlie. He had insisted each time that he really wanted to go. And it had been very wonderful to have him there, always within her sight. He had even danced once with her at Lady Trent's and been subjected to quite merciless teasing for the rest of the evening from Captain Norton and Lord Eden and Lieutenant Byng.

She had recovered from the vague and terrifying fears that had succeeded her return from England with Jennifer, the fear that something had changed, that something indefinable was missing, that something dreadful was going to happen. It had been the going away that had done it. When one lived with an army from day to day, one became accustomed to the dangers and the uncertainties. One learned to live with them. Being away for a while had brought to the surface all the latent anxieties that she was normally unaware of.

"I enjoyed last evening," she said.

"Did you, lass?" The captain smiled at her. "Just being at home with me? It wasn't very exciting for you, was it?"

"It was," she said, moving her head a little closer to his and batting her eyelids, "very exciting."

He laughed. "Even after five years, sweetheart?" he said. "Do you think Jennifer really had the headache?"

"I think not," she said. "She knew that you would have gone to that moonlight picnic only because you love the two of us, Charlie, and she knew that I would go only because I love her. And she has grown up a little in these weeks. She did something for us. She developed a headache and took herself off to her room. You have a kind daughter, sir, and I would say that she comes by it quite honestly."

"You must come with me afterward," he said, "and I will buy her that tortoiseshell brush she admired. Do you know the shop?"

Lord Eden was strolling along behind them with Jennifer. She had lost a good deal of her shyness with him, though she still blushed if he let his eyes rest on her for too long. And though she talked freely with him, she did not prattle as she tended to do with that group of young ensigns who liked to crowd around her, or with some of the younger lieutenants, like Penworth.

He had grown fond of her. She was a sweet girl, and a very pretty one. But he had not allowed himself to fall headlong in love with her as he would have done a few years before. He wanted to be more cautious. He wanted to make sure that he really wished to be in love with her. And he wanted to wait to see if he was in any fit state to court her after this confrontation with the French was over. If he were dead, of course, there would be no decision to make.

But there were some things worse than death for a soldier. He might not wish to inflict himself upon any wife.

"I missed you at the picnic last evening," he said. "I thought you were to be there."

"Yes," she said. "I looked forward to it because I have never been to a moonlight picnic before. But Ellen would have had to come, and Papa would have come to keep her company. And they are such strange people. If you would believe it, they would far prefer to stay at home together. And they have been so very good to me. I have been allowed to go everywhere. So I had the headache last night and retired early to my room."

"Did you?" he said, looking at her with some amusement. "And did you sleep?"

"No, I did not," she said. "I wrote a long letter to Helen West, my particular friend at school, but I had to shade the candle so that Ellen and Papa would not see it shining under the door, and then I could scarce see the paper to write. I was feeling thoroughly cross and sorry for myself by the time I went to bed." She looked up at him and giggled merrily.

"Well," he said, speaking more incautiously to her than he had ever done before, "I was feeling cross and sorry for myself too by the end of the evening. You were not there."

She blushed and looked away.

But it was true. Not, perhaps, that he had been out of sorts just because of her absence. But he had definitely been out of sorts. He had found himself almost literally bumping into Susan Jennings wherever he turned, and somehow turning aside her veiled suggestions that they stroll and enjoy the moonlight together. Lieutenant Jennings was apparently about official business and had been unable to accompany his wife to the picnic.

Moonlight picnics could get one into more trouble than just about any other entertainment.

He looked down at Jennifer Simpson again, some light remark on his lips. But it froze there when he found her tight-lipped, tears glistening on her lashes.

"What is it?" he asked in some concern.

"Those horrid women," she said. "I hate them."

He looked his amazement.

"Did you not see?" she asked. "They walked quite pointedly past Ellen and Papa and made a great to-do about acknowledging you."

"Those two ladies we just passed?" he asked in some astonishment. "Because I have a title, perhaps, and they think me vastly superior to the ordinary run of mortal." He grinned down at her.

"Because Ellen is the Countess of Harrowby's daughter," she said, "and they think her a little worse than the dirt beneath their feet. The two of them together do not possess as much worth as Ellen in her little finger." Her tone was quite vehement.

He frowned in incomprehension and glanced ahead to Mrs. Simpson, who was saying something to Charlie and smiling.

"And Ellen persists in not noticing," Jennifer continued. "And Papa says that those people are not worthy even of our contempt. I would like to spit in their eye, and I would do so too if it would not create a huge scandal and hurt Ellen worse than their snubs."

"I am sure your father is quite right," Lord Eden said, "though your anger on your stepmother's behalf does you credit. But the Countess of Harrowby is still alive."

"Do you know her?" she said. "Papa told me when I asked—though he said he should not be telling me such things—that Ellen grew up thinking herself the daughter of the earl. But then the countess had a terrible quarrel with him and told him before she ran away with someone else that Ellen was not his daughter. And when Ellen found out, she insisted on going to her real father, who had always been a friend of the family, although the earl wanted her to stay and still be his daughter. She went to Spain, and she met Papa there. And I am glad she did, because they are happy together. And I love her."

Her voice was shaking. Lord Eden held her arm more firmly to his side. "Mrs. Simpson is a lady, no matter what the story of her past," he said. "You must disregard those who would snub her. They are beneath notice."

"Yes, I know," she said. "But I hurt for Ellen's sake."

Lord Eden looked ahead to Mrs. Simpson, who was now laughing at something Charlie was saying. Yes, the girl was right. They were happy together, those two. And it was right that they be so. Charlie was the kindest of men, even to the soldiers of his company. He deserved happiness in his personal life. And Mrs. Simpson, from what she had said about herself, and from what he had just heard, had not had an easy life. Yet she had not let herself become embittered. She was a kind and dignified lady. She deserved happiness too. She deserved Charlie.

He felt a twinge of the old envy. Perhaps he had never done anything himself to deserve such love from a woman.

He was glad that she had recovered from that embarrassment that had made them awkward in each other's presence for a few days. He did not like to feel uncomfortable with Mrs. Simpson. He did not like to be aware of her as a woman, lovely as she undoubtedly was. Such awareness seemed disrespectful to her and disloyal to Charlie.

She was Charlie's wife, and it was perfectly right that she be so.

"There is going to be fighting soon, isn't there?" Jennifer said.

"It is possible," he said. "But not just yet. You need not worry."

"That is what everyone tells me," she said. "But I do worry. And it all seems so senseless. I wish people did not have to fight."

"Most of us agree," he said. "But I am afraid we live in an imperfect world."

"I think Papa is going to send me home," she said. "I don't think it fair. Ellen will be staying, and she has been with the army since she was younger than I am now."

"Your papa will doubtless worry less if you are safe in England," he said. "And women who stay close to the fighting do not have an enviable lot, you know."

She looked annoyed, and he realized he had said the wrong thing. "Do you think it is easy for women to be in England," she said, "where we do not hear of a battle until days after it is all over? Do you have any idea what it is like waiting to find out if one's father is alive or dead? And this time it will be worse because I know more men than just Papa. It is not fair to treat us as children who will be safe as long as our bodies are not harmed."

"I am sorry." He touched her hand. "But we men are brought up to feel protective of women, you see. And sometimes the best we can do is to protect them from physical harm. It is not easy for us, either. I have a mother and a sister who will be scarred for the rest of their lives if I die. That is no easy knowledge to have on my mind as I face battle."

She nodded. "No one has it easy at such times, I suppose," she said. "So the best way I can help Papa is to go meekly home when he tells me it is time?"

He nodded. "I'm afraid so."

"I'm afraid so too," she said ruefully.

They smiled at each other.

She was not such a child after all, Lord Eden thought. Not as fragile and helpless and as much in need of a man's protection as he had thought.

6

ELLEN HAD NOT FLINCHED FROM THE HEIGHT-ened preparations for war that she had seen happening around her. She had given in to her fear during that one evening at home with her husband, but she would not do so again. Besides, she had found from past experience that the closer a pitched battle drew, the calmer she became. It was as if the inevitability of it all finally convinced her that anxiety was a pointless luxury.

They were walking in the park beside the lake. She had met the captain there after he had finished duty for the day. Jennifer and Lady Anne Drummond, Lord Eden and Lieutenant Penworth were watching the swans on the water.

"Jennifer has taken it well, hasn't she?" Captain Simpson said. "I expected that there would be many more tears than there actually have been."

"I think she was consoled when she knew that Lady Anne and several of her other friends are also going home," Ellen said. "And I think she is a little frightened, Charlie. She is very young, after all."

"I don't know how to thank Lord Amberley enough," he

said. "We scarce know him apart from our connection with Eden. It was exceedingly kind of him to agree to take Jennifer home to England with his own family."

"I think that has helped Jennifer too," Ellen said. "The prospect of being able to help the countess and her nurse with those children is very appealing. She adores the baby."

"I don't suppose I can persuade you to change your mind and go too?" he asked tentatively.

"Absolutely not!" Ellen smiled at him. "Save your breath, Charlie."

"Well," he said, "I would not be doing my duty as your husband if I didn't try, lass, but you know I would be quite lost if you went. You see how selfish I am?"

"Then thank heaven for selfishness," she said fervently, and they both laughed.

"Ellen," he said, glancing ahead to make sure that the other four were out of earshot, "we must talk. Perhaps I should wait until we are quite alone together, but I have more courage in public like this."

"The usual talk?" she asked, keeping her tone light.

"Yes, and a little more," he said.

"You have provided for me and for Jennifer," she said. "If anything happens to you, I am to go to your sister in London and visit your solicitor or wait for him to call on me there. I understand, Charlie. But I do not need to, for you will be here afterward and we will travel to England together."

"Yes," he said, patting her hand. "But I have been thinking, Ellen. It never seemed important before, with Jennifer at school. But she is a young lady now and needs to be provided for as well as possible. It's time I forgot my pride. If you are alone—afterward—I want you to communicate with my father. Will you? Dorothy will help you."

"Oh, Charlie, I could not!" Ellen looked at her husband in dismay. "He has had nothing to do with you all these years. He has not cared about you or about Jennifer."

"He is her grandfather," he said gently. "And your father-in-law. He will not turn his back on you if you appeal to him. We have both been too stubborn. Neither of us willing to make the first move to the other."

"Well," she said with determined cheerfulness, "you can go and see him yourself when we return to London, Charlie."

"Please, sweetheart?"

She looked ahead along the path. "For Jennifer?" she said. "Very well, then. You have my promise."

"Thank you," he said, squeezing her hand. "He is not an ogre, you know. We had a good relationship when I was a boy. I had a happy childhood. But he expected a great deal of me since I was the elder son. Things were strained when I joined the army instead of going to university as he wished—can you imagine me in university, lass? But the break didn't come until I married Jennifer's mother."

He had never mentioned her before. Ellen continued to stare along the path ahead of her.

"She was a pretty little thing," he said. "A foolish unhappy girl when I met her. I wouldn't mention this, Ellen, except that I must. For when you talk to my father and my brother—if you ever talk to them—they may try to tell you that Jennifer is not mine. Her mother was a dancer, you see, but she could not make a living from her dancing alone. She was not a bad girl, just a girl who needed to eat to live. She was not with anyone but me after I married her, and Jennifer was born a little more than nine months after that. She is mine, Ellen. Even if she were not, I would love her all the same, because she cannot help her birth, can she? But she is mine. She should be acknowledged by my father."

"I will see that she is." Ellen did not know how she forced the words beyond the lump in her throat. "Is that why you loved me, Charlie? Because I could not help my birth?"

He laughed and patted her hand again. "My heart was touched by a pretty, rather grubby little girl crying over a dusty hairbrush," he said. "But she grew up to be the treasure of my life. The love of my life. That is what you are to me, my lass. It doesn't matter who you are. You are not letting those tabbies bother you, are you?"

She shook her head. "No," she said. "I lived through all the pain of that situation years ago. A little spite now has no power whatsoever to wound me. Oh, heavens, no. You are not to think it. I have you and Jennifer and all our friends. I am a very happy person. I have heaven on earth, Charlie."

"You will do that for me, then?" he asked. "For Jennifer? I wish I could do more for you, Ellen. I wish I had a million pounds to leave you. I wish I could have—"

"To have known you and been your wife has been more to me than a million pounds and everything else in the world," she said quickly. "And to be your wife for the rest of my life is all I could possibly wish for—a fortune beyond price, Charlie. Hush now or you will see me cry again. And you hate to see me cry, and I have promised myself not to. Tell me something. Tell me something funny that has happened in the last week. You are always so full of stories."

"Hastings blew a hole in Walker's cap when he was cleaning his gun a few mornings ago," he said. "Did I tell you about it? Fortunately, Walker's head was not inside the cap at the time. But I think Hastings might have wished it had been after Walker had finished with him. And then Eden started in on him—a few choice words from him can reduce even the most hardened soldier to jelly. Poor Hastings was almost in tears."

"But how fortunate that no one was hurt," Ellen said. "The poor man would never have lived with himself afterward, would he?"

"Let's go back to the lake," he said, "and find out what is amusing those four so much."

ALTHOUGH THE RUMORS and false alarms and panics became more and more numerous as June went on, and although the army and the artillery continued to pour into Belgium, and although even the most hardened cynics admitted that there must be some truth to at least some of the rumors, surprisingly few civilians left Brussels for the safer shores of England. It was as if they refused to believe that danger could ever seriously threaten them, the British, who had always been protected by their own shores. Or as if the Duke of Wellington had acquired in their eyes the stature of an invincible god.

Although the Earl of Amberley did not leave for Antwerp with his family, his servants, and Miss Jennifer Simpson until Monday, June 12, there were no delays or impediments to their journey, as there surely would have been had they waited just a few days longer.

Madeline, who had remained adamant in her decision to stay in Brussels as long as her twin was there, had arranged to move in with her friend, Lady Andrea Potts, who was quite as intrepid as she was herself and would tell those French a thing or two, she declared in her loud, rather masculine voice, if they dared set foot in Brussels and tried to do any looting in Colonel Lord Potts's home. Lord Eden himself was to move into an officers' billet with Captain Norton.

Christopher Raine, Viscount Cleeves, seemed blissfully unaware of the preparations for departure going on around him the day before they left, or of the heightened emotional tensions in his father's drawing room as Lord Eden prepared to remove himself to his new billet. The boy was crawling about among chair legs and table legs, quietly intent on a private game. He was clucking his tongue to represent the sound of horses' hooves.

"Well, old pal," Lord Eden said, "are you going to shake hands with your uncle?"

"Old pal," the child said, coming to his feet, his game and his horses abandoned for the moment. He put his hand in his uncle's large one. "Big ship."

Lord Eden stooped down on his haunches. "You are going in a big ship," he said. "Tomorrow, you lucky lad. Do you have a hug and kiss for Uncle Dom?"

The child put two chubby arms around his neck and squeezed tightly, puckered his mouth, and kissed Lord Eden wetly on the lips. "Old pal," he said, and spread his arms to begin a new game. He was perhaps a ship in full sail.

Lady Caroline Raine was lying in her father's arms, staring unblinkingly into his face, although occasionally her eyelids drooped. Having been fed a half-hour before, she was patiently awaiting sleep.

"A smile for Uncle Dom?" Lord Eden asked, taking her tiny fingers on one of his. But though she clutched it and shifted her eyes to his face, she remained solemn. "No? Well, no matter. The young bucks are going to be lined up at Papa's door sixteen years or so from now just for a glance from those eyes, little beauty." He bent and kissed her forehead.

A moment after he had turned away to speak to the countess, the baby looked back to her father and favored him with one of her rare, brief, and total smiles.

"Wicked little princess," he murmured.

Lord Eden had both of his sister-in-law's hands in his. "Thank you for coming, Alexandra," he said. "I cannot tell you what it has meant to have my family close to me. Have a safe journey home and give my love to Mama and Aunt Viola and Uncle William. And to Anna, of course. She is having a successful Season, I would wager. I will see you all again almost before we know it."

"Yes." She smiled. "Your mother will be so very happy to see you again, Dominic. But she just could not come, you know. She would rather worry in private. Take care of yourself."

They were in each other's arms suddenly, their eyes tightly closed.

"Dominic," she said, "we love you so very, very much."

"I'll remind you of that when I come home," he said, "and demand all sorts of favors as proof." He lifted his head and grinned down at her. "And why did you choose Edmund rather than me if you love me so very, very much? I offered for you too, if you remember."

"Oh," she said, flushing, "because I love him so very, very, *very* much, I suppose." She turned to take the almost-sleeping baby from her husband.

Lord Amberley got straight to his feet and took his brother unashamedly into his arms. They hugged each other wordlessly for some time. There was so much and so little to say.

"I am proud of you, Dominic. You know that," Lord Amberley said.

"You will tell Mama . . . ? You will tell her what needs to be said?" Lord Eden said.

"Of course," his brother said. "She is proud of you too, you know, and always will be, no matter what."

"Yes." Lord Eden released himself from his brother's embrace and grinned. "It is as well I take my leave now. You will have enough to do tomorrow just taking yourselves off with all your baggage and the children. And Miss Simpson. Thank you for taking her with you, Edmund."

His brother shrugged. "She is a pleasant young lady," he said. "And anything for you, Dominic, as you know. She is important to you?"

Lord Eden looked guarded. "She is Charlie Simpson's daughter," he said.

Lord Amberley chuckled. "There is no pinning you down, is there, Dominic?" he said. "But don't worry. Alex and I will take good care of her and deliver her safe and sound to her aunt. On your way, then. Nothing can be gained from a prolonged parting, can it?"

Lord Eden turned to his twin, who had sat in stony silence throughout the previous scene. "See me to the door, Mad?" he said.

She rose and preceded him from the room.

"You will not reconsider?" he asked when the door was closed behind him. "No, of course you won't. You have a splendid courage, Mad, and I honor you for it. I will come to see you every day, shall I?"

"If you don't," she said, "I shall come and find you out."

"Don't do that!" he said. "You will be all right with Lady Andrea? She has always reminded me of a horse, I must say."

"I have always been fond of horses," she said. "Dom, you will come to me before you have to go?"

He did not misunderstand the meaning of her vague words. "If there is any chance," he said, "I will come to you, Mad. But don't hate me for the rest of your life if I don't. There may not be time."

"I love you," she said, putting her arms up around his neck despite the presence of a footman who was waiting to open the door into the street for Lord Eden. "If you don't have time to come, that is all I want you to know and take with you. I love you."

"I know that, you goose," he said, hugging her briefly but hard. "I am just a little fond of you too, if you would believe it." He grinned at her and was gone.

Madeline resisted the urge to throw something at his retreating back only because there was nothing within her reach to throw. She sighed and turned back to the drawing room.

LORD EDEN CALLED at Captain Simpson's rooms on the Rue de la Montagne that same evening, though he was not sure that they were to be at home. He might have been sure before the arrival of Miss Simpson, since Charlie and his wife far preferred to sit at home together in the evenings than to seek out some entertainment. But things had changed, of course, with the arrival of that young lady.

He wanted to take his leave of her. And he wanted it done that day rather than wait until early the following morning before she left with Edmund and Alexandra. He wanted it all over with. He wanted them gone. And how could he admit as much even to himself without sounding as if he were lacking in natural affections?

Lord Eden had always found leave-takings painful. He would have liked to walk out of Edmund's house that afternoon without saying a word to anyone. He would like to avoid this farewell to Miss Simpson. Saying good-bye was difficult at any time. Saying it when one knew that it might well be forever was grueling beyond words.

He wanted to be free of all ties of affection. He wanted to be able to concentrate his mind and his emotions on what was coming. He wished Madeline had decided to go home too. He did not want her there in Brussels, making a constant claim on his emotional energy. And how ungrateful that sounded when she was risking her very life just so that she might stay close to him. She would never understand if he tried to explain to her. She would think that he did not care for her. And she would start hurling things at his head and yelling unladylike imprecations, and otherwise showing him that she was deeply hurt.

It was at times like this that he was glad that he was not married or even deeply attached to one woman. For he had found from past experience that before a major battle he must blank from his mind all the people who were most dear to him. He must live as if they did not exist. The men under him must become his family, the only persons for whose safety and welfare he had any concern. His commanding officers must become the only persons who had any claim on his loyalty and obedience and trust.

He did not envy Charlie at such times. Mrs. Simpson was always with him. How would it be possible to take one's leave of one's wife and go immediately into battle? How would it be possible to concentrate on the task at hand when one knew her to be very close and like to get hurt if the tide of battle went against one's own army? He shuddered.

He had watched them once, when they had come out of Charlie's tent with perhaps one minute in which to say their farewells. They had clung wordlessly together, the faces of both pale and totally without expression, so that he had turned away from the sight, more pained than embarrassed that he had been the unwitting witness to such an embrace between husband and wife. And it had taken Charlie a good ten minutes to come out of his stupor and become his usual cheerful, determined, even reckless self as he rushed into battle.

The three of them were at home when Lord Eden arrived at his friend's house. But he did not stay long. Conversation was labored. All four of them were fully aware that there was so little time left in which to talk. And how could one talk meaningfully when constrained to do so? He took tea with them and rose to leave. He held out a hand to Jennifer and smiled at her.

"I will wish you bon voyage, Miss Simpson," he said, "and hope that you will not be seasick on the return journey."

Charlie drew his wife into an adjoining room, he noticed, leaving the door open between.

"I am sure I shall not," she said, "now that I am a seasoned traveler." She placed her hand in his.

"I am glad you came," he said. "I have been happy to make your acquaintance."

"And I yours," she said. "I hope this horrid war comes to nothing after all."

He smiled. "There are many soldiers wishing differently," he said. "There are many wanting just one more chance to score a big victory against Bonaparte."

"And you?" she said. "Are you eager for battle?"

How could he explain to her that it was a necessity of his nature to fight for his country and all it stood for, with his life if need be? That there was almost an exhilaration now, a need to assert what he believed in?

"Not for the killing," he said. "But I want to be part of this fight against tyranny."

"Well, then," she said. "Good-bye, my lord. I will pray that you will be kept safe."

"Will you?" he said. "And may I call on you when I return to England?"

She flushed as she looked up at him. "If you wish," she said. "I would like that."

He lifted her hand, which still lay in his, and kissed it. "I do wish it," he said. "I am glad you are to travel with my brother. I will know that you are safe."

"He is very kind," she said, "and her ladyship. I like them."

"Good-bye, then," he said. And he squeezed her hand until he was aware of her wincing. He released it immediately.

Her eyes filled with tears. "Please keep yourself safe," she said. "Please!" And she lifted both hands and placed her fingertips lightly against his cheeks for a brief moment. She looked over her shoulder rather jerkily. "Papa," she called. "Papa, Lord Eden wishes to say good night to you." And she was gone from the room almost before Charlie was back in it.

Damnation to all leave-taking, Lord Eden was thinking a few minutes later as he strode down the street in the direction of his new billet. Now what had he done? Had he raised expectations? Was he now honor-bound to make her an offer when he returned to England? And did he want to? He was not at all sure. And he did not want to be plagued by such thoughts, such problems, such doubts. He wanted to be free of all emotion.

Devil take it. He had only just stopped himself from scooping her into his arms and pouring out his love for her and his desire to keep her safe from anxiety for the rest of her life. Would he never learn? Did he love her?

He did not know and did not want to know at that particular moment. He would not think of it. How much longer before they were finally engaged against the French? A week? Two? It could not be soon enough for him. He was ready. He was restless. He needed to get at it, this great battle that he had decided would be his last in one way or another. Time enough afterward to think about love. Not now!

He was glad to find his friend at home in the rather sparsely furnished and very masculine rooms that were now his new home too. Captain Norton's boots, none too clean, were crossed at the ankles on the table before him. His hands were clasped behind his head as he contemplated a corner of the ceiling. There were a half-empty bottle of cognac and a glass on the table.

"Old Picton is due to arrive in Brussels any day," Lord Eden said, flinging his hat onto a chair that was already overloaded with discarded clothes. "Newly appointed commander of the Fifth, in case you had forgotten, Norton my lad. You had better not thrust those boots into his face the way they look now if you know what is good for you."

"Why polish them before it is absolutely necessary to do so?" his friend asked cheerfully, a slight slur to his speech. "Find a glass, Eden, and pour yourself some cognac. Hate to drink alone. There should be one underneath all those papers on the chair. Letters from m'mother and the girls. They all write books instead of letters. I must read them sometime. Remind me."

Lord Eden found a glass, carefully avoided inspecting it

too closely for cleanliness, settled at the table, his own highly polished boots joining those of his friend, and reached for the bottle.

ON WEDNESDAY, JUNE 14, the rumor began to circulate that the French army was concentrated about Mauberge to the south and had even crossed the frontier into Belgium. Word had it that Bonaparte himself was at its head. If it was true, people said, old Boney had done it again. He had taken his fellow generals of Europe by surprise.

It was ridiculous to say such a thing, of course, when the whole spring had been taken up with nothing else but preparations for just such an eventuality. But still, people said, when every day brought a dozen rumors, truth took one rather unawares. The duke, of course, had his spies and would not be so dependent upon rumor as almost everyone else. But the duke had really expected that the attack would come from the west and the north, had he not? That was where he would attack if he were Bonaparte. He would try to cut off the allied army from the channel coast.

But then, Bonaparte could never be relied upon to behave with predictability and good sense. That was the very fiendishness and brilliance of the man, depending upon whether one feared or admired him more. Those people in Brussels in June 1815 tended to fear him.

And of course, no one knew for certain that this rumor was true, except perhaps the duke himself, and everyone knew how tight-lipped he could be. The more he smiled and looked relaxed, the more truth there was likely to be in what they had all heard. And the duke was looking very relaxed these days. There were those who began nervously to pack their belongings and choose their route to the coast, either to Ostend or to Antwerp.

At three o'clock in the afternoon of June 15, word reached the Prince of Orange as he sat at dinner with the Duke of Wellington that the Second Prussian Brigade of General Ziethen's First Corps had been attacked by the French army during the early morning and that the attack was being directed on Charleroi.

At four o'clock the duke received a dispatch from General Ziethen himself to say that Thuin had been captured. But Wellington was reluctant to act too hastily. Although he did not doubt the truth of either piece of news, he was not sure that the attacks were not merely a ruse to draw off the major portion of his army to the south while Bonaparte himself came along the expected westerly route of attack.

The duke made quiet plans to send his troops into action while waiting, patiently or impatiently—who could tell which with the duke?—for more definite word from Grant, his intelligence officer at Mons.

How did word of these matters leak out into the streets and salons of Brussels? Who knew? But leak out it did, causing excitement, exhilaration, despair, panic, just about every extreme emotion of which man is capable. On the whole, the troops hoped it was all true and that they would see action before another day had passed. The period of waiting was telling on taut nerves.

Most of the women felt despair. Some clung tearfully to their menfolk. Some demanded to be taken from the scene of the danger immediately. Some, especially those who had had experience with army life, began busily and quietly to prepare and roll bandages, bought at chemists' shops or torn from sheets and shirts. Some continued with their lives as if nothing unusual were happening. And perhaps nothing was. The spring had been full of such false alerts.

Plans proceeded unchecked for the grand ball to be held that evening at the Duchess of Richmond's house on the Rue de la Blanchisserie. Everyone who had any claim to gentility had been invited. And it was said that the Duke of Wellington and all his personal staff had every intention of attending even if the French were already in Belgium and part of the Prussian army put to rout.

Ellen and Captain Simpson decided not to go to the ball, though they had been invited and had considered going. They sat at home hand in hand until he put his arm about her shoulders and drew her closer. And they talked about any piece of nonsense they could lay their minds to.

Charlie was eager to be on his way, Ellen knew, as he always was at such times. And she must sit with him, quietly cheerful, doing and saying nothing that might distract him from the concentration he was beginning to build inside himself for what was to come. She knew and she understood that he grew away from her at such times. He was as affectionate, as loving. But he always talked to her of what he had done to provide for her in the event of his death—though the possibility was never expressed baldly in words like that—several days before there was any real chance of active service. Never, except under the severest surprise attack, at the last moment.

Before seven o'clock the duke had ordered the Second and Fifth divisions to gather at Ath in readiness to move at a moment's notice. Most of the officers remained in Brussels, and many of them intended to go to the ball. But the time had definitely come. There would be no more waiting around.

It was almost a relief. Ellen rested her head against her

husband's shoulder and closed her eyes. They lapsed into silence. Neither made any move to go to bed, though the hour was late. They would not make love. The time for such intimacy was past, even if it had not been the wrong time of the month for Ellen. They would wait. Charlie would be called before morning came. Better to be up and ready. Her arm stole around his waist, and he kissed her forehead and patted her shoulder.

They both rose to their feet quite calmly when Lord Eden's knock sounded at the door. They had expected it. The moment had come.

7

*L*ORD EDEN HAD DECIDED TO ATTEND THE
Duchess of Richmond's ball even though his division was already under orders and it was perfectly obvious
that he would be on the march before the night was out.
The house on the Rue de la Blanchisserie was, in fact,
crowded with officers of all ranks. The entertainment was
perhaps the perfect outlet for nervous energies that found
it difficult, if not impossible, to wait quietly.

Lord Eden danced and smiled and conversed with the
ladies, and listened to numerous conflicting reports of
what was happening and what was about to happen on the
borders between France and Belgium. He was as eager as
anyone else for some definite word, and he looked, as
everyone else did, for the duke, and wondered what his absence might mean.

He happened to have Susan Jennings on his arm when
some Scottish soldiers, splendidly clad in their kilts and full
Highland dress, marched into the ballroom to the music of
the bagpipes and entertained the company with reels and
strathspeys. It was difficult to imagine that the same soldiers might be in battle before another day was done.

Difficult, that was, unless one stood quite still for a moment and felt the very tangible tension behind the surface gaiety of the ballroom.

"How wonderful they are!" Susan said. "I wish I were Scottish every time I see them."

"I think I am glad I was never called upon to use my wind to blow into those pipes," Lord Eden said. "Has your husband left already, Susan? I have not seen him."

"He is still here," she said. "And please do not talk about his leaving or anyone else's leaving. I shall faint quite away at the very thought."

"You, Susan?" he said, smiling down at her. "You have a great deal more courage than you will admit to, my dear. You were in Spain. And you have remained here."

"I try," she said, raising large tear-filled eyes to his. "I try to be brave, my lord, but I am just a poor timid thing, as you must know. I must be a burden on those who know me."

"I am sure you are not," he said. "I am sure your husband honors your courage, Susan. It takes far more fortitude to appear brave when one feels afraid, you know."

"I try to be brave," she said, one tear spilling over and down her cheek. "You understand how hard it is for me, my lord. Thank you. My husband is sometimes rather brusque with me. Though I do not believe he means to be unkind."

Lord Eden smiled and was relieved to see that the orchestra was ready to begin the next set of dances. He was engaged to dance it with Madeline.

The Duke of Wellington, looking as genial and relaxed as he always did in society, arrived at the ball soon after midnight. But any hope—or fear—that the latest rumors and panic were as ill-founded as all those that had preceded them was almost immediately put to rest. The duke, normally reluctant even to mention military matters at a social event, admitted that the troops were finally off to war the next day.

Later, during supper, a dispatch was delivered to the Prince of Orange with the news that Charleroi had fallen and that the French were already twenty miles into Belgian territory. But the news caused a sensation only to a very depleted gathering. Most of the officers had already taken their leave in order to rejoin their regiments.

Lord Eden sought out Madeline before he left. He drew her into the hallway beyond the ballroom, but there was no chance of any great privacy. It did not matter. Under the circumstances, two people could find all the privacy they needed merely by looking into each other's eyes.

She clung to his hands. "You are going, Dom?" she said. "I am glad I have stayed. I have always hated you for this, you know, and have thought it all so senseless. But sometimes the most senseless and brutal deeds are necessary. And this is. I can see it, having been here for a while. You have every reason to go. You are using your life heroically. I am very proud to be your twin."

He was rather white-faced. "Mad," he said, and swallowed, "I always hate this business. You know that. What can I say that will have any meaning?"

She smiled. "Nothing," she said. "We don't need words, you and I. Just go, Dom. Go now, my dear."

He squeezed her hands until she bit her lip with the pain. "Don't grieve too much for me," he said. "If anything happens, go on living, Mad. And be happy. This is something I want to do, and I do not regret what it may cost me."

"Go," she said, still smiling. "Kiss me once and go."

He held her hands still as he kissed her. "I'll be back," he said with a sudden grin before turning and hurrying away down the stairs. "I have no intention of relinquishing my claim to be the elder twin, you know."

She stood smiling after him until he was out of sight. And then the fan that she held broke in two in her hands.

Lord Eden hurried back to his billet to change out of his ball clothes, and found Captain Norton all ready to leave, alert and smartly dressed now that it was time to go into action.

"You go on ahead," Lord Eden said when it seemed that the captain would have waited for him. "I promised to call on Simpson if there was need. We will catch up to you somewhere."

His friend grinned at him. "Don't delay too long," he said. "You might miss all the fun."

"Not a chance!" Lord Eden said with a laugh, hurling a silk shirt to the floor and trampling over it a moment later as he went for his boots.

Charlie was not in bed, he found less than half an hour later as he knocked on the door to his rooms. There was light within. If he knew his friend, he was probably all ready to leave.

Their faces were very set and without expression, he saw immediately when Charlie opened the door. He tried to smile. "It's time to go," he said.

He would have turned and left, but Charlie went from the room, and Mrs. Simpson stood looking at him. Her face was quite composed and quite without color. She held out both her hands to him.

"You will take care of yourself," she said.

"Yes." He smiled and took her hands. "And you, ma'am."

There was a wonderful comfort in her presence. He never had known what caused it. He would have avoided taking any leave of her if he could. But he was not sorry now that he was holding her hands and looking down into her eyes. Perhaps Charlie was to be envied after all. He squeezed her hands.

"Come home again," she said quietly. "Please come back again."

"Yes," he said.

And when he released her hands, she came into his arms and raised her face for his kiss. And he felt none of the terrible sick panic he had felt with all the others—with Edmund and Alexandra and the children, with Madeline. Only a certain peace as he kissed her and then hugged her to him and breathed in that fragrance from her hair that had haunted him for a few days. And a release of new energy that was no longer nervous energy, but a purposeful desire to go out and do the job that he was trained to do.

He smiled down at Ellen Simpson as she released him. "Thank you, ma'am," he said. And he looked up briskly at his friend, who had been standing quietly in the room since she had spoken her last words. "I'll see you outside in a few minutes, Charlie."

Ellen turned to her husband and looked at him as if down a long tunnel. He held out his arms to her.

"Well, lass," he said.

"Charlie." She put herself against him, her face pressed to his shoulder.

And he rocked her in his arms. They communicated at a level far deeper than words. He put her from him eventually and held her face in his hands.

"My precious, precious treasure!" he whispered, and kissed her once, briefly, on the lips. "My sweetheart."

"Go now," she said as she always said to him on such occasions.

And after the door had closed quietly behind him, she

squared her shoulders and lifted her chin. She did not dare move. Not yet.

So. It was done. She had sent her men on their way, and there remained only the wait to see if either or both of them would come back to her again.

Charlie, her love. The light of her life. The precious only light. The only person on this earth she would gladly, gladly die for. The only person she could not—dared not—contemplate living without.

And Lord Eden—Dominic. Her husband's friend. Her friend. Beautiful, smiling, charming Lord Eden, whom she had seen reluctantly, unwillingly, in the past weeks as a man. As a very attractive man of her own age. And now he was going with Charlie into the carnage of war. She might never see him again.

And so she had sent him on his way with her love. She had kissed him as a mother might. As a sister might. And perhaps a little differently from either.

And Charlie was gone.

Charlie was gone.

She continued to stare at the door even when, eventually, it blurred before her eyes.

THE FOLLOWING DAY was the worst waking nightmare Madeline had ever lived through. She began the day badly, rising for an early breakfast, though she had hardly slept at all. Lady Andrea's manner, she found, was as brisk and as heartily cheerful as it ever was, though the colonel too had left from the ball to join his regiment, without returning home to change from his evening clothes. The two ladies were alone in the house apart from the servants. Mr.

Mason, Lady Andrea's father, was already out seeing what news he could discover.

And they were to spend the day, Madeline discovered, laying in as many supplies as they could, both of food and of medical necessities, clearing rooms of unnecessary furniture, and gathering as many sheets, blankets, and pillows as they could lay their hands on. It mattered not at all that there were servants in the house who might be set to performing these tasks.

"Soon it will not signify whether we are tavern maids or the Queen of England or anything else in between," Lady Andrea said. "They will send the wounded back here, you know, and before we know it, there will be scarce room even in the streets for them all. We will be ready to take in as many as we can."

Madeline blanched at the mental image of wounded soldiers—those same soldiers whom she had seen thronging the streets and dancing at the Duchess of Richmond's ball only the day before.

"There will be surgeons?" she asked.

"They will probably all stay at the front," her friend said, seemingly quite unmoved by the horror of her own words. "The wounded who are sent back here will be dependent upon our care. We must be ready for them."

"I have no experience. I will not know what to do." Madeline swallowed awkwardly.

Lady Andrea allowed herself a short bark of laughter. "Yes, you will, my dear," she said. "Of course, I forget that you are raw out of England. Believe me, Madeline, my dear girl, by this time tomorrow or the day after, you will know exactly what to do. You will see need and you will be there to supply it. We do not know what inner resources we have until they are called upon."

But she had none, Madeline thought. She would not even be able to shut herself away in the kitchen and cook broths for the wounded. She did not know how to cook. And the sight of blood made her feel faint.

"Don't worry," Lady Andrea said, patting her on the arm and rising resolutely from the breakfast table. "When the time comes, you will be far too busy to remember that you are a delicately nurtured young lady."

Perhaps there was some truth to that, Madeline thought as the day proceeded and she rushed about without maid or chaperone, though the streets were far more crowded than usual. Although a surprising number of people seemed to be going about their business as usual, there was also an unusual press of vehicles in the streets, piled high with baggage and furniture, often pulled by fewer horses than was customary with the particular conveyance.

People were leaving Brussels in droves. But it was not easy, one chance-met acquaintance told Madeline. Some other mutual acquaintances who had tried to leave by barge on the canal to Antwerp had found that there were no barges available. They had all been commandeered under the duke's orders for the purpose of bringing artillery up to the front. Horses were selling for a king's ransom, and the crudest wagon for a fortune. People were panicking.

Madeline was glad that she had more than enough to do. There was no time to panic or to worry about Dom. She would not think of Dom. She bought all the bandages and all the laudanum that one chemist was willing to sell her and hurried back home with them.

There was no news, though Mr. Mason made frequent outings during the day and both ladies were constantly in and out of the house bound on some errand. But the guns began in the afternoon. Madeline was outside and looked up in some surprise to find that indeed there were no clouds either above or on the horizon that could presage a thunderstorm. And then she realized that the sound was not thunder and felt her knees turn to jelly and her stomach perform a somersault.

And it was not quite accurate to say that she could hear the guns, she realized. She could feel the guns. The sound was too deep and too distant to have any great effect upon the ear. But the echoes and vibrations could be felt to the very marrow of the bones.

Dominic!

She was greatly relieved to recognize Mrs. Simpson hurrying across the street toward her, head bent.

"Good afternoon, ma'am," she said, catching the lady by the arm. "Can you hear them too?"

Ellen looked up, startled. "Oh, Lady Madeline," she said, "it is you." And she stopped walking and looked more closely. "Oh, my dear," she said, "you have never experienced this before, have you? Are you going to faint? Bend your head sharply forward and take some deep breaths. Come, I shall walk with you for a little way. I was on my way to a grocer's. My poor maid had the hysterics this morning. She is fresh from England, poor girl. I succeeded in getting her a place on the cart of a neighbor, bound for Antwerp and home."

Madeline was glad of the quiet cheerfulness of her voice. "I am very silly," she said. "I am ashamed of myself."

"It would be a great deal more shameful to feel nothing when you hear those guns," Mrs. Simpson said. "But you must not worry about being missish. When the wounded begin to arrive, as they surely will by tomorrow, you will find that you have a strength you did not even suspect, and that there is no room at all for squeamishness."

"That is what Lady Andrea Potts says," Madeline said. "I am afraid I will disgrace myself."

Ellen squeezed her arm, which she had taken for support. "You will not," she said. "And if you do vomit at first, you will pick yourself up after and do what the rest of us will be doing. I have every faith in you."

"Do you think they are up there where those guns are?" Madeline said. "Dominic, I mean. And Captain Simpson."

"I don't know," Ellen said. "There is no way of knowing at the moment. And that is the very worst of battle—the not knowing. You must train your mind not to think of it. Deaden your mind. Once the wounded begin to arrive, it will be better. You will have no time to think. Each wounded soldier will become your brother, and you will care for him because he might be your brother and because some other woman somewhere may be doing for Lord Eden what you are doing for him."

"Yes," Madeline said. "That will help, will it not? Is that how it is done? Do you see your husband in every wounded soldier? I think perhaps I will not faint or vomit if I can see Dom each time. Will there be very many, do you think? Oh, how very senseless it all is. Yesterday they were here with us. Today we are feverishly gathering bandages and whatever else we can in the certainty that the city will be filled with the wounded. And what about the dead? Will they be brought in too? Or are they left where they are?"

Ellen had a very firm grip on her arm. "No," she said. "No. Deaden the mind. Keep yourself busy. Dominic will come back to you, even if only in the wounded, thirsty body of a stranger—they are always thirsty, poor souls. He will come. I promise. Do you wish me to take you home?"

"No." Madeline shook her head and smiled as brightly as she was able. "That would be shameful. I would never be able to look you in the eye again. Here is a grocer's shop. This is what you need, is it not? Good-bye, then. I shall see you probably within the next few days. And thank you."

And what was shameful, she thought all the way home, and scolded herself roundly with the thought, was that she had forgotten her own errand. Why was she out wandering alone about the streets? There must have been a reason when she left the house. She concentrated on her own stupidity as she hurried along, and even had an inward laugh at it, imagining herself telling the joke against herself years in the future to Dom and Edmund and Mama.

She could feel the guns from the brim of her bonnet to the toes of her slippers.

THE BATTLE WAS RAGING on two fronts. And the Duke of Wellington had been taken by surprise after all. The whole of the French forces were concentrated to the south. Bonaparte himself led the charge against the Prussians at Ligny, dispelling any suspicion that he might be waiting with the flower of his army on the western border. Seven miles away Marshal Ney led the attack against the few allied troops who were in position at the crossroads of Quatre Bras. Most of Wellington's army was still on its way from Brussels and Nivelles and other points to the north.

The fun and games would probably all be over by the time they got there, the men in Lord Eden's company grumbled as they trudged south in the dust from Mont St. Jean, where they had been halted for a long time awaiting orders. Here they had been sitting around on their rear ends for weeks, some of the men complained to their sympathetic mates, with nothing to do except watch the Dutch wenches and try to learn enough of their language to bring a blush to their cheeks.

And standing around half the bleeding night, a young private added while desperately trying to walk with the swagger and talk with the careless assurance of the veterans surrounding him, when they might have been amusing themselves with some of those wenches without the need of any tongue at all.

"Yer mean yer hain't never used yer tongue on a wench even when yer can't talk ter her?" some wag called from several lines behind the unfortunate private, and was rewarded for his wit by loud guffaws of rough laughter. "Yer should go back ter school and do some real learnin', lad."

All they would get from this march would be holes in their ruddy boots, another soldier complained to anyone who cared to listen. Most of them were listening to the guns ahead of them. "Johnny'll be beat before we come up to 'im, and all we'll 'ave to amuse ourselves with is diggin' pits to shovel in the dead. You mark my words."

It seemed that several did mark his words. There was a murmur of grumbled assent.

However, even the most eager rifleman of the Ninety-fifth saw all the fighting he could desire before the day was over. By the time they arrived at half-past three in the afternoon, the situation for the allies was looking somewhat grim. The Brunswickers and the Nassauers had been severely battered and the Duke of Brunswick even killed. The Ninety-second, the Gordon Highlanders, had been almost cut to pieces. And the cavalry had still not arrived. Only the constant presence of the Duke of Wellington, riding coolly up and down the line, always where the action was thickest, seemingly quite unconcerned for his own safety and leading his usual charmed life, had prevented a rout, so it was said.

They must be thankful, it seemed, for the rolling nature of the country. If only Marshal Ney could have seen clearly ahead and been sure that the Duke of Wellington was not up to his old trick of keeping the bulk of his army hidden behind a rise and ready to attack at a moment's notice, then surely he would have pressed on with far more boldness than he did. And he would have swept to certain victory.

As it was, the Ninety-fifth was sent straight into action, and it was many hours before those who were still alive could look about them to discover the fate of friends and comrades, not to mention that of their whole army. Had they won or lost? They were still in the same position as they had taken up in the afternoon, and the French had retired for the night. But what would happen in the morning? Would old Ney push on again at first light? And were there enough of them left to hold him? And what had happened over at Ligny, where they had heard old Boney himself was attacking the Prussians?

Trust old Blücher to hold him, some said. But Bonaparte himself was leading the attack, others added. There seemed to be no answer to that one.

However it was at Ligny or with the army generally, most of the men were concerned first and foremost with themselves and with those who had fought elbow to elbow with them for hours. There was an appalling number of dead. Everyone looked about him warily and anxiously to see who was left and—more significant—who was not. One grieved for a close friend who had fallen, once the day was over and one had leisure to grieve, that was. One did not grieve for a fallen comrade, but merely assured those close by that it was tough luck; old so-and-so had been a good lad. Unnecessary grief put too much of a strain on the emotions. One buried one's dead comrades if they were close enough to the lines to be reached in safety. One left them where they were if they were not.

And one looked to the wounded, trying to find a stretcher for those too badly hurt to fend for themselves, encouraging those who were at least on their feet to begin the tramp back behind the lines or even all the way to Brussels if it seemed that they would not be fit for action on the next day. Those who were hurt only slightly, or those who were too tough to admit that their wounds were severe, bound up their cuts as best they could and jested to one another.

"Yer'd better get some mud on that bandage," someone called to a brave lad who stayed at the front though he had a nasty slash on the forehead, "or Johnny'll be usin' it fer target practice."

"It's the merest scratch," the same private who knew of no other use for his tongue than to talk with assured the burly sergeant who bound up his arm for him. "Scarcely even needs a bandage."

The sergeant, more kindly than some of his peers, looked closely at the youth and did not remark, as well he might, that the boy's face was almost of a color with the bandage. He ruffled the boy's hair when he was finished and said gruffly before moving away, "You'll do, lad."

Lord Eden found Captain Norton and Captain Simpson and breathed with something like relief before squatting down beside the latter. "A close thing," he said.

"Just a nice little skirmish to warm up with," Captain Simpson said. "Good practice for the boys."

Lord Eden grinned. "You don't think this is it, then,

Charlie?" he asked. "You don't think Boney will turn tail and run now?"

The captain chuckled. "Will the sun fall from the sky?" he said. "Scared, Eden?"

Lord Eden squeezed his friend's shoulder and rose to his feet again. "Only a Johnny Raw ever answers no to that question," he said. "You can't catch me out with it any longer, Charlie. My knees are knocking, if you want the truth. And my teeth clacking. I am trying to get them coordinated so that at least there will be a pleasing rhythm."

"Stay close," his friend said. "I'll add my stomach rumblings to the music. Excuse me. I have to go over to talk to that young private over there who is pretending not to be sniveling. Poor lad. He wants his mother, I'll wager my month's pay. He was doing well until the guns stopped."

Lord Eden smiled without a great deal of humor as he turned back to his own company. It did not seem so long before that Charlie had been comforting another lad— though not such a young one—who had wanted his mother after his first taste of action. And without in any way belittling or humiliating him. He wondered if anyone had done as much for Charlie Simpson when he was a raw recruit.

It was time to snatch some sleep, he thought, looking down at the hard, uninviting ground ruefully and trying not to look at the faces around him or—more to the point—the faces that were not around him. Like Captain Simpson and unlike many other officers, Lord Eden had always made a point of bivouacking with his men under exactly the conditions they experienced, instead of using his rank to commandeer more comfortable accommodation.

• • •

ELLEN WANDERED OUT into the streets the following morning, unable to remain indoors. Any news she heard might be wildly inaccurate, but even rumors and distorted truths seemed preferable to the silence that had haunted her all night after the guns had stopped. And even the night had not been totally silent. There had been noises, frightening noises, that she had resolutely ignored.

There had been a panic, she learned from one acquaintance, in the very early morning when heavy artillery being moved through Brussels toward the front was thought to be in retreat. And further panic when a troop of Belgian cavalry had galloped through the city shouting that all was lost and the French on their heels. But the French were still not there.

The Prussians had been defeated at Ligny, she heard later, and General Blücher severely injured. No one seemed to know what was happening at Quatre Bras, except that casualties had been heavy.

Ellen did not listen too closely. She watched the walking wounded who were beginning to trickle into the city, a sad and tattered remnant of those who had marched out so gallantly less than two days before. She looked closely at each separate one, her heart thumping painfully, and she found herself taking the arm of one soldier around her own shoulders to relieve his companion, who was himself wounded. She sat with him on the stone steps outside a house and wiped the dust from his face with her handkerchief and some eau de cologne. But he would not let her touch his dangling arm. It was broken, he said. He must reach his brother. Fortunately the brother was found just emerging from his home one street away.

She must go home and fetch bandages, Ellen decided, hurrying along toward the Rue de la Montagne and looking anxiously into the faces of the men about her. But she recognized no one. There was a young soldier wandering alone not far from her own door.

"A drink of water, lady," he said as she came up to him, his voice apologetic and not very hopeful.

"Of course," she said, touching his one arm and noticing the blood caked on the sleeve of the other. "Oh, you are hurt. Do you have a billet here?"

"I live in Somerset, lady," he said. "A drink of water, please."

"Come," she said, setting her arm about his waist and guiding him to the door of the house in which she had rooms. "Come, my dear. I will soon have a soothing bandage on that arm and a warm, comfortable bed for you to sleep in. And you shall have your drink."

He was a child, she thought in some horror. She doubted that he was sixteen. And his eyes were already brightening with fever.

She lowered him carefully to the sofa in the parlor and went for a glass of water before removing his boots or tackling the sleeve that was stuck firmly to his right arm together with a heavy bandage.

"They removed the ball," the boy said. "I thought they was going to take my arm off. I reckon they was too busy. Don't touch me, lady. Let me be. Don't touch me."

"You shall lie down in bed," she said gently. "I will not hurt you, my dear. And you will feel so much better afterward. I promise you. I have nursed many boys like you, you know. You must pretend that I am your mother. Do you have a mother?"

She coaxed him to the bed that had been Jennifer's and stroked her hand gently over his dusty hair on the pillow until the panic had receded from his brightened eyes.

"There, there," she said, smiling at him, "it will be all right, my dear. No one is going to hurt you anymore."

Was some woman murmuring comfort to Charlie somewhere in the city? Was he too badly hurt or too delirious to remember where he lived? Was some woman trying to cleanse and bind Lord Eden's wound, wincing herself at every hurt she knew herself to be inflicting on him?

Or were they out there somewhere unhurt, preparing to fight again? Or actually engaged in battle? But there was no sound of guns today.

Or were they lying dead somewhere?

Deaden the mind.

Remove the sleeve and the bandages inch by cautious inch to reveal the red and swollen flesh. Murmur comfort to the boy who had fought like a man the day before and who was trying very hard not to sob like a child. Keep talking to him. Smile kindly into his eyes. Let him know himself loved.

And deaden the mind.

8

THE NINETY-FIFTH DID NOT SEE A GREAT DEAL of action the following day. The French forces under Bonaparte's direct command had won a complete victory at Ligny, with the result that the tattered Prussian army was in full retreat north to Wavre and their commander lying severely wounded in a farmhouse, though he stubbornly refused either to die or to give in to his condition. Marshal Ney had not broken through the British and allied lines at Quatre Bras, but he had battered and bruised them and stood a good chance of shattering them completely on Saturday, June 17.

But surprisingly, no attack came during the morning, and the Duke of Wellington was able to withdraw all his troops in good order northward to a position he had picked out weeks before, a position on the crossroads south of the village of Waterloo and the Forest of Soignes and north of the inn La Belle Alliance on the main road to Brussels.

The men of the Ninety-fifth were the last to retreat, with the cavalry, having been assigned the unwelcome task in the morning of forming burial details to go out between the lines and try to give their own dead some sort of decent burial. The men in Lord Eden's group dragged a pair of boots from under one bush to find a French cavalry officer at the end of them, still breathing. Those few men who were new to the company were surprised when their lieutenant ordered three of them to lift the Frenchman carefully and carry him to a nearby farmhouse, where some of their own wounded were being tended.

"I said carefully!" he barked before turning to lead the way.

One veteran grinned at a new recruit. "If you was to arsk," he said, "you would be told that the bleeding orfficer ain't a Frenchie or an Englishman but an 'uman being." He tapped his temple several times and looked significantly at the recruit.

"Crazy?" the lad asked.

The veteran continued to grin. "But you never says it out loud," he said, "or one of us is likely to flatten your nose level with the rest of your face, see."

They had a miserable retreat of it. It started to rain before they were even on their way, and it was like to rain for the rest of the week, the men predicted gloomily, gazing up at the angry clouds and noting that there was a full-blown storm coming up. They forgot that the week was already ending. One tended to lose track of what day or date it was when one was on active duty.

And as if the marching and the getting soaked were not enough troubles, men with more energy than others grumbled, they were getting thoroughly peppered from behind by those damned French. Indeed, most of them agreed, the only fun they had all day was watching and cheering and jeering the Guards—the Hyde Park soldiers, as they were contemptuously called—driving the advancing French back from the village of Genappe, where the duke had spent the night before. They did all right, those cavalry Guards, despite the rain and the slithering mud. But it was quite hilarious to see the scarlet of their smart uniforms and the shine on their polished boots disappear beneath a liberal coating of mud.

It was enough to drive them all home bawling to cry on their mammies' shoulders, one witty rifleman bellowed to an appreciative audience. But there was no other fun at all. Only the interminable trudging and mud, and the blinding flashes of lightning and the crashes of thunder that made their backs twitch, so much like the heavy guns did they sound. And at the end of it all they found a nice muddy bed for the night at a crossroads in the middle of nowhere. And no rations. Trust the bloody commissary wagons to have trundled off to Brussels by now, grumbling voices too weary to be mutinous murmured to comrades. Or Ghent. Or Ostend. Or perhaps they were being loaded onto bleeding ships already to feed the bleeding sailors.

And the rain kept sheeting down.

LADY ANDREA AND Mrs. Simpson had been right, Madeline thought when she had the luxury of a moment in which to think. The first terrible feeling of panic and nausea and light-headedness when the wounded began to arrive passed almost before it was felt. The urge to go out into the street to find if she would recognize any of the poor men dragging themselves into the city or being half-dragged along by comrades in little better case than they was stronger than the desire to rush up to her room to bury her face in a pillow and clamp her hands over her ears.

And once out there, though none of them was Dom or

any other soldier she knew, there was no going back in again. Someone else had been right too—but she could not remember who had said it; they were all thirsty and begging for water. And while rushing in and out of the house with slopping pails of water and smelling salts and bandages, she quickly forgot everything but the need to quieten pathetic pleading voices, to help someone limp along, to help another sit down in the roadway for a moment, to wave smelling salts beneath the noses of the fainting, to wipe a dusty face with a damp cloth. And always to help the men to a drink.

Her senses were allowed to accustom themselves gradually to the gruesome sights. Those who arrived first were those who could still somehow drag themselves along, the somewhat lesser wounded. It was later in the day before the worse cases began to arrive, those too weak to move themselves. They came by the cartload, right into the city and onto the streets, many of them, though by the afternoon, tents for the wounded had been set up at both the Namur and the Louvain gates.

And then it began to rain. Men who must have welcomed the cooling drops at first were soon soaked through to the skin, muddy, and shivering. And women tended them with sodden skirts and hair that plastered itself to their heads and faces and dripped streams of water down their necks.

Lady Andrea and Madeline began to move inside as many of the men from the street in front of the house as could move of their own volition or with a little help. A few, those with unhurt legs, were put to bed upstairs, with no thought to the mud that quickly transferred itself to the delicate silk sheets. Others stretched themselves out on the carpets downstairs and counted themselves blessed.

Madeline hauled off mud-caked boots, cut uniforms from congealed or still-flowing wounds, bathed and bandaged cuts and gaping holes, soothed fevered brows, held reaching hands, spoke quiet words that she could never afterward recall, once closed eyes that would never close themselves again—with a hand that scarcely trembled. And always, constantly, held weakened hands and heads so that the cup of water might reach thirsting mouths.

She scarcely thought of her twin all day. There was no time to think. And it was not desirable to think. Mrs. Simpson had been right about that too. But she saw him in every face around her, in every lifted arm. She heard him in every muffled moan and plea for water, in every gasp of thanks.

She did not know when night came. She did not even know that the rain still lashed down outside. There was no leisure in which to wonder if her brother was still alive to feel all the discomfort of a night spent outdoors during the final hours of a lengthy thunderstorm.

LORD EDEN WAS very definitely alive. And uncomfortable. And hungry. He had a chance to share a scrawny fowl and a bottle of wine with Colonel Barnard of his regiment in the small cottage the latter had commandeered for the night. But with one last regretful look Lord Eden waved a dismissive hand, said that the bird was not nearly plump enough for his delicate palate, grinned at the other two officers gathered there, and returned to his hungry, sodden men.

"A strange fellow, Eden," the colonel said before turning his attention to the pathetic feast spread before him.

Lord Eden and Captain Simpson spent a tolerably comfortable night huddled beneath two blankets, a thick layer of clay spread over the top one for warmth and waterproofing, their heads resting on saddlebags. Those poor devils who had never been on a campaign before! Charlie remarked before yawning loudly and falling asleep just as if he were lying on a feather bed. They must be suffering. If one just ignored an empty, protesting belly and the muddy ground, and pretended that one was not wet through to the bone, one could not ask for greater comfort, Lord Eden agreed, sliding into oblivion only moments after his friend.

But the morning was a different matter. Although the rain had stopped, everyone and everything was wet and muddy. And shivering. Guns were unfit to be fired. Stomachs were so empty that they felt and sounded like echoes in a hollow cave. And when might the French be expected to attack? They had bivouacked alarmingly close to the allied lines and would surely want to make an early push for victory.

But the attack did not come all morning. Somehow, despite the prevailing wetness, fires were built and stiff hands warmed and sodden clothes steamed. Guns were carefully cleaned and polished by thawing hands. And finally the commissary wagons appeared from somewhere and the men had breakfast.

But one did not feel quite as one would like to feel before a major battle, Lord Eden thought, walking among his men to see that the proper preparations were being made. But then, one never did. And the consolation was that the enemy would feel no better. And he did not doubt that this would be a major battle, perhaps the biggest of his experience. They certainly could not retreat any farther without losing Brussels.

The morning was a long one. Let them get started, he thought constantly, and heard as constantly on the lips of the men about him. Even though we aren't as ready as we would like to be, let them get started.

But when the attack did begin, all the activity was directed far to the right of their position at the crossroads. The French were trying to take the villa of Hougoumont, and the British and German defenders were just as determined that they would do no such thing.

"Poor devils!" one rifleman commented.

"Wisht they'd come this way," another said, staring off to the right with narrowed eyes, though the lie of the land blocked the view of the villa from his sight.

It was half-past one in the afternoon before the heavy French guns, amassed on the slope to the south of the allied lines, all opened fire at once in the most deadly bombardment that even the oldest veteran had ever experienced. Men died and men cursed in impotent rage. There was nothing that could be done to defend oneself against such attack. The bombardment was a sure prelude to an infantry attack, to be followed doubtless by a cavalry attack. Let them come on, then. Enough of this!

The men of the Ninety-fifth were ordered back from the road behind a rise of land, where they could lie down in relative safety from the relentless pounding of the guns. But still men died.

The survivors felt enormous relief and a deep, knee-weakening dread when the guns stopped suddenly and the French drums could be heard heralding the approach of infantry. And their position, which had sheltered them from the cannon, made matters more nerve-racking now, for they were crouched down behind the rise and could not see who—or what—was approaching.

It was three solid phalanxes of infantry that were coming, each twenty-five men deep and one hundred and fifty men wide. All yelling their bone-chilling battle cry, *"Vive l'empereur!"* But the riflemen were unaware of the statistics when they were finally given the order to rise and fire. They saw only masses of the enemy alarmingly close and soon falling in satisfying heaps to the first volley from their faithful Baker rifles.

Volumes might be written in years to come about the fortunes and misfortunes of that fateful Sunday, June 18, on which the battle was fought that the Duke of Wellington later dubbed the Battle of Waterloo, according to his custom, after the village where he had stayed the night before. But to the men who fought in it there were only themselves and their immediate comrades, their weapons, and the interminable noise and smell, and the day that seemed a week long.

In all the noise and smoke of battle, and the crowds of milling soldiers and the piles of dead and wounded, it was impossible for an individual to know how the battle was going. All each man could know was that he was there and had not yet given an inch of ground, that his comrades were ranged around him, and that his officers were still giving orders that he obeyed without question.

Had Hougoumont fallen? The men of the Ninety-fifth did not know, and probably did not care. Would La Haye Sainte, the farmhouse in front of them being held by a company of German soldiers, hold? It was their job to see that it did. And may pity help them if it did not and the French had a chance to move their guns into the courtyard. They would be blown off the face of the earth.

Had the Prussians come from Wavre? Were they on their way? The lines were getting thinner and there seemed to be no more reserves to move up. But who knew? Perhaps farther along, the line was as solid and thick as ever. Or perhaps there was no other line beyond the little stretch that they could see to either side of them. Perhaps everyone else had fled as Bylandt's Belgians had done right next to them during that first charge of the French infantry.

General Picton was dead. They all saw him fall a moment after yelling encouragement to his men to push back the advancing French infantry lines. That was real to them.

And then late in the day La Haye Sainte did fall to a concerted attack, and the last surviving defenders fought their way out and back to the crossroads.

"Now all hell will break loose!" someone at Lord Eden's elbow remarked, and was proved right without further delay.

The men fought doggedly on, all the odds against them. Yet when it seemed they must break, encouragement came that no British soldier could ever resist.

"Stand fast, Ninety-fifth," the steady voice of the Duke of Wellington said above the din. "We must not be beat. What will they say in England?"

The men fought on, the duke with them, until it was clear to him that they would not break.

But the battle and the world ended for Lord Eden during a momentary lull in the action. A swift glance to either side of him revealed Charlie Simpson lying on the ground, a corporal kneeling over him. Lord Eden elbowed his way through the throng of his own men and fell to his knees beside his friend.

"You have been hit, Charlie?" he asked unnecessarily. "Lie still. I'll have a stretcher brought up. We'll have you back from here before you can count to ten."

But there was that long-familiar look in his friend's face. The look of sure death.

The glazing eyes searched for his and found them. "I'm done for, lad," Charlie said.

And they were too old and experienced soldiers to live a lie. Lord Eden closed his mouth, which had opened to make a hearty protest. He took his friend's limp hand in his own.

"I'm here, Charlie," he said.

"Ellen." The voice was faint, dreamy almost. "Jennifer."

Lord Eden leaned forward until his face was a few inches from Captain Simpson's. "They will never be in need," he said. "I swear that to you, Charlie. I will always take care of them. Do you hear me?"

But Charlie was looking through him, beyond him, with eyes that were fast clouding. And then the eyes were lifeless.

His friend was dead.

Lord Eden fought panic and tears. There was no leisure now to grieve. He grasped his sword and started to get to his feet.

And then he knew, with some surprise and no pain at all, that he had been hit. There was a rush of warmth about his ribs. His eyes widened before he fell forward across the body of his friend.

ELLEN KNEW THAT she could not shut herself into her rooms tending the needs of one poor boy. There were more men out there, men in the hundreds, perhaps thousands, and they would need all the nurses that could be found. Besides, Charlie might be out there. She must look for him. Or other men of her acquaintance. She must look for them. Lord Eden might be out there.

And so she ventured out in Saturday afternoon's torrential rain when the boy had settled into a rather fevered sleep, his arm swathed in a fresh bandage, swollen and angry-looking, it was true, but with the wound clean. She had hopes that she could save him from amputation. It was amazing that the arm had not been sawed off before he left the battlefield. The surgeons had not had time to amputate, the boy had said. In her experience, the very fastest treatment field surgeons knew for arm and leg injuries was amputation. But most of them were unnecessary, she had always felt. She would save the boy. She did not know his name.

The wounded were being carried inside the cathedral not far from where she lived. She stepped sharply over to one sodden bundle whom no one was making any attempt to move. He was Charlie, she thought with a sick lurch of the stomach. But he was a stranger. She knelt and put a hand to his wet brow. He stared straight through her arm.

"Carry this man inside out of the rain," she called in French to a man who had just emerged from the cathedral.

"It is not worth disturbing him," the man said, not unkindly. "He will not last."

"But he will not die untended and unloved," she said, rising to her feet and running back in the direction of home. A few minutes later she was hurrying back again with two of the menservants from the other part of the house in which she lived. And together they carried the soldier to her rooms and set him down on the bed that had been the maid's.

"Thank you," she said as the two servants withdrew, but she did not take her eyes from the wounded soldier, who had not made a sound beyond one faint moan when they had first lifted him. His eyes were open, but they were neither living nor dead.

"It is all right, my dear," she said softly, taking a towel

and dabbing lightly at his wet face and hair. "You are safe now. No one will harm you."

His boots came off easily, she was thankful to find. She set herself the task of cutting the rest of his clothes away so that she would not have to move him. It looked as if no one had tended his wound, a gaping hole in the stomach that should surely have killed him instantly. Ellen patted him dry and went for one of Charlie's silk shirts to make a light pad to set over the wound. She covered him with a blanket and smoothed her hand over his bald head. He must be of an age with Charlie.

His eyes were on her, she saw.

"You are dry now," she said, "and warm. You are safe now. I shall care for you. No one will harm you."

He continued to look at her. She did not know if he heard her or saw her.

"I will bring you some water," she said. "You are probably thirsty."

And the boy was thirsty, she found, and tossing feverishly on his bed and groaning when his bandaged arm touched the mattress. She spent some time with him, straightening the sheets, smoothing back his hair, bending to kiss his forehead when he looked up at her with a boyish trust and hope in his fevered eyes.

Before the day was out, the door to her rooms was permanently open. The house became one again as it filled with wounded and Ellen was called upon to give advice from her experience with tending injured soldiers. Servants from the house watched over her wounded when she occasionally went outside that day and the next and the next. A great battle was raging to the south, she heard. A great disaster. A great defeat, perhaps. No one knew, and the wounded brought conflicting reports, though most seemed agreed that it was going badly for the allies.

But she no longer cared for news. Only for the suffering in the city and her own helplessness to alleviate more than a very small portion of it. And her obsession with looking into the faces of all the soldiers stumbling past or stretched on straw beds in the streets.

Was some other woman caring for Charlie? she wondered as she hurried back along the Rue de la Montagne after an hour away early on Monday morning. Was he well and still fighting somewhere? Was the battle still on? Was he dead?

Deaden the mind. She hurried on.

But she looked up sharply at a group of horsemen proceeding slowly along the street, all in military uniform. The one in the middle was slumped forward in his saddle. The soldier to his right held a steadying hand against him. She felt all the blood draining from her head.

"Do you know this man, ma'am?" the soldier on the left called, touching a hand to his shako. "He said the Rue de la Montagne, but that is all he seems to remember. I don't think he even knows his own name any longer."

"Eden," she said past lips and a tongue suddenly dry and feeling twice their size. "He is Lieutenant Lord Eden. Yes, this is where he belongs. Bring him in, will you, please?"

The soldier who had spoken to her saluted more smartly. "This is the house, my lady?" he said. "We are going to have a hard time. He can't move. All swollen up. Is there anyone who can help?"

"Go inside and call some servants," she said. She was alongside the horse, touching his boot, seeing that indeed his legs were badly swollen, seeing too that he was not quite unconscious. His breath was being drawn in labored rasps.

"You are home," she said softly. "You are home now, my dear. We will have you inside and in bed in no time. Just a few minutes more and then you can rest."

She did not know if he heard her. The same two servants who had helped her carry the man from outside the cathedral came out of the house. Ellen had to turn her back and bite her lips as the four men eased Lord Eden from the saddle. He screamed when they first touched him, and moaned with every agonized breath after that.

She led the way up the stairs and into her own bedchamber.

"Set him down here," she said. "Oh, how am I to get his boots off?" His legs were so swollen that the boots were cutting into his calves.

"I'll fetch a knife and cut them off, ma'am," one of the servants said.

"May we leave, my lady?" one of the soldiers asked. "Is there anything else we can do?"

"No," she said. "You have your duty to get back to, doubtless. I shall care for him now."

"Lucky man to have his wife here," the other said before the two of them withdrew.

And yet again she set about the task of cutting away an entire uniform. She washed the caked mud from his body and patted gently with a towel. She winced at the sight of the heavy bandage around his ribs and over his chest and at the sticky mass of blood that had oozed from the bandage and run down his right side and thigh. He moaned constantly.

"You are home, my dear," she said, washing his face finally and looking down into the pain-racked eyes she had been afraid to look into until that moment. "You are home and safe now. And may rest. I shall not change your bandage until later. You are safe. No one is going to harm you now."

"Safe," he said thickly. "Always safe. Here."

"Yes," she said, touching his fair wavy hair and putting it back from his brow. "Safe, my dear. You are always safe here. Do you know where you are? Do you know who I am?"

His breathing was labored again. He closed his eyes and moaned. She stroked his hair.

"Charlie," he said.

Her hand fell still. "Yes," she said. "I am Charlie's wife. And I am going to look after you."

"Charlie," he said. His eyes were open again, glazed with pain.

"Yes?" she said softly. His hand was waving weakly above the blanket she had laid over him. She took it in both of hers.

"Gone," he said. "He's gone. I was with him."

"Yes." She was stroking the back of his hand. "You must not let it worry your mind any longer. Rest now. You shall tell me all about it later. Thank you for bringing me the news. Is that why you directed those soldiers here? Thank you, my dear. You must sleep now. Sleep now." She smiled down into the eyes that were looking into hers. "Sleep now."

The boy was calling for water.

LORD EDEN HAD COME to himself in a farm cowhouse at Mont St. Jean, seven hundred yards behind the crossroads. The shells were falling more thickly there, someone was saying, than at the front itself. He looked about him. The ground was thick with wounded. Was he one of them?

His chest felt so swollen that he could hardly breathe. He could feel blood oozing down his side. He was lifted to a table eventually. He rather thought that the scream he heard had come from his own mouth, though it was not by any means the only one he had heard during his half-hour of returned consciousness.

The surgeon who looked down at him with weary eyes was splattered with blood from head to waist. Lord Eden closed his eyes and gritted his teeth and concentrated on not shaming himself any more, now that he was expecting pain and it was not to take him by surprise.

He was fortunate enough to faint while the flattened ball was cut from his chest, but the gush of clotted blood that came from the wound brought consciousness and relief from the terrible pressure at the same moment. He heard himself groan, and cut off the sound in the middle as hands lifted him from the table and set him on the floor again.

It was amazing how small the world became when one was in pain, he thought. He was shuttered and enclosed by it, an agony of knifelike pain. He must have broken ribs.

He did not know how long he lay there before hands were lifting him again and setting him astride a horse.

"It's not the best, sir," a voice said. "But the roads are so clogged up that it might take you days to get through on a wagon. You are one of the lucky ones."

One of the lucky ones. The words ran like a refrain through his muddled, fevered, agonized brain for the rest of the night. He did not know where he was or who was with him. He did not know where he came from or why he was on this ride.

But there was something ahead of him. Someone. Someone he must reach, and then he would be safe. All would be well. Mama? She was in London. Edmund? Yes,

Edmund. Alexandra would look after him, and Edmund would make everything right, as he always had done. A big boat, Christopher had said. A big boat. Edmund was gone.

Madeline? He had to reach Madeline. She would be worried. He had promised not to die. He mustn't die. Madeline would be fit to throw hatchets if he did. He had to get to Madeline. Where was she? Not at Edmund's. Edmund was gone. Where was she? Had she gone too? Was she in London? At Amberley? She shouldn't have gone. He needed her. She should have stayed.

Charlie. He would go to Charlie. The Rue de la Montagne. He must remember that. Rue de la Montagne. He said it over and over to himself. He said it aloud. There was comfort there. He would be able to rest there. *She* would be there, and she would not fuss him or talk too loudly. She would look after him. Yes, she was the one he had to go to.

He had something to tell her. She would look after him, but he had something to tell her first. He couldn't remember what. He would remember when he saw her. The Rue de la Montagne. The Rue de la Montagne.

And then he heard her voice. But he could not move. He did not dare move. Someone was touching him, pulling at him. They would kill him. Where had she gone? Was that him screaming again? Not again. He must not do that again. He would frighten her and disgust her perhaps. But who was making those sounds?

His body was on fire. It felt as if it must explode at any moment. He fixed his eyes on the only comfort there was. A face bending over him. Busy at something. And there was some comfort. The terrible pressure of his clothes and boots against his body had gone. And there were cool cloths against him. And was that a pillow beneath his head?

She was there. He could relax now. She was there, and her cool hand was on his brow.

He had something to tell her.

"Charlie," he heard someone say. And then he remembered.

And he told her.

Had he told her? She was looking at him with a calm marble face. She smiled. She told him to go to sleep. And then she lifted his hand to her cheek, kissed the back of it, laid it down on top of the blanket, and was gone.

But she was there. He was home now. He could not sleep, but he could retreat into his pain again. She was there.

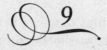

9

MADELINE WAS AT A LATE BREAKFAST OR an early luncheon—no one bothered to give names to meals any longer—when she was called out into the hallway of Lady Andrea Potts's house. At some time during the night—she had no idea when—Lady Andrea had appeared at her shoulder after having been absent for some time and ordered her to go to bed.

"I have just had a refreshing four hours of sleep," she said. "Now it is your turn. You will be no earthly good at all to these men if you collapse with exhaustion, now, will you?"

Madeline had gone because she was too tired to argue. But Mr. Mason had already brought the news from somewhere outside the house that the fighting was over and the French in full flight and the Prussian army in pursuit. A great victory, he had announced heartily, to the faint cheers of the lesser wounded.

A great victory indeed, she had thought, stepping carefully among the living bodies strewn over the drawing-room carpet so that she would not step on an outflung arm or leg. Was this what a great victory was?

And somehow even more wounded had been carried into the house while she slept. They were in the salon by the front hall, with only one thin blanket apiece, a weary-eyed maid had told her, and no pillows. She had not been in there yet.

Who could be wanting to talk to her? she wondered, hurrying into the hall when she was summoned, her stomach lurching inside her at all the possibilities. But it was only a strange manservant with a note. He handed it to her and waited. There was no empty room to which to withdraw.

Dominic had been brought in earlier that morning, Mrs. Simpson had scrawled. He had a chest wound that she had not yet examined, though it had been tended on the field. He was in a high fever, but was safe and warm in a bed in her rooms. Nothing else. No indication of whether he would live or die. Madeline surprised the servant by laughing suddenly. How could one tell if any of these men would live or die? Two had died in this very house the day before, and one of those had walked inside without assistance. And there were a dozen at least for whom it was a miracle that this day had dawned. If it had dawned. She had been sleeping for five hours and had not yet checked on them.

"Tell Mrs. Simpson that I will be there as soon as I am able," she said, folding the note carefully. She was surprised to find that her hands were quite steady.

She turned and walked into the salon, and was greeted by a chorus of requests for water. She was soon so busy that she abandoned her plan to ask Lady Andrea if she might be excused for an hour. How could she leave when there were so few hands to help? Dom was as safe as he could possibly be. Mrs. Simpson would care for him.

Before approaching the final silent bundle by the window, she opened the door and yelled at a servant who happened to be passing through the hallway to run up to her room and bring all the pillows and blankets from her bed and the cushions from the daybed. Then she turned back to him. She knew he was not dead; his hand was twitching. But his head and one side of his face were swathed in fresh bandages, and the single blanket draped over his body was flat to the floor where his right leg should have been.

She knelt beside him and took his hand in hers. "I shall have a pillow for your head and another blanket for you in a moment," she said gently. "Would you like a drink?"

His one uncovered eye was closed. He did not answer her. But he clawed weakly at her hand. She turned and lifted the cup she had set on the floor beside her and slid her free arm beneath his head to raise it slightly so that he might drink. And as he did so and some of the water dribbled from the sides of his mouth and down his neck, she realized that he was Lieutenant Penworth. That vigorous, eager boy.

"Here," she said as the servant picked her way over to her side, her arms laden, "I shall put a pillow beneath your head. And an extra blanket over you. You are shivering. It is Madeline Raine, Lieutenant. You are safe now. And will be more comfortable than you have been, I think."

She touched the backs of her fingers lightly to his cheek and turned to look at the men about her and to decide which were most in need of the single pillow, two frilled cushions, and two blankets still piled in the servant's arms.

Dominic was forgotten about. Or at least pushed to the back of her mind. There were more pressing concerns to occupy her for the moment.

• • •

THE DOOR THAT SEPARATED Ellen's rooms from the rest of the house remained open as she and the other occupants shared the care of the wounded. But she did not go out into the streets again. She felt no more need to do so, and the house was as full as it could be. No one else that she knew came to the house until Lady Madeline Raine came that evening. But then, she was expecting no one she knew. No one at all.

Lord Eden was delirious with a high fever by afternoon and had not been quite rational even when they had carried him in. But he was right about that one thing. No one else came at all. And she felt that he was right. She had not doubted it from the moment he had told her. There was no lingering hope, no part of her that listened for footsteps even against reason.

She was not expecting anyone else. And it did not matter. She would not think of it. She had plenty to do. More than enough. The boy, though not nearly as highly fevered as he, was fretful. She had to make frequent calls on him to soothe him, to give him drinks and set his blankets straight, to smooth back his hair and kiss his brow.

And late in the morning she sat with the other man, the one who always watched her with his eyes though he showed no other sign of consciousness or of life. She held his hand and smiled at him and said a prayer over him and told him that he was safe with her, together with a dozen other murmured consolations, until he died. And she closed his eyes, covered him with the sheet, and sent a manservant to find someone whose job it was to take away the dead.

But it was he who drew her constantly. Lord Eden. Dominic. She was frightened, but she would not admit to her fear. He was going to die. The fever raged in him. He did not sleep, but he knew nothing. He did not know her. She changed his bandage when the boy had sunk into an uneasy sleep and the other man had been taken away. And she winced at sight of the wound and the purple-and-green bruising around the broken ribs. And her hands trembled slightly when he began to groan with every labored breath.

"I will have a clean bandage on you in a moment, my dear," she said. "Bear with me for one minute more. Soon you shall rest again."

She sat with him whenever she could and bathed his face with a cool cloth.

No surgeon came all day long, though they had sent for one the day before, and again that morning.

Lady Madeline came in the evening, a shawl thrown over her hair, her dress crumpled and none too clean.

"Where is he?" she asked as soon as she set eyes on Ellen. "I could not get away before now. Is he . . . ?"

"He is in my room." Ellen took her visitor's arm and guided her in the right direction. "He is still alive."

"Still?" Madeline's voice sharpened. "You did not expect him to be? Oh, but how foolish. I know how it is. Was ever anything more dreadful? Is it always like this, or is this worse? Oh, Dom!"

She was into the room and across it and bending over the bed without even thinking to wait for an answer.

Ellen stood in the doorway and watched the other woman take up his hand and hold it to her cheek and talk to him. But although his eyes were open and bright, he did not know his twin. His breathing was labored.

"He needs a surgeon," Ellen said quietly, "but I am afraid they are all far too busy to come. I have changed his bandage and tried to get him to drink. There is precious little else I can do."

"I know." Madeline straightened up, though she continued to gaze down at her brother. "I know. One is so helpless. Dom, you must not die. Do you hear me? You fought out there. Now you must fight in here too. You must. You mustn't die. I don't want to be the elder twin, Dom."

She set his hand down gently at his side eventually and turned to Ellen. "It was kind of you to send," she said. "And I can see that you have been giving him the best of care. He is clean. I cannot stay. It would be selfish of me to move here merely because my brother is here. There are so many thousands . . . and so many in Lady Andrea's house, and so few to tend to them all. Lieutenant Penworth is there. He has lost a leg. And an eye. I must go back."

She was surprised to hear the sob in her throat. She had thought herself past feeling.

"Yes, you must," Ellen agreed. "I have help here in the rest of the house. And I will care for him, you know. He has been like part of my own family for the past three years."

"Yes," Madeline said. And then, as she took one agonized look back at her brother and pulled her shawl over her head again: "Your husband? Have you heard? Apparently they are all gathering at Nivelles and pushing on to Paris."

"Is the battle over, then?" Ellen asked. "Yes, I have heard. Lord Eden brought word. He is gone."

"To Par—?" But Madeline had looked into Ellen's face. "Oh, no. I . . ."

"Don't!" Ellen spoke sharply. "You must go now. Lady Andrea will be looking for your help. And I have a boy in the other room who will have kicked his blankets into knots by now. He is just a child. A frightened, hurt child. I am going to fight the surgeon when he comes, for his arm is swollen, you know, and they are bound to want to take it off. But it is clean, and I am sure the swelling will go down. I am going to fight for his arm." She laughed. "Do you think I should have a sword to wield?"

Madeline had turned very pale. But she drew back her shoulders and smiled in return. "A pair of scissors perhaps?" she said. "And a very ferocious frown."

"I will try it," Ellen said, standing in the doorway to watch her guest run lightly down the stairs. "I shall send word if there is any change, you may be assured."

The boy was sleeping, she saw. She did not disturb him even though the blankets were twisted awkwardly about him.

She stood beside Lord Eden's bed and smiled into his fevered eyes that were turned on her.

"I am here, my dear," she said softly. "I will bathe your face and turn your pillow for you. Perhaps you will be more comfortable then."

He closed his eyes when she had finished and sat down beside his bed. He seemed a little quieter. Ellen fell into a doze.

A SURGEON ARRIVED during the afternoon of the following day. He was an army man, a hearty, loud-voiced soldier who appeared to believe that by talking loudly he would penetrate the fever and pain of his patients.

And yet he was not ungentle. He removed the bandage carefully from the boy's arm, talking and laughing in an apparent attempt to distract the youth's attention. But the boy was terrified. He clung unashamedly to Ellen's hand and gazed at the doctor with eyes like saucers.

"Hm," the surgeon said, prodding and poking at the swollen arm until the boy squirmed and Ellen began to change her mind about his gentleness. "Nasty enough. Well, lad, it's not putrid, but it well might be soon. We'll have the arm off, shall we, and be done with it? I'll have someone come for you."

"No," Ellen said quietly. "If amputation is not yet necessary, we will wait. I shall keep the wound clean and covered and hope for the best. His fever has already subsided considerably."

The surgeon frowned. "Are you family, ma'am?" he asked.

"No," she said. "But he is in my home, and for the time being I stand in place of his mother."

The man threw back his head and roared with mirth. "Oh, mothers!" he said. "Enough said. I am wiser than to fight against a mother. Why do you think I am with the army, ma'am? The lad is going to wait, is he? He might be sorry."

"Perhaps," she said. And she turned to tuck the blankets around the boy while the surgeon bandaged his arm again. He looked up at her with wide, panicked eyes. She smiled and even winked at him.

The surgeon shook his head when he looked at Lord Eden. He removed the bandage gently enough and peered closely at the wound.

"Abscess forming," he said, and shook his head again. "Well, we can't amputate this one, can we, ma'am? So we have no cause to quarrel." He laughed heartily at his own joke. "Nasty fever. I'll have to bleed him."

"Has he not lost enough blood?" she asked.

"Apparently not," he said. "Or he wouldn't have such a raging fever. Here, you can hold the bowl for me."

Lord Eden did indeed seem more restful after the bleeding was finished. But it was a rest of extreme weakness,

Ellen thought. She had no time to worry about it. She had performed her task so unflinchingly, it appeared, that the surgeon soon sent for her from the other part of the house to take the bowl from a trembling maid's hands while he bled most of his patients there.

He would be back the next day if he could, he said as he left the house and hurried along to another. He would bleed those patients again and see how that arm was looking.

The boy was calling for her as she reached the doorway into her own rooms.

LORD EDEN CLUNG to life. Sometimes it would have been easier to let go. Sometimes he wanted to claw at the heat and the pain, to climb outside them, to run away, to be free. Something in his chest felt as if it were swelling and swelling until it must burst and fling him in a thousand directions. And sometimes he forgot who he was and where he was and why he was there.

Only one thing kept him pinned to life. Only one person. Sometimes when he came to himself she was not there. He would try to close his eyes, to lie quietly until she came. Sometimes he lost himself again while he waited. Sometimes she came hurrying, a look of concern on her face, and he knew that he must have called out. Sometimes he could not remember who she was.

In fact, most of the time he could not remember who she was. He could not put a name to her face. But it did not matter. He was safe when she was there. He was at peace. Sometimes when he came back to himself she was sitting beside the bed sewing or holding his hand. And always smiling. Not with merriment. But with gentle affection, as if he were someone very special.

Was he special? To her? Who was she? He could not remember. But it did not matter.

The ceiling did not move down toward him when she was there. The furniture did not move about.

"Everything will stay still now," she assured him, her cool fingers smoothing through his hair. "I am here. I am going to stay with you for a time."

He could close his eyes and perhaps sleep for a while. If only someone would lift the great weight from his chest. Was it too heavy for her to remove? She was only a slender woman. It was hard for him to breathe with that weight on him. He was going to suffocate.

"I will wash you off with a cool cloth above and below the bandage," she said, folding back the blanket. "That will help lessen the weight. Does that feel better?"

And it always did. The weight was still there—it must be too heavy for her—but some of the heat had gone. He thought he might sleep.

Sometimes there was a lamp burning in the room. It must be nighttime. He listened. There was no sound at all except for a clock ticking somewhere. She was asleep in the chair beside his bed, her head fallen awkwardly to the side. She should be lying in a bed. She must be tired. He was thirsty. But he must say nothing. She would jump up and fetch him a drink. But she was sleeping. He lay and watched her. He was comforted by her presence. Was it a live coal that was on his chest?

Sometimes he knew who she was. She was Madeline. She was telling him that he would be proud of her if he could only see her all day long nursing the wounded.

"And I haven't had a fit of the vapors even once, Dom,"

she said. "Poor Lieutenant Penworth does not have the will to live, I think. But I will nurse him back to health despite himself. You have the will to live, Dom. I can see it. And you are going to win too. I know. Oh, I know, you horrid pestiliential man, you! How dare you put me through this! I hate you."

He felt a grin, but there was too much effort involved in transferring it to his face.

Nursing what wounded?

Sometimes she wasn't Madeline. And he didn't always want her to be. She was more peaceful than Madeline. She never cried, as his sister had cried when raging against him. She soothed him. She fed him cold water and . . . What? Toast? And she came with the cooling cloths and the comforting words and the gentle hands. Even when she hurt his chest, he learned to grit his teeth and endure. For he always felt better afterward.

"I will be finished in a moment," she would say quietly. "One minute more, and then you can rest again."

And it was always true. He could trust her word. And everything stayed still around him when she was there.

"Put out the fire."

"I will open the door wider," she would say, "and bathe your forehead. You will feel cooler."

"Take off some blankets."

"I will fold it back to your waist," she would say. "Is that better, my dear?"

"Can't you find someone to lift this weight off me?"

"I will bathe your shoulders and your arms with cool water," she would say. "Perhaps that will help."

"You are tired. Do you never sleep? Do I keep you up? Is it nighttime? You should go to bed."

"I shall sit beside you here and rest," she would say. "The

chair is very comfortable. Don't worry about me, my dear. Try to sleep."

He was on fire. It must be a red-hot coal. But he would not say anything to her. She was doing too much. Always busy. Always cheerful. Always smiling.

Who was she? He could not remember.

He clung to life for her. She made life bearable despite all. Despite the heat and the weight and the feeling that his chest must explode.

And sometimes there was Madeline.

But always there was her.

The surgeon bled him four times in ten days despite Ellen's tight-lipped disapproval. The fever raged and he weakened. He was almost constantly delirious. All he had eaten was toast dipped in weak tea.

After two weeks the abscess burst and the matter within it flowed. Ellen was with him at the time. She called to one of the servants in the house and sent him running for the surgeon—if only the man could be found. And she bit hard on her lower lip as she cleaned the wound. He was moaning with each breath.

It had happened at last. His chest had exploded, and the pain knifed and knifed at him, robbing him of breath and of all power to think or even to see.

But the weight was lifting too. She was bending over him, and she was taking the weight away. And she must have put out the fire and taken off all the smothering blankets. He felt light and cool, pinned in place only by the searing pain.

"Mrs. Simpson?" he said.

She lifted her head sharply from what she was doing and looked into his face. "You know me?" she said. She put a cool hand against his brow. "The fever has broken. It has gone with the abscess."

"I was wounded," he said. "How did I get here?"

"You rode here," she said. "With some help."

"How long ago?" Where had he been? The last thing he could remember was trudging along a muddy road with his men. There had been jokes about Hyde Park soldiers.

"You have been here for two weeks," she said.

Two weeks? The pain was like a knife. But such a lightness. He could breathe despite the pain.

"There was a weight," he said, "on my chest."

"It has gone," she said. "You will feel better now."

"Am I going to die?" he asked. He could not keep his eyes open. He was falling into deep soft darkness. He did not hear her reply, but her hand on his brow again was part of the softness. It was not a darkness to be feared.

"Hm," the surgeon said, probing around the area of the burst abscess with a finger that Ellen would dearly have liked to dip in her washtub. "He is a fortunate young man, I would say. It looks as if he might live after all. And the fever has gone. It is the fever that has been the great killer. So many good men in the last two weeks, ma'am."

"He will live?" she asked.

He shrugged. "He is young," he said, "and big and strong. He will live if he wants to live, I would reckon. Not that I am God, ma'am. I have seen worse cases recover. Keep him on toast and tea. I will come back tomorrow and bleed him again."

Ellen swallowed. "Is he unconscious or sleeping?" she asked.

The surgeon pursed his lips. "Perhaps a bit of both," he said. "Men don't sleep properly when they have the fever. He will probably be dead to the world for a few days.

Figuratively speaking, we hope." He laughed heartily so that Ellen glanced anxiously down at Lord Eden.

"Yes, he needs sleep," she said.

"And so do you, ma'am, if you don't mind my saying so," the doctor said, his manner suddenly kindly. "And you won in the case of the boy, didn't you? A nasty blow, that, to my professional pride, you know. So the lad will march home with two arms. What happened to him?"

"Someone came for him," she said. "A lieutenant in his regiment. Apparently the boy had been a stable lad at his father's house. The lieutenant was taking him back home again. He had been wounded too. A nice happy ending, was it not?"

"Aye," the surgeon said with a sigh. "There have been precious few of those in these last days, ma'am. Good day to you. I'll call again tomorrow."

"Thank you," she said.

She felt bone-weary. She leaned over Lord Eden to observe that he was still in a sleep so deep that it frightened her. And then she went to fetch blankets and a pillow from another room and curled up on the floor beside his bed. She was asleep long before her body could make any protest against the hardness of the floor.

THE EARL OF AMBERLEY met his wife and children and his mother in the hallway of his London home. They were returning from an early-afternoon walk in Hyde Park.

"Well, tiger," he said, scooping up his son, who hurtled toward him across the tiled floor, "did you have a good walk?"

"Horsies!" the child cried excitedly.

"Were there?" his father said. "Lots of them? And how is

my princess? A big smile for Papa again? I am in favor these days. And here is Nanny Rey to take you both back to the nursery. Are you sleepy, tiger? No, that was a silly question, wasn't it? Why would a big man like you be sleepy in the middle of the day? I tell you what. You pretend to sleep for Nanny while she rocks Caroline. See how long you can keep up the game. All right?"

The child giggled and squirmed to be put down. He was soon laboriously climbing the stairs ahead of his nanny and the baby.

Lord Amberley turned to his wife and his mother with a smile. The latter was looking thin and drawn, he noticed not for the first time in the month since he had been home. And even Alex had lost some of her bloom.

"Would you like to step into the library for a moment?" he said. "Was the park crowded?"

The two women exchanged glances as they followed him across the hall to the library. Neither answered his question. Edmund only ever smiled like that when he was troubled.

"Dominic?" the dowager Countess of Amberley asked as a footman closed the door behind them.

"Sit down, Mama," the earl said quietly. "I have just had a letter from Madeline. It was written three weeks ago, if you would believe. Dominic is in Brussels. He has a quite severe chest wound and broken ribs and was in a high fever when she wrote."

The countess crossed the room to his side and laid a hand on his arm.

"So he is not on his way to Paris with the rest of the army," the dowager said brightly. "And we have been wrong to blame him for being thoughtless and not writing."

"And Madeline's silence is explained too," her daughter-in-law said. "Everything has been chaos. She must have written immediately. So she is with him, Edmund?"

"Apparently not," he said. "He is at the Rue de la Montagne with Mrs. Simpson. Madeline cannot leave Lady Andrea's. It seems the house has been turned into a hospital, and Madeline is being rushed off her feet."

"But he is in good hands," the countess said. "You would like her, Mama. She is quite charming and very calm and sensible. Did Madeline say if Captain Simpson is well, Edmund?"

"Killed, I am afraid," he said.

"Oh." His wife looked, stricken, up into his face. "How dreadful. They were so devoted."

The dowager countess rose restlessly on her feet. "The news is three weeks old, Edmund?" she said. "And he was badly hurt. And fevered. The news is so old."

"Will you go to him, Edmund?" his wife asked. "Oh, I wish now that I had insisted that you stay."

"The chances are that he is better by now and on his way home," the earl said, covering her hand with his own. "But, yes, I think I will go, my love, if you will not mind being left."

"Foolish!" she said.

"I am going too," the older lady said, her voice trembling quite noticeably. "I should have gone earlier in the spring and stayed. It just seemed that if I remained in the sanity of London, everything would be all right. You must take me to Brussels, Edmund."

"It is a long and tiring journey to make just to find that perhaps he has gone already, Mama," the earl said.

"Gone!" she said. "But he is my boy, Edmund. My son. I

am going to him even if I have to go alone. I must go home immediately to get ready."

The earl crossed the room to her and put an arm firmly about her shoulders. "We will leave in the morning, Mama," he said. "You and I together. There will be plenty of time to have your bags packed. I shall order the carriage in a little while to take you home. But first you must sit down and have tea with us. You see? Alex has rung the bell for it already. And that is an order from the head of the family, my dear."

His mother collapsed against him. "I thought I would be relieved once I heard," she said. "No matter what the news was. As long as I knew, I thought. But I still do not know. Three weeks, Edmund. And he had a high fever."

He kissed her forehead and held her to him. "No, don't choke back your tears, Mama," he said. "I shall feel remarkably foolish for my own if you succeed in controlling yours. Tomorrow we will be on our way. Then at least we will be doing something. And soon enough we will know."

He looked at his wife through his tears as he held his mother's head to his shoulder and rocked her against him.

10

*H*E WAS STILL SLEEPING WHEN SHE WOKE UP.
It was a deep and peaceful sleep. There was none of
the tossing and turning of his head and the heightened
color and the mutterings that she had become used to in
two weeks of nursing him. He was sleeping. He was going
to get well again.

Ellen was feeling cramped from lying on the hard floor.
But she did not move for a while. She lay still and looked at
him. Would she even call him handsome if she were to see
him now for the first time? His normally fair wavy hair had
not been washed in two weeks, except at the forehead and
temples with the damp cloths she had used so often to cool
his face. He had a two-week growth of beard. And his face
was thinner than it had been. Even his arm and hand, flung
out on top of the covers, were thinner.

But he had come home, and she had fought for his life.
And he was going to live. The question of whether he
looked handsome or not was supremely irrelevant.

Ellen gazed at Lord Eden for a long time without moving. It seemed that she had slept for the first time in a long,
long while. And she felt refreshed. There was a deadness

somewhere inside her, an enormous load that might weigh her down if she dwelt upon it. But she would ignore it for the present. It was not time yet to take it out and explore it. She had slept and she was refreshed and she would allow herself to regain strength and energy before looking too far inward.

She had washed and changed and was folding the last blanket that had covered her on the floor when she turned her head to find him looking at her.

"You are awake," she said.

"Did you sleep there?" he asked. "It must have been very uncomfortable."

"Perhaps it was," she said. "But I was sleeping too soundly to notice."

A ghost of his old grin flashed over his face. "Have I been a hard patient?" he asked. "I can remember only that the furniture was walking about the room. Most disconcerting, I assure you."

"You have not been a difficult patient," she said.

He looked keenly at her for a few moments. "Two weeks I have been here?" he said. "There have been others too? You look run into the ground."

"There have been others," she said. "There still are in the other part of the house. They are all recovering."

He closed his eyes.

"You should not talk," she said. "You are very weak."

"And will be as long as I lie here sleeping and saying nothing," he said, opening his eyes again. He felt his jaw. "Ugh! I must look like some sort of monster. May I trouble you for some water and a towel, ma'am? And can you possibly lay your hands on some shaving gear?"

"I will bring them," she said, picking up her blankets and pillow and leaving the room. But when she came back with the things he had asked for and took hold of his blankets to fold them back, she found one of his hands on each of her wrists.

"I shall do this myself," he said. "I gather that for the last fortnight you have cared for every single one of my needs. It quite puts me to the blush to think of it. But no more, ma'am. I thank you, but I shall see to my own bodily needs from now on."

"You are weaker than you think," she said. "You will exhaust yourself."

"Then I shall sleep afterward," he said. "I have a comfortable bed in which to do so."

Ellen hesitated.

"I am ravenously hungry," he said. "Do you have any food in the house, ma'am? Do you have any money? I am afraid I have no way of knowing if I do. Do I?"

"The surgeon said you are to have only tea and toast," she said. "I shall bring you some. He is coming sometime today to bleed you again."

"Devil a bit!" he said. "I feel as weak as a baby. I don't think I can spare any surgeon one drop of my blood. I need it all myself, and a beefsteak and some porter sound altogether more palatable than tea and toast."

Ellen felt herself smile. "Perhaps some eggs with the toast," she said. "And some milk instead of the tea."

When she entered the room next, he was lying on the bed, his eyes closed again. But he was clean-shaven, and his hair was damp and clean. He was looking very pale.

"I feel as if I had done a week's work," he said. "Damnation! This weakness. Pardon me, ma'am. My brain must be addled. Can't think what I am about, using such language in a lady's hearing." He did not open his eyes.

"You must sleep," she said, crossing the room and laying

light fingers against his forehead. But it was quite cool. "You shall eat when you wake up again."

"You cannot know how tempting your suggestion is, ma'am," he said. "But I need to eat if I am ever to get up off this bed without coming nigh to fainting."

"I shall fetch the tray then," she said. "It is all ready."

By the time she came back with it he had managed to drag himself into a half-sitting position, with two pillows behind him. And he felt as if he must scream with the pain and faint from the exertion. He gritted his teeth and smiled at her. Boiled eggs had never looked so appetizing, he thought. Two of them with two pieces of toast and a large glass of milk. He thought he could probably eat the plate and glass as well.

"The beefsteak for dinner?" he asked.

"I shall see what the surgeon says," she said.

He kept talking to her as he ate. She stood beside the bed for a while, her hands folded in front of her, and then she sat down and watched him quietly.

As she had done for the two weeks previous. He could remember that too. And her face bent over his. Always soothing him. He could not remember quite how. He could not recall all she had done for him. But there appeared to be no servant in the house. She must have done everything. And even though his hair had been unwashed and his beard of two weeks' growth, the rest of him had been perfectly clean, he had discovered when he had washed himself, including his bandage and his large nightshirt.

He owed her everything. And he was embarrassed, self-conscious. They were alone together in her rooms, as far as he could tell. She was beautiful. He must have noticed that before. She was pale and thin. There were dark shadows below her eyes. And the eyes themselves were tired. But she was beautiful. And she must be no older than he. She should not be nursing him.

He had been wholly dependent on her for two weeks. She had talked to him. He recalled that now also. Her voice soothing and caressing. He could still hear it, though he could not hear any of the words she had spoken. He must have called to her often. He could remember her sleeping in the chair in which she now sat.

What was he doing there? Why there in particular? Madeline was still in Brussels. Mrs. Simpson had sent to her the night before, after his fever broke, she had told him. Why was he not with Madeline? He was about to ask as he talked on about nothing in particular. But something stopped him. There had been a reason. He could not remember what. He *would* not remember what. He did not want to remember. Not yet. He needed some of his strength back before he could cope with that memory.

"Damnation!" he said, looking down at his tray and realizing that both plate and glass were empty. "I have never felt so tired in my life. Did you give me a sleeping potion, ma'am?" He was aware of a noisy and inelegant yawn, which he supposed came from his own mouth.

"No," she said. "It is just that your body has a little more sense than you have, I believe."

The tray was gone from his hands. There was an arm behind his shoulders, and when it eased him back, his pillows were flat on the bed again. And cool and comfortable. And her hand on his forehead was light and cool. He sighed with contentment. "Magic hands," he murmured, and let himself fall into a deep and welcome nothingness.

• • •

LORD EDEN WAS still sleeping when his twin arrived during the afternoon, hurried and breathless.

"You must think I do not care," she said to Ellen. "I cried so hard when I received your letter last evening that Lady Andrea misunderstood and launched into a speech about how Dom was better off where he was than suffering on unnecessarily. And I cried and laughed all night long. I would have come early this morning, but Lieutenant Penworth needed me again. The poor man. He has no will to live, you know, and no one can do anything at all for him but me. He refuses to eat or drink or even move for anyone else. He needed me this morning. His leg was paining him again, or rather the stump of his poor leg. And I knew that Dom was out of danger and in good hands. I am prattling, am I not?" She burst into tears.

Ellen put her arms about her and hugged her. "Yes, he will live," she said. "And it is only after a long period of anxiety is over that one realizes how much of a strain one has been under. I have never doubted your devotion to your brother. Not for one moment. He is sleeping. Go and see him."

"You have shaved him," Madeline said with a laugh when she came back out of the bedchamber. "And did not cut his chin even once. How clever of you."

"I was allowed to do nothing for him this morning except bring him a food tray," Ellen said. "If he had had his sword beside him, I believe he would have held me off with that."

Madeline laughed again. "Oh, you do my heart good," she said. "Dearest Dom. And I suppose he was demanding kidneys and ale for breakfast?"

"Beefsteak and porter, actually," Ellen said.

Both women giggled and felt strange doing so, as if they

were performing some long-forgotten skill. They looked at each other in some embarrassment, and both ended up with tears in their eyes.

"I do wish Lieutenant Penworth were roaring with such discontent," Madeline said. "Oh, I do wish it. But then, his injuries are in many ways worse than Dom's, though I do not believe he was ever as close to death. He has to learn to live without a leg and an eye. It is bound to take longer, is it not?"

"He is fortunate to have someone who is willing to spend her time and sympathies on him," Ellen said with a smile.

"And Dom is fortunate," Madeline said. "But I cannot help feeling that we are imposing upon you now, Mrs. Simpson. Perhaps you would like to be free to leave here. Shall I make arrangements to have him moved to Lady Andrea's? I am sure she will not mind. I was hoping to have heard from Edmund in England by now, but still there is nothing. I suppose the mails have been disrupted in the past two weeks."

"I have no plans," Ellen said. "And I would not want Lord Eden moved before he has regained some of his strength. Please leave him here." Her voice shook a little. "I believe I need something to keep me occupied for a while yet."

Madeline bit her lip and looked away. "Yes, of course," she said. "I shall leave him here, then. And thank you. Will you tell Dom that I have been? The lieutenant was asleep when I left, but he does not sleep for long. He will be needing me again. I shall call again tomorrow if I may."

She hurried away again soon after, eager to return to her main patient. She felt so very sorry for him. He was very young to have lost both his looks and his fitness. And he had been a vigorous young man who had enjoyed exercise and outdoor activity more than anything. She tried to imagine the same thing happening to Dom, and she knew that he would rather be dead. As Lieutenant Penworth would. He had told her that more than once.

He needed her now. She was the only person he would respond to, the only one he would listen to. She sat by his bedside sometimes for an hour or more, chattering away about her childhood, her girlhood, Amberley, the strange circumstances that had brought Edmund and Alexandra together, anything she could think of to distract his thoughts for a few minutes. And talking was something she had always been good at.

It felt lovely to be needed. Although she would many times prefer that the lieutenant had not been so wounded, since he had, she was glad that chance had brought him to Lady Andrea's house and her. For the time, at least, purpose had been given to her life. It would be many weeks, perhaps months, before he would be fit enough to return to England. In the meanwhile, she would stay with him. Lady Andrea had no intention of removing from Brussels while her husband was with the army in Paris anyway.

She herself had nothing to return to England for. Even when Dom was well enough to travel, he would have Mama and Edmund to go back to. She would not be essential to him. She would be her old restless self again. Here she would be needed, perhaps for the rest of the summer.

And it was good to be needed.

She wondered why Edmund had not written. She wondered if he had yet received any of the three letters she had sent. But it did not matter. Dom was safe. And she was so busy that she had very little time to fret for family and home.

• • •

LORD EDEN MADE A determined effort over the next few days to regain some of his health and strength. His chest wound was healing nicely now that the abscess had broken, and his ribs were knitting together again. But there was still an annoying amount of pain. He could not move without wincing and gritting his teeth.

He was appalled at his own weakness. Just the effort of standing to wash himself in the mornings exhausted him. He could not walk without leaning heavily on Ellen's shoulder, and the ten steps to the doorway of the bedchamber and back were almost beyond his endurance. After sitting up in bed for a meal he would slide gratefully back to a lying position again. And he seemed to be sleeping his life away.

He offended the doctor the afternoon after his abscess burst by flatly refusing to be bled, and added insult to injury by laughing at the man outright when he had turned to Mrs. Simpson and recommended a continuance of the diet of toast soaked in weak tea for another two weeks at the least. The surgeon washed his hands of him there and then and did not return after.

He determinedly ate whatever was put in front of him, and would several times have asked for more had he not had the uncomfortable feeling that he was living on Mrs. Simpson's charity. She had not answered his question about whether he had any money or not. He had no idea where his clothes and gear were. His coat at least, he supposed, must be in sorry shape if the appearance of his chest was any indication.

But he did not worry a great deal about anything except regaining his strength. Those days seemed almost suspended beyond time, and he was not sure that he craved the day when he would be ready to leave those rooms and return to normal life.

They were alone together. Only once—on the morning after his first full day of returned consciousness—did a manservant appear from the other part of the house to stay with him while she went out, presumably to buy more provisions. He told her afterward that he had felt decidedly uncomfortable with the man standing silently just inside the door of the bedchamber, just like a large and humorless jailer. She laughed and left him alone after that during the few spells when she was out of the rooms. Madeline, of course, made whirlwind visits about every second day.

Most of the time, however, he and Mrs. Simpson were alone together. But his self-consciousness disappeared after the first day, once he had taken over looking after his own bodily needs. And he found her a cheerful and gentle companion. She spent most of her days in the room with him, sitting quietly sewing much of the time.

They talked. He told her—at her request—about his childhood and all the numerous scrapes he and Madeline had almost constantly been in. She even told him something of her own childhood, a happy one, she claimed. The man she had called father had always been kind to her, though as the years went on she had seen less and less of him, and sometimes when he came he had been in his cups. He had never mistreated her even then, she said, but she had not liked his glittering eyes, the smell of liquor on his breath. Her mother had always been a lovely, vivacious, seldom-seen presence, admired and adored from a distance.

"It is only looking back from an adult vantage point that I can realize what an unhappy household it was," she said quietly, stitching at her embroidery. "Children very readily accept almost any kind of life as normal. I used to hate to hear them quarrel, but I did not hear it so very often. Tell me more about your own parents. It must have been dreadful to lose your father when you were only twelve."

And so he talked on and sometimes even brought a smile to her eyes and a laugh to her lips.

But they did not always talk. Sometimes she sat quietly, her head bent to her work, and he watched her until he fell asleep. And sometimes he would open his eyes to find her sitting watching him.

It should have been embarrassing, the silences, the meeting of eyes in a quiet room in an empty house. But it was not so. Not at all. Sometimes their eyes would hold for several seconds before one of them would say something or smile or before he would close his eyes. There was never any feeling of discomfort.

She was an amazingly strong woman for someone so slender and of no more than average height. She never stumbled, though he leaned heavily on her at first when he walked. And she could take much of his weight on her arm as he sat up in bed or lay down again, so that he would not have to put so much strain on his chest muscles.

Often when she thought he slept, he would hear the rustle of her skirts and feel the coolness of her hand on his brow, checking for a return of his fever. He would never show her at such moments that he was not sleeping. He liked the nearness of her, the touch of her.

IT WAS FIVE DAYS after the end of his fever when he woke up one night to the sound of his own voice. He was sitting up in bed, the pain from his ribs only just penetrating his consciousness and robbing him of breath. He was cold with terror.

Ellen had been sleeping in Jennifer's room, as she did each night, the doors open so that she would hear him if he called. He had yelled several times in succession, and she had come running.

"What is it?" she said. She bent toward him in the darkness, a hand on his shoulder. "Is there something wrong?"

"God!" he said, gasping through his pain. "God!"

"Was it a nightmare?" she asked. Her other hand was cool on his brow.

"God!" he said again. He had been bending over dead eyes with all hell breaking loose about him. "Yes, a nightmare."

"It will be all right now," she said gently. She helped him to lie down again, and smoothed the hair back from his brow. She was leaning right over him, a slim young woman with a shawl thrown over her white nightgown, and heavy fair hair falling forward on either side of her face and over her shoulders. He could see her quite clearly, used as his eyes were to the darkness.

He felt instantly comforted. "I woke you," he said. "I am sorry."

"You need not apologize," she said. She was stroking his cheek with her fingertips. She had done that before. He could remember. "Would you like me to sit by you for a while?"

He shook his head. "I have kept you up long enough," he said. He did not know he had lifted his hand until he saw it put one side of her hair back over her shoulder. He touched the backs of his fingers to her cheek. Soft warm skin.

She did not move. His fingers were warm and gentle on her cheek.

"Ellen," he whispered.

Neither of them knew afterward if he drew her head down or if she brought it down of her own accord, or if perhaps they both moved with that strange togetherness that had grown between them in the past days. However it was, their mouths met. And held together. And opened and caressed and explored. And one of his arms moved around her shoulders and the other hand to cup the back of her head. Her hands were on the pillow at either side of his head. Her wrists rested against his shoulders.

Thick silky hair. The scent of her that he had been aware of for weeks. The beauty and warmth and softness of her. The gentleness and sweetness and womanliness of her.

"Ellen." His hand was at the buttons down the front of her nightgown, and she raised herself on her arms to help him. She was not stopping him. She was helping him, encouraging him. "Ellen."

He pushed the linen away from her shoulders to her arms and took her breasts in his hands. Full and firm. Silky smooth. Nipples already taut. Taut for him. She wanted him.

She wanted him. His hands were warm and gentle, as she had known they would be. They knew where to touch her. How to touch her. His thumbs brushed the peaks of her breasts, creating a sweet agony that rose into her throat and spiraled down into her womb.

"Ellen." He was staring up into the shadows of her eyes. She had raised herself the full length of her arms, but she made no attempt to cover herself or move away from him. He reached across himself to grasp the bedclothes and pull them back. She looked down at them and stood up beside the bed. She wriggled her shoulders so that the nightgown slid down her arms and fell away from her completely, and she accepted his invitation by climbing into the bed beside him. He covered her with the sheet and turned onto his side, biting his lip as he did so.

He could feel the heat of her as soon as he touched her, the tautness of her, the eagerness to find his mouth in the darkness. She was warm, soft, shapely. Eager for him. Not with the feigned eagerness of the numerous courtesans with whom he had lain in the past, but with the hot straining eagerness of a woman for her lover.

She came to him, put herself against him, felt the warm length of his limbs, felt his arms close about her, his mouth reaching for hers. And there was no thought to holding back. She gave herself fully and eagerly. This was what she had wanted. What she had always wanted. She had always wanted him. Always loved him. And there was an enormous hurt somewhere that he would soothe for her. That he would take away.

He covered her mouth with his and traced her lips with his tongue before plunging into the warm, moist cavity beyond. She was beautiful. All woman. All eager hot yielding woman. Eager and hot for him. Yielding to him.

And he wanted her. God, he wanted her. Had wanted her for days. For weeks. All his life. He had always wanted her. Always searched for her. Only for her. He took fire.

And turned her beneath him on the bed. And rolled heavily on top of her and lay still until he could get the pain under control. He could not lift his weight away from her. He was forced to crush her into the mattress.

But she did not complain. She wrapped her arms about him, opened herself to him, raising her knees to his hips. And she lifted her face to his again.

"Ellen." He kissed her, deeply, deeply. And moved his hands down her warm sides, past her breasts to her slim waist, over the very feminine curve of her hips. And beneath her. She hugged him with her thighs. And he found her in the darkness, the entrance to her, and he hid his face in the soft silkiness of her hair and pushed himself into the blessed deep heat of her.

They both gasped.

"Dominic. Dominic."

Her hands were roving over his back, above and below the bandages, and she tilted herself to meet him, moved against him and with him so that he clenched his teeth and closed his eyes very tightly and willed control on himself.

"Yes. Oh, please. Yes."

"Ellen. So beautiful. Oh, my love."

"Yes. Dominic. Oh, please. Please."

They found a rhythm together, and he moved his hands up into her hair and took her mouth with his again.

And this. Oh, yes, this. Dominic. He was loving her and she him. This was as it had to be. As it had always had to be. Dominic loving her and she loving him. Nothing held back. Giving and receiving. Together. Loving. Yes. Oh, this. Surely some part of her had always known.

He turned his face into her hair again and drove into her and into her until he lost himself—long before he wanted to and long before he was sure she was ready. He took all that she had to give and gave her all of himself until he lay throbbing and spent in her, all of his weight pressing down on her.

He rolled away from her, biting down hard on both his lips so that she would not hear his pain, and keeping one arm beneath her head. He pulled the bedclothes as neatly as possible around them and looked at her. Her eyes were open, he could see.

"I squashed you?" he asked, putting her hair back over her shoulder with his free hand.

"No." She traced the line of his lower lip with one light finger and then closed her eyes.

There was a bewilderment. An emptiness. A disappointment. She had not been ready to let him go. And yet there was an exhilaration. A warm glow. A satisfaction. He was her lover. He loved her. He had been inside her. There was still the throbbing, the aching pain where he had been. And his arms still held her. She breathed in the warmth of him.

And she loved him.

She slept almost immediately. He could tell from the evenness of her breathing. He was breathing shallowly, waiting for the pain to recede, knowing that it must do so eventually if he lay very still.

And he watched her the while in wonder. Wonder at himself that he had not recognized her until that night. He had known her for a long time, had liked her, respected her, admired her. Even felt the pull of an unwilling attraction. But he had not recognized her. For three weeks while he had lain in this bed he had come to depend upon her, to feel comforted and happy only when she was there. And yet he had not recognized her. For days he had drawn closer to her, felt her beauty, the sweetness and strength of her character, known that he did not want these days to end. But he had still not recognized her.

He had searched for her for years. And he had persisted in looking for her in young girls who were frail and in need of his protection. But she was strong and had sheltered him with her protection. And she was no girl. He simply had not recognized her.

But here she was anyway, in this bed, in his arms, warm

from his lovemaking. The woman of his life. The love of his life. Ellen.

He tested a somewhat deeper breath. The pain was receding.

Was she always as wildly passionate? Had she been like this for Charlie?

No, no, *no, no. No!* Lord Eden found that he was shaking his head from side to side on the bed and gritting his teeth. Not yet. Not that name. Not yet. He was not ready yet.

He gazed at Ellen and knew beyond any doubt that this was no brief passion for him. He loved her. She had just given everything with no demand for anything in return. But he would give anyway. All of himself. All that he had. It was all hers. He had searched all his life for her. Now that he had found her, all he had, all he was, was hers.

Ellen.

His pain had gone. Her bare legs felt warm and smooth against his own. He could smell her fragrance again. She felt very, very good.

He closed his eyes.

11

*M*ADELINE CAME VISITING THREE TIMES. And Ellen went out each morning to buy food and to have some fresh air and exercise, and once she went to bid farewell to Mrs. Byng, who was going to join her husband in Paris. But apart from that they were alone together for six days. Six days and nights of magic that they both knew must come to an end but did not wish to end. Six days during which they both held at bay what both knew must be faced soon. Six days of wonder and of love.

Ellen had woken during that first night and removed herself from the bed and the room without waking him. And she had lain awake until dawn, not even trying to sleep, not wanting to sleep. There was too much wonderment to feel.

He was still sleeping the next morning when she plucked up the courage to take warm water and his shaving things in to him. But it took a great deal more courage to go back in with his breakfast tray. She could hear him moving about in his room. And she did not know how she should behave when she went in there, what she should say.

She need not have worried. He was lying in bed again,

and he watched her come into the room as he always did, and he smiled as he always did and bade her good morning. And he sat up without her help, gritting his teeth so that she would not know that he was in pain—foolish man to believe that she did not know. The only thing different from usual was that when she set the tray across his lap, he took her hand and lifted it to his lips, kissed the palm, and smiled up at her. And she leaned forward, without any thought at all, and kissed him briefly on the lips.

They said nothing beyond the usual. She sat with him while he ate, and told him some of the gossip she had heard at market that morning, told him he was foolish when he announced that he was going to walk right out into the parlor that day and back again without any assistance, and said that, yes, there were more kidneys in the pan and he might have them, since all the food he had put inside himself in the last week had not yet killed him. And, no, she did not want them herself. How could he even think of eating kidneys for breakfast?

For six days they lived much as they had lived before, except that each day he sat and walked a little more than he had the day before, though each day he swore just as fiercely at his own weakness and his seemingly insatiable need of sleep.

Ellen sat with him through much of each day, sewing when he rested or slept, waiting to leap to her feet and run to his assistance when he walked, talking and listening tirelessly when he sat or lay awake. She listened avidly to stories of his childhood and boyhood, a time of great freedom and happiness, it seemed, except for the great blot of his father's death and his mother's near-breakdown for a year afterward. But he had had his brother—only nineteen at the time of their father's death, but a rock of strength and cheerfulness and dependability, it seemed. And he had had his sister.

She told him more about her own girlhood, even up to the pain of that final dreadful quarrel, after which her mother had left, not to return. And during which she had told her husband that Ellen was not his daughter. Perhaps she would never have known, Ellen said, if her father—the earl, that was—had not been drunk at the time and had not come crying to her. He had told her and spent the following week drinking and crying and begging her not to leave him but to be his daughter anyway. But she had left.

Her father—her real father—had been a family acquaintance for years. He had been in London at the time, on leave from the army. She had gone to him and persuaded him to take her with him when he left again. He had never been unkind to her. He had always made sure that she had the best of care and all the necessary clothes and possessions. He had made an effort to spend time with her and to show her affection. But it had been difficult for both of them to suddenly play the role of father and daughter after so many years.

She never took her stories closer to the present than that. Neither of them told stories of the present or recent past. But the long-ago past was safe. And it drew them closer together. They came to know each other better, to like each other more.

Sometimes he held her hand as she sat beside his bed. And sometimes lifted it to his lips and kissed it, and her fingers one by one. Sometimes they smiled into each other's eyes and let their eyes rove over each other's faces. And never with embarrassment. Ellen even wondered about it when she was alone. Usually it was uncomfortable to look at someone without speaking. She never felt uncomfortable with Lord Eden, no matter how long the silence.

She called him that most of the time, though he always called her now by her given name. She called him by his only when he was making love to her. And they made love each night after that first. She did not know quite what to do the next night, but he called to her as she was putting out the lamp in the parlor, and she went to him, and it seemed perfectly natural to climb into the bed beside him.

She stayed with him for the whole night after that first time. And after that first time it was truly beautiful. He took her slowly and seemed to sense at each stage of their lovemaking when she was ready to move on to the next. On the second night and every night after that she came to him, shuddering and calling his name, while he still moved in her.

She had not known there could be such physical passion, such longing indistinguishable from pain, such a peace beyond the crest of her longing. She had never experienced real passion before. And yet, though the physical sensations were intensely personal, there was a meeting too of selves and emotions as well as bodies. It was true that man and woman could become one. She was always most intensely aware of him when she was being released into her own pleasure and when he was coming to his.

She loved totally. She felt cheated if she slept soundly the night through after their lovemaking. She liked to lie awake and watch him sleeping beside her. She liked to feel her love for him almost an ache in her. And she liked to feel the warmth from his body, to know that she might reach out and touch him, that she might wake him and know that his eyes would focus on her and smile.

She loved him with a totality that could come only from

the unreality of the moment. Because it was unreal. And sometimes, before she firmly shuttered her mind, she knew that it was unreal, that there was a world beyond their doors, and that because of their humanity they were part of that world and at some time must go back out into it again. But not yet. Oh, please, not yet. She needed this time out of time. She needed him. She loved him.

And Lord Eden, frustrated by his great weakness and the slowness of his recovery, was nevertheless living in an enchanted time. He had been in love before, constantly, routinely, as a younger man. Painfully in love, living for one daily sight of his beloved, pining for one kindly look from her eyes. But he had never loved, he realized now; he had merely played with sentiment.

He loved Ellen Simpson. He did not think he could ever have his fill of gazing at her, of watching her about some ordinary task like her sewing, of listening to her talk and discovering her past and her background, of talking to her and watching her changing expressions that told of her interest in him.

He could never have his fill of loving her, of making love to her. It was a heady experience, a totally erotic experience, to make love with a woman rather than to her. And quite unexpected. He had never thought of such a thing, had never expected it even of his dream love. To find that Ellen wanted him, burned for him, urged him on to giving her satisfaction, and showed that satisfaction with a quite uninhibited pleasure, more than doubled his own delight in her. He could not now imagine that he had never known there could be such loving.

He loved her. It was for her that he washed and shaved himself and ate and drank and walked laboriously and painfully around and around his bedchamber and eventually out into the parlor. He would exhaust himself, cause himself unnecessary pain and shortness of breath, but he would get well for her. He would regain his strength. And when the time came that he could venture beyond these rooms and get his life back to some normalcy again—he did not like to think about the time—then he would learn to love her in an everyday setting instead of this magical one.

He would sell out of the army and marry her and take her into Wiltshire with him and settle in the home that he had never really made his own. And he would have children with her and spend his life restoring her faith in the happiness and stability of family life. Mama would love her—how could anyone not? He thought that Edmund and Madeline already did like her exceedingly.

He said nothing to her. By unspoken consent, neither of them spoke at all about the future or about the present or immediate past beyond the haven of their rooms. They lived their love, but they spoke of it only in murmured love words as they lay entwined on the bed, words that neither of them remembered afterward.

He lay holding her hand one afternoon. They had fallen quiet after talking for a while. He felt drowsy and closed his eyes. But he squeezed her hand and tugged on it slightly.

"Lie down beside me," he said.

"The doors are all open," she said, squeezing his hand in return. "And it is daylight."

He opened his eyes and smiled sleepily at her. "Just on top of the covers," he said. "I want to feel your head on my arm. Won't you humor a poor defenseless wounded soldier and help him fall asleep?"

She laughed. "The description will not suit you for much longer," she said. "You will soon be as fit as I, sir. . . . Just for a little while, then."

He turned onto his side and stretched his arm along beneath the pillow. She settled her neck comfortably against it and smiled at him.

"The surgeon never did recommend this as suitable therapy," she said.

"The old quack did not know what he was talking about," he said. "He would have bled me dry by now, and I would still be watching the wardrobe performing a *pas de deux* with the washstand at the foot of my bed. I much prefer this. You wouldn't care to join me underneath the covers, I suppose? It is warm and cozy in here, Ellen."

"No, thank you," she said. "This is far more respectable for an afternoon."

He smiled at her and kissed her lightly on the mouth. And continued to do so, teasing her lips with his, touching them with his tongue, drawing his head back to smile at her. There was no passion between them. He was still feeling drowsy, and she looked as if she might sleep too. There was just a warm affection, a comfort, a happiness. He continued to kiss her and murmur nonsense into her ear. She made sounds of deep contentment in her throat.

And then a movement beyond her head drew his eyes to Madeline standing in the doorway. She flushed a deep crimson as her eyes met his, and took a backward step.

"Oh, pardon me," she said. "The door was open. I . . ."

He laughed softly. "I never thought to see you so discomfited, Mad," he said. "My apologies. This is all my fault."

But even as he spoke, Ellen scrambled off the bed, resisted his attempt to catch at her wrist, and was through the door past Madeline before he could finish his words and try to make both women feel less uncomfortable.

"You had better come in and sit down," he said to his sister. "I'm sorry. Ellen told me the door was open. Now I have hopelessly embarrassed both of you. No, do come. I'll talk to her afterward. For now, doubtless, she will be glad of some time in which to find a place to hide her head."

"Dom." She closed the door of the bedchamber and came to sit on the chair beside his bed. "What was that all about? You are not dallying with her, are you? She has been very good to you."

He smiled and clasped his hands behind his head. "I was not dallying," he said. "Neither was she."

She looked closely into his face. "Oh, Dom," she said in some wonder. "It has happened to you, has it not? And I am so pleased. I could not have chosen anyone better for you myself. She is a lovely person. I admire her excessively."

"I love her," he said. He reached for her hand. "I love her, Mad. If I were only a little stronger, I would climb to the highest rooftop in Brussels and yell it to the world."

She sat smiling at him, his hand clasped in both of hers.

"I am going to marry her," he said. "I didn't know it could be like this, Mad. I have always dreamed of it, but I didn't know. I had no idea. I am going to marry her as soon as I can get out of this infernal bed without feeling like a rag doll after five minutes. God, but I love her."

"She has said yes?" she asked.

"I haven't asked her." He smiled sheepishly at his twin. "I have been too busy loving her to think of anything so mundane as asking her to marry me. But she will, Mad. She loves me too. That is what is so wonderful about it. Can you imagine?"

"Of course I can imagine, silly," she said. "Girls have been falling in love with you for years. Sometimes it does not seem fair that the most handsome man of my acquaintance is my own brother."

"Then you can't imagine," he said. "I mean, she loves me,

Mad. She is not just *in* love with me. Oh, I can't explain. You will understand one day."

"I am very happy for you," she said, lifting his hand and laying it against her cheek. "So both of us are going to be married soon, Dom."

He looked his inquiry.

"I am going to marry Lieutenant Penworth," she said.

"Penworth?" he said. "I thought he didn't want to live."

"He doesn't," she said. "But he will live, of course. And he has come to depend upon me. He needs me, Dom. I don't know how he would go on without me. I am going to look after him for the rest of our lives."

"You love him?" he asked.

"Of course I love him," she said. "He needs me, Dom. It is a wonderful feeling to be needed, you know. I am going to devote my life to him."

"I don't think you love him," he said flatly. "It would be a mistake to marry a man because you pity him, Mad. Don't do it. Break the engagement before it is too late."

"There is no engagement," she said. "Not yet." She laughed softly. "He does not know yet. But he will marry me. I shall show him that he does not need to go through life alone and miserable. I shall be there for him. It will be a good thing for both of us, Dom. I will have something, someone, to live for."

"It's the most cork-brained thing I have ever heard of," he said. "It won't do, Mad."

Her eyes filled with tears. "Don't be horrid," she said. "I have been glad for you. I have told you so. And all you can tell me is that I am being cork-brained."

"Well, that is because you are," he said. "Heavens, where is Mama? And Edmund? They won't allow it, you know."

"I am five-and-twenty," she said indignantly. "They have

nothing to say to the matter. And they will not be so horrid. They will welcome the lieutenant into the family even if he is crippled and has had his face disfigured."

"Lord!" he said. "Do you think I do not want the man as a brother-in-law just because he does not have the full quota of legs and eyes? I would welcome him with no legs and no eyes, Mad, if I thought you could not live without him."

"You are horrid!" she said, rising to her feet and looking down at him with hostile eyes. "After all you have been through, Dom, I thought you would have some sympathy for a fellow sufferer. But it is all right for you. You still have all your good looks, and you will have back all your old strength and physique. Lieutenant Penworth will not. He needs me. And I don't care what you say. I am going to marry him. I don't need your approval, or even your love. Someone else will need me, and that will be enough."

"Little goose!" he said fondly, reaching for her hand again. But she snatched it away. "If you are determined to have him, Mad, I will say no more. Only I want to see you happy, as I am going to be happy. I care about you, you know. Whoosh! Good God! Do be careful."

This last was said as she almost threw herself on him and planted a kiss firmly on his cheek.

"I knew you would understand," she said, "once you got used to the idea. I knew you would. I am going to be the happiest person in the world; you will see. And you are going to be happy too. I could hug the life out of you, but I am afraid that Mrs. Simpson will come in here brandishing some weapon if I make you yell out again. I am going to love her as a sister-in-law, Dom. I really am. And I won't say anything to her on the way out, since you have not asked her yet. I must go. He will be needing me."

She kissed him again on the other cheek, smiled gaily down at him, and was gone.

Lord Eden clasped his hands behind his head again and smiled at the door. Should he get up and go and find Ellen? She was probably still hiding her embarrassment somewhere. It was just a very good thing that she had refused to join him beneath the covers. Both she and Mad would have had an apoplexy apiece. He grinned at the canopy above him.

He closed his eyes and felt his drowsiness return. Lieutenant Penworth indeed! Mad had scarce looked at the man twice when he had two legs and two eyes. What a disaster she was going to make of her life if he could not talk her out of marrying Penworth just because she pitied him. Silly goose! He yawned loudly. He should go and find Ellen. He could just open his mouth and yell for her, but he should exert himself and get out of the bed and go to find her. Another silly goose. He was going to enjoy kissing away her blushes and explaining that Madeline was just his twin. Nobody any more formidable than that.

But when he opened his eyes, it was to find that she was standing silently in the doorway looking at him, her face a pale and expressionless mask.

"Ellen!" he said, sitting up sharply and wincing. "You have not taken it so much to heart, have you?"

"What have we done?" Her voice was toneless.

"What . . . ?" He frowned at her.

"We have been living here together for almost a week," she said, "like a pair of carefree lovers. You are Charlie's closest friend. I am his wife. What have we done? He trusted us both. We have both cheated him."

"No." He stood up and reached out a hand to her, but she did not move from where she stood. "No, that is not true,

Ellen. I never . . . Good God, I never thought of you in this way while you were married to Charlie. You never thought of me in this way."

"I am an adulteress," she said.

He passed a hand over his eyes and felt for the edge of the bed with the backs of his knees. "No," he said. "Of course you are not. Calm down, Ellen. You were always a faithful wife. I always admired you for that. So did everyone who knew you."

She laughed harshly. "A faithful wife indeed," she said. "I have been lying with you in that bed each night, taking pleasure from you. As if pleasure were relevant to my life at present. In that bed. My husband's bed. Oh, my God!"

He sat down heavily. "Don't make it sordid, Ellen," he said. "Please don't do that. It has not been a matter of simple pleasure. You know that. It has been love. I have loved you in the past five days. You have loved me."

She laughed again. "Love!" she said. "I do not love you, my lord. You are a very attractive man. I have given in to the power of your attraction. And you do not love me. I am the woman who has nursed you during your recovery from injury. You have seen no other woman in three weeks, except for your sister. Did you not know that men always fall in love with the women who nurse them? This has not been love. This has been lust. And sordid. Oh, yes, very sordid."

He was angry. He surged to his feet and grasped his side. The wind felt as if it had been knocked out of him for a moment. "So you would spoil it all," he said, "because my own carelessness and the arrival of Madeline earlier embarrassed you. I am sorry about that, Ellen. But don't make something ugly about what has happened here. It is not ugly. We love each other."

"I love Charlie!" she cried. "I love him. I worship him. He

is twice the man you are. And now what have I done to him? What have I done?"

"You have done nothing," he said. He took a few steps toward her. "Charlie is dead, Ellen."

She stared back at him, her mouth open. The color that had returned to her face with her anger fled again.

"He is dead," he said dully. "Charlie is dead, Ellen. He died on the battlefield south of Waterloo. I was with him."

She closed her eyes and swayed on her feet. But when he took another step toward her, she looked up and held a hand in front of her.

"Don't come near me," she said. "Don't touch me." She swallowed more than once and looked down at herself. "I am dressed in green. Green. The color he liked me to wear. Not in black. I have known for almost a month that he is dead, and I am not wearing black. And I have not gone out as other women have on the fruitless search for his body. I have allowed him to be buried in an anonymous grave. I have refused to open the doors of my mind to the truth. He is away with the army, I have persuaded myself. A month, and I am not in mourning." She smiled.

"Ellen," he said, "come and sit down."

"You knew he was dead." She looked up at him, the strange smile still on her face. "You knew he was dead, my lord. You were with him. You brought me the news. And yet this is what you have done to his memory?" She pointed to the bed behind him.

He shook his head slowly. "Don't," he said. "It has been with me as with you, Ellen. He was my closest friend. I watched him die. I told you—I did, didn't I?—and then I let go of the knowledge."

"So," she said with a little laugh. "We are a pair of fools, my Lord Eden. And a pair of sinners."

"No," he said, "not that. We would not have done what we have done if Charlie were still alive. Both you and I are incapable of that. You know it. This has not been wrong, Ellen. Only very poorly timed. We should have waited—for a year, perhaps. But love will not always wait. And we have needed the comfort of each other."

She held her hands palm-up before her and looked down at them. "Charlie is dead," she said. "This time he is not coming back. I will never see him again. There will be no cottage in the country. No safe and secure times together. Only the past. Only memories. He's gone."

"Come over here, Ellen," he said softly, reaching out a hand to her again. "Let me comfort you. Let us comfort each other."

Her eyes were brimming with unshed tears when she looked up. "You cannot comfort me," she said. "He was my husband. My life. I loved him."

"I know," he said. "I know you did. And he was my friend, Ellen. You are my friend. Let me hold you."

"You are not my friend," she said. "Not any longer. Not ever again. You are my guilt. For all during these months in Brussels I have wanted you. I have looked at you and touched you and wanted you. Even though I had the best man in the world as a husband. Even though I loved him more than I love life."

He put his head down and rubbed at his eyes with the heels of his hands. "We each need some time alone," he said. "The atmosphere is too charged at the moment for either of us to talk sense. Let us not say anything that we will forever regret, Ellen. Let's talk later."

When he looked up, she was staring down at her hands again, her expression stony. One tear had escaped and was trickling unchecked down her cheek.

"There is nothing to say," she said.

"Only perhaps that I love you."

She shook her head. "Not even that," she said. "You will see that it is not true when you have had time to think. There is nothing to say, my lord. Nothing at all."

She turned without looking at him and left the room.

He was sitting on the bed, his head in his hands, when he heard the outer door of her rooms open and close and knew himself to be quite alone.

12

SOMEWHAT LATER THE SAME EVENING
Madeline was summoned downstairs in Colonel
Potts's home. She closed the book she had been reading
aloud from, smiled cheerfully at Lieutenant Penworth, who
was lying staring at the canopy over his bed with his one
good eye, and promised that she would return in time to
make him comfortable for the night. She ran lightly down
the stairs.

And positively hurtled down the last ten, shrieking in
a manner quite unbecoming a house in which there was
sickness. Her arms wound themselves around the Earl of
Amberley's neck, and he lifted her from two stairs
up and twirled her around twice before setting her on
her feet.

"Edmund!" she cried. "I was never more happy to see
you in my life. I thought you must have disappeared from
the face of the earth. And Mama!" She shrieked again and
threw herself into her mother's arms, laughing and crying
all at once.

"My darling girl," her mother said, hugging her very
tightly. "Looking creased and uncombed and quite hagged.

And behaving like a hoyden. And more dear than you have ever looked in your life."

"Have you just arrived?" Madeline asked eagerly. "Why did you not let me know you were coming? Why have you not answered any of my letters? Oh, do come into the salon."

"Your first letter reached us the day before we left," the earl said, taking his mother's elbow and following his sister across the hallway to the salon, from which the wounded had long ago been moved. "We thought we could get here faster than the mail. Dominic?" His voice was tense.

"Oh!" Madeline said. "You have read only my first letter? How dreadful! Dom is well on the road to recovery, I do assure you, and has been for almost two weeks. He has totally defied the surgeon who was calling on him, and is eating like a horse and prowling around his room like a caged bear."

The Earl of Amberley took his mother by the arm again. Her hands had gone up to cover her face. "Thank God!" he said, drawing her into his arms. His voice was shaking and his own eyes suspiciously bright. "Thank God."

"What dreadful suspense you must have been living in!" Madeline said. "My first letter must have been dreadfully gloomy. And the second. He was gravely ill, you know. The surgeon told Mrs. Simpson that we must expect the worst."

The dowager Lady Amberley pushed herself away from her son, searched in her reticule for a handkerchief, and blew her nose. "But Dominic would not give in," she said. "He is positively the strongest and most stubborn boy I have known. I was not glad of it three years ago, but now I am. We were afraid to go to Mrs. Simpson's first, Madeline. We did not know what we might find."

Madeline smiled brightly. "I was there this afternoon,"

she said, "and was taken quite by surprise. I am not at all sure that the scene would have been good for you, Mama. Dominic and Mrs. Simpson have fallen in love with each other and are to be married. Except that Dom has not asked her yet. But she is sure to say yes, he says. And I have never seen him so glowingly happy."

Her mother looked inquiringly at the earl, who was frowning. "This is rather sudden, is it not?" he said. "I have the greatest liking and respect for Mrs. Simpson, but she lost her husband just a month ago. Can she be thinking of remarrying already?"

"It is just like Dominic to be so impulsive," his mother said. "Will she suit, Edmund?"

"Oh, assuredly," he said. "She is not at all Dominic's usual type."

"That sounds decidedly promising," the dowager said with a smile.

"I shall fetch a shawl and bonnet," Madeline said, "and walk there with you."

Her brother held up a staying hand. "I think we must curb our impatience to see him," he said, "especially since he is out of all danger. It is rather late in the day to be paying social calls. Besides, Mama and I have not even found a hotel yet. We shall take rooms at the Hôtel d'Angleterre if there are any available and pay our call at the Rue de la Montagne in the morning."

"Yes, I think it would be best," his mother agreed. "As it is, we have disturbed Lady Andrea's household."

She kissed and hugged Madeline again, as did Lord Amberley, and they parted for the night. Madeline ran up the stairs again to share her good news with the lieutenant. She chattered brightly to him as she washed him with deft and gentle hands, straightened out his bedclothes, and turned and plumped his pillows.

She resisted the urge to kiss his forehead as she was leaving the room. She had not yet done so, and he might think it forward of her. He did not yet know that she was going to marry him and look after him for the rest of his life.

Neither did Mama and Edmund. She sobered somewhat as she reached her own room. It was going to be tricky. She hoped they would not voice some of the same silly notions that Dom had had. But she did not care anyway. She loved Lieutenant Penworth with a deep tenderness. And she would be able to pour out her love for him for the rest of their lives. He would always need her.

THE EARL OF AMBERLEY and his mother were surprised the following morning when they arrived at the Rue de la Montagne to find that Mrs. Simpson looked far from being a woman newly in love and planning a marriage. She was dressed in deepest mourning, her hair pulled severely back from her pale, drawn face. She looked as if she were close to collapse.

"Mrs. Simpson." The earl held out both hands to her and took one of hers within their clasp.

"Good day, my lord," she said. "You have come. Lord Eden will be glad." Her voice was totally devoid of expression.

"My very deepest sympathies, ma'am," he said. "Your husband was one of the kindest gentlemen of my acquaintance, and I know you were devoted to him."

"Yes," she said. "Thank you."

"May I present my mother, the dowager Countess of Amberley?" he said. "Mrs. Simpson, Mama."

Ellen curtsied.

"You have been wonderfully kind to my boy," Lady Amberley said, stretching out both hands to her new acquaintance. "And oh, my dear, how you have been suffering on your own account." She gathered the other woman into her arms when Ellen's face crumpled. "Oh, my poor dear. My poor dear child."

Lord Amberley walked quietly past them and on to the closed doors that must lead to the bedchambers. The second one he opened showed him his brother, standing at the window, his back to the room, looking somewhat thinner than he had looked five weeks before.

Lord Eden's shoulders tensed when the door opened, and he turned slowly. His brother looked at him in shock. He had expected to see him looking somewhat less than his usual fit, ebullient self. But he had not expected to see the pale, haggard face, the haunted eyes.

"Edmund," Lord Eden said. "God, Edmund!"

He took two steps forward, but his brother was across the room before he could move any farther, and had him in a close embrace. Lord Amberley felt a nasty lurching of his stomach when his brother leaned his head on his shoulder and broke into racking sobs.

"Dominic!" he said, aghast. "My God, is this what war does to a man? Well, you are with me now, and I am going to take you home with me no matter what ideas anyone else may have. I have never interfered with what you want of life, and have no right to do so now. But I will use all my influence on you, and set Alex to using hers, to persuade you to sell out of this infernal life."

Lord Eden straightened up. "I never thought to make such a prize idiot of myself," he said. "If you only knew how I have longed and longed this morning to see just your very person. I am so helpless here on my own, Edmund. As weak as an infant. I doubt I could get down the stairs to the street without assistance."

"You are on your feet and standing straight," his brother said, "when two weeks ago, by all accounts, it was just as likely you would not even live. Don't rush things, Dominic. Let us be thankful for great mercies. Your strength and freedom of movement will return."

"Take me away from here," Lord Eden said. "Will you? Today?"

Lord Amberley frowned and looked closely at him. "You are that restless?" he asked.

"I am imposing on her," his brother said. "I have no right here. She has her own life, her own grief. She will be wanting to return to England."

"Mama is with her now," the earl said quietly. "She is very broken up, Dominic. But it is hardly surprising. They were a devoted couple." He watched his brother.

"Mama?" Lord Eden frowned. "Mama is here? And I suppose I have eyes as red as a petulant schoolboy's. I must get over to that washstand. Mama! Whatever possessed her to leave England?"

"Merely a son who was at death's door," Lord Amberley said. "I want to see that wound, Dominic, and more to the point, I want a physician to see it. I hear that you sent the army surgeon packing."

"So would you have," Lord Eden said, gasping as he dashed a handful of cold water onto his face. "Having blood pumped from you daily and toast and weak tea pumped back in again is not conducive to good health, I would have you know. I would still be flat on my back. Or else six feet under."

"I am sure we can manage better than that," his brother

said. "Do you think you can travel in a hired carriage? We have one outside. What about Mrs. Simpson, Dominic? Is she fit to be left alone? Will she need help in returning to England?"

"You can ask her," Lord Eden said. "Will you, Edmund? I can't. I mean, I am in no shape to offer anyone help, am I?"

There were a dozen questions racing through the earl's mind. He asked none of them. He watched his brother sit heavily on the bed and stretch out on it, wincing slightly, and turned to leave.

His mother was sitting on a sofa next to Mrs. Simpson, holding both her hands and talking to her.

Ellen looked up. "You will want to see your son," she said. "I am sorry. I have been keeping you from him."

"You must not apologize," the dowager said, squeezing tightly the hands that she held. "Gracious heavens. When I think of how much I am in your debt, my dear, dear child!"

She rose to her feet and hurried to the open doorway of Lord Eden's room.

Lord Amberley stood looking down at the fair head of Mrs. Simpson.

"I cannot thank you enough for what you have done for my brother," he said. "I shall always consider myself in your debt."

She looked up at him with reddened, miserable eyes. "You must not do so," she said. "It is the role of army women to tend the wounded, my lord. There is nothing out of the ordinary in what I have done."

"Ah, but to me there is," he said. "For you have tended my only and very dear brother, ma'am. And at a time when the burden of your own grief has been very heavy on you. Is there anything I can do for you, my dear?"

"No," she said. She rose to her feet. "I thank you, but no, there is nothing."

"I shall be taking Dominic away with me," he said, "as soon as I can return to the Hôtel d'Angleterre and bring back some clothes for him. Apparently you had to cut away his uniform? So one burden at least I can remove from you, ma'am. We have imposed upon your hospitality long enough." He watched her closely.

"It has been no imposition," she said. Her eyes were directed at his waistcoat.

"What will you do?" he asked. "Will you return to England?"

"Yes," she said. "I have my stepdaughter to look after. And I promised my husband that I would go to his sister in London if anything happened to him." Her voice wavered slightly.

"May I arrange for your passage?" he asked. "I wish I might offer you the protection of our company on the way home, but I believe it might be several weeks before my brother is fit enough to travel."

"Thank you," she said, "but I will be able to manage quite well on my own."

"Yes, I am sure you will," he said, wishing there were some way to discover her financial circumstances and to offer her money. "One thing you must allow me to do, though, if you please. I will hire a maid to accompany you. Please?" He added the final plea hastily, noting that she was about to open her mouth in protest.

She looked up into his eyes and nodded briefly. "If you wish," she said. "Thank you."

She stayed in the parlor, sitting quite still, when he left to fetch clothes for Lord Eden. And she stayed there when the dowager countess joined her as Lord Eden dressed with his brother's assistance. She got to her feet and moved to a shadowed alcove by the fireplace when the door opened again.

"Will you be able to descend the stairs, Dominic?" his mother asked anxiously.

"Quite easily," he said, "with Edmund's help."

His face was very white and set. Mother and elder son exchanged glances.

Lord Eden looked about him until he saw Ellen in the shadows. He crossed the room to stand in front of her. She was staring down at her clasped hands.

"Good-bye, Ellen," he said. He was almost whispering, though his mother had begun to talk in a quite loud voice to his brother. "I am sorry. I am truly sorry. For the timing. The timing was all wrong. We protected ourselves so carefully from the painful truth that we ignored it entirely. But what happened was not sordid, for all that. And I do not love you any the less for all the guilt I feel and all the suffering I know I have caused you. May I see you in England? After several months perhaps, or even a year?"

"No," she said. "I do not want to see you ever again, my lord. It is not that I blame you or hate you. I blame myself, and I hate myself. But I will not see you again. Good-bye."

He stood silently before her for several moments before bowing as well as he could with the fresh bandages that Edmund had secured tightly about his ribs, and turning away.

Lady Amberley took Ellen's hands in hers again. "I will call on you tomorrow again, my dear," she said. "Perhaps just seeing another person will help you somewhat. Though that is a foolish thing to say, I know. I lost my husband very suddenly, and I know that it is the world's loneliest and most wretched feeling. The only consolation I can offer will seem like no consolation at all at the moment. It will pass, my dear child. The pain will go away eventually. I promise you it will." She leaned forward and kissed Ellen's pale cheek.

Lord Eden and his brother had already left the room, Ellen was relieved to see. She sank to the sofa when their mother too had left, and sat there for a long time, too deeply miserable even to cry.

LORD EDEN WAS stretched out on his bed at the hotel, one arm flung across his eyes.

"I don't want anything, Mama," he said. "I am not hungry."

"You have not eaten all day," she said. "Are you feeling unwell?"

"Just tired," he said. "The move here was more exhausting than I would have thought."

She touched his hair and looked down at him, troubled.

"Nothing," she said a few minutes later when she had rejoined her elder son in the sitting room. "He will not even look at a tray."

Lord Amberley got to his feet. "Teatime," he said, "and my arms feel dreadfully empty. No tiger to undo my waistcoat buttons and remember too late that his bread and jam have not been wiped from his fingers. And no princess to stare me down and then smile like an angel when I am vanquished."

"And no Alexandra," his mother added with a smile.

The earl groaned. "And no Alex," he said. "Devil take it, but I miss her, Mama. Is it normal?"

"Perfectly, I am afraid," she said. "Are you going in to him, Edmund?"

"Yes," he said, "as soon as I have flexed my elder-brother muscles. We seem to have arrived at quite a time of crisis, do we not?"

"A good time, I think," she said. "He is going to need us. But that poor child. She is so very alone."

The Earl of Amberley stood looking down at his brother a couple of minutes later. Lord Eden's arm was still over his eyes.

"Do you want to talk about it?" the earl asked, pulling up a chair to the bed and seating himself.

"About the battle?" Lord Eden did not change his position. "Not really. It is hard to have clear memories of such a thing. It is all noise and confusion at the time. All I can ever see clearly afterward is the dead eyes."

"I didn't mean the battle," the earl said.

Lord Eden took his arm from his eyes and stared upward. "I suppose Mad has been talking," he said. "I made a mistake, that is all, Edmund. She has a husband's death to grieve for. I fancied her because she has been my only nurse for a month and I saw no one else. It's over now and really does not signify at all."

"If you could have seen your face and Mrs. Simpson's face this morning," the earl said, "you would not have said that it does not signify, Dominic. You care for her deeply?"

Lord Eden stared upward. His jaw had tightened. "Yes," he said.

"Do you have any reason to believe that she returns your feelings?" his brother asked.

"I cannot speak for Ellen," Lord Eden said. "She loved Charlie. There can be no doubt about that."

"No," Lord Amberley said. "There cannot. You have been in love before, Dominic. Dozens of times before you reached your majority, even. Is there any chance that this one will go the way of the rest? Sometimes a lost love is painful at the time, but quickly recovered from."

"I love her," Lord Eden said. "I am not just in love with her."

"Ah, yes," his brother said sadly. "I am sorry, then, Dominic. I don't know what happened exactly between the time when Madeline called upon you yesterday afternoon and the time when we arrived this morning. And I won't pry. But I am sorry. Is life very hard to face at the moment?"

"There does not seem much point to it," Lord Eden said. "And I am not being self-pitying, Edmund. I don't plan to pine away. But today I can't force myself to live. I don't want to. Those damned French never could shoot straight. It was pure chance they got Charlie. They bungled badly with me."

Lord Amberley rose to his feet and placed a hand on his brother's shoulder. "Do I have your word that tomorrow you will force yourself?" he asked. "So that I won't have to hold you down while Mama shovels food inside you?"

Lord Eden laughed unexpectedly. "Yes," he said, "you have my word. You would do it too, wouldn't you, the pair of you? And have Mad stand at the foot of the bed, as like as not, chattering her head off to distract my mind. What would I ever do without a family to torment me? God, Edmund"—his voice shook suddenly—"I'm glad you came. I don't know what I would have done if you had not. Sent for Mad and thrown myself on the mercy of her horsey friend, I suppose."

Lord Amberley patted his shoulder and left the room.

Lord Eden swung his legs over the side of the bed and eased himself first into a sitting position and then to his feet. He began to pace the room diagonally. He had to regain his health. It would be stupidity in the extreme to allow himself to fall into a decline.

He had thought he could draw her out of her terrible sense of guilt. He had thought that perhaps he could comfort her to a certain extent for her loss of Charlie. He had thought that perhaps he could make her realize that what had happened between them had occurred because they loved each other. He had thought that he might suggest that they wait for a year, see each other during that time only under controlled circumstances, and then get together again and marry and have children together and share their love for a lifetime.

His own sense of guilt was a terrible thing. He had loved Charlie with a deep affection. Charlie had been friend, father, and brother all in one. And yet for a month, two weeks of that time free from fever, he had not given him one conscious thought, or shed one tear of grief. And he had allowed himself to fall in love with Charlie's widow and to become her lover. He had dreamed of an immediate marriage with her.

All as if Charlie had never lived and loved her. And as if she had never loved him.

And yet, he had thought after she had left him the previous afternoon and after he had heard the outer door close and knew she had gone out, even the fact that they had not mentioned or thought about Charlie in a month proved their love for him in a strange way. They had both known in a part of themselves deeper than thought that coping with the knowledge of his death would be difficult. He had had his physical weakness to contend with. She had had patients to tend. And so they had kept their knowledge and their grief at bay. But just a little too long. Six days too long. They had been lovers for six days.

He had thought he might explain those things to her when she came back. She would have calmed down by that time. He had calmed down. Yet when he had heard her come home and gone out into the parlor, he had found himself looking at a woman wearing deep mourning and a face of marble.

"Can we talk?" he had asked, knowing that it was hopeless, that there was no way to get past the defenses she had built in the space of a few hours.

"There is nothing to say," she had said. "I am sorry I am late with your dinner. I will have it ready soon."

"I am not hungry," he had said. "Ellen, let me grieve with you. Let me comfort you if I can."

"There is no grieving to be done," she had said, "and no comfort to be offered. I am not worthy to grieve for Charlie. And you are not worthy to offer comfort to anyone for his death. I shall show the outer respect of wearing these clothes for him for the next year because he deserves that respect. I would prefer it if you stayed in your room, Lord Eden. We can have nothing more to say to each other, you and I."

They were ridiculous words, of course. She must have realized it herself before the evening was out. Of course she would grieve for Charlie. She had loved him. Her grief was only just beginning. But he knew that there was no getting past that barrier she had set up between herself and him. Certainly not that evening. Perhaps not ever.

He had had no choice but to return to his room and remain there, careful to have his back turned or his eyes closed every time she came in after that on some necessary errand. He had been desperate over his own helplessness by that morning. Edmund had seemed like an angel sent from heaven.

And so he had lost her. There was a vast and painful emptiness inside him that threatened to turn to panic. She did not wish to see him ever again, she had said that morning. And she had meant it.

He would never see her again. Never talk with her and laugh with her. Never sit in comfortable silence with her. Never explore her lovely face and figure with his eyes. Never sit quietly holding her hand. Never kiss her or touch her. Never make love with her.

The emptiness yawned.

But Lord Eden paced on. He had promised Edmund that he would be ready for life again by the next day. And by God, he would be ready. He was not going to pine his life away for any woman. Not even for Ellen. And if he must continue living, there was no point at all in putting it off until the next day. He opened the door of his room.

"I hope you have chosen a hotel with a decent chef," he said when his brother looked up from a book in some surprise. "I could eat a horse."

"Ah," Lord Amberley said. "Was that to be boiled, stewed, or roasted, Dominic?"

ELLEN WAS STANDING at the rail of the packet from Ostend, feeling the strong wind of the channel catch at her breath and whip her cloak against her. Her new maid, Prudence, an English girl excited to be returning to her own country, stood at her side. The Earl of Amberley had hired the girl, bought her passage, and paid her first year's salary in advance. It was a comfort to have a companion, not to be entirely alone.

She would not look back to the coast of Belgium. She set

her face for England, invisible still beyond the haze of the horizon. But she would not look back.

She had left them there, both of them. Forever. Charlie in an unknown grave on a battlefield she had roamed over for several hours three days before, Lord Eden recuperating from his wounds in Brussels with his brother and mother. She would not see either again, the one because he was forever beyond her sight, the other because she chose not to do so.

Charlie was dead. She recited the fact to herself almost constantly and was continually amazed that she lived on. That she could live on. She had not thought that she would be capable of doing so without him. But she was living. She was dreadfully lonely despite the friendly sweetness of Prudence, despite the visits in Brussels in the week before she had left, daily by the dowager Lady Amberley and twice by Lady Madeline. There was no longer that sheltering, all-encompassing, totally unconditional love that had been Charlie. But she was living.

And she would live. She still had someone to live for. Jennifer was in London, doubtless distraught over the death of the father she had only just begun to really know. Jennifer would need her, even if Ellen was not nearly old enough to be a real mother to the girl. She could be a friend instead, the closest living link with the girl's father.

And there was Lady Habersham, Charlie's sister, who had been kind to him through the years, who had always kept Jennifer when her brother was not in England, who must have agreed to give a home to Ellen in the event of Charlie's death in battle. She would be grieving. She too would be a friend.

And then there was her final and reluctant promise to Charlie. The promise she had not wanted to make. The one she did not want to keep. But she would keep it for all that, for she had truly loved Charlie, and she had wronged him terribly after his death, and she would do this last thing for him with all the determination that it might take. She would see to it that Jennifer met her grandfather, that he acknowledged her and took charge of her future.

She would do that much for Charlie. And for Jennifer. And then, if there was enough money, she would buy a cottage in the country. And she would live there for the rest of her life. She would even be happy there eventually, once the terrible pain of her grief had passed off. It did not feel now as if it ever would, as if she would ever wake up again in the morning glad to be alive, looking forward to what the day might bring.

But the older Lady Amberley had said that it would pass. And common sense told her that it would. Charlie was gone. And she lived on. So be it.

So be it. She would live on.

And as for that other, she would put it from her mind, and that too would fade with time. The guilt would fade. The memory of him and what she had known with him for six days would fade. A more heightened sensuality than she had ever dreamed of with Charlie, contented as she had been with every facet of their life together.

She would not think of it any longer. Or of him. It had not been love, or anything approximating love. It had been all purely physical, and therefore not anything of any lasting value.

She was sorry to have lost a friend, to have bitter memories of him instead of sweet ones, connected with the times he had shared with her and Charlie. But that was all her fault. She had spoiled their relationship. And, of course, they could never be friends again.

She would not think of him any longer.

And she would not look back to a past that could never again be her present or her future. She would look ahead.

"When may we expect to see the coast of England?" she asked Prudence, raising her face resolutely to the wind. "Do you know?"

Sometimes the pain was a real and a physical thing. Sometimes it was almost past bearing.

13

ELLEN SAT DOWN FACING HER SISTER-IN-LAW, Lady Habersham, and smiled. "The house is suddenly quiet with Jennifer gone out. She seems almost her old self again," she said. "I am so glad the Misses Emery have taken to her and she to them."

"They are sweet girls," Lady Habersham said. "And of course I have known Melinda Emery for more than twenty years. We were girls together. It will do Jennifer the world of good to spend the afternoon shopping."

"I had no idea when I came home that she would be quite so broken up," Ellen said. "I expected tears, Dorothy, and regrets. But not all the rest."

"She always worshiped her father," Lady Habersham said, "and lived for the day when she would be free of school and free to live with him all the time. She used to talk of it when she was here, you know. It has been a terrible blow, losing him like this just when it seemed that her dream was coming true."

Ellen smoothed the black silk of her dress over her knees. "I didn't expect to be the way I have been, either," she said. "I had thought of it many times during the five years of our marriage and wondered how I would react. Quite honestly, I did not think it would be possible to live on with Charlie dead. And when it did happen and I knew that of course I would survive, I thought I could fight the grief and the emptiness. I remember standing on the boat from Ostend thinking that once I set foot on English soil I would be able to put it all behind me and start life again. I even made plans. I knew it would be hard, but I thought it would be possible. That was two months ago. And I have done nothing."

Lady Habersham picked up her embroidery frame and began to stitch. "Losing a husband is the very worst thing that can happen in the world," she said. "I know, dear. And, believe me, you are doing remarkably well. You have allowed Jennifer to lean on you, and have been a pillar of strength for her. If it were not for your face and your loss of weight, Ellen, no one would have an inkling of how deeply you are suffering. But it is time to start living again, is it not?"

"Yes." Ellen stared down at her hands. "You know, the very worst thing is finding myself storing up some silly little incident in my head to tell Charlie later, and then remembering that I won't be able to do so. Ever. Oh, dear, I must stop this. You are quite right, Dorothy. It is time to live again. Where should I start, do you think?"

Lady Habersham kept her head bent over her embroidery. "Papa wants to see you," she said.

"Your father?" Ellen looked up wide-eyed. "He wants to see me, Dorothy? Why?"

Her sister-in-law set her work down on her lap. "You are Charlie's widow," she said. "Charlie was his favorite child, Ellen."

"His favorite child?" Ellen's eyes flashed with indignation. "Yet he did not talk to him for almost twenty years?"

"He would doubtless have forgiven Charlie a long time ago if he had only loved him less," Lady Habersham said sadly. "Family members sometimes do dreadful things to one another. Now that it is too late, of course, Papa is almost prostrate with grief. He has worn mourning ever since he heard. He asked me two months ago, and has been asking me ever since, if I would persuade you to meet him. I have not thought that you were ready for such a thing. But now perhaps you are. Will you, Ellen?"

Ellen drew in a deep breath. "I promised Charlie I would try to get his father to receive Jennifer," she said. "It was my last promise to him, and it was one of those things on the boat home that I was going to do without delay. And now it has been made easy for me. No, not easy. It will be one of the hardest things I have ever done in my life."

"I will arrange for you to take tea with him tomorrow," Lady Habersham said with a smile that showed her relief. "He will want Phillip and Edith to be there too. You might as well meet all the family at once, Ellen."

Charlie's younger brother, Phillip. He had figured in most of those stories of childhood that Charlie had told her so many times.

"I wonder how Jennifer will feel about going," she said. "Excited, do you think, Dorothy? Nervous? I do not know if she even knows much about her grandfather."

Lady Habersham picked up her frame again in nervous hands. "Papa wants to meet you, Ellen," she said. "He has not mentioned Jennifer. Let's take it slowly, shall we? Perhaps after he has met you and grown to love you, as he is bound to do, then he will be willing to meet Jennifer too."

Ellen stared at her sister-in-law. "He does not want to

meet his own granddaughter?" she said. "He is grieving for Charlie, but he does not want to meet Jennifer?"

"Do you know the whole story?" Lady Habersham's attention was concentrated on her work.

"Yes." Ellen looked at her sister-in-law, aghast. "Charlie was right, then? His family believes that Jennifer is not his daughter? Is that what it is?"

"I believe that she is," Lady Habersham said. "Perhaps Papa does too in his heart. They had been married long enough when she was born. But, Ellen. She was a prostitute." She flushed and lowered her head even further over her work.

"And Jennifer is to be held to blame for that?"

Lady Habersham looked up in some distress. "You must understand," she said, "that Papa and Charlie were very close. Papa had great hopes for him. And then he insisted on enlisting in the army. Then that marriage. And the birth just a little too close for comfort afterward. Oh, Ellen, it is so easy to judge other people. Papa is not a monster."

"I will not visit him," Ellen said, "unless he also receives Jennifer. She is his flesh and blood, Dorothy. I am merely the widow of his son. No, I will not go. I will see her respectably married on my own after our year of mourning is at an end and then carry on with my own life. I don't need your father. I don't need anyone. Only Charlie, and he is gone."

"Don't upset yourself." Lady Habersham pulled a handkerchief from her pocket to dab at her own eyes. She looked up at Ellen, who had got to her feet and was looking back at her, unshed tears brightening her eyes. "I will talk to Papa. He is so stubborn, Ellen. And so hurt. Oh, dear, I don't know what to do."

Ellen closed the distance between them, and laid a hand

lightly on the other's shoulder. "This is hard on you, Dorothy," she said, "being a go-between like this. I understand, and I honor you for remaining loyal to both sides all these years. But I can't make it easy for you, I'm afraid. I can't go and visit him without Jennifer."

Their conversation was interrupted at that moment by the entrance of the butler, who presented a card on a silver salver to his mistress.

Lady Habersham picked it up, read it, and smiled up at Ellen. "This should cheer you up," she said. "You have a visitor, my dear. Is he waiting downstairs?" she asked the butler.

"Yes, ma'am," that individual said, bowing.

"Who?" Ellen asked.

"Charlie's friend," Lady Habersham said with a bright smile. "The one Jennifer was taken with. The one you nursed in Brussels. Lord Eden. Show him up, Hancock."

"No!" Ellen spun around to face the butler. "No. You will tell him, if you please, that neither I nor Miss Simpson is at home."

"Ellen, dear . . ."

"We are not at home," Ellen told the butler firmly.

He looked inquiringly at Lady Habersham, bowed, and left the room.

"But why?" Lady Habersham's voice was puzzled. "I thought you would be delighted to see him, Ellen. Was he not a very close friend of yours and Charlie's?"

"Excuse me." Ellen did not turn around to look at her sister-in-law. "Excuse me, please, Dorothy. I, er . . . We . . . Excuse me, please." She hurried from the room.

Lady Habersham was left to stare after her in some dismay. Clearly Ellen was not as far along the road to recovery as she had hoped, if she went to pieces like this at the prospect of meeting someone who would remind her of Charlie and the events surrounding the Battle of Waterloo.

LORD EDEN HAD SPENT almost a month in Brussels with his mother and brother before they felt that he was fit for the journey home. There he had concentrated all his energies on his physical health, forcing himself every day to greater and greater effort, priding himself on the gradual return of stamina and weight and muscle.

He had set goals for himself. By such and such a day he would be able to set foot outside the hotel, or walk for fifteen minutes or half an hour, or ride a horse. By such and such a day he would be ready to return to England. Edmund's frequently woebegone expression spurred him on to the last goal. Edmund was missing his family, though not by a single word would he ever have admitted the truth.

They had come home eventually, leaving Madeline behind. She was still busy nursing Lieutenant Penworth, whose recovery was necessarily slower than his own, and was made slower by the patient's own lack of will to live. Madeline had refused to listen to any of the advice she had been given, gently by her mother and older brother, scathingly by him. She was convinced that she loved the lieutenant and would be happy with him for a lifetime. And when Mad once got a notion into her head, Lord Eden had to admit at last, there was no shaking it.

Perhaps she was right. Perhaps she really did love the man. And perhaps she would live happily ever after with him. Who knew? And who was he to judge? He was no great expert on love and happiness.

He had been back in England for a month. Back in London. Getting himself out of the army and back into civilian life. It was unusual for his brother to spend much time away from Amberley, especially during the summer months. But on this occasion he did stay, with Alexandra and the children. And so did the dowager, with whom Lord Eden took up residence. And his uncle, Mr. William Carrington, was there too, with Aunt Viola and Walter and Anna. They had come to London in the spring for Anna's come-out Season. They had stayed after the Battle of Waterloo in order to have news of him. And then they stayed until he came home. And now they were staying— as was the rest of the family—for Madeline's return.

His physical recovery was progressing daily. Provided he walked and rode and exercised in moderation, he could almost forget his injuries. It was only when he forgot and exerted himself too much that he felt the old twinges and aches in his side and the old breathlessness. And only when he caught sight of himself shirtless in a mirror that he was reminded of the ugliness of his wound.

His emotional state he did not explore too deeply. In Brussels he had had to block thoughts of Ellen from his mind. They were too painful, and threatened his physical recovery. After the first week, when his mother finally informed him that she was no longer in Brussels but had gone home to England, he felt some relief. There was no chance that he would come face-to-face with her if he went outside.

And back in England he kept up the mental block. He would not think of her. He would put her behind him with all the other pain and nightmare of the Battle of Waterloo. He would not think of Charlie because doing so reminded him that he had lost a friend so dear that he had felt almost like a brother. And he would not remember Ellen because doing so reminded him that he had lost what might have been the happiness of the rest of his life.

He would not think of her.

And when he did—as he inevitably did every single day and every single hour—it was to admit that she had probably been right. He had loved her because she had nursed him with such gentleness and devotion. Because they had been cut off together from the rest of the world. Because she was beautiful and had great strength of character. Because they had both been carrying the burden of a great grief that they were afraid to admit even to themselves and had turned to each other for comfort.

It had not been love. It had not been lust either. But definitely not love. Not the sort that could last a lifetime through the daily routine of marriage.

When the pain was gone and he could eventually think quite openly about their affair, he would be able to remember it and her with some pleasure. But it was an affair for memory only. It was not something that he would want to revive.

He had promised Charlie, as his friend was dying, that he would look after his wife and his daughter, that he would see to it that they were never in need. It was very possible that Charlie had not heard. He had almost completed his journey into death when the words were spoken. But that did not matter. The fact was that the promise had been made and that it was binding.

And so it nagged at Lord Eden's mind for the month after his return to England. And he knew that he could never know peace of mind until he had called upon Ellen and Miss Simpson to satisfy himself that they were not in need. But always he would pay that call tomorrow. There was always a good reason why it should not be made today.

It was Susan Jennings who finally decided him that the visit could be postponed no longer. Susan too had lost her husband at Waterloo. She was in London, staying at the home of Lord Renfrew, her brother-in-law. Her mother, Mrs. Courtney, had come up from the country to be with her.

The two of them had called a couple of times on Alexandra while he was still in Brussels, and once since to inquire after his health. And they called again a month after his return, while he himself was also at his brother's house.

"It is so lovely to see you home safe and sound again, my lord," Mrs. Courtney said in her motherly way, squeezing his hand and patting it. "And quite as handsome as ever. Though thinner, I believe. Is he not thinner, ma'am?" She turned to the dowager Lady Amberley for confirmation.

Susan withdrew a lace handkerchief from her reticule and dabbed at her tears. She gazed at him with large soulful hazel eyes.

"I would not have called, my lord," she said, "if I had known that you and her ladyship were also visiting. I would not have intruded. Mama and I merely wished to hear how you did. I am very, very happy that you escaped the fate of my dear husband."

She dissolved into further tears and was comforted by her mama.

She looked remarkably pretty, Lord Eden thought, even in her mourning. The unrelieved black of her dress made her look more fragile than ever and complemented the auburn of her hair.

But it was not Susan he saw in his mind after she and Mrs. Courtney had taken their leave. He saw Ellen as he had seen her last, also in black, hiding herself in the shadows of her living room in Brussels. She would still be wearing mourning. So would Miss Simpson.

He must call upon them. She had told him, of course, that she never wanted to see him again. But he had promised Charlie. Besides, she had spoken at an emotionally charged moment. Despite everything that had happened between them in those rooms, they were still friends of long standing. He owed her a courtesy visit. He must put it off no longer.

Even so, he had to use all his willpower the next day not to make excuses yet again for staying away from the house on Bedford Square. He could feel his heart thumping in his chest as he handed his card to Lady Habersham's butler and asked if he might wait upon Mrs. Simpson and her stepdaughter.

It was strange, he thought as he left the house a few minutes later, having left his card and the message that he would call again the next day. He had rehearsed several scenes that might develop from his call. He had pictured Ellen upset or angry or cold or even glad, and he had dealt with all those possibilities in his mind. But he had not at all prepared himself for finding that she was from home. He had not prepared his mind for perhaps having to go through the same ordeal all over again.

Or perhaps she was at home. Perhaps she would not see him. He would find out the next day, he supposed, when she would be expecting him. He mounted his horse and turned its head toward the stone gateposts and the square beyond.

ELLEN STOOD LOOKING DOWN at him. He was wearing very fashionable civilian clothes. She had never seen him out of his officer's uniform. Except in those last few weeks, of course.

He looked strange. Different. And very, very familiar.

She wished she could relive the past few minutes. She would not behave in the same way. She had been very foolish, very uncontrolled. But he had taken her by surprise. She had not expected him. And so she had reacted by instinct. And instinct had made a coward of her. She had run from him.

She would not have expected to act that way. In two months she had worked him out of her system. Her grief at her loss of Charlie had outweighed all else in her life. It had been far, far worse than she had expected even in her worst nightmares. It had paralyzed her, taken away all her will to live, to do, and to plan.

She had put Lord Eden out of her mind, out of her heart. And she had forgiven herself for what they had done together. In the absence of anyone to confess her guilt to—in the absence of Charlie—she had forgiven herself. He had been right about that one thing. Neither of them had been ready to face the truth, and so they had turned to each other. They had become lovers briefly.

There had been no love involved, only a physical and emotional need. They had filled the void for each other for a few days.

There was no point in carrying around a burden of guilt with her for the rest of her life. No point at all. And so she forgave herself. And him. She did not hate him. But she did not love him either. She had no feelings for him. He had been Charlie's friend. That was all.

But she did not want to see him again. She did not want to be reminded either of those days when he had been almost a part of their family or of the days after Waterloo.

She did not want to see him again. And she had assumed that honor would make him respect her final refusal to allow him to see her.

She had been taken by surprise. And instead of receiving him downstairs in Dorothy's presence and conversing politely with him for half an hour, she had run like a frightened rabbit to hide in her room.

Except that her room faced the front of the house and she had been unable to resist the temptation to cross to the window, standing well enough back so that she would not be observed from the outside, in order to see him when he left.

Just like a lovesick schoolgirl!

He looked so very familiar, despite the unfamiliarity of the clothes. Certainly no worse for his ordeal, though she could not, of course, see his face. He looked quite as splendidly built as ever.

Would he come back? She must prepare herself. She must know very clearly how she would react next time. She must certainly not rush away like that again. Dorothy would think she had taken leave of her senses. Or would perhaps suspect the truth. And Jennifer might begin to wonder. It was a good thing she had not been at home this first time.

She must prepare to meet him as an old acquaintance. She must inquire about his health and about the members of his family. She must prepare herself to look him squarely and coolly in the eye.

It should not be difficult. She had known him and been on friendly terms with him for more than three years. There had been only six days of the other. No more.

Of course there was a good deal more. Ellen's hand was

spread below her waist as she watched horse and rider leave the square and disappear from sight.

A great deal more.

Her mind had been in a deep torpor for two months. She had made no plans whatsoever for her future apart from the ones she had made on the boat home. It was as if life had been suspended. And yet all the time—a great irony indeed—life had been developing. New life. Her future.

There was no doubt left in her mind. And there was no panic and no fear either, though perhaps there had been a little of both at the end of the first month. No thought to how she would cope with the reality, how she would explain to other people. To Jennifer and to Dorothy.

She was going to have his child. Lord Eden's child. There. She had said it in words in her own mind. Charlie and the army surgeon had been right. It had been something to do with him. Not with her. She was able to conceive, and she had conceived at some time during those six days.

She was going to have a child. And she must be taking leave of her senses—she was glad! There was an excitement in her that she had not until this moment admitted to herself.

Here was her future. Something—no, someone—to live for now that there was no longer Charlie. She could wish fiercely that the child were his, but it was not, and it could not have been. And so she could not after all feel as sorry for that affair as she should have felt, for without it she would be without this child growing in her. She would be without a future. No, not that. She did not think she was the sort of person who could ever give up entirely and permanently on life. But without the child she would be starting at the age of five-and-twenty with a blank life ahead. A frightening prospect.

She would have her child to live for. And it did not matter that it was not Charlie's. It did not matter that it was Lord Eden's. What did matter was that it was a living being and growing in her, that it would be hers, and that it had been conceived at a time when her love for Charlie had been too great for her mind to be willing to let him go. And at a time when she had felt a great tenderness for its father.

For the child had not been conceived out of lust. She had been wrong to say that. There had been a closeness, a tenderness. Nothing that would last. Nothing that could be called love. But not just lust, for all that. Nothing ugly. Nothing sordid, despite what she had said to him at the time.

Ellen's free hand joined the other over her abdomen.

LORD EDEN WAS RIDING along Oxford Street when he spotted his cousins Anna and Walter Carrington walking along toward him, Walter's arms loaded with parcels. Anna saw him, smiled dazzlingly, and waved.

"Dominic," she called when he drew rein beside them. "You wretch. You have been going to take me walking this age. But I might be sitting at home gathering dust for all you care. So I have come shopping with Walter."

"And I can see why you need him," Lord Eden said, grinning down at them. "I suppose you can't balance something on your head too, Walter, so that Anna can buy a few more things?"

Walter grimaced.

"And besides, Anna," Lord Eden said, "once when I

called, you were entertaining a dozen guests, at least half of whom were male and young. And another time you were out driving with young Pendleton. I concluded that a mere cousin was of no account now that you have grown into the beauty I always told you you would grow into, and have been the belle of a London Season."

"Oh, nonsense!" she said. "You know that I would have consigned Mr. Pendleton to the bottom of the sea, Dominic, if I had known you were going to choose just that afternoon to come for me. And you really must not smirk at me in that odious way, Walter, as if I were a child still."

Walter turned and smirked instead at his cousin, who grinned back.

Three young ladies were coming out of a shop just behind Anna and Walter, one of them wearing deep mourning. Miss Jennifer Simpson, by some strange coincidence, Lord Eden saw when he looked more closely. She saw him at the same moment, smiled uncertainly, and blushed. He swept off his hat, which he had returned to his head after greeting Anna.

"Miss Simpson!" he said. "Well met. I have just come from your aunt's house, but neither you nor your stepmother was at home."

She curtsied and looked up at him. "You have been to call on us, my lord?" she said. "But Ellen is at home. She had no intention of going out."

"I left my card," he said, "and told your aunt's butler that I would return tomorrow."

"I shall look forward to that," she said, her voice breathless. She looked over her shoulder, but her two companions had strolled on. "And I am sure Ellen will too."

"May I present my cousins?" he said. "Anna Carrington

and her brother, Walter. Miss Jennifer Simpson is the daughter of an army friend, Anna. She was in Brussels earlier this spring."

Anna smiled. Walter dropped two parcels and took Jennifer's hand in his. She looked at him and blushed anew.

"I have not had a chance to express my sympathies," Lord Eden said. "I do so now, Miss Simpson. Your father was a fine man."

"Yes." She smiled briefly up at him and stooped at the same time as Walter, to pick up one of his parcels.

"I shall hope to see you and your stepmother tomorrow, then," Lord Eden said. "Perhaps you would care to join me for a walk in the park?"

"Thank you, that would be pleasant." The slight breathlessness was back in her voice.

As Lord Eden gave his horse the signal to move on, Anna was linking her arm in Jennifer's. "Where is your carriage?" she was saying. "We will walk you to it, since your companions have left you behind. Won't we, Walter? You must not worry about my brother's having to carry so many parcels, Miss Simpson. They are all as light as a feather."

Anna was laughing merrily as Lord Eden rode away.

So she *was* at home. She had refused to see him.

Miss Simpson was very pretty. It was sad to see her in black, and to know that she wore it for Charlie. Lord Eden recalled the very last time he had seen the girl. She had begged him to keep himself safe. And he had asked if he might call upon her in England. He had had every intention at that time of falling in love with her, of courting her as his bride when he came home.

He hoped she had not realized that. He hoped that by planning to call upon her the next day and even take her walking, he was not about to get himself into some nasty tangle.

Would Ellen refuse to see him the next day too?

JENNIFER'S FACE WAS GLOWING with color and her eyes sparkling when she returned from her shopping trip with the Misses Emery, Ellen was happy to see. It seemed a long time since the girl had looked on life with her characteristic eagerness.

"Did you have a nice time?" Ellen asked. "And did you buy anything?"

"I bought a comb that matches exactly the tortoiseshell brush Papa bought me in Brussels," Jennifer said. "Nothing else, Ellen. I won't need anything else until next summer, will I?"

No, they would not need anything new until the following summer. They had quite enough black outfits.

"You will never guess whom I met." Jennifer caught at Ellen's hands, the color in her cheeks heightened.

"Who?" Ellen smiled at her.

"Lord Eden!" The girl paused for effect. "Looking quite, quite gorgeous, Ellen, even though he was not in uniform. But he said he had called here and we were both out. Did you go somewhere?"

"I was here," Ellen said. "I am afraid I turned craven, Jennifer. I could not face meeting him."

"Of course," the girl said, squeezing Ellen's hands and looking at her with sympathy. "I am being insensitive, am I not? It will bring back so many painful memories for you to meet him again, won't it?"

"But he is coming back tomorrow," Ellen said. "I will

pluck up the courage then. We will meet him together, shall we, Jennifer?"

"He wants to take me walking," the girl said. She smiled. "You too, Ellen, probably. You always came with us in Brussels, did you not? Will you come tomorrow too? He presented me to two of his cousins. Anna Carrington is very lovely, Ellen. She made her come-out during the spring. She told me that she is going to marry Lord Eden, but her brother just laughed at her and told me that that is her idea, and she has had it since she was ten years old. I like them, Ellen. I don't think they take life too seriously. They laugh a lot. They both said that they hope to meet me again, and I think they meant it."

"I am sure they do," Ellen said. "And I hope you do meet them again, Jennifer. It is time you started enjoying yourself again just a little, though of course you may not go to any formal party or anything like that for a long time."

"And have no wish to do so," Jennifer assured her. "Oh, Ellen, I wish Papa were here. He could come with us tomorrow, and the two of you would be able to walk ahead of Lord Eden and me in the park, and I would be able to watch you talking and laughing together. Oh, I do wish Papa were still here . . . But I am sorry. I should not say such things any longer, should I, for it only makes you feel sad. Forgive me, Ellen. I am so self-indulgent. I won't say such things again, I swear I won't."

Ellen smiled and kissed her and asked to see the tortoise-shell comb.

14

$\mathcal{L}$ORD EDEN DID NOT AFTER ALL CALL AT Bedford Square the following day. He sent a note excusing himself after his mother received a hastily scrawled letter from Dover to say that Madeline expected to be home sometime that day.

She arrived late in the afternoon in a carriage belonging to Mr. Septimus Foster, the cousin with whom Lieutenant Penworth was to stay in London. She was looking tired but incredibly happy.

"Mama!" she cried, hurling herself into her mother's arms. "It seems like forever. Oh, how good it is to be home. And Edmund and Alexandra have come too. But not the children?" She hugged both of them hard and turned to her twin. "Dom. Oh, you horrid man. You look quite as healthy as you have ever looked. And when I think of the fright you gave me in Brussels!"

She was in his arms then, and he was rocking her against him. "You are looking pretty good yourself," he said. "I have been expecting to see you a mere wraith of your former self after months of playing nurse. But you look as if you are in the middle of a very successful Season."

"Allan and I are betrothed," she said. "It was all decided before we left for home. The official announcements are to be made as soon as he has spoken with you and Edmund, Mama. He does not have to do so, of course, because I reached my majority long ages ago, but he is going to do so anyway. Wish me happy?" She smiled brightly and a little uncertainly around the room.

Lord Amberley got to his feet again and put an arm about her shoulders. "You look quite happy enough already, dear," he said. "And of course I have never wanted anything else but your happiness. If you have decided upon Penworth, then he is a fortunate man."

"I could not have said it better myself," the dowager said, beaming at her daughter.

"Where is he?" Lady Amberley asked. "When are we to meet him? If I had only known back in the spring that he was to be your husband, Madeline, I would have taken far more notice. I can picture only a very young man in scarlet regimentals."

Madeline glanced at her twin, and he smiled and stretched out a hand to her.

"The journey was a great ordeal for him," she said. "I don't think I stopped talking for a single moment all the way from Dover. I was trying to keep his mind from his own discomfort and pain. We went straight to Mr. Foster's, and then I came here. It feels strange to be without him after so many months." She looked again at her brother, rather uncertainly, and took his hand.

"If you are happy, Mad," he said, "then I am too. Are you satisfied now?"

She nodded.

"Well," the Earl of Amberley said, seating himself next to his wife, "we might as well enjoy this unusual interlude of brother-and-sister amity, Alex. I am sure the two of them will be at each other's throats before another day has passed, and we will know that all is back to normal."

The dowager rang the bell to summon the tea tray.

"Now," Madeline said brightly, "I want everyone to tell me everything that has happened since I saw you last. Everything. Have the children grown, Alexandra? And will Caroline smile yet for anyone but Edmund?"

"She was very uncertain when he came home from Brussels after such a long absence," the countess said with a smile. "But seeing Christopher launch himself onto Edmund's back and me clinging to one of his arms must have reassured her. She gave him the smile I had not seen for weeks. It really is not fair, is it? Who feeds the child, after all?"

"It is just that she recognizes a handsome man when she sees one," the earl said.

Although there was so much to say, so many questions to be asked and answered, they all recognized that Madeline was very tired. Half an hour later she was climbing the stairs to her rooms, her arm linked through her twin's.

"How are you, Dom?" she asked as she closed the door of her sitting room behind them.

"As you see." He spread his arms to the sides. "As good as new, Mad. And in civilian clothes, you will be delighted to observe."

"I am." She crossed the room and patted the lapels of his coat. "And it is just as well for you that you are. I would declare open warfare on you if you had not sold out already."

"Ooh," he said, grinning. "A narrow escape indeed."

"What I meant to ask," she said, "was how *are* you? I mean really, Dom."

"You are asking me about Ellen Simpson," he said. "I was planning to call on her this afternoon. For the first time, and because I promised Charlie that I would look after the two of them if there were need. I have not seen her since Brussels, Mad. It is all over. It was just an unreal episode from a time of great crisis. Sweet at the time, but best forgotten." He smiled.

"Was it?" she said sadly. "But it seemed so real at the time. You looked so very happy. What happened, Dom?"

"We both woke up," he said. "That is what happened. It was inevitable." He shrugged. "It was no big thing. It only seemed so at the time. There is one thing I must know about you. Did Penworth ask you to marry him, or did you ask him?"

She blushed and giggled. "You could not expect him to ask me," she said. "He still does not particularly want to live, except that now I think he has realized that he must do so whether he wants to or not. He certainly does not think he has any worth left as a man. He is unwilling for anyone to see him. And he won't go home to Devon. He cannot face the pity of his family, he says. All absurd, of course. I shall talk him out of it all eventually. It will take time."

"So you asked him," he said. "Do you love him, Mad? Or is it pity?"

"I love him," she said. "He has filled my whole world for three months, Dom. I can't imagine life without him now. You are not going to be difficult, are you, just because he has lost a leg and an eye?"

"No, I am not going to be difficult." He took her by the shoulders and shook her gently back and forth. "You are as old and as wise as I, which is not saying a great deal, I suppose. But if you say you can be happy with Penworth, then

I daresay you can be. And all I can do is repeat what I said downstairs. If you are happy, then so am I."

She hugged him hard and rested her head on his broad shoulder. "Oh, Dom," she said, "it is so very good to be home. So good to have you alive and safe at last. And I am so tired. I feel as if I have not slept for months."

"Don't fall asleep on my shoulder, then," he said. "I'm sure your bed will be far more comfortable. Stand up now, or sit down if you will, and I will ring for a maid."

Madeline yawned loudly and inelegantly and sat down hard on a chaise longue.

ELLEN WAS SITTING DOWNSTAIRS in the morning room finishing off a letter to her friend Mrs. Cleary, who was still in Paris. She had the house to herself apart from the servants. Dorothy and Jennifer had gone out soon after breakfast, in order to accompany the Emery ladies to the library and the shops.

She and her stepdaughter were both recovering their spirits, she had just written to her friend. Her husband had left her an independence, and she hoped soon to buy herself a cottage somewhere in the country and move there. She was not sure about Jennifer. The girl might stay with her aunt. Or perhaps she would move to her grandfather's house.

Nothing was as certain as that in reality, of course. Dorothy had said no more about the visit to Sir Jasper Simpson. Perhaps she never would. Perhaps Charlie's father would refuse to receive Jennifer, even if that meant that he could not meet his son's widow either.

But Ellen was determined that matters would not be left at that. She had made a promise to Charlie, and she was going to keep it. His father would not reject them if appealed to, Charlie had said. Well, if necessary, she would go to Sir Jasper herself—not to take tea, but to plead with him to accept his granddaughter. If he had really loved his son, as Dorothy claimed, and if he truly grieved for him now, then surely he could not refuse to meet the daughter whom Charlie had loved, even if there really could be any doubt about her birth.

She would allow one more week to pass. If Dorothy had not said anything more in that time, then Ellen would take action herself. She felt better having decided so. She felt as if she were coming back to life after a long time. She reached for the blotter and carefully dried the ink on her letter.

She had taken action on something else too. She had told Dorothy the day before about the child. She had been feeling unusual tiredness during the days, and frequently felt nauseated and dizzy in the mornings. She needed to tell someone. She had told no lies. She had said nothing about the baby's paternity and had said merely that it was expected sometime early in the following spring. She had not told the truth either, of course.

Dorothy had been overjoyed, and had hugged her and kissed her and laughed and shed tears.

"Oh, I am so very happy," she had said. "I have hoped for it ever since Charlie married you, Ellen. And now it has happened just when it seemed too late. I am so very happy for you. But have you seen a physician?"

Ellen had shaken her head and agreed that she would see Dorothy's doctor later in the week, as soon as it could be arranged.

She felt uneasy about the deception. But what could she have done? How could she have told Charlie's sister the truth? On the whole, it felt good to have her secret off her chest. Though it was not entirely so.

"Please don't tell Jennifer yet," she had said.

"But why ever not?" Lady Habersham had asked. "She will be thrilled to know that she is to have a sister or brother."

"I will find the right moment to tell her," Ellen had said.

Jennifer's brother or sister! She had felt very uneasy and guilty again. But if only she could bring about this reconciliation with Sir Jasper, then she could remove to the country, and she would be free to tell everyone the truth. The time would come soon, she hoped, long before her child was born.

Yesterday had brought one other relief from a burden, although Jennifer had been disappointed. An unexpected commitment had forced Lord Eden to cancel his plan to call on them during the afternoon. There had been no other explanation. It must be that he had realized that she was at home when he had called before, that she had refused to see him. It must be that he had changed his mind about forcing his company on her.

There was enormous relief in the knowledge. She really did not want to see him. And there had been a certain pain in the prospect of his seeing Jennifer again. It had seemed for a while in Brussels that the two of them might be developing a *tendre* for each other. And at one time she had hoped it was true.

She would not think of such things. Jennifer was not unhappy. She had her friends, and she was very young. There would be time enough for beaux and marriage after her year of mourning was past.

Ellen sealed her letter and got to her feet. She stayed standing despite the wave of nausea that had her bending her head forward and closing her eyes for a moment. She would hand the letter to a footman and it would go with the day's mail. Strange to think that she would be in Paris herself if Charlie had still been alive. No, she would not think of it. She hurried out into the hallway.

And collided head-on with a man standing just outside the morning-room door.

"Oh," she said, looking up sharply as he caught at her arms to steady her.

"Ellen," he said.

She looked up into his face through a long, dark tunnel. There was a buzzing in her ears. She clasped her letter to her bosom.

"Ellen," he said again. "How are you?"

"Well," she said, but no sound came from her mouth. "Well," she repeated.

He was still clasping her arms. He let her go suddenly, and they stared at each other foolishly, both seemingly incapable either of moving or of mouthing some commonplace.

"I have just sent the butler upstairs with my card," he said eventually.

"I was writing a letter," she said, holding it out almost as if she were offering it to him.

Her voice sounded very far away. She listened to it as if it were someone else forming the words. And the buzzing in her ears became a roar even as she felt her face grow cold and her vision recede.

"Ellen!" someone was saying very, very far away. "Sit on the stairs for a minute." And someone was holding her sagging body in very strong arms and lowering her to a sitting position on the stairs. And someone's warm hand was at the back of her neck, forcing her head downward. And someone was stooping down in front of her. She was breathing in the fragrance of a familiar cologne.

"She has fainted. She will come around in a moment." The quiet voice was close to her ear.

"May I fetch something, my lord?" The voice of the butler.

"A glass of water, perhaps." Strong, warm hands took one of hers between them and began to chafe it. "Keep your head down, Ellen," he said. "Take slow, deep breaths."

Dominic's voice. It was Dominic. And she had fainted! She was sitting on the second stair in the hallway, the butler hurrying up with a glass of water, and Dominic down on one knee in front of her, taking the glass in his hand, covering her own cold and shaking hand over it, and helping her to lift it to her mouth.

She had fainted. She did not think she would ever be able to raise her head.

"How foolish of me," she said. "I am quite all right now."

But a firm hand on each of her shoulders held her down when she would have got to her feet.

"Just sit there for a moment," he said.

And then the front doors were being opened and Dorothy and Jennifer were there, and her humiliation was complete.

"My lord?" Jennifer said. "And Ellen? Whatever is the matter?"

"She has fainted," Lord Eden said. "But I believe she has almost recovered now."

"Ellen!" Dorothy said, hurrying over to her. "One of those dizzy spells again, dear?"

Don't say anything!

"I am fine," Ellen said, trying again to rise, and feeling those strong hands close again about her shoulders, holding her down. "I cannot think what came over me. Please forgive me. I shall go up to my room."

"I shall carry you there," Lord Eden said.

"Yes, you must lie down," Lady Habersham said. "You really should be resting more, dear."

Don't say any more. Please don't say any more!

"Thank you," Ellen said, "but I have quite recovered now, my lord. I do not need your assistance."

"I shall come with you, Ellen," Lady Habersham said. "You must lie down until luncheon time. And I shall send for my physician. It is high time you consulted him."

Please, oh, please, don't say any more!

Ellen collapsed facedown on her bed a few minutes later and stayed there as her sister-in-law removed her slippers and tiptoed from the room.

If she tried very hard from now until doomsday, she could not possibly think of a greater humiliation than what had just happened. He had appeared again, and she had swooned—literally swooned—at his feet. Whatever would he think? He was bound to draw all the wrong conclusions.

She had been feeling dizzy before she left the morning room. She had not been expecting him. She had not had time to prepare herself for that first face-to-face encounter. If only she had known, she would have received him with admirable coolness. He had taken her by surprise.

And she had swooned!

How would she ever be able to face him again? As if it had not been hard enough to do so anyway. But would she have to face him again? Would he not now realize that she just did not want to see him?

Or would he feel obliged to come back to inquire after her health?

Lord Eden, downstairs with Lady Habersham and Jennifer, was expressing concern about Ellen's health.

"She has been feeling indisposed for some time," Lady Habersham said. "It is doubtless no more than the stress caused by my brother's death. I will make sure that she sees a physician and rests more."

"I did not know that Ellen had been feeling unwell," Jennifer said in some distress. "She has not said anything to me, Aunt Dorothy. I have been selfish, as usual, have I not? I have been thinking about only my feelings."

"You are absolutely not to blame, my dear," her aunt said briskly.

Lord Eden got to his feet. "I was hoping that you and Mrs. Simpson would be free to walk with me this afternoon," he said to Jennifer. "But I will, if I may, call tomorrow to see how your stepmother does."

He made his bows and took his leave.

Had he done that to her? he wondered as he rode away. Had she really been unwell, as Lady Habersham had said? Or had it been a sickness that only the sight of him had brought on?

Should he call the next day? Would it be kinder and more honorable to stay away? But he would have to go. He would have to assure himself that she was feeling better.

He had dreaded making the call. He had dreaded that first moment of looking at her again with all the necessity of appearing cool without seeming careless, of appearing friendly without seeming heartless. He had dreaded having to form those first words to say to her.

But he had thought it was possible. He had rehearsed the meeting many times, expecting that it would be in the presence of other people. He had not expected to stare dumbly at her, his mind paralyzed so that no words had come at all, except her name.

He had behaved like a schoolboy with his first infatuation. It was quite ridiculous, especially when he had had more than two months in which to recover from their liaison. Especially when he had convinced himself that she did not mean any more to him than any of the other several women who had been his mistresses for varying lengths of time.

He would have to do much better the next day.

LADY HABERSHAM SUGGESTED a short walk in the park in the afternoon. If Ellen was feeling well enough, that was.

"Of course I am feeling all right," Ellen assured her. "I had been bent over the desk writing for an hour this morning and jumped to my feet too quickly. That was all. It was very foolish of me to faint in the hallway."

"And there was the shock of finding that young man there," her sister-in-law said with a nod. "He was a very close friend of Charlie's, was he not, Ellen? It must be hard for you to know that he survived when Charlie did not. But he is a very amiable young man, and very handsome too. You were quite right about that, Jennifer."

The girl blushed.

Five minutes after they had entered the park, a curricle drew to a halt beside them, and Jennifer recognized Anna and Walter Carrington.

"Do join us in a turn about the park, Miss Simpson," Anna said after introductions had been made. "The seat is narrow and we will be horribly squashed. But you will be doing me a great favor. Walter declares that I have not a word of sense to say, which is very nasty and ungentlemanly of him, and no other gentleman of my acquaintance has ever said such a thing. But Walter is my brother and thinks it quite unexceptionable to be as rude as can be to a mere sister."

She laughed gaily while her brother looked indignant and jumped down to the ground to lift Jennifer up.

"You would be doing me a kindness too, Miss Simpson," he said, "by rescuing me from a shrew. With your permission, ma'am?" He did not seem to know whether he should look to Ellen or Lady Habersham for permission, so smiled at both.

"How pleasant for her," Lady Habersham said a minute later as the curricle moved away along one of the carriage paths. "I am glad to see her make some friends, Ellen. And they seem like very pleasant people indeed."

"Yes," Ellen said. "But I am not surprised, you know. Jennifer was very popular in Brussels."

Lady Habersham linked her arm through her sister-in-law's. "I am glad we have a few minutes together," she said. "I have talked with Papa. He wants you and Jennifer to take tea with him two days from now. Phillip and Edith will be there too. You will come, Ellen?"

Ellen smiled brightly. "Jennifer too?" she said. "He has changed his mind about her? Oh, yes, Dorothy, of course we will go. I am so very glad. And thank you for speaking up for Jennifer."

"Well," Lady Habersham said, squeezing Ellen's arm, "I think Papa would have accepted any conditions at all as soon as he heard the news."

"The news?" Ellen felt herself turn cold.

"About his expected grandchild," her sister-in-law said. "I don't recall ever seeing Papa quite so excited about anything, Ellen."

"You told him," Ellen said, closing her eyes briefly. "Dorothy, I asked you not to tell anyone else yet."

"No, dear." Lady Habersham stopped walking. Her voice was full of concern. "No. You asked me not to tell Jennifer. I did not realize that perhaps you would wish to be the first to break the news to Papa too. But of course. It was thoughtless of me, wasn't it? Of course you would want to tell him yourself. And now I have spoiled it for you. Oh, I am so sorry, Ellen."

"No." Ellen put one hand over her face and shook her head. "No, it is not that, Dorothy. I am sorry. I'm not angry with you. I am just being silly about this whole thing, I suppose. I want to keep it a secret, when it will be quite obvious to anyone who cares to look within the next month or two."

"It is just that you are so very alone," her sister-in-law said. "If Charlie were only with you, Ellen! Oh, I can imagine just how proud and happy he would be. But we are your family too, dear—Papa and Phillip and I. And Jennifer, of course. We will help you to feel the happiness of the event, even though, of course, there is bound to be a great deal of sadness for you too."

"You are so kind to me," Ellen said, looking up at Lady Habersham. "I really don't deserve . . . Oh, dear."

"Well," her sister-in-law said, "in two days' time you will meet Papa and Phillip. And all will work out well, you will see. Papa is not a monster, you know. Not at all. And he is going to love you. And Jennifer too."

"Has he agreed to receive her only because he wants to meet me?" Ellen asked.

Lady Habersham squeezed her arm again. "Never mind about motives," she said. "It is the results of the meeting that will be important, Ellen. He will not be able to help loving her once he sees her."

"So he will meet the grandchild of questionable legitimacy in order to be sure of meeting the one of whose birth there can be no doubt," Ellen said quietly.

Lady Habersham patted her arm. "Ah, here they come again," she said. "And all laughing merrily, as young people should. Is not Anna Carrington a very pretty young lady, Ellen? Her hair is as dark as Jennifer's, but cut very short, if I am not mistaken. And Mr. Carrington is a very presentable young man too."

MADELINE RODE BESIDE her brother during the carriage ride to Bedford Square.

"I really appreciate this, Mad," he said. "I owe you a favor."

She grinned at him. "I shall not forget," she said. "But this is no burden on me, Dom. Allan was tired this morning when I went to read to him, and decided that he will rest this afternoon. And I wish to see both Mrs. and Miss Simpson again. I liked them both in Brussels."

"When is Penworth going to admit any visitors but you?" he asked. "And when is he going to venture outside?"

"It will take time," she said. "He will do both eventually, Dom. Have patience with us. Please?"

"I want to talk to him," he said. "If he is to be my brother-in-law, I want to get to know him. And he should meet Mama and Edmund."

"He will," she said hastily, laying a hand on his sleeve. "He will, Dom. Do try to put yourself in his place. How would you feel?"

He looked at her silently for a few moments and then

turned to look out the window at the passing streets. "Probably much the same," he said. "Except that I don't think I would have betrothed myself to anyone."

"Only because there are not as many women who are as impudent as I," she said. "It quite puts me to the blush to know that I proposed to my future husband. But if I had not, he would never have married me. So I am not sorry. Will Mrs. Simpson receive you, do you think?"

"I don't know." He grimaced. "And I don't at all know if I am doing the right thing, coming here again like this. But I have to make sure that she has recovered."

"And you really feel nothing for her, Dom, beyond the concern you would naturally feel for your friend's widow?" she asked.

"No, nothing," he said. "I have known her for several years, remember. That foolishness lasted only a few days. I just need to make this one visit. Then it will all be over."

"Oh, liar, Dom," she said, settling her shoulders against the corner of the seat and looking steadily at him. "I am Madeline, remember? Your twin."

He glared back. "I brought you with me for moral support," he said, "not as father confessor. And on this one you are wrong anyway."

She shrugged and said nothing. But she made him feel uncomfortable all the rest of the way by sitting sideways and staring at him.

She still said nothing as they waited for Lady Habersham's butler to take Lord Eden's card upstairs. But it most certainly helped to have her with him when they were shown into an upstairs salon. He could collect his breath and his thoughts while presenting his sister to Lady Habersham and while waiting for the effusive greetings Madeline exchanged with the other two ladies.

He bowed over Jennifer's hand and acknowledged Ellen's curtsy with a nod.

She sat down with a straight back, not touching the back of her chair. She folded her hands quietly in her lap. Lord Eden took his courage in both hands and crossed the room to take a seat beside her. Madeline began to talk with animation to the room at large.

Her face was thinner and had lost color. Her gray eyes, by contrast, looked larger and more luminous as she rested them steadily on Madeline's face. Her fair hair, smooth and shining, was drawn back from her face in the old simple style, resting in a knot at the back of her neck.

Unbidden memories came to him of her face flushed and animated at a ball and heavy-eyed with passion on a pillow, that hair framing her face like a shining halo.

"I trust you are feeling better, ma'am?" he said. Words of ridiculous formality. He had murmured love words into her ear, against her mouth.

"Yes, I thank you, my lord." She lowered her eyes away from Madeline and looked to the side. But not at him. "I was very foolish. I had been bent over a letter for more than an hour."

She had cried out her love to him, murmured his name over and over again.

"I hope you have recovered thoroughly," she said. "You are looking well."

How did she know? She had not looked at him.

"Thank you," he said. "I have made every effort to regain my health."

The hands in her lap looked relaxed until one observed closely and saw the whiteness of her knuckles. She had sat beside him many times with one of those hands in his, smiling at him while he kissed each finger separately.

"I felt that I must call on you and Miss Simpson," he said, "to see that you have settled comfortably in this country."

He had dreamed once of settling her on his own estate in Wiltshire. He had told her about it once when she lay in his arms, her hand smoothing gently over the bandages on his chest. He had told her how it had been his since the death of his father but how he had never really thought of it as home. But he had dreamed of doing so then with a wife of his own to take there. Though he had not said that to her.

"That is very kind of you, my lord," she said. "We have settled well. My sister-in-law has been very good to us, and tomorrow we are to take tea with Sir Jasper Simpson."

"With Charlie's father?" he asked in some surprise.

The name brought spots of color to her cheeks and increased his own discomfort. The name of her husband, his friend.

"Yes," she said, "we are to meet him tomorrow."

He had dreamed of presenting her to his own family. As his future wife. He had dreamed of how his mother would love her, of how Edmund would approve his choice, of how Alexandra and Madeline would become her close friends.

He had dreamed a whole lot of dreams that he had never experienced with his other mistresses. But then, she had not been his mistress. It was an unsatisfactory word applied to her, suggesting a kept woman.

Ellen had been his lover. For a brief time. In the past.

"Miss Simpson will come with us, Dom," Madeline's bright voice said, reminding Lord Eden that he was in a room with other people as well as her. "And will you, ma'am?" She smiled at Lady Habersham. "And you, Mrs. Simpson? But you were talking with Dom then and did not hear. We are going to drive to Kensington Gardens and walk there awhile."

"I am afraid I have another engagement later this afternoon," Lady Habersham said.

"Then Mrs. Simpson must come," Madeline said. She smiled engagingly. "You really must. I have just come home and I have recently become betrothed to Lieutenant Penworth and I simply must have someone to boast to."

"You are betrothed to Lieutenant Penworth?" Jennifer said with a smile. "How splendid! He must be considerably better, then? I cried when Ellen told me about his injuries. I could not help remembering how he loved to talk about riding and sailing and playing sports at home in Devon."

"You will come?" Lord Eden asked Ellen.

He watched her draw in a slow breath. She looked across at Madeline, her expression quite calm.

"Thank you," she said, "that would be pleasant. I shall come as chaperone for Jennifer again."

Madeline laughed. "You must come as our friend," she said. "I would be quite chaperone enough for Miss Simpson, you see. Shall we leave? And then we will not keep you from your other appointment, ma'am." She smiled at Lady Habersham.

Lord Eden got up as Ellen rose to her feet and left the room for a bonnet and shawl. Jennifer smiled brightly at him and followed her stepmother.

Lord Eden's eyes met his sister's smiling ones across the room.

15

MADELINE SAT BESIDE ELLEN IN THE CARriage, Lord Eden and Jennifer opposite them. Madeline talked brightly to all three for a few minutes before the conversation divided itself into two pairs. Then she talked to Ellen about her betrothal.

Ellen did not know quite how it had come about that she was sitting in the carriage at all. She had been prepared for Lord Eden's calling at Dorothy's. She had been prepared for his asking Jennifer to go walking with him. And she had even considered the possibility that he would extend the invitation to include her too. She had had her answer all ready. A maid could accompany Jennifer.

In the event, a refusal would have been even easier than anticipated. Her stepdaughter would not have even needed a maid as chaperone, since Lady Madeline was to be with her.

Yet here she sat, Ellen thought ruefully. And how did one avoid altogether looking at a tall and fashionable gentleman who sat opposite, his knees almost touching one's own? And more to the point, why would she wish to avoid looking at him? She should look across, meet his eyes, smile coolly, and dispel this terrible embarrassment and awareness that were making her extremely uncomfortable.

She kept her head turned and her attention focused on Madeline beside her.

"He is beginning to realize," Madeline said in response to Ellen's question, a twinkle in her eye, "that short of suicide, he is doomed to live on for a time at least. He realizes that he must somehow make that life worth living. He can never do any of the things he enjoyed doing before, of course. He has to begin life anew. I have been reading to him. I have been encouraging him to paint and concentrate on music. He is apparently accomplished in both, though of course the painting may be more difficult now that he has only one eye. But the foolish man, of course, does not see those as manly accomplishments."

"It has been only three months," Ellen said. "I believe that if the lieutenant is already beginning to think that there is a future to plan for, then he is doing remarkably well. I am sure that having you has helped him enormously, of course."

Madeline laughed. "You would not think so if you had ever heard him arguing with me," she said, "and trying to send me away. The very worst thing for him, you see, and the one he will perhaps never adjust his mind to, is his appearance. He will not receive company or go outside his cousin's door. He will not inflict the sight of himself on other people. The foolish man."

"He was a good-looking young man just a few months ago," Ellen said gently. "It must be hard for him."

"Yes, it is," Madeline said. "But he need not fear. I am going to spend the rest of my life looking after him and making life easy for him." She smiled at her companion. "I am very happy, Mrs. Simpson."

"I am glad." Ellen smiled back. "Everyone deserves to know some of that kind of happiness in life."

Madeline opened her mouth and closed it again. Her eyes saddened. "It will happen for you again," she said very quietly.

Lord Eden helped all three ladies from the carriage when they reached Kensington Gardens, Ellen last. By the time she stepped down onto the pavement, she was dismayed to find that Madeline had already linked her arm through Jennifer's and was walking off with her. She drew a steadying breath.

"This is what you did not wish for, is it not?" Lord Eden said, offering her his arm. "I must confess that I had hoped to avoid it too. It is difficult to meet again."

Well, Ellen supposed, if they must speak to each other, it was probably better to speak openly like this rather than in the stilted manner in which they had conversed at Dorothy's. "Yes," she said.

"Do you blame me for coming?" he asked. "Do you wish I had not?"

"Why did you?" she asked. "Nothing can be accomplished by our meeting again. Only embarrassment for both of us."

"I had to come," he said. "I promised Charlie that I would see you and Miss Simpson safe."

She felt her stomach lurch and was afraid that she was going to be overcome by dizziness again.

"We must not avoid his name," he said. "He was my friend. The two of you were my friends, Ellen. I would hate to think that a few days of thoughtless madness have wiped out three years of friendship."

She said nothing for a while. "But they did," she said at last.

"Yes, I suppose so." He looked about him at the grass dotted with fallen leaves. "I had hoped that perhaps we could still be friends. But I suppose we can't. We can make all sorts of excuses for what happened between us, but the fact is that it happened and will always be there, a shared embarrassment."

"Yes," she said.

He drew an audible breath. "So what are your plans now?" he asked. "You are going to call on Charlie's father, you said?"

"Yes," she said. "I promised Charlie that I would. But as it happens, Sir Jasper has been the one to make the first move. I am hoping that he will take Jennifer in and take charge of her future."

"And you?" he asked.

"Charlie left me an independence," she said. "I will buy a cottage in the country and move there. I don't know exactly where yet."

"Alone, Ellen?" he said. "It will be a lonely life."

"I think not," she said. "It is what I want."

"You will not stay with your father-in-law?" he asked. "You are very young still."

"I would rather be independent," she said. "And what about you, my lord? You have sold out of the army?"

"As you see," he said. "I think I will be moving to my property in Wiltshire soon. It is time I stopped wandering and settled down. I would think that Edmund will be removing his family back to Amberley soon, now that we are all safely home from Belgium. I don't know about Mama and Madeline. I suppose a great deal depends upon Penworth. I will be going soon, I think."

And there seemed to be no more to say. Ellen held to his arm and was reminded of the walk they had taken in the

Forest of Soignes the day after she had become physically aware of him for the first time. Oh, no, they could never become merely friends. Because she could never again be without this almost sick awareness of him when he was close, this urge to flatten her palm and her fingers more firmly on his arm, to close her eyes and lay the side of her head against the broad shoulder so close to it.

Dear God, she thought, it was this man's child she was carrying in her womb.

They could certainly never be just friends again.

"Why did you faint?" he asked abruptly.

"I have not been in the best of health," she said.

"You have lost weight," he said. "You have suffered, Ellen."

"You must understand," she said, "that he was my world. I have lost people before, by death and otherwise. But they were always a part of my life, not life itself. Charlie was my life. The world is a very empty and a very frightening place without him."

"Yes," he said, and laid a warm hand over hers. She did not try to pull away from it. "I can believe that, though fortunately I have not experienced it. Not directly. I remember my mother after my father died. I'm sorry, Ellen. And more sorry than I can say that I am unable to offer any of the comfort I might have been able to offer had I remained just Charlie's friend."

She drew a deep breath. "I have forgiven you for that," she said. "And myself too. I would rather not dwell on it. And you are not to think that I am a broken woman. I am not. I have lived through two months of intense grief, when the pain of living at times seemed almost too much to bear. But I am through them now and on my way back to life. I will live again if only for Charlie's sake. He would have been upset to see me as I have been. But for my own sake too. Life is too precious a gift not to be lived. You are not to feel sorry for me, my lord."

He smiled. "I remember your saying those exact words in Spain," he said, "when you were soaked to the skin after fording a river at night, only to discover that your servant had lost your tent in the crossing. And Charlie was off somewhere else on duty. Of course, your teeth were chattering so loudly that it was hard to hear the words. Do you remember?"

She looked into his face for the first time that afternoon. She gave him a fleeting smile. "Yes," she said, "though it was a good thing that you had to ride off immediately. I believe I spent the rest of that night howling with self-pity and huddling over an inadequate fire."

She looked away again when his green eyes crinkled at the corners and smiled back at her.

"Here comes Susan," Madeline said suddenly, looking back over her shoulder at Lord Eden.

The lady who was approaching on the arm of a portly gentleman of haughty bearing was also in deep mourning, Ellen saw. She was small and dainty. She carried a lace-trimmed handkerchief in her free hand. It was impossible to see her face until she drew close, as she wore a heavy black veil over it.

She was also a wilting little creature, Ellen discovered, noting the contrast between her affected greeting of Lord Eden and his sister and their effusive greeting of her. And then Ellen recognized her as the pretty auburn-haired lady who had spoken and danced with Lord Eden at the Duke of Wellington's ball in Brussels.

"Well, Susan, how do you do?" Lord Eden asked when

Ellen and Jennifer had been introduced on the one side, and Lord Renfrew on the other.

"Quite as well as can be expected, my lord," Susan said, dabbing at her eyes beneath the veil. "It is quite devastating to be without my poor dear husband, but my brother-in-law has been kind. I am sure you must quite know how I feel, Mrs. Simpson."

Ellen inclined her head.

"Your mother is here with you too, Susan?" Madeline said. "I have been meaning to call upon the two of you. I shall do so one day, and bring Mama or Dom with me."

"Oh, that is very kind of you, I am sure," Susan said, large hazel eyes gazing soulfully at Lord Eden. "But I would not put you to any inconvenience on my account."

"It will be no inconvenience at all, Susan," Lord Eden said with a bow. "Perhaps we may call upon you tomorrow?"

"How very kind!" Susan murmured. "I find it very hard not to be able to venture outdoors until his lordship has the time to take me. Even a simple visit to the library becomes out of the question. Oh, Mrs. Simpson, we take husbands so very much for granted until they are no longer there at our convenience, do we not?" Another dab of the handkerchief.

Ellen inclined her head again.

Lord Eden was smiling. Ellen could hear it in his voice. "If it is the library you wish to visit, Susan," he said, "your need is easily answered. I shall accompany you there tomorrow morning while Madeline converses with Mrs. Courtney."

Hand and handkerchief flew to Susan's mouth. "Oh, my lord," she said. "I could not so impose upon your time. I would have said nothing if I had thought you would feel obliged to make the offer."

"It is no imposition at all," he said. "We will see you in the morning." He nodded to Susan's silent companion. "Renfrew?"

"As if she could not go to the library or anywhere else, for that matter, with Mrs. Courtney!" Madeline said indignantly when they had walked on a little way. "Or with a maid. Oh, really, Dom, Susan has not changed one little bit since she was a child."

Lord Eden chuckled. "But it is a very little thing to accompany her to the library," he said.

"Hm," Madeline said in some disgust.

Ellen was relieved to find that her walking companion was now Madeline. And Madeline was soon laughing gaily and drawing smiles from Ellen over a trio of gorgeous dandies who were mincing along the pathway ahead of them.

When the carriage stopped later outside Lady Habersham's house on Bedford Square, Madeline smiled eagerly at both Ellen and Jennifer. "It has been so pleasant to meet you again," she said. "Let us not make this the last time. Will you come to tea? I know that Mama will be delighted to see you again, Mrs. Simpson. And of course she has not met Miss Simpson at all. Will you come? Tomorrow?"

"We have another engagement tomorrow," Ellen said, feeling rather than seeing the stillness of the man opposite her.

"But we can come the next day." Jennifer was flushed and bright-eyed. "Can we not, Ellen?"

"Yes." Ellen smiled at Madeline. "That would be very pleasant. Thank you."

Lord Eden vaulted from the carriage to help them down.

"Was not that just a lovely afternoon?" Jennifer said to Ellen when they were inside the house. She looked quite her old exuberant self, Ellen thought, despite the black clothes. "Suddenly there are things to do, Ellen, and friends to be with. And all without any effort at all on our part."

"I am very glad for you," Ellen said. "It is time you had some brightness in your life again. Mr. and Miss Carrington are to call for you tomorrow morning, did you say?"

The girl nodded happily. "Isn't Lady Madeline just lovely, Ellen? I wish I could have her beauty and her charm and poise."

"You will." Ellen smiled as she removed her bonnet. "All she has that you don't, Jennifer, is extra years and experience."

"Lord Eden is excessively handsome even now that he is not wearing a uniform, is he not?" Jennifer said. "I just wish I did not feel like such a child when I am with him. I always have done. I don't feel that way with other gentlemen. I don't feel blushing and tongue-tied with Mr. Carrington, for example. Of course, he is not near as handsome as Lord Eden."

Ellen had never been sure how her stepdaughter felt about Lord Eden. She hoped now that the girl would not develop a *tendre* for him. Oh, she hoped not. She did not think she would be able to bear that. But most of all, she hoped that Jennifer would not have a chance to develop a *tendre* for him. Would they see much more of him? She hoped not. If it had not been for Lady Madeline issuing that invitation to tea, she did not think that he would have suggested any further meeting. He had realized, as she had, that there could never be anything between the two of them but awkwardness and embarrassment.

She did not think that the visit had been his idea.

"Are you playing devil's advocate, Mad?" Lord Eden was asking his twin in the carriage.

"Whatever are you talking about?" She looked at him with wide innocent eyes.

"That look won't work," he said. "This is me, remember?"

She grinned at him. "I wish you could have seen yourselves," she said, "seated side by side in Lady Habersham's salon. It was a sight for sore eyes, Dom. You were behaving like the stiffest of strangers."

"It is called embarrassment," he said, his voice testy. "But I notice that you did not do much to rescue me, Mad. You made very sure that we walked together in Kensington Gardens."

"Look me in the eye," she said, "and tell me that you did not want to talk privately with her, Dom. And while you are about it, tell me that you have no spark of feeling left for her. Do it. Come on. And I shall call you liar."

"She was my friend for three years," he said in exasperation. "She nursed me when I was close to death, and I fancied myself in love with her for a week. Of course I have feelings for her."

"You were lovers too, weren't you?" she asked more gently.

"No, of course we weren't," he said.

"She was lying on the bed with you, Dom," she said. "You were kissing her. I am not a green girl."

"If you know so much, then," he said irritably, "why did you ask?"

She shrugged. "I like her," she said. "She is so different from your usual type of flirt, Dom. I think she is perfect for you. And though she undoubtedly was very devoted to

Captain Simpson and has suffered a great deal since his death, I think perhaps she could come to love you too. She would not have become your lover lightly. So, yes." She smiled rather impishly. "I was playing devil's advocate. Or heaven's angel, perhaps."

"I think you had better concentrate all your angel-of-mercy tendencies on Penworth in future," Lord Eden said. "And leave me to look after my own affairs."

"And talking of affairs," she said, "you are not about to pick up with Susan again, are you, Dom?"

"To what?" he said, frowning.

"She had you wrapped about her little finger before you bought your commission," she said. "She started it again this afternoon, and you came running like a little puppy dog."

"Because I said I would take her to the library?" he said. "What nonsense are you talking, Mad?"

"You have always had a dreadful weakness for helpless females," she said. "You used to fall in love with them routinely, Dom. You know you did. I was very much afraid a few years ago that Susan was about to net you. You would have been miserable for the rest of your life. Now she is going to be after you again."

"What nonsense you talk," he said. "I am taking the woman to the library, not the altar!"

"I hope so," Madeline said before transferring her gaze beyond the window.

ELLEN'S FLUTTERING HEART was calmed the following afternoon by the necessity of dealing with Jennifer's extreme nervousness.

"Will he like me?" she asked her stepmother over and over again, her dark eyes huge with anxiety.

"If he does not," Ellen said eventually, "then he does not deserve to be liked either, Jennifer. Just be yourself and don't worry."

"Papa never told me why he quarreled with Grandpapa," the girl said. "But I think it was because of Mama. It was, wasn't it, Ellen?"

The girl was no child to be comforted with some soothing story. "I think she was part of it," she said. "But listen to me, Jennifer. Your papa married your mother even in defiance of his own father, and he loved you dearly until the day of his death. You know that. You have nothing to feel anxious about. If your grandpapa does not like you, then that is his problem, not yours. But let us not judge him ahead of time."

Jennifer sighed. "I will be so glad to have this over with," she said. "Thank goodness I was busy this morning and unable to brood on this afternoon. Mr. Carrington and Anna are such good company, Ellen. And Mr. Phelps, Anna's friend, is an amiable gentleman too. I enjoyed myself so much. Was it not a happy coincidence that we also met Lord Eden and Mrs. Jennings? Though we knew yesterday, of course, that he was going to escort her to the library."

"I am glad you had a happy morning," Ellen said.

"Do you think Aunt Dorothy was offended that I could not eat much luncheon?" Jennifer asked. "I did not have any appetite, I'm afraid, after the six of us went to a confectioner's for cakes. Mrs. Jennings was very friendly, Ellen. Her father is a tenant of Lord Amberley's, you know. She has known Lord Eden and Lady Madeline all her life."

Ellen was content to let her stepdaughter prattle on happily about the morning's events until they were in the carriage with a rather tense Dorothy on their way to Sir Jasper Simpson's residence on Clifford Street. And her own heart began to thump again.

She would have known he was Charlie's father, she thought later as they were ushered into the drawing room, even if the room had been full of people. The same height and build. The same open, jovial face. His head was somewhat balder.

She curtsied and felt her stepdaughter doing the same beside her.

"My dear!" The elderly gentleman crossed the room and took Ellen's hands in both of his. He stood shaking them up and down and looking into her face. "So you are Charlie's wife. So young and so pretty. You are looking at a foolish old man, my dear. A foolish old man."

Ellen smiled uncertainly at him. He was dressed in deep mourning, she noticed. "I am pleased to make your acquaintance, sir," she said. "I promised Charlie that I would, if it was possible."

"If it was possible!" he said, wringing her hands. "I am a foolish old man, my dear."

Dorothy had already presented both of them to her father. But Ellen turned her head toward Jennifer and smiled. "Will you not meet your granddaughter?" she asked.

Sir Jasper released her hands and turned to Jennifer. "Let me look at you, my dear," he said. He nodded. "Very pretty. Very pretty indeed. So you are Charlie's girl, are you? Well, do you have a kiss for your grandpapa, child?"

"Yes, Grandpapa," Jennifer said, leaning forward to place a kiss on Sir Jasper's cheek. "You look very like Papa."

"Do I?" he said. "Even to the bald head? Did your father lose his hair?"

Jennifer nodded.

Sir Jasper turned to the couple standing silently behind him with Lady Habersham. "Meet your aunt and uncle, my dear," he said. He took Ellen's hand in his as Jennifer curtsied and smiled uncertainly at the strange couple. "Meet your brother-in-law, Phillip, and his wife, Edith, my dear. It is high time, is it not?"

Mr. Phillip Simpson took Ellen's free hand in his and laid his other on top of it. He looked closely into her eyes. "You are Ellen?" he said. He did not smile. He was not wearing mourning, though there was a black band on the sleeve of his coat. "I am glad you have come. Old quarrels should not go on for twenty years and more."

Edith Simpson pecked her on the cheek and expressed pleasure at meeting her.

Ellen was directed to a seat, and found herself in conversation with her brother-in-law and his wife while tea was served. Phillip did not look anything like Charlie, she thought. He was thin and narrow-faced and sandy-haired. His wife looked remarkably like him.

They were a perfectly civil couple even if there was no great warmth in their manner. They told her about their two sons, both away at school. Charlie's nephews. Ellen wondered how much Phillip regretted not having seen his brother again before his death. They had been close as boys. Most of Charlie's stories had included his younger brother.

Jennifer, she was pleased to hear, was chattering with some animation to her grandfather. From the few snippets of their conversation that she heard, Ellen gathered that the girl was telling him about her schooldays and about her stay in Brussels.

"Well," Sir Jasper said eventually, his raised voice drawing the two groups together, "we must repeat this pleasure.

We must have tea again. And perhaps I will organize some sort of dinner and evening party that will be suited to our state of mourning. Something to celebrate my reunion with my daughter-in-law and my granddaughter."

Lady Habersham took his words as a signal to rise and take their leave.

"I must not lose you again now that I have found you," he said to Ellen as he was squeezing her hand at the doorway of the drawing room when she was leaving. Dorothy and Jennifer had already started on their way down the stairs. "I have been a foolish old man. I have been all these years without my own son. But I will not be without his children. I swear it."

Ellen smiled and swallowed. "I am glad we have met," she said. "Charlie would be glad."

"Is this one to be a son?" he asked, patting her hand.

Ellen shook her head. "I don't know," she said.

"Well," he said, "we will hope so, my dear." And he leaned forward to kiss her cheek.

Ellen scurried down the stairs in pursuit of the other two.

MADELINE HAD FINALLY PERSUADED her betrothed to venture beyond the doors of his cousin's house. He was to take tea with her at the Earl of Amberley's town house. Her mother was to be there too.

But if he was feeling nervous, then she was feeling no better, she thought, seating herself beside him on a love seat, almost but not quite touching him, resisting the urge to take his hand in hers. She was chattering brightly to Alexandra and Edmund and to her mother.

Edmund had chosen a downstairs salon in which to

entertain his guests, Madeline had been relieved to discover. And he had not offered to help Allan into the room. Neither had she, but she had hovered at his side as he had moved awkwardly on his crutches, ready to help him if he had needed her assistance.

"I can manage," he had said to her, looking somewhat tight-lipped. He had thought she was about to reach out to him. "You need not concern yourself, Madeline."

So she had smiled brightly and seated herself beside him and begun to chatter. Thank goodness Dom was not there. She had forbidden him to come, but whether for Allan's sake or for her own, she did not know.

She was not doing very well, she knew. She was taut with worry that someone would ask her betrothed some personal question that would embarrass him. She found herself jumping in with answers to every question directed his way. She knew she was doing it, but she could not stop herself. She could feel him growing tenser beside her.

"I hope you do not mind our children being in the room, Lieutenant," Alexandra said with a smile. "We always have them with us at teatime. I am afraid we are unfashionably attached to our offspring."

"Oh, no," Madeline said cheerfully, "Allan does not mind, do you, Allan? They are such well-behaved children. One would hardly know they were in the room."

"It seems that the Battle of Waterloo is going to be seen as something of a landmark in history," the earl said to the lieutenant. "One does wonder what Europe will do without Bonaparte to worry about any longer. How long will it be, I wonder, before someone else comes along to take his place?"

"One would like to believe in universal and everlasting

peace," Lieutenant Penworth said. "Unfortunately, human nature inevitably gets in the way. It is my feeling—"

"Goodness," Madeline said, smiling about her, "must we be so gloomy? I think we should all take a drive out one afternoon to see the trees before they have dropped all their leaves. Has anyone noticed how lovely they are?"

"Your home is in Devon?" the dowager asked a few minutes later. "Your family must be quite anxious to see you again."

"But Mr. Foster quite insists that Allan stay in London a little longer, doesn't he, Allan?" Madeline said.

She noticed the look Edmund and Alexandra exchanged across the room and bit her lip. This was not working at all. If Allan was ready for such a visit, she certainly was not.

The earl got to his feet and went to stoop down in front of his daughter, who was sitting on the floor playing with some toys. "Why do you not fetch that letter from your brother, Alex?" he said. "I am sure Mama and Madeline and the lieutenant will be interested in hearing of his adventures. My brother-in-law has been in Canada for more than three years, Lieutenant, or rather, far inland beyond Canada."

"Will you be interested?" the countess asked with an apologetic smile. "I naturally find the letter quite exciting and fascinating. But then, I am partial. James is my brother. And this is the first letter I have had from him this year."

For once Madeline let her betrothed answer the question. Alexandra disappeared from the room.

"He works with a fur-trading company," Lord Amberley explained to his guest. "And he has chosen to live in the wilderness where the furs are gathered and traded. Quite an adventurous life, it seems."

"Your wife must miss him," the lieutenant said. "I have

three brothers and two sisters at home. And though we fight almost constantly when together, I must confess to beginning to miss them just a little."

"Here it is," the countess said, coming back into the room.

Madeline was watching her brother talk quietly to the baby and lift her high into the air when she smiled and reached up her arms to him. She chuckled and reached down to grab his nose.

The winters were so cold where he stayed that any exposed part of the flesh would freeze in less than a minute.

Edmund sat down with his daughter and held out a toy to her.

Tears froze on one's eyelashes. Sometimes if his bed was pushed too close to the wall of the hut in which he lived, the bedclothes would be frozen to the wall in the morning.

Caroline was chewing on the toy.

He traveled around by dogsled and snowshoes. Native women netted the latter and sewed moccasins for his feet.

Christopher was pulling at the leg of his father's breeches and gazing soulfully up at him.

He was in the Athabasca country, thousands of miles from Montreal. He had traveled the whole distance by canoe.

Edmund was ruffling the child's hair and lifting him up to sit on his other knee.

"The rest would be of no interest to you," the countess said, smiling at the lieutenant. "It is just inquiries about our parents and the rest of my family. He does not even know about Caroline. News takes such a very long time to travel back and forth."

"My mother did not know for a whole month that I had survived the Battle of Waterloo," Lieutenant Penworth said.

"And that news had to cross only the English Channel, ma'am."

"Oh," the dowager countess said, "it was three weeks before we heard about Dominic. I can certainly sympathize with your mama, Lieutenant."

Madeline smiled brightly. "Are you tired yet, Allan?" she asked. "Are you ready to leave? I am sure Edmund and Alexandra will excuse you if you are."

16

*J*ENNIFER SLEPT LATE THE FOLLOWING MORN-
ing. Lady Habersham was in the morning room going over the weekly accounts with the housekeeper. Ellen
was restless.

She should never have begun the deception. She should
have told the full truth from the start. Now it was becoming increasingly difficult to do so. She should tell Dorothy
immediately. And she should take a maid and pay a call on
Sir Jasper that very morning and tell him. She should trust
that Jennifer would be well enough looked after by her aunt
and her grandfather, and she should make immediate plans
to leave. She could find somewhere to live until she could
settle in a more permanent home.

But she knew that she would do none of those things.
She would put them all off until the next day, fully aware of
what she was doing. Sometimes, she thought, it is so much
easier to know what one should do than to do it.

And then there was the afternoon's visit to the dowager
Countess of Amberley's home. She had no idea if Lord
Eden would be there or not, but it really did not matter. She
should not go. She did not want any further involvement

with either him or his family. And yet Jennifer was eager to make the visit. And Jennifer was becoming friendly with his cousins and had sat in a confectioner's with them and with him the morning before.

Life was becoming hopelessly tangled.

Ellen was normally of a frugal nature. She had always had to be. There had never been a great deal of money to waste. But just occasionally she had the urge to go out and spend money. Charlie had laughed at her sometimes, when they were in a town, Madrid or Badajoz or one of the others, and she had come back to their rooms loaded down with small items that she did not need at all—bright and cheap earrings, a gaudy shawl, some sweet-smelling lotion for him, a new fob for his watch. And he had always kissed her and called her his treasure and told her that she should enjoy herself more. He had always teased her out of the pangs of guilt she would feel at her extravagance.

She was in that mood now. And she would not stop to talk sense into herself, she decided as she hurried out into the hallway to order the carriage brought around, and upstairs to put on a pelisse and bonnet. She would not even take a maid with her.

She had Dorothy's coachman take her to Oxford Street. She bought two lace-edged handkerchiefs that she did not need, and spent many minutes at a jeweler's looking at a bracelet that would very nearly match the earrings Charlie had bought for her. But they were too precious a gift to be matched with anything of her own choosing, she decided at last. She bought instead a small porcelain jar with a lid to keep the earrings in.

She was coming out of the shop when a carriage pulled up in the street beside her and the Earl of Amberley leaned out of the window and hailed her. The countess was beside him, smiling. Ellen walked closer.

"How do you do, ma'am?" the earl asked. "Alex said it was you, and she was quite right."

"I have not seen you for an age," the countess said after Ellen had bidden them both a good day. "I met you and your stepdaughter once in the park, if you recall, but that must be well over a month ago. And you have still not called for tea." She smiled.

"I am sorry," Ellen said. "I have no excuse. We have been somewhat preoccupied, I'm afraid."

"That is quite understandable," the earl said gently. "Is Prudence giving you good service?"

"Yes, I thank you," she said. "She is a very sweet girl. I have become quite attached to her."

"Christopher—our son—asked for Miss Simpson several times after we came home," the countess said. "She had endless patience with him on the journey back, when Nanny Rey was busy with Caroline and Edmund was busy with me. I was very sick on the crossing, I'm afraid. Your stepdaughter was proud of the fact that she was not. Will you come and take tea with us one afternoon?"

"We would be delighted," Ellen said.

"Let us make a definite day, then," the countess said. "Are you free on Tuesday next?"

Ellen inclined her head.

The countess smiled at her.

"We will expect you then, ma'am," the earl said. "And if I do not give my coachman the order to drive on soon, someone is going to come to fisticuffs with him for blocking the roadway."

They were gone almost immediately. And there she was again, Ellen thought ruefully, with yet another involvement with Lord Eden's family. The sooner she found some quiet corner of the country in which to hide herself, the better.

To hide herself? Was that what she was trying to do? How despicable! She did not need to hide herself. And she would not do so. She would remove herself from London to the cottage of her dreams when she was fully ready to do so.

She went inside another shop, scarcely looking to see what type of wares it dealt in. She came out ten minutes later, smiling to herself in some amusement. She must be perfectly mad. Dorothy and a thousand other women would doubtless screech in horror at the way she was so tempting fate. She had bought a pair of tiny leather baby boots. A ridiculous, pointless extravagance. How did she know what size her child's feet would be? Maybe they would never be quite that small. How could any feet be that small?

Perhaps, the superstitious would say, there would be no baby to wear the boots and the question of their size would be quite irrelevant.

But she had bought them anyway. And she was not sorry. She would doubtless keep them in a drawer beside her bed, in the drawer where she kept her Bible. And she would take them out night and morning to look at them and touch them.

She was not at all sorry. Or sorry for the fact that her purse was considerably lighter than it had been when she left home. She bought a plain ivory fan for Jennifer and a small vial of perfume for Dorothy.

She was balancing five packages in her arms as she walked along, telling herself with a smile that it was a good thing she had not brought more money with her. If she had, she would doubtless be lost behind a mountain of boxes by the time she reached the carriage.

She was still smiling when she collided with a large gentleman who was on his way out of a bootmaker's. Two packages flew off in opposite directions, and the other three slid to her feet.

Ellen bent with anxious haste to retrieve the perfume and the porcelain jar.

"Beg pardon, ma'am," the gentleman said, stooping down at the same moment. Ellen grimaced at the strong smell of brandy on his breath and realized that the collision had been caused not so much by her own carelessness as by the fact that he was foxed.

"There," he said, holding out to her the two packages that she had not retrieved herself. "I hope there's nothing in them to break, ma'am."

Ellen stood staring stupidly at him and made no move to take the parcels that he held out to her. His eyes were glittering as they always had done when he was in his cups. His cheeks were perhaps a little more flushed than they had used to be. They were certainly more fleshy. And he was altogether heavier. His double chin looked strangled by his cravat.

He looked at her, his eyelids rather heavy. He frowned. "Do I know you?" he asked. "Deuced if I can place you, ma'am. I've had one too many, I'm afraid."

"I'm Ellen," she said.

"Ellen." His hands, which had been holding out the parcels to her, dropped to his sides. "Well. You grew into a beauty after all. I knew you would. I'm foxed, I'm afraid. I wouldn't have taken a drop if I had known I would bump into you. Ha! I really did bump into you, eh, Ellen?"

"Yes," she said. *My lord? Sir? Father? Papa?*

"Who died?" he asked, indicating her black clothes with a somewhat uncoordinated wave of an arm.

"My husband," she said.

"A soldier, wasn't he?" he said. "I'm sorry, Ellen. Did he treat you right?"

"Yes," she said.

"Better than your father did?" he asked. He grinned suddenly and hiccuped. "Pardon me. Indigestion. You don't know to which father I refer, do you?"

"How are you?" she asked. Her lips and her jaw felt stiff. They would not quite move as she wanted them to move.

"As you see," he said, making that expansive gesture with his arm again. "Not a care in the world, girl. That's me."

"I'm glad," she said. And then she became aware of the world around them again. "I must be on my way."

"Oh, yes," he said jovially. "Mustn't keep you."

But after she had hesitated and hurried past him, he called to her.

"You forgot your parcels," he said, holding them at the ends of outstretched arms. And when she walked back to retrieve them, "Do you have a kiss for your papa, Ellen?"

She looked mutely at him.

"I was your papa," he said, his arms still extended. Attracting attention. "You don't always have to beget a child to be its father, Ellen. Wasn't I a good papa?"

"Yes," she said, taking her packages from his hands. "Most of the time."

"I was human," he said. "We are all human. Come and see me. Will you come to see me, Ellen? I will stay sober if I know you are coming."

"Yes," she said. "I will come. Tomorrow. Shall I come in the afternoon?"

"For tea?" he said. "We will have a tea party, Ellie. Just the two of us."

Ellie!

"Yes," she said. "Just the two of us." She had forgotten, completely forgotten, that old pet name. His arms were still spread out to both sides. A few pedestrians had been forced to step from the pavement into the roadway in order to pass him. He had drawn several curious glances.

Ellen turned and hurried away from the Earl of Harrowby. Her legs felt decidedly shaky by the time Dorothy's coachman had helped her into the carriage and closed the door behind her.

"Perhaps I should have called on them myself before now," the Countess of Amberley was saying to her husband. "It is so hard to know what is the thing to do. They both looked so completely broken up when I met them in the park—you were still in Brussels at the time—that I felt it would be intruding to call on them. Especially when they did not call on me, as I had invited them to do."

"She was looking quite cheerful this morning," the earl said. "It is to be hoped that she is recovering, my love."

"Do you think Dominic just imagined that she returned his feelings for a while?" she asked. "I still find it hard to believe, Edmund. She was so devoted to Captain Simpson, and he had been dead for only a month when you arrived there. Surely she could not have fancied herself in love with Dominic or anyone else, could she?"

"I really don't know," he said. "I know only what Dominic went through."

"I would be so prostrate with grief if anything happened

to you," she said, "that I don't think I would even know that anyone else existed in the world."

He took her hand in a warm clasp. "It is impossible to know how one would act in a situation of such extreme catastrophe," he said. "Impossible, Alex."

"You are telling me that I am judging her too harshly if it all turns out to be true, then," she said. "And you are right, of course. I am afraid my upbringing still clouds my vision at times, Edmund. I still tend to see things in very black-and-white terms, as Papa always does."

"Mama and Madeline are entertaining the Simpson ladies this afternoon," he said. "Did I tell you that?"

"No," she said. "I didn't know. Dominic is in communication with her, then? Or with Miss Simpson, perhaps. He seemed very fond of her when we were still in Brussels. This is all very intriguing, Edmund."

"Perhaps we should take up matchmaking," he said, easing the kid glove from her hand and laying his own fingers the length of hers on the seat between them. "With whom shall we match Dominic, Alex? With Miss Simpson, Mrs. Simpson, Anna, or Susan Jennings? We have quite a choice, don't we?"

"I wouldn't dream of even trying to interfere," she said. "What a dreadful idea, Edmund. He will never marry Anna, though. He has never had any sort of *tendre* for her. Besides, she is your first cousin. And he would never seriously consider marrying Susan, would he? Oh, I do hope not. She is such an artificial little creature. And why are you grinning at me in that perfectly odious way?"

He made a kissing gesture with his mouth. "You fall into a trap so easily, Alex," he said, lacing his fingers through hers and carrying her hand to his lips. "I love you."

"Horrid man!" she said, maintaining her dignity and turning to look out the window.

ONE FACT WAS CLEAR to Lord Eden. He was still in love with Ellen Simpson. He wished it were not so. And he had really convinced himself that his infatuation with her had been a purely temporary thing brought on by the stress of circumstances. Until he saw her again, that was.

But it was not so. He loved her and had not slept at all during the night following their walk in Kensington Gardens. He had scarcely slept the night before, either, and even when he had, he had woken several times, his mind grappling each time with the question of whether he should be in his mother's drawing room when she came to tea with her stepdaughter.

Something else was clear to him too. If he saw much more of Miss Simpson, there would be people to think that he owed the girl something. Like an offer of marriage. He had come perilously close in Brussels to committing himself. He did not want to put himself into the embarrassing predicament of feeling honor-bound to offer for the stepdaughter when he loved the stepmother. And had been her lover.

Then, of course, there was Anna. She had never made any secret of the fact that she intended to marry him when she grew up. But what had always amused him when she was a girl was somewhat more serious now that she was a lovely young lady who had made her come-out and who was definitely on the market for a husband. One of these days he was going to have to have a good talk with Anna. And she was coming to tea as well, with Aunt Viola.

And when he had escorted Susan to the library, he had

somehow found himself also inviting her to join him and Edmund and Alexandra at the theater one evening. He did not quite know how he had come to do such a thing, since Susan had spent almost the whole of their outing worrying about how she was imposing upon his time.

He had almost married Susan once upon a time. And now she was a widow and in a delicate emotional state. He really did not harbor any leftover feelings for her, beyond the fondness he had always felt for her, even when she was a child. He did not want to marry her.

Ellen was the only woman he wanted to marry, and that was out of the question.

Somehow, he thought, life had been far less complicated when he had first bought his commission and gone off to Spain and there were only the French and the mud and the heat and death to worry about.

He did attend his mother's tea, even though he knew he would be the only man present. And he very deliberately seated himself beside Ellen when she arrived, and conversed with his aunt, who sat on his other side. Anna and Miss Simpson had their heads together and looked quite pleased with themselves.

"William has decided that we are going home soon," Mrs. Carrington said, "and I can't say I am sorry. Two months were all we expected to be away. But thanks to you, my dear"—she patted Lord Eden's hand—"we extended our stay. And here we still are. Anna and Walter don't want to go home, of course. But when Papa speaks, they have no choice."

"In my experience," Lord Eden said, grinning, "when Uncle William speaks, Anna starts to twist him about her finger."

"Gracious, Dominic!" she said as Madeline laughed, and

tapped him sharply on the hand. "You must not say so, especially when she is like to hear." She glanced at her oblivious daughter. "Poor William is too indulgent by half."

"So you are going home," he said. "Edmund and Alexandra too, I believe. And I plan to take myself off into Wiltshire within the next week or so. I have a home and an estate to make my own."

"You have decided, then, Dominic?" his mother asked. "I had hoped that you would wait until after Christmas, dear. But I daresay you will come to Amberley for the festivities, anyway."

"Perhaps," he said. "But I have a life to get on with. And I feel quite fit again and eager for something definite to do."

"I was very pleased to see the progress Lieutenant Penworth has made," the dowager said to Mrs. Carrington. "There has been a marked improvement since I saw him last in Brussels."

Madeline focused her attention on that line of conversation.

"I will be taking myself out of your life soon, you see," Lord Eden said quietly to Ellen, smiling down at her.

"Yes," she said.

"You will be glad of that."

Her cup rattled ever so slightly in its saucer as she set it down. "Yes," she said.

"I think it very likely that I will not see you again after today," he said. He looked at her for a silent moment. "Ellen, are you quite sure that you are not in need at all? I suppose you would not allow me to help you anyway. But I am worried about you."

"You need not be." She looked up at him, her jaw very firm. "Do you think it possible that Charlie, who knew for years that he might die at a moment's notice, would not have made adequate provision for his daughter and me? We are not in any kind of need, my lord."

"I am glad, then," he said.

She moved her eyes to Madeline, who was talking to her aunt and her mother, but he could tell that she was not listening. His own eyes moved over her profile, over her hair, as if to commit all the details to memory.

How could he have known her all those years, been frequently in company with her, and not known? It seemed incredible now that he could ever have looked at her and not known.

Her head moved jerkily and her eyes met his, wavered for a moment, and held. She swallowed and licked her lips. His eyes dropped to follow the movement.

"I met my father this morning," she said hastily.

His eyebrows rose. "The Earl of Harrowby?"

"The earl, yes." She flushed.

"Did you, Ellen?" he said. "I am glad for you. Should I be glad?"

Her gray eyes were wide and fully focused on him. "I have not seen him since I was fifteen," she said. "I told you about that last meeting, didn't I? He hasn't really changed. He looked very familiar. I am going to visit him tomorrow."

"Are you?" He clenched into a loose fist the hand that had been about to reach out to cover one of hers.

"Is it the wrong thing to do?" she asked. "He is not my father. Is it foolish to revisit the past? It was my home. And now I am going there as a visitor. Should I have refused?"

He shook his head. "No," he said. "I can see in your eyes that this is very much something you want to do, Ellen. Then you should do it. And he was your father for fifteen years, even if he did not beget you. You had good times with him. You told me about some of them."

She half-smiled into his eyes.

"What does your sister-in-law say?" he asked.

She shook her head. "I have not told anyone else," she said. "I was alone this morning. I think I want to go. I want to have someone of my own, even if he is not quite mine. Do you know what I mean?"

He nodded. "Families can be the plague of one's life," he said. "But I cannot imagine a worse fate than to be totally without mine. You must go, Ellen. He invited you?"

She nodded.

"Then you must go."

If he held his breath, perhaps the spell would never be broken. They were smiling into each other's eyes, not saying anything, but unembarrassed nonetheless. Just as they had done frequently through almost two weeks. She was talking from the heart, just as she had done then. He felt almost that he could reach out for her hand and she would give it to him and let it rest companionably in his.

And he had just told her that he would probably not see her again.

"Dominic!" Anna's voice was laughing and exasperated all at the same time. "Are you deaf? I suppose you and Mrs. Simpson are deep in war reminiscences. Could I please have a little of your attention?"

Ellen's eyes widened before dropping away from his. She flushed.

"Sorry," he said. "What is it, Anna?"

"Jennifer is coming to the Tower with Walter and me tomorrow," she said, "and Mr. Phelps cannot come. It would be very lowering for me to have to go along with a mere brother, Dominic. You must rescue me. Will you? If you come, I will instantly become the most envied female in

London, for you are easily the most handsome gentleman in town." She laughed gaily.

"I can resist anything but flattery," he said, "and the chance of having a pretty lady to escort about London."

"Oh, splendid!" she said, smiling back at Jennifer. "And we will charm the men into taking us to Gunter's for ices."

"At this time of year?" Lord Eden asked. "You must be mad, Anna."

Ellen, he noticed, had been drawn into conversation with his mother, his aunt, and Madeline. He did not talk with her again until she and her stepdaughter rose to take their leave.

"I shall see you tomorrow," he said to Jennifer as he took her hand in his. "It is years since I saw the Tower."

"And I have never seen it," she said, her face bright and eager. "I shall so look forward to the outing, my lord."

"Good-bye, Ellen," he said, taking her hand in a quite tight grasp and looking closely into her eyes. There was nothing else to be said. They were surrounded by members of his family and Miss Simpson, all talking at once, it seemed. And this might be good-bye indeed. There were a thousand things to say. He felt panic rise into his throat.

"Good-bye, my lord." She returned the pressure of his hand. And then drew it free and turned to smile at his mother.

"What a very prettily behaved young lady Miss Simpson is," the dowager said after all her guests had left. "It is quite a pity that Anna has not had her for a friend for longer. And Mrs. Simpson is quite charming, and looking very much better than when I saw her in Belgium." She looked curiously at her son.

"Yes," he said. "She is too strong a person to crumble even under the cruelest blow. I saw her comfort men in

Spain after enduring exactly the same adverse conditions as they."

"You were talking with her," she said. "Has the bitterness been put an end to, Dominic? I do hope so, for both your sakes."

"Yes," he said. "I don't think there is any left, Mama."

"And is there any chance," she said, "that after her year of mourning is at an end you can mean more to each other?"

He shook his head. "No," he said. "I think it unlikely that I will meet her again. I am quite serious about leaving for Wiltshire next week."

She sighed. "What a shame!" she said. "I have not met a young woman I would like better as a daughter-in-law since I met Alexandra."

"Well," he said, putting an arm about her shoulders and hugging her, "we cannot load you down with new relatives, now, can we, Mama? Penworth is next, I believe. Then it will be my turn, perhaps, if I can persuade anyone to take me on."

Madeline made a sound very like a snort. "Just whisper that you are on the market, Dom," she said, "and there will be girls and their mamas lined up outside your door for the distance of half a mile."

He chuckled, and felt rather as if his heart had turned to stone inside him.

MADELINE ARRIVED AT Mr. Septimus Foster's house the following day after luncheon and was shown into a salon on the ground floor, where she found her betrothed sketching on a piece of paper with some charcoal.

She leaned over his shoulder and kissed his forehead. "The fireplace," she said, "in minutest detail."

He tossed the paper aside and looked up at her. "Madeline," he said, "I told you that Septimus and his wife would be from home this afternoon. You should not be here."

"Oh, faradiddle!" she said. "I am five-and-twenty years old, Allan. Years past the necessity of having armies of chaperones trailing along behind me."

"Even so," he said, "I don't want you talked about. You are Lady Madeline Raine. Someone special."

"Do you think so?" she said, sitting down beside him. "How very flattering, sir."

"Not just to me," he said. "You draw admiration wherever you go. It's not just your looks, though they are quite good enough. There is a sparkle about you, something that draws the eyes. I really shouldn't have allowed you to betroth yourself to me. It's not right, Madeline."

"Are we going to have this argument again?" she asked, smiling at him and taking one of his hands in hers. "Because you are missing a leg, Allan? And an eye? I don't care about those things. I shall be your missing leg and eye."

"But you shouldn't have to be," he said. "You shouldn't be tied to a cripple. And besides, no one can be a missing limb for someone else. I have to learn to cope with my own disabilities."

"Oh, you are cross today, Allan," she said, kissing the back of his hand. "Would you like me to read to you?"

"No, I would not!" he said. "I can read for myself when I want to."

"But your eye tires. You have told me that," she said. She laid her cheek against the back of his hand.

He turned his head to look at her. "Oh, Lord," he said. "I am treating you abominably, aren't I? My leg has been aching all morning. I would swear it is still there. It has definitely been aching. And I have been thinking again. That is always a fatal thing to do. And I am thoroughly out of sorts with the world and sorry for myself. And I am taking it all out on you. When you have done so much for me. You brought me back to life when all I wanted to do was die. Forgive me?"

She turned her head and kissed his hand again. "I understand," she said. "I do, Allan. And I am not hurt or offended. It is all right."

"But it is not," he said. "You should not be tied to me or subject to my moods of irritability. You should be free to enjoy life again."

"Oh," she said, smiling, "if you only knew how little I have enjoyed life in the past few years, Allan. It was all surface enjoyment and gaiety. I am not complaining, because it was a life of privilege and I know thousands would give a great deal to have just half the pleasure that was mine. But there was something missing. Some substance. And I have found it with you. Maybe I helped you back to life. But you have given meaning to my life. You have. So don't talk anymore about my going away to enjoy myself. I *am* enjoying myself—with you."

He sighed and withdrew his hand from hers in order to put his arm about her shoulders. "I just hope that in five years' time," he said, "or ten, you will not feel tied down by the fact that you are married to me. But look, Madeline, you ought not to be here alone with me. If you won't go away as you ought, then we must go out. A carriage ride in the park?"

"Are you sure you feel well enough?" she asked, sitting upright. "Are you willing to venture out, Allan? I know you did not enjoy the visit to Edmund's a few afternoons ago."

"Only because you are so anxious to protect me from embarrassment that you would not let me speak a word," he said. "You must learn not to do that. But we argued that out quite effectively at the time. We don't need to reopen that quarrel. Yes, let's go out. If we go in a closed carriage, I won't have to inflict the sight of me on anyone. Though of course in a closed carriage you really should have a maid. I'll ring for a carriage to be brought around."

"I'll do it," she said, leaping to her feet. "You sit there."

"I said I'll ring," he said testily, and pulled himself slowly upright with the help of his crutches. "Oh, Madeline, pull the bell rope, will you? I'm sorry. And I have the feeling I am going to be apologizing to you for the rest of our lives."

17

JENNIFER AND ANNA, WALTER CARRINGTON, and Lord Eden spent more than an hour at the Tower of London, inspecting the armory and gazing at the crown jewels.

"It makes one wish there were some eligible princes floating around waiting to be married, doesn't it?" Anna said to Jennifer. "Can you imagine wearing all that finery?"

"It would be splendid," Jennifer agreed rather wistfully.

"But you would get very bored sitting on a throne all day," Walter said, drawing a giggle from both girls, "drumming your jeweled fingers on the carved arm. Picture it. No freedom to walk in the park. Or to eat ices at Gunter's."

"Perhaps those princes would not be very handsome anyway," Anna said, linking her arm through Lord Eden's. "Now, what was that about ices?"

"You will freeze your insides," he said. "But so be it. And you chose an open barouche too, Anna? At the end of September?"

"Anna is always gasping for air in a closed carriage," her brother said, "and convinced that she is missing all sorts of spectacular sights, since she can look from only one window at a time."

"I have a new bonnet," that young lady said gaily, "and I want the world to see it. Do you like it, Dominic?"

"Very fetching," he said. "But I don't want you bending forward when you are within twenty feet of me, Anna, if you please. That feather would take my eye out."

They decided to drive through Hyde Park before going to Gunter's, since the leaves, according to Anna, were too lovely to be missed. There they met the closed carriage in which Madeline was riding with Lieutenant Penworth. Madeline let down the window in order to exchange greetings with the occupants of the barouche. The lieutenant stayed back in the shadows and said nothing.

Jennifer leaned forward and smiled. "How do you do, Lieutenant?" she called. "I am very pleased to see that you are out again. Do you remember me?"

"Of course he does," Madeline said with a smile. "We decided to take advantage of a beautiful day and come out for a drive."

Jennifer gazed in at the man who had raised a hand in acknowledgment of her greeting. She would not have known that it was he. This man looked thin and pale, and half his face was completely covered by a type of bandage. She remembered a lithe, good-looking, high-spirited young officer who liked always to be active.

"We are on our way to Gunter's," Lord Eden said. "Would you care to join us, Penworth? Madeline?"

"Perhaps some other time," Madeline said quickly.

"Thank you," Lieutenant Penworth said at the same moment. "That would be pleasant."

She looked at him, surprised. "Are you sure you will not mind?" she asked.

"No," he said abruptly. "Will you?"

"We will meet you there in a few minutes, then," Lord Eden said as Madeline flushed and withdrew her head back inside the carriage.

"So I am finally to meet my future brother-in-law," Lord Eden said as they drove on. "Madeline has been keeping him hidden."

"I have been dying of curiosity," Anna said.

"Poor man," Jennifer said. "How can war be so cruel?"

"You did not wish to go," the lieutenant was saying in the other carriage. "For my sake, Madeline? Or for yours?"

She looked at him in dismay. "For yours," she said. "You have been unwilling for anyone to see you. And Gunter's is a very public place. Allan, you don't think I am ashamed of you, do you?"

"No." He reached out a hand for hers. "But you have spent so long nursing me, that I think perhaps you are trying to protect me from all harm, physical and otherwise. It is exhausting for you when other people can see me, is it not? But I cannot keep you from all normal daily activities, Madeline. These are your family and your friends. You should spend time with them. If I am to be your husband, I must spend time with them too."

She squeezed his hand.

A few customers at Gunter's turned to watch the entrance of a rather grim-faced Lieutenant Penworth a few minutes later. He crossed without assistance to the table at which the other four were seated and took the only empty chair at one end of the table, the one next to Jennifer. Madeline, having made the introductions, was forced to sit at the opposite end of the table.

The conversation was bright and hearty for a few minutes. There was much laughter at the table. Then Anna launched into a description of the crown jewels and a lament over the fact that her papa had said they were to go home to the country within the next week or so.

"Well, Edmund and Alexandra and the children will be going as well," Madeline said soothingly. "And I am trying to persuade Allan to come too for a while. He has not said no, so I hold out great hopes." She smiled the length of the table at her betrothed, who was talking with Jennifer.

"Are you feeling better?" Jennifer was asking. "I was sorry to hear of your injuries, sir."

"Thank you," he said without looking at her. "I am fully recovered." His face was pale and grim. He was not at all the same young man as the one she had danced with and walked with in the Forest of Soignes.

"Will you be returning to Devon soon?" she asked him. "I remember your telling me about your family and about how you loved your home."

"I have no intention of taking myself back there in the foreseeable future," he said.

"Oh," she said, and took a mouthful of her ice. She had lost touch with the conversation that the others were engaged in. Lord Eden, she saw, was watching them from beside his sister.

"Your mother must be anxious about you," she said. "And your papa and all your brothers and sisters."

"Doubtless," he said. "I would be the object of their pity for the rest of my life. They were proud of me."

Jennifer played nervously with her spoon. She wished he had sat somewhere else. "Are they not proud of you now?" she said.

"Oh, yes." His voice was cold. "I am their wounded hero."

"Why do you wear such a large bandage?" she asked, and flushed at the rudeness of her question.

"My face is not a pretty sight," he said.

"Have the wounds not healed?"

"As well as they ever will, I suppose," he said. "Which is not to say a great deal at all."

"Would it not be better to wear just a small eye patch?" she asked. "The sun and air would help the other scars to fade, would they not? And if you were to ask me, I would say that the bandage is far more noticeable than a few scars would be."

"If I were to ask you," he said so quietly that she was not quite sure that she had heard the words correctly. She felt acutely uncomfortable for the rest of their stay at the confectioner's.

"Were you very badly snubbed by Penworth?" Lord Eden asked her with some sympathy in the barouche later.

"I deserved it, I'm afraid," she said. "I should not have asked him any personal questions. He seems to have recovered from his outer wounds quite well. But there are other wounds, far deeper, that have not even begun to heal yet."

"I must confess I was very embarrassed," Anna said, "and annoyed with myself for being so. I was so afraid of saying something that I should not say."

"How would one face life?" Walter said. "Only one leg. Only one eye. Ouch! I think I would rather be dead."

"What nonsense!" Jennifer said, and flushed again at yet another rudeness. "There are a great many things one can do in life without a leg or an eye. I do feel sad for Lieutenant Penworth, for I knew him as he was before. But I also feel a little angry that his attitude has become bitter and cynical. No, not angry. It all happened to him only three months ago. But I would be angry and doubly sad if I were to meet him in a few years' time and still found him bemoaning his loss and not getting on with his life."

"I'm sure you're right, Miss Simpson," Walter said. "But, gad, how would one get on with one's life without a leg? No riding. No sports. It doesn't bear thinking of."

"Poor man," Anna said.

Lord Eden was smiling at her, Jennifer saw.

ON THE SAME AFTERNOON, Ellen called upon the Earl of Harrowby. She took no one with her and even thought, as she raised the brass knocker outside the huge double doors of his house, that perhaps it was improper to visit him alone. But she smiled at the thought. This had been her home for fifteen years. He had been her father.

He had been drinking again, she could see as soon as he hurried down the stairs to meet her instead of waiting for his butler to show her up to the drawing room.

"I wouldn't have touched a drop if I had known for certain that you would come, Ellie," he said, flashing her a smile as he offered his arm. "I thought you wouldn't, once you had thought about it."

"But I did come," she said, looking about the drawing room and finding it exactly as it had been the last time she saw it, except that perhaps the carpet was slightly more worn and the draperies at the windows more faded.

"I didn't invite anyone else," he said. "I hope you don't mind. It will be just you and me, Ellie. Besides"—he smiled apologetically—"there are not many ladies who would accept an invitation from the Earl of Harrowby these days. I am not considered quite respectable, y'know."

"Are you not?" she said, looking at the marked signs of dissipation about his face and figure as he stood with his back to the fire. They did not speak as the housekeeper—like the butler, someone she did not know—brought in the tea tray. She felt awkward. She did not know what to call him. "Shall I pour?"

"If you had not left me," he said, extending one hand to indicate that she should take a seat behind the tray, "I would not be the wreck you see. I loved you, girl. You should not have left."

"You did not take up drinking just after I left," she said, holding up a full cup and saucer to him. "Now, be honest with yourself. I do not need the blame for that heaped on my shoulders."

His smile was almost boyish. "You are quite right," he said. "But you were always good for me, Ellie. You never did put up with any nonsense. You always said what was what. You used to tell me to go away when I was in my cups. Do you remember?"

"Yes," she said.

He laughed. "Sometimes, not often, I admit," he said, "I used to stay sober just so that I could come to the nursery or the schoolroom and see you. And then I would drink afterward. But not so much in those days, girl. Not so much then. Have some cakes."

They looked at each other.

"You were always my St. George," she said, "who would slay all my dragons."

"Was I, Ellie?" he said. "Was he good to you?"

She knew he was not referring to Charlie. "Yes," she said, "he was good to me."

"But he didn't slay any dragons?" That boyish smile again.

"I was older," she said. "I knew that no man is infallible. Not even fathers."

"Tell me about your life," he said. "It is as if you were dead, Ellie, and have come back to life again."

She told him about Spain and about Belgium. She told him about Charlie and Jennifer and her other friends. She must have talked for half an hour, she realized with something of a jolt as she finished telling him about her meeting with Sir Jasper Simpson. But he was interested. He had scarcely moved or withdrawn his eyes from her face.

"It is me you should be turning to for support, Ellie," he said, "not him. Do you feel that he is more your father than I am?"

How could she answer the question? "He is Jennifer's grandfather," she said. "That is why meeting him is so important, Papa." And she bit down hard on her lip and closed her eyes.

"Perhaps I am too," he said. "Perhaps I am your papa, Ellie. But the important thing is that I was for all those years. I was your papa. I loved you. I wasn't perfect, but I didn't ever mistreat you, did I?"

She shook her head, her eyes on the silver milk jug on the tray.

He got to his feet and pulled on the bell rope for someone to come and remove the tray. He rested an elbow on the mantelpiece and tapped one knuckle rhythmically against his teeth as he waited, saying nothing. But he turned back to her when the footman had disappeared, and came to sit down beside her.

"Don't go yet," he said, taking one of her hands in his. "Stay and talk awhile longer, Ellie."

She looked down at his hand, fatter now than it had been, but a hand she would have recognized anyway, with its blunt, dark-haired fingers, the nails broader than they were long. Hands that had held her as a child, hands that she could remember clinging to sometimes as she walked, though she could no longer remember where it was they had walked.

"What did you mean," she asked, "that you might be?"

He looked at her with his heavy-lidded, rather blood-shot eyes. "Your mother and I," he said. "We always said what would most hurt, even if it were not always the truth. You might be mine, Ellie."

"She said not," Ellen said. "And he did not argue."

"When your mother was expecting you," he said, "I never did so much as think of questioning whose you were. I would have if there had been any chance of your not being mine, wouldn't I? I always knew when she had someone else. I knew she had lovers. But I wasn't suspicious at that time. Besides, your mother was a careful woman. She would have made sure that you were mine. You were our first—and our only, as it turned out. You might have been a boy, Ellie. You might have been my heir. I think you are mine."

"But why would she have said such a thing?" Ellen asked.

"To hurt me," he said. "She must have been feeling particularly vicious. She knew you were the only person I ever really loved. She wanted to turn me against you. You weren't supposed to know. But I came and told you, didn't I? I suppose I was foxed at the time. And then your mother went off with Fenchurch and I haven't seen her since. She was in Vienna for the Congress the last time I heard of her. With someone I have never heard of. We weren't a pretty pair, girl. It wasn't all her fault, what happened. But you are the one who suffered most."

"Yes," she said, "I did. But everything in life has a purpose, perhaps. I would not have met my husband if I had not gone to Spain. And I would hate to have gone through life without knowing him."

He patted her hand. "Say it again," he said, "what you let slip a little while ago. It sounded good, Ellie."

She looked at him and swallowed. "Papa?" she said. "I didn't ever call him that, you know."

He patted her hand again.

She looked at him. And looked beyond the bloodshot eyes and the flushed cheeks, and the double chin. He had been her papa. She had curled up on his large lap and played with the chain of his watch. And had felt as if nothing on this earth could ever harm her.

"I am with child," she surprised herself by saying suddenly. "And it is not my husband's. I conceived it from a lover less than a month after his death. And now I have started to let people think it is Charlie's, and I don't know what to do."

Take all your problems to Papa, Ellen. And climb into his lap and let him soothe them all away.

"Are you, Ellie?" he said, his free hand smoothing over the back of hers. "The important thing is, are you happy about it? Did you love him?"

"Yes, I did," she said. "Totally and passionately, Papa. Nobody else existed in the world for a week. Just for a week. Less, even. He was a friend of Charlie's and of mine. And then, before either of us knew what was happening, we were lovers. But it was all wrong. I loved Charlie. Or thought I did. Now I am so consumed with guilt and confusion that I no longer know what love is."

"Well," he said, patting her hand, "you will have a child to love soon, Ellie. You will find out. Does he know?"

"No." She gripped his hand. "I couldn't possibly tell him. I don't want him ever to know."

"It is sad, Ellie," he said, "to be deprived of your child. Does he love you?"

"No," she said. "Oh, he did for that week, as much as I loved him. But love is the wrong word. It was not love. And he does not feel whatever it was for me any longer. He is leaving London soon."

"And you will be staying," he said, "with relatives of your husband's and a child of your lover's. Well, girl, you will sort out your own future. You always did. I have great faith in you. But you know, you can always come here, Ellie. This will always be your home. And I will always be your papa even if I didn't beget you. But I think I did."

"Oh," she said, lifting their joined hands so that her lips rested against his knuckles, "if you knew what a burden has been lifted from my shoulders just by telling you all this! I think there is still a little of St. George in you, after all."

He laughed with some amusement and she smiled up into his eyes.

"You'll come back again?" he asked. "You won't disappear altogether again, Ellie? You'll come back to see me?"

She nodded and got to her feet. "I have been here much longer than I planned," she said. "I'm glad I came, Papa. You are really the only person of my very own left."

"Come and be hugged, girl," he said, and waves of memory washed over her as his arms closed about her and rocked her against him. Memories of bedtime, when her mother had been too busy getting dressed for the evening's entertainment to come to the nursery to kiss her good night. Even the same smell, some curious mixture of brandy and snuff and cologne.

"Oh, Papa," she said, giving in finally and totally to self-pity and really not caring for the moment, "how am I going to bear it when he goes away forever?"

"You'll have your child," he said, "and your papa. You'll do, girl. You'll do."

THE EARL OF AMBERLEY was sitting sprawled on a sofa in a room adjoining the nursery of his house, his arms stretched out along the back. He was half-smiling as he watched his wife nursing their daughter.

"She is sleeping," he said.

"I know." She sighed. "And I should put her down, shouldn't I? She is going to have to be weaned fairly soon. She is seven months old already. It is not fair, Edmund. Children should remain tiny babies for far longer than they do."

"Well," he said, "when Caroline has finished at your breast, Alex, we will just have to see about putting another child there, won't we?"

She flushed. "Will we?" she said. "Oh, Edmund, you have me tingling right down to my toes."

He grinned. "It seems a shame to waste the moment, doesn't it?" he said. "And Caroline is asleep. However, I have just recalled that the minute I step back out into the nursery, I will have to give Christopher that promised piggyback ride. And I am talking about giving you more children?"

"We are really going back to Amberley next week?" she said, smiling. "I won't believe it until we are there. Home again. It will be bliss."

"I was somewhat surprised that Lieutenant Penworth has agreed to come along with Madeline, weren't you?" he said.

"Yes," she said. "But I am glad. I want to get to know him better. And having him to tea does not accomplish that.

Madeline is so very careful to protect him from any awkwardness."

"And only succeeds in making the whole situation impossibly awkward," he said. "Amberley will be good for him. I think he has what it takes to cope with his handicaps if he is left to himself, Alex."

"You mean if Madeline will stop coddling him," she said.

"I don't want to be unkind to her," he said. "She has done wonders for him, I believe, and she is wholly devoted to him. I have never seen Madeline so unfocused on herself."

"Will they be happy?" she asked.

He shrugged. "If they want to be, I suppose," he said. "Being at Amberley should help them to get to know each other better. I mean, in more than a nurse-patient sort of relationship. The Simpson ladies will be here later. You are sure you want to invite them to Amberley too, Alex? I did not talk you into it?"

"You know I would have argued if I had disagreed," she said. "I don't. But I am not sure they will come, for all that, Edmund."

"Dominic has made a definite decision to go into Wiltshire," he said.

"But Mrs. Simpson is bound to feel awkward with us," she said. "We are his family, after all. It would be lovely if they would come, though, Edmund. It was an inspired idea on your part. Madeline is friendly with both of them, and Anna has become very close with Miss Simpson. And Walter too, it seems. And it would be good for them to have the greater freedom of a country estate during the time of their mourning. And I like them. I would enjoy their company."

"I feel under a great obligation to Mrs. Simpson," the earl said. "I am still of the opinion that Dominic might well not be alive today if it were not for her. I would like to show my gratitude in some way."

"Then we shall ask them when they come to tea," the countess said. "I hope they say yes. You speak to them, Edmund. You are much more persuasive than I am."

"Am I?" he said, getting to his feet and taking the sleeping baby from her arms. "I don't suppose I can persuade my son to forgo his piggyback ride and my wife to visit our bedchamber with me, can I?"

She laughed. "No, you certainly may not," she said. "You will behave yourself until the decent hour of bedtime, my lord."

"I didn't think I would succeed," he said with a sigh.

JENNIFER WAS BUBBLING with high spirits. She still had moods of guilty remorse and would shed tears when she remembered that she was in mourning for her father. But Ellen did not resent the fact that the girl was returning to her youthful enthusiasm for life. Those two intense months they had spent grieving were quite enough for one so young.

Everything seemed to be going well for Jennifer. She had made friends and was having numerous outings. She had a few admirers, though Ellen did not think she was attached to any one of them. Including Lord Eden, she was relieved to find. Jennifer did not talk of him any more than she talked of Walter Carrington or Anna's friend Mr. Phelps. And she did not appear to be nursing a private *tendre*.

They had visited Sir Jasper Simpson more than once, and Mr. Phillip Simpson on one occasion. And Sir Jasper appeared to have accepted Jennifer as his granddaughter. Indeed, the girl confided to Ellen after one visit, he had told her that she had the look of her grandmother when she smiled.

And he was as good as his word. He was holding a dinner and quiet evening party in honor of his newfound relatives. He had asked both of them if there was anyone in particular that they wished him to invite. Ellen had said no, but Jennifer had had her grandfather smiling indulgently as she had eagerly listed almost all of her acquaintances: Lord Eden, Anna and Walter Carrington, Mrs. Jennings, Lady Madeline, the Emery sisters.

"Lady Madeline is betrothed to Lieutenant Penworth," she had said. "I knew him in Brussels, Grandpapa, but he was badly wounded and he does not like to be seen in public now. I don't believe he would come."

"But I will send him an invitation anyway," the old man had said with a chuckle.

Ellen would have been alarmed at the mention of Lord Eden had she not known that he was as eager to avoid meeting her again as she was to avoid him. And he was planning to go into the country soon. She need not fear. He would refuse his invitation.

She could not bear it if he came. It was not that she was afraid to meet him. She had recovered from that sort of dread after her humiliating fit of the vapors. But she had accustomed her mind to the idea that she would never see him again. The wound was beginning to film over. Very thinly, it was true. But she did not want it rubbed raw again.

She did not fear the visit to the Earl and Countess of Amberley's. She liked them very much and remembered the kindness and the tact the earl had shown her during those dreadful days in Brussels. She did not think that they would embarrass her by inviting the earl's brother to tea as well. And Jennifer was excited at the prospect of the visit. She was hoping to see the children again.

She was not to be disappointed. Christopher was tugging at her skirt, waiting for her attention, when she was still exchanging greetings with her host and hostess. She stooped down as soon as she was able and hugged him. And then he was off again, in pursuit of his game.

The countess looked at her husband a few minutes later and raised her eyebrows when Caroline hauled herself up on her knees beside Ellen, clung to her skirt, and gazed up solemnly into her face. Ellen did not withdraw her attention from the conversation, but lifted the child onto her lap and opened her reticule so that the baby could rummage through its contents.

Ellen was taken totally by surprise when the invitation to stay at Amberley Court was issued. She had already expressed envy when the countess had mentioned the fact that they were removing to the country. And she had told them that it was the dearest wish of her heart to live in the country herself.

"Oh," she said when the earl asked her and Jennifer to join them for a few weeks at Amberley. And could think of nothing else to say.

Jennifer was not so tongue-tied. "Oh, may we go, Ellen?" she asked, sitting on the edge of her chair, her cheeks flushed. "Oh, please, may we? Amberley is by the sea, is it not? You told me about it, ma'am, on our journey back to England, and Anna has told me about it. It sounds so perfectly splendid."

"You are very kind," Ellen said, looking from the earl to the countess. "But you really do not owe me anything at all. I did no more than hundreds of other women in Brussels."

"Indeed you did," the earl said. "The hundreds of others

did not nurse my brother back to health, ma'am. But our obligation aside, we would enjoy entertaining you. And so, apparently, would our daughter. You would not realize how very rare it is for her to associate with anyone except her parents and her nurse. I suppose she would befriend her brother too if she could only catch him occasionally."

"Oh, do say yes, Ellen," Jennifer begged.

Ellen looked at the earl and the countess, both of whom were smiling at her.

"Madeline will be there," the countess said, "and her betrothed. Dominic will not, of course, as he is going to his own estate within the next few days."

"The prospect of a few weeks in the country is an appealing one," Ellen said with the utmost sincerity.

Jennifer beamed with pleasure and sat back in her chair again. The countess smiled more broadly. It seemed that her answer had been made, Ellen thought.

"Splendid!" the earl said. "Alex and I always enjoy showing off our home to guests. That is settled, then. And from the noise on the stairs it is my guess that we are about to be invaded."

The doors to the drawing room opened to admit the butler, only one step ahead of Anna and Walter Carrington, Susan Jennings, and Lord Eden. Anna's voice, as usual, preceded her into the room.

"It is beginning to rain, Alexandra," she was saying, "and we were riding in an open barouche. The question was where to go. And your house was the closest of anyone we knew. So we decided to invite ourselves to tea. You do not mind, do you? And how could you possibly say so now, even if you do mind? Oh!" She clapped a hand over her mouth. "You have visitors already."

But when she saw who they were, the twinkle was back

in her eyes, and she was across the room to sit beside Jennifer.

"Walter and I had an invitation this morning," she said. "From your grandfather. Did you know? We answered it right away and said we would come."

"That is a relief," Jennifer said. "The Misses Emery, my friends, have another engagement for that evening."

Everyone else exchanged greetings. Lord Eden took a seat across the room from Ellen. And the film had been rubbed away from the wound. She wished she had not said that to her father about not knowing what she would do if she never saw him again. She had not admitted anything to herself before that moment. And it was better so.

She must count the days patiently until his departure for the country.

Anna was squealing. "Walter," she said, "Jennifer and Mrs. Simpson are coming to Amberley for a few weeks. Is that your doing, Edmund? You are my very, very favorite cousin, I do assure you. I shall not mind half as much having to go home now, and I shall tell Papa so. He threatened this morning to stuff his ears with cotton if I complain about it one more time."

Ellen and Lord Eden were regarding each other across the room.

"Why don't you come too, Dominic?" Anna said. "Then I would be totally happy. It is very unsporting of you to take yourself off to Wiltshire when you can quite easily postpone going there for a few months."

"No," he said, still looking at Ellen. "I will not be at Amberley before Christmas, Anna."

"I have had an invitation to Sir Jasper Simpson's for dinner and cards," Susan Jennings said to Ellen. "It is very obliging of him, I am sure. And all because of my friendship with your dear stepdaughter, ma'am. It will be difficult to attend, of course, as I have no one to escort me, with my dear husband gone."

"Are you coming, my lord?" Jennifer asked Lord Eden eagerly.

"I have not answered my invitation yet," he said guardedly.

"It is the day before you plan to leave town," Anna said. "I worked it out in my mind when I read my invitation. You must come, Dominic."

"You will understand if I refuse my invitation," Susan said gently to Ellen, "that it is not that I wish to appear ill-mannered to your dear father-in-law, ma'am. But you will know just how very alone one is when one's husband is gone. You at least are fortunate enough to have a step-daughter to give you some company." She lifted a delicate handkerchief to her eyes.

"I will take you up in my carriage, Susan," Lord Eden said. "We will go together."

"How very kind you are," she said. "But I would not wish to impose upon you, my lord."

"It is no imposition at all," he said.

His eyes, when they looked back to Ellen, were inscrutable.

The wound had been rubbed quite raw again.

The conversation had moved on to another topic.

18

SIXTEEN PERSONS SAT DOWN TO DINNER AT Sir Jasper Simpson's town house several evenings later. It would not, unfortunately, be a merry gathering, he told his guests in the drawing room before they moved into the dining room. There would be no dancing. A number of them were in mourning. But he had given in to the desire to honor the daughter-in-law and the granddaughter whom he had met for the first time only recently, and to meet some of their closest friends.

He knew almost everyone, Lord Eden discovered. He did not know Sir Jasper himself or Mrs. Edith Simpson, but he had seen Phillip Simpson at White's a few times in the past. And he was acquainted with Mr. and Mrs. Everett, cousins of Charlie's. Young Mr. Lawrence Winslow he had not seen before, but he did know Viscount Agerton. And there was a great deal of loud talk and laughter and back-slapping when that last gentleman and Walter recognized in each other old school fellows.

Anna and Susan and Madeline were present too, of course, and Penworth, much to Lord Eden's surprise. Madeline had announced at home the day before that he had decided to attend the dinner. She had been sparkling with exuberance, and yet she had expressed some uneasiness to him when they were alone together. Was he up to mingling with such a gathering for a whole evening?

There was only one way to find out, he had told her, his arm about her shoulders. Was she up to it? That was more to the point. She had thrown him an indignant look, and he had guessed that he had hit on a raw nerve.

Lord Eden should have felt quite comfortable at the gathering. In fact, he felt quite the opposite. He was mingling with Charlie's family. And he was intruding yet again on Ellen's presence, when he had told her the week before that he would probably not see her again. He had said good-bye to her.

He was still not quite sure why he had accepted the invitation. Had it been Susan's plight? Or Anna's persuasions? Or Miss Simpson's eager expression? Or was it his own weak and selfish need to torture himself? And perhaps Ellen too?

However it was, he felt uncomfortable and wished himself anywhere but in that particular place. He was thankful that his trunks were packed and arrangements all made for his departure the next day. Temptation would be taken out of his grasp then. He could begin the process of forgetting her and starting a new life.

In the meantime, he decided as Sir Jasper took Ellen on his arm to lead her into the dining room, and he offered his own arm to Susan, he would stay far away from Ellen for that evening. He would show her feelings that much respect, anyway.

He seated Susan as far from the head of the table as possible and set himself to charming both her and Lady Habersham on his other side. He concentrated the whole of his mind on his conversation with those two ladies and on Winslow and Mrs. Everett opposite. And soon, he thought after an interminable hour, the ladies would withdraw, and if he was fortunate, Sir Jasper would be the type of man who liked to sit over the port and the male conversation for at least an hour more.

But Sir Jasper rose to his feet before Edith Simpson could give the signal to the ladies. He wished his guests to join him in a few toasts, he said. They all dutifully raised their glasses to his granddaughter, whom circumstances had kept from him all her life, and to his dear daughter-in-law, who had comforted the last years of his son.

The old man paused, his smile directed at Ellen. Lord Eden allowed himself to look fully at her for the first time that evening. She was sitting very upright in her chair, her face pale and tense, her eyes wide and pleading on her father-in-law. One hand began to reach up to him but joined the other in her lap again.

Lord Eden frowned.

"And a very special toast," Sir Jasper said, "to a third person, one who is with us tonight and makes our numbers a very awkward seventeen." He smiled kindly down at his daughter-in-law.

She closed her eyes.

"To my future grandchild," Sir Jasper said. "To my grandson, it is my fondest hope. My heir."

There was a buzz of voices about the table and a scraping of chairs being pushed back. And a clinking of glasses. Lord Eden found himself on his feet and doing what everyone else did. He even heard Susan say that she was never more surprised in her life. And one part of him noticed Jennifer with both hands to her mouth, crying.

He stayed on his feet, bowing and smiling as the ladies

left. And he even found himself participating in a conversation about the races and the quality of the cattle that were up for auction these days at Tattersall's. He had no idea if the gentlemen sat over the port for ten minutes or thirty, or for a whole hour.

But Sir Jasper did eventually suggest that they join the ladies in the drawing room.

JENNIFER SAT BESIDE ELLEN until the gentlemen joined them. Most of the other ladies were gathered about the pianoforte. Several of them played.

Jennifer was feeling happier than she had felt for months, she told Ellen more than once. Why had Ellen not told her before? She was so very happy.

"I have been feeling so sad for you in the last few weeks, Ellen," she said. "I have new friends and have been going about a great deal more than you have. And I have realized that losing a husband is very much worse than losing a father. I have wished and wished that there were something or somebody for you. But though you are young and very lovely and will undoubtedly remarry eventually, you could not think of doing so yet, could you? But now you do have someone. Your very own child. Oh, Ellen, I know why you did not tell me when we were alone at home. I would have screamed and danced you about the room. I don't blame you for preventing that."

"Jennifer." Ellen looked acutely distressed. "I did not want you to find out like this. I wanted to tell you myself. I wanted to tell you the whole of it. There is a great deal to be said."

Jennifer smiled brightly at her. "And I want to hear it all," she said. "You shall tell me all about it sometime when we have the leisure. There will be lots of time, Ellen. Three weeks at Amberley Court. Oh, life suddenly seems very good again. But you are not looking happy. I am being very insensitive. There is a sadness for you too, as well as happiness. Papa isn't here. He would never have known, would he?"

Ellen shook her head. "No," she said, "he did not know."

Ellen rose as soon as the men came into the drawing room, and stood behind the bench at the pianoforte, watching Madeline play. Jennifer stayed where she was, feeling her own happiness. Just a few months before, her world had seemed to end when her papa died. And yet she was now surrounded by family and friends at a party that was being given partly in her honor. And Grandpapa had said that she and Ellen must come to live with him when they returned from the country.

And Ellen was to have a child. She would have something of Papa left.

But Lieutenant Penworth was sitting alone in the darkest corner of the room. And he was shifting about as if he could not find a comfortable position, as if he were in some pain. Jennifer crossed to the tea tray, took two cups from her Aunt Dorothy's hand, and carried them over to the corner. She took a seat close to his and smiled.

"Would you care for some tea, sir?" she asked.

"Thank you," he said. "But you do not need to bother yourself waiting upon me, you know. You should be enjoying yourself with the other young people."

"I can enjoy myself here," she said, "with another young person."

"There is no enjoyment to be gained here," he said. "You should be at the pianoforte, singing or playing, and being admired."

Jennifer laughed. "I am afraid that if I sang or played," she said, "I would not be admired, sir. Would you not like to be closer to the pianoforte yourself?"

"It is better if I sit here," he said. "If I went over there, everyone would be falling over themselves to find me a chair and to speak kindly, as if I were an infant."

"You don't like kindness?" she said.

"Not particularly," he said.

"You would prefer that people ignored you or kicked your leg from under you?"

He stared at her rather coldly from his one eye. "You cannot possibly understand," he said. "When you have been in the best of health, when other people have treated you as an equal, then it is hard to find that everything—and everyone—has changed."

"But everything has changed," she said. "Nothing can be quite the same for you again. But people have not been unkind to you, have they? Perhaps you should be thankful for that at least."

"The very worst way in the world to be treated," he said, "is with pity."

Jennifer stirred her tea and lifted the cup to her lips. "You are right," she said. "I don't understand. I don't know what it would be like to be in your place. But I would think that the very worst thing in the world is to feel self-pity."

He was very angry. She could see that from the set of his jaw. "Self-pity!" he said. "To know that any stranger looking into my face for the rest of my life will either grimace with distaste or smile with embarrassed pity. To know that I will never again walk properly, never again ride, or sail a boat, or play cricket, or run. Or a hundred and one other things. I would be better off dead."

"My father is dead," she said, setting cup and saucer

down carefully beside her. "He will never see the sun again. Or feel its warmth. He will never see Ellen again, or me. He will never know love again or laughter or tears. And we will never have him with us again. Only a great heavy emptiness where he used to be. And you dare to envy him?"

"Yes, I do," he said curtly.

"Then you are greatly to be pitied," she said. "Not because you have lost a leg, and not because your face has been disfigured. Not because your life must change beyond recognition. But because you do not have the character to cope with those changes. Because you have allowed yourself to crumble beneath adversity."

"A very eloquent speech," he said with heavy sarcasm. "I thank you."

"I try to recognize the man I knew in Brussels," she said. "I liked him. He was sunny-natured, and he had a love of life, and a passionate desire to serve his country. I think I even felt a little jealous at one time that he seemed to prefer Lady Madeline to me. I can see him sitting before me, even though one side of his face is covered with bandages, and a pair of crutches rests against his chair. But I have mistaken. He is not the same man. I am sorry. I would have mourned that man with my father if I had known that he died at Waterloo."

His jaw was set very hard. He was choosing his words with care, she could see. But they were interrupted.

"Jennifer has brought you a cup of tea, Allan?" Madeline said, smiling warmly down at him. "That was kind of her. Did you hear me singing? I did so just for you. You are in some discomfort, aren't you? Shall I take you home? I am sure everyone would understand."

"We will stay here," he said. "I want you to enjoy the evening, Madeline."

"But I don't mind leaving," she said. "I don't want you to be in pain."

"We will stay," he said, his eye straying to Jennifer. "I will play a hand of cards as soon as the tables are set up. I am sure I can see well enough to do that."

"But of course you can," Madeline said, laughing in some amusement.

Jennifer excused herself and moved away. How unforgivably rude she had been. She had said herself just a few days before that Lieutenant Penworth would need more time to adjust to the harsh circumstances of his future. And yet she had just ripped up at him as if he were a sullen schoolboy.

Perhaps she should go back to him and apologize, she thought. But no, that would doubtless make matters worse. He would think she was pitying her. She went to the pianoforte and seated herself on the bench beside Anna.

ELLEN TOOK A SEAT between Edith and Mrs. Everett, and talked with them while they drank their tea. It seemed a safe place to be. But when their cups were empty, Edith took hers and Ellen's and crossed the room to return them to the tray. And she stayed there to talk with Dorothy. And Mrs. Everett was called away to play the pianoforte while Anna and Jennifer attempted a vocal duet.

The rest of the company were beginning to take their places at the tables for cards.

Ellen did not react fast enough. One of the empty chairs beside her was taken. And they were somewhat removed from both the pianoforte at one end of the room and the card tables at the other. Ellen clasped her hands in her lap and focused her attention on one of the tables. Lieutenant

Penworth was to have Susan Jennings for a partner, and Lord Agerton had Madeline.

"Well, Ellen," Lord Eden said quietly from beside her.

There was no reply to such a greeting, was there? Or if there was, she could not think of it. She said nothing.

"It appears you forgot to tell me something," he said.

"My lord?" Her eyes shifted to his legs, clad in blue knee breeches, but could not lift to his face.

"You forgot to tell me that our liaison had consequences," he said.

"You are referring to Sir Jasper's announcement at dinner?" They were very foolish words, she knew. But she could think of no others.

"I suppose there are not many men," he said, "who find out in just such a way that they have fathered a child. But under the circumstances I suppose I should be thankful that I found out at all. Tomorrow your secret would have been safe. Tomorrow I leave for Wiltshire."

"My secret?" she said. "It has not been a secret, my lord. I have told a few people. I had no occasion to tell you."

"Ah, of course," he said. "How foolish of me to think that I am of any importance in this matter. I merely planted the seed. I am merely the father. A quite irrelevant person once the seed has been sown. It is conceited of me to feel that I should have been told."

"I think you are under a misapprehension," she said. "It is Charlie's baby."

She could feel him looking at her. She watched the card games in progress at the other side of the room.

"I see," he said. "It was a happy coincidence, then, that after five years of marriage he finally got you with child at the last possible moment. Nothing shows yet. It must have been the last moment."

"Yes," she said. "A happy coincidence."

"Happy for the Simpson family," he said. "Very happy for Sir Jasper, who has a new grandchild to look forward to. Someone to replace the son he has lost and comfort him in his old age."

"Yes," she said.

"And happy for Miss Simpson, who will have a new brother or sister."

"Yes."

"Happy too for Mr. Phillip Simpson, who has thought himself his father's heir since June. He must be hoping with his father that the child is male so that the family property and fortune will be restored to Charlie's line again." He leaned toward her suddenly. "What did you say?"

She tried again. "Yes," she said.

"Ellen," he said, "I never thought you a coward. I have seen proof time and time again that you are capable of extraordinary courage. Now I see you are capable of extraordinary cowardice too."

She looked at him for the first time, her eyes flashing. "Prove it!" she said. "Prove that I am lying. Prove that the child is not Charlie's. That I am too cowardly to admit the truth. Prove it!"

He shook his head. "I cannot do so," he said, "and would not, even if I could. But you and I both know the truth, Ellen. You are carrying a child that is mine and yours. And it always will be ours, however much you wish it could be Charlie's, and however much you look for signs of him in the growing child. You will be fortunate indeed if it does not have green eyes."

"Charlie did not have green eyes," she said, "and I do not."

His eyes passed slowly and almost lazily over the other

occupants of the room, none of whom were paying them any attention. "You know, Ellen," he said, "you are fortunate that we are in such a public place and must pretend to be holding an amiable and quite unimportant conversation. Very fortunate. For the past hour or so, I have been in shock. I am only just beginning to feel anger."

"You have nothing to feel angry about," she said. "This has nothing to do with you, my lord."

"I want to pick you up with my two hands," he said quietly, "and shake you until your teeth rattle. I want to take you across my lap and beat you until you are too sore to sit down. Both of which acts I am saved from committing under present circumstances. And it is as well. I have never abused a woman physically and have never thought to. But I want to do you terrible violence, Ellen. And I am deadly serious despite the amiable expression I must put on for the other occupants of the room."

"I think we have already said everything that needs to be said between us," she said, hearing her own breathlessness, and unable to control it. "You should not be here, my lord. You said good-bye to me at your mother's house."

"We have not said one fraction of what needs to be said between us," he said. "I did not know at that time, Ellen, that you have my child inside you. You had chosen to deceive me, to keep from me what every man has a right to know. We have not by any means finished speaking, you and I. And will not be until you have the courage to look into my eyes and tell me the truth so that we can discuss like rational beings what we are to do about our child."

"My child will be well-cared-for," she said. "By me. You need have no fear of that."

"But this child is not yours," he said. "It is ours. It will be well-cared-for, Ellen. By you and by me. We will jointly decide where and how it will live."

"We will see," she said. "I believe you will find that you will not be allowed to harass me."

"I will take the risk," he said. "I have a child of mine to consider."

They sat side by side, both watching the card players, both apparently relaxed, both taut with anger and tension and awareness of each other.

"Ellen," he said at last, very quietly, "tell me the truth. Please? I loved you for those six days, and you loved me. It was a kind of love, anyway. At the time, it was very precious to both of us. It has gone and can never be rekindled, I suppose. But there has been that between us. Tell me the truth. I will not make trouble for you with your family. You may do what you wish with regards to them. But look at me and tell me the truth."

She felt quite incapable of either moving or opening her mouth. It would be so easy to do. And the right thing to do. It was what she wanted to do, to have part of the burden of a secret guilt removed. Even if she could not look at him. Just to say the words—*It is your child, Dominic.* Just to say them. It should be so easy.

She said nothing at all.

"The silent treatment, then?" he said at last. "That is all I am worth to you, Ellen? You cannot even look me in the eyes and tell me once more that I am mistaken?"

She stared straight ahead, her mind forming the words, knowing exactly what the words should be. Knowing how few and how simple they were and how much better she would feel after saying them. Knowing how the words needed to be said. Knowing that he had every right to hear them.

She said nothing.

He got abruptly to his feet. But one of the card games had come to an end without their noticing the fact. Susan Jennings had crossed the room toward them.

"Such a pleasant evening," she said, taking a vacant seat and smiling up at Lord Eden, who resumed his own seat. "Of course, Mrs. Simpson, you must feel, as I do, that it would be easier to remain at home alone and grieve. But one must make an effort to continue with life, mustn't one?"

"Yes," Ellen said.

"You are in many ways fortunate," Susan said, unfurling a fan and fanning herself slowly with it. "You have a daughter to take about with you. And you have another event to anticipate." She glanced archly at Lord Eden and laughed. "But we must not put his lordship to the blush by discussing such matters."

"Is Mrs. Courtney staying in town long, Susan?" Lord Eden asked.

"She talks about going home," she said. "Papa and the boys are so helpless when she is not there. But she knows that I need her. And she will not abandon me in my time of great need. It is a great comfort to have one's mother close, Mrs. Simpson."

Ellen inclined her head.

"You are going into Wiltshire tomorrow, my lord?" Susan said. "Your family will miss you dreadfully, I am sure."

"After Christmas," he said abruptly. "I will be going into Wiltshire after Christmas. I plan to spend a few months first at Amberley Court."

Susan's face brightened. "But how happy your mama must be," she said.

"Yes," he said. "She will be happy to have her family all together again at Amberley."

"Of course," Susan said, "I must be going into the country soon too. Mama is restless, and Lord Renfrew is about to betroth himself to Lady Penelope Varley, I believe, though he has been obliging enough to assure me that I may always have a home with him. I shall doubtless spend what is left of my year of mourning quietly at home."

"Then I shall look forward to seeing you there, Susan," he said.

"You are very kind," she said. "You will like Amberley Court, Mrs. Simpson. The valley and the beach and the cliffs. I am afraid of heights, of course, and can never enjoy the cliffs. I hope you are not as silly as I. I am sure I spoil everyone's enjoyment. You will find plenty to do there. And the young people will amuse themselves. Your stepdaughter will be happy there."

"I rather think Mrs. Simpson might qualify as one of the young persons, Susan," Lord Eden said.

Susan looked at him with large, remorseful eyes. "Of course," she said. "Pardon me, ma'am. I did not mean to imply . . . Why, I daresay you are not above five or six years older than I. It is just that you were married longer, and your husband was older than mine. And of course, you are *enceinte*. But I did not mean to imply that you were old."

"Mrs. Jennings, ma'am." Sir Jasper was smiling down at all three of them suddenly. "Mr. Winslow is in need of a partner for the next hand. Would you oblige?"

"Why, certainly," she said. "It is very kind of you to ask, I am sure, sir."

Lord Eden too got to his feet, though he stayed for a moment when the other two had moved away.

"You will be able to get out the words at your leisure,

Ellen," he said. "You are to be at Amberley for three weeks? Or do you plan to change your mind about going? Do so, if you will. But you will not escape from me. You will tell me the truth, with your eyes on mine, before you can hope to see the last of me."

"I shall be going to Amberley Court," she said. "I do not change my mind as easily as you seem to do, my lord."

He nodded and turned away. "We will talk further there, then," he said. But he turned back after taking only one step in the direction of the tables. "Have you seen a physician, Ellen?"

"Yes," she said.

"And is all well?" he asked. "There have been no recurrences of the fainting spell? I assume it was your condition that caused that."

"The doctor says I am in the best of health," she said.

He looked at her broodingly before moving away abruptly.

ELLEN DID NOT SLEEP at all that night. The accusation of cowardice had cut to the heart of her guilt. And the more so because she had no defenses against it. He had been quite right. She was a coward.

Less than a month after the death of her husband she had conceived another man's child. And rather than admit that fact to the world, she had allowed other people—members of Charlie's family—to believe that it was his. She had never lied to them. But she had allowed them to believe a lie, and that was just as bad. Now she seemed to be in a quite hopeless situation.

But worse had happened. She had finally lied outright. She had told Dominic that the baby was Charlie's. A pointless and an unnecessary lie. Why had she said it? She could not answer her own question. It had been wrong, of course, to withhold the truth from him in the first place. She had realized that all along. But to lie to him when the truth was out was utter madness. And she did not know why she had done so and why she had not been able to put the matter right when he had given her the chance to do so.

Oh, yes, she was a coward. She had prided herself so much on her independence, on her ability to survive even the crushing blow of Charlie's death. And yet she was too cowardly to admit that the child she was carrying was illegitimate. Even though she was not ashamed at all of its illegitimacy. Even though she had loved its father when he had begotten it in her.

She slipped out of the house the following morning and had the carriage drop her outside the Earl of Harrowby's house. She willed him to be at home, not to have departed for one of his clubs already. But she need not have feared. It was too early for him to be abroad. She had to wait in the morning room while his valet hastily dressed and shaved him.

Ellen was nervously pacing the room when he finally made an appearance. She shot across the room almost before he could get any greeting out, and straight into his arms.

"Ellie?" he said, one large hand going to the back of her head. "What is it, girl?"

"He has found out," she blurted into his neckcloth, "and I lied to him and told him it is Charlie's. And if it is a boy, he will be Sir Jasper's heir. And Phillip will be defrauded. Papa. Oh, Papa, I have made such a mess of things. And me five-and-twenty years old. I have made such a mess of things."

"Ellie," he said, rocking her comfortingly in his arms,

"we all make a mess of life sometimes, girl. But there is usually a way out if we want it dearly enough."

She closed her eyes and let the comfort of his arms flow over her.

"Come into the breakfast room with me," he said. "Have you had breakfast? And you shall tell me what it is you were trying to tell me just now. It didn't make much sense, Ellie, girl. It is the father who has found out?"

She nodded against his neckcloth and lifted her head away from him. "I didn't have breakfast," she said.

Sometimes, she thought afterward, one did not need anything more to help one solve one's problems than a truly sympathetic ear. Her father had said very little. She had done most of the talking. He had not given any advice or any comment on what was right or wrong. He had offered to go with her to Sir Jasper Simpson's, and she had been very tempted to say yes. But she had not. She had decided herself what must be done, and she would do it alone. She was very much afraid, but she would do it.

"Papa," she said when she was leaving, wrapping her arms about his neck and standing on tiptoe so that she might lay her cheek against his. "Papa, the very worst thing I ever did was to turn my back on you, thinking that somehow it was the honorable thing to do. I don't care if you are my real father or not. I really don't care. You are my papa, and that is all that matters."

"And this is your home," he said, patting her reassuringly on the back. "You must come here, Ellie, when you come back from Amberley's home. You must not rush into buying a place that you may not really like. You must come here. I'll stay sober if you come home, you know."

She withdrew her cheek from his and smiled up into his

face. "No, you won't, Papa," she said. "Be honest. But it does not matter. I love you anyway."

He smiled a little sheepishly.

And so the visit to her father-in-law was made, where Ellen lived through surely the most uncomfortable half-hour of her life. And could not collapse with relief even when it was over, because it had to be repeated with her sister-in-law.

She asked only that Jennifer not be told. She would tell the girl in her own time. At the end of the visit to Amberley, she planned. Indeed, she was somewhat surprised that someone did not suggest that she was no fit companion for Jennifer and should not accompany the girl into the country. But no one did say that. In fact, Dorothy was not even unkind and did not order her from the house.

It had all been a lot easier—and many times worse— than she had anticipated.

LORD EDEN HAD a few confrontations of his own to face before leaving London behind him.

His twin did not even allow him the night in which to get used to the totally new fact of his life. She came to his dressing room soon after he had escorted Susan home, and came inside without waiting for his valet to answer her knock. He dismissed his man.

"Dom," she said, leaning back against the door, "did you know?"

He did not pretend ignorance. "No," he said.

"It is yours?"

"She says not," he said.

"I saw you talking to her." She pushed away from the

door and came toward him. "Is there any chance that she is lying, Dom? You were lovers, weren't you?"

"She says it is Charlie's," he said, turning away from her.

"Oh, Dom," she said, "I am so very, very sorry. And tomorrow you leave. And you will never see her again."

"I am going to Amberley," he said.

"Oh." There was silence for a moment. She sounded almost her normal cheerful self when she broke it. "You are going to fight, then. I am glad to hear it. She is by far the most sensible female who has ever taken your fancy, Dom."

"She has not taken my fancy," he said. "There is nothing between us, Mad. Except this, of course. There are a few matters to settle, that is all."

"Yes," she said, "that is all." She reached up to kiss him lightly on the cheek and whisked herself from the room. She paused as she was closing the door. "But that is quite enough, Dom. I know it. I feel it in my bones." She laughed lightly as she shut the door.

Edmund was not nearly so sympathetic or so easy to deal with. It was a mere courtesy call Lord Eden made to inform his brother of his intentions. He found him in the library.

"What is happening?" the earl said with a frown. "You are coming to Amberley, Dominic?"

"You don't need to look quite so enthusiastic," Lord Eden said with a grin.

"I am not particularly enthusiastic," his brother said. "We have invited guests. I think you know that one of them may not welcome your presence there too."

"Ellen?"

"Well, you tell me," the earl said. "Will she mind your being there, Dominic? I don't know quite what happened in Brussels, and I do not know what has happened since. And

I would not presume to pry. But she did not look overjoyed to see you when you arrived here a few afternoons ago."

"She knows I am going," Lord Eden said, "and says that she is still planning to go too."

Lord Amberley looked uncertain. "Well," he said, "there is not much I can say, then, is there? Amberley is your home, Dominic. I would never dream of closing its doors to you. But I will make one thing clear. I will not have Mrs. Simpson harassed. Is that clear?"

"I feel like a young boy who has been hauled onto the carpet," Lord Eden said. "I will not harass her, Edmund. But I have to be there. Do you understand?"

"No, quite frankly, I don't," his brother said. "But you are an adult, Dominic. I will not even try to tell you how you should behave, beyond what I must do to protect a guest in my home, of course."

"Of course," Lord Eden said. "I will take myself off, then, Edmund." But he paused with his hand on the library door. He did not turn his head. "You will doubtless hear it from Madeline or Anna. I might as well tell you myself. She is increasing."

He continued on his way out of the room.

19

*B*EING AT HOME AGAIN AFTER SUCH A LONG absence was a pleasure too deep to put into words, the Earl of Amberley found. Fortunately for him, he was able to communicate with his wife at a level beyond words, and he knew that she shared his happiness. It seemed incredible to him that there could ever have been a time without Alex. Yet they had been married for only a little longer than three years.

His guests arrived only a scant day after his own family, and at the same time the Carringtons were coming home, bringing with them Walter's friend Lord Agerton. And Susan and Mrs. Courtney had decided to travel down in their company.

There were visits to receive—from large, genial Mr. Courtney, who was beaming with delight at the prospect of having his beloved daughter and his wife home once more, and from the rector, who brought the local news, including the fact that Miss Letitia Stanhope was recovering from a severe chill and that his dear helpmate was in expectation of a happy event. The happy event had been an annual one for a number of years.

And there were visits to be made—to the Mortons and the Cartwrights, to the Misses Stanhope and the rector's wife, to Mr. Watson. And to his dearest friend, Sir Perry Lampman, and his family. And of course to the laborers on his estate.

There were guests to entertain. He spent the whole of a morning showing off Amberley Court to Mrs. Simpson and her stepdaughter. And he spent more than an hour of the afternoon showing Lieutenant Penworth the music room and the long gallery, before the latter tired and sat at a window in the gallery to look out along the valley that led to the sea and the cliffs. Madeline stayed there with him.

The earl and countess organized a dinner party on the first full day their guests were in their home. There were to be twenty persons present.

"Twenty!" the countess said in some amazement. "Is it possible, Edmund? There seemed to be only a handful when we listed them off. But now when I write the names down, I find there are twenty."

"It is just that we are familiar with almost all of them, Alex," he said, "and do not feel there will be any great effort involved in entertaining them all. Now, twenty strangers would be a formidable prospect."

"Yes," she said, "I suppose you are right."

The Carringtons were invited with Lord Agerton, Mr. and Mrs. Courtney with Susan and their eldest son, Howard, Mr. Watson, and Sir Peregrine and Lady Grace Lampman.

Ellen was enjoying herself in a somewhat tense sort of way. It was not comfortable to be in the same house as Lord Eden, of course, and she fully expected that he would find the opportunity soon to carry out some of the threats he had made at her father-in-law's house. But so far he had stayed away from her. He had been out visiting friends much of the time. He had sat talking with his sister and the lieutenant for hours on end. He had accompanied Jennifer to the Carringtons'.

But if she could ignore what she knew must be coming, she could feel a certain contentment. The house and its surroundings were quite magnificent, though she had not yet seen the sea or been up onto the cliffs or been inland along the valley, all of which she had been told they would do during the next few days.

And the earl and countess were kindness itself, and treated her as a real friend rather than merely as a guest in their home. The countess had taken her to the nursery to see the children, and had marveled again that the baby was willing to come to her, though she did not smile. She rarely smiled for anyone except her father, Lady Amberley had explained.

The dowager countess was equally kind, as was Lady Madeline, though her time was taken up mainly with her betrothed.

And yet they must all know. They must know that she was with child. And they must suspect that it was not her husband's. Yet nothing was said, and there was no detectable hostility in their manner.

She sat between Mr. Carrington and Sir Peregrine Lampman at dinner and was thoroughly entertained by the humor of both. She could not remember when she had laughed quite so much.

And after dinner, when some of the young people went downstairs to the music room and Susan Jennings held court to Mr. Watson, Lord Agerton, and Sir Peregrine, telling them of her dreadful experiences in Spain, Ellen sat with Lady Amberley and Lady Lampman, who talked of their children.

"We are being dreadfully rag-mannered," the countess said after a few minutes. "I am afraid, Mrs. Simpson, that we mothers of young children become dreadful bores when we discover other ladies in like case. Grace has a daughter just a little older than Christopher, and a son a little older than Caroline. And I must make sure, you see, that my two cut their teeth and smiled and crawled and slept through the night, and so on and so on, at no later an age than hers. It would be shameful to find that mine had lagged behind." Her eyes twinkled as she spoke.

"We have to make a desperate effort not to match Christopher with Rose and Paul with Caroline," Lady Lampman said. "It would be the depths of degradation for us to become matchmaking mamas, Mrs. Simpson. But Paul's fair coloring would be a wonderful complement to Caroline's dark beauty, Alexandra."

All three of them laughed.

Ellen liked Lady Lampman. At first she had thought the Lampmans quite mismatched. Sir Peregrine, with his laughing eyes and relaxed, amiable manner, must be several years younger than his wife, whose slim, upright figure and narrow face and dark coloring gave her a rather severe appearance. But there was a quiet charm about her that became obvious on closer acquaintance.

And Ellen had noticed an exchange of looks between husband and wife at the dinner table. There had been nothing very significant. She had not smiled, though there had suddenly been a great depth to her gray eyes. He had smiled, though more with his eyes than with his facial muscles. It had been an entirely private and very brief interchange that had made Ellen's stomach quite turn over inside her with a longing and a nostalgia.

"You must tell me something about yourself, Mrs. Simpson," Lady Lampman was saying now. "You lost your husband at Waterloo, I understand. I am so very sorry. Is it painful for you to talk about him?"

"No." Ellen smiled. "For a few months I thought of him continuously and unwillingly—it hurt quite dreadfully. But I am beginning to remember with some pleasure. He was, I think, the kindest man I have known." She proceeded to tell them about Charlie's habit of buying her gifts for no reason at all except that he felt like doing so and knew they would give her pleasure.

And then the moment came. Just at a time when she was relaxed and enjoying the company of the two ladies who she felt could be real friends.

"Would you care to walk in the formal gardens, Ellen?" Lord Eden was standing in front of their chairs, his head inclined toward her. "Susan and Agerton, Anna and Howard have decided that they must take the air."

Ellen looked at him and nodded, resisting her first impulse to make some excuse—any excuse. The moment must be faced. There was no point in putting it off. Somehow tonight she must find the words to tell him what he wanted to know, and what he had a right to know.

"You will need a cloak," he said. "There is no wind, and it is rather a lovely evening. But of course it is autumn."

"I will fetch one," she said, getting to her feet and turning to the other two ladies to excuse herself.

JENNIFER HAD GONE downstairs to the music room with Anna and Madeline, Mrs. Carrington, and the dowager countess. She listened while her two friends played on the pianoforte, and stayed at the instrument after they had crossed the room to sit with their mothers.

She had never been an accomplished musician. The music mistress at school had despaired of her when it seemed that she always had an excuse for having neglected her practicing. She would be sorry one day, the teacher had warned, when other young ladies were playing their way into the admiration of handsome young men.

It had sounded a little silly to Jennifer. Was the playing of a pianoforte the only way to a man's heart? And did only handsome men appreciate good music?

She sat down on the bench and played quietly to herself from the music that was propped against the stand. She was quite competent enough to play for her own amusement. She had no wish to play for an audience anyway.

"Are you going to play again?" a voice said from behind her when she was finished, and she jumped and turned in some embarrassment to find Lieutenant Penworth standing there, leaning on his crutches.

"Oh," she said, "I did not know anyone was listening. I'm afraid I am not good."

"Fairly competent," he said. "There was something missing in the expression and feel for the music, I must confess."

Jennifer was unreasonable enough to feel offended. "The piece is rather difficult," she said. "Perhaps there is something easier in the pile." But even as she reached out for it, she turned and looked at him again. "You are wearing just a small eye patch. I saw it as soon as we arrived, but have not had a chance to tell you that I had noticed."

He propped one of his crutches against the pianoforte and seated himself at the end of the bench next to her. "Everyone has noticed," he said. "How could they fail to do so? My face is a repellent sight. I wish now that I had not come."

"Repellent?" she said in some surprise. "It is a great improvement on those bandages."

He gave a bitter little laugh.

"Let me see." She leaned forward over the keyboard so that she could see the right side of his face, which was turned away from her. "It is indeed a nasty scar. It curves all the way around from your eye to the corner of your mouth. And it is rather livid at present. That is because it is still quite new and because you have kept it covered for so long. In time it will fade, no doubt."

He laughed again.

"I think," she said, still peering around into his face, "that in time it will not be unsightly at all. In fact, I think it might make you look rather distinguished. And certainly very heroic."

"Don't mock me," he said.

She clucked her tongue. "Your sense of humor is something else you left behind on the battlefield of Waterloo," she said. "You really should learn to laugh at yourself a little, sir. And if you find people shunning you, you know, it is only because you have such a ferocious and morose manner. It is not because of your appearance. I feel sad for you."

"Don't pity me!" he hissed vehemently through his teeth. "For God's sake, don't pity me. I am mortally sick of being pitied."

"I have no intention of pitying you," she said tartly. "One has to like someone in order to pity him, does one not? You go out of your way to make yourself disagreeable, sir. I really do not know how Lady Madeline can tolerate you."

"Perhaps because she is a lady," he snapped back.

"And I am not," she said, straightening her back. "Perhaps

you had better move away, sir. I am about to murder your ears with my music again. Unless you want to turn the pages for me, of course. I suppose you can be a gentleman even if I am not a lady."

"My right hand is occupied," he said, indicating the crutch that he still held, "and my left hand is clumsy. But I will try."

"Are you always going to have your crutches?" she asked. "You would have your hands free, would you not, if you had an artificial leg?"

"And I would doubtless fall flat on my face with every step I took," he said. "I think not, Miss Simpson. Other people can find some other spectacle with which to amuse themselves."

"Did it ever cross your mind," she asked, "that other people might have better things to do with their time than stare at you?"

"Meaning that I have a false sense of my own importance," he said. "Thank you, ma'am. You are always so very pleasant."

"There is nothing forcing you to stay here," she said, beginning to play, and finding that every finger was on the wrong note. But she played valiantly on. "I can turn my own pages, thank you very much. And you see? I am playing abominably and no one is noticing. It is a foolish and a conceited thing to imagine that everyone's attention is focused on oneself."

"Oh, my dear," Mrs. Carrington called, smiling kindly and nodding from the other end of the room, "that is a difficult piece of music, is it not? Would you like Anna to help you find something simpler?"

"No, thank you, ma'am," Jennifer called back, lifting her

fingers from the keyboard immediately. "I have just finished."

She looked at the lieutenant out of the corner of her eye, and the next moment they were both bent forward behind the music rest, tortured by smothered laughter.

"Let me try it," he said, "and see if I can do a little better."

All of Jennifer's amusement fled. "Oh," she said, "I suppose you are an accomplished musician, and I shall end up feeling doubly mortified?"

He did not say anything, but slid along the bench when she rose to stand behind him. He answered her question by playing the piece without a single error and—worse—by making sheer music of it.

She was very glad to see Madeline strolling across the room toward them. She was thereby released from the necessity of making some comment when he had finished.

"You play so well, Allan," Madeline said when he had finished, one hand resting on his shoulder. "You are a real musician."

"I have something to amuse myself with, you see," he said, "even if I cannot indulge in more manly pursuits."

"What a good thing it is," she said, "that you have real talent."

Jennifer admired Madeline's endless cheerfulness and patience. She would have retorted that of course it was considerably more manly to play cricket, chasing a hard ball around a field for a number of hours, than to create beauty with one's hands. And her own tone would have been quite as heavily sarcastic as his had been when he spoke to Madeline.

What a horrid man he was, she thought. And felt guilty at her own intolerance. He had suffered a great deal. And he had made a fast physical recovery from his injuries. It was all very well for her, with two arms, two legs, and two eyes, to criticize. She would do well to learn from Madeline, to become more ladylike and more compassionate.

"Are you tired, Allan?" Madeline was asking. "Shall I help you to your room? I will make your excuses to Alexandra. She will not mind at all."

"Yes, I will withdraw," he said. "But I can manage quite well on my own, thank you, Madeline. And I will stop in at the drawing room to bid Lady Amberley good night. Miss Simpson?" He nodded curtly to Jennifer.

"It was nicely done," Ellen said when she was standing with Lord Eden out on the terrace. "I could scarcely say no in front of your sister-in-law and her friend, could I? And I suppose we are to take a different direction in the formal gardens from that being taken by the others?"

The other four were making their way along the gravel walks in the direction of a stone fountain at the north end of the gardens.

"Precisely," he said. "Take my arm, Ellen, and let us relax and enjoy the coolness of the evening for a time. My anger has cooled too since the last time we spoke. I am not planning either to shake you or to beat you, if that is what you are afraid of."

"I am not afraid," she said. "I am not afraid of you, Dominic."

They walked along the paths; the sound of their own footsteps and the faint sounds of the conversation of the other group were the only things to break the silence. They were making their way toward the companion fountain of the other, at the south end of the garden.

He broke the silence at last, when they had rounded the

fountain and were out of sight of the others. He set his back to the stone basin and crossed his arms on his chest.

"Well, Ellen," he said, "I have something to say to you."

"Yes," she said. She was facing away from him, looking along the valley.

"It is not, perhaps, what you expect," he said. He laughed softly. "My brother has told me in no uncertain terms that I will not harass you while you are a guest in his home. Besides, I have had time to think. Time for both shock and anger to have receded."

She said nothing. She continued to gaze along the darkened valley.

"Ellen," he said, "I know that it is my child you are expecting. We both know that. And I want to have some say in the future course of my son's or my daughter's life. But there will be time for that. Time for arguments and quarrels. It is not an urgent matter. The child is safe with you for another six months. A mere father is very irrelevant in that time."

She turned to look into the shadows where he was standing.

"I liked you, Ellen," he said. "I don't know of a woman whom I have more admired and respected. You are a very strong person. There was a peace and a comfort in your presence. I did not fully realize at the time that you were part of the reason why I liked to come home with Charlie. I think you liked me too. You always made me welcome. You never made me feel that I was intruding. You never made me feel foolish when I fell asleep in your rooms. You used to laugh at me, and at Charlie. What happened to our friendship?"

"You know very well what happened to it," she said. "We

destroyed it. Together. I don't blame you any more than I blame myself."

"By sleeping together," he said. "By turning to each other for physical comfort when we should have contented ourselves with emotional comfort."

"Yes," she said.

"Three years," he said, "balanced against six days. Should we let a bitterness, an estrangement, stand between us when we had three years of friendship and only six days of the other?"

"I can't look at you without remembering," she said. "I can't just pretend it did not happen."

"But there is a friendship even apart from that," he said. "There was even during those days, Ellen. It would be wrong of us to remember it only as a physical passion. I want to know you again. I want to know what you have been through during the past few months. I want to become your friend again during your weeks here. Do you think it is possible? And before you answer, I want to tell you this. If you say no, I will leave here tomorrow. That is a firm promise."

"Dominic!" She came toward him, and stopped a few feet away. "I don't know if it is possible. I don't know."

"Are you willing to try?" he asked.

She bit her lip. "I don't know."

"Do you want me to go away?"

"No," she whispered. She stared at him in the darkness. "But I cannot promise ever to be comfortable with you. I cannot promise that we will ever be friends again."

"I can't either," he said, and he reached out to brush the backs of his knuckles along her jawline. "But I want us to be, Ellen. I want to be able to see my child after it is born, and it will be easier to do if I am on friendly terms with its mother."

She said nothing.

"It is my child, Ellen, isn't it?"

She was a long time answering. "Yes," she said finally.

There was a further silence.

"Well," he said at last. "I did not mean to force that out of you. I have not been setting a trap for you. We will talk about it much later. Just before the child is due to be born, perhaps, unless you broach the topic with me before that. For the time, let's try to pretend that none of that happened between us, shall we? Let's be friends."

She drew a deep breath. "I'll try," she said. "Yes, I want to try, Dominic. I was very fond of you. Charlie loved you as a son, or as a younger brother."

He set his hands on her shoulders suddenly, bent his head, and kissed her once, hard and briefly, on the lips. "Let the healing start tonight, then," he said. "The Battle of Waterloo left so many wounds behind, Ellen. Those of us who survived are only beginning to realize how deep some of them went. Look at poor Penworth. And look at us."

They were interrupted at that moment by the sound of a bright and laughing voice from the other side of the fountain.

"I am very jealous," the voice of Anna said. "Dominic has disappeared from sight with a lady who is not me. If it were anyone but Mrs. Simpson, I should be sharpening my claws."

She was laughing when she came around the fountain on the arm of a rather shamefaced Howard Courtney. Lord Eden was standing upright. Ellen was again several feet away, looking down the valley.

"Anna," Lord Eden said, "I would tell you to watch your manners if I thought you had any to watch."

She laughed again. "Howard thinks I am horribly wanting in conduct too, don't you, Howard?" she said. "And you are quite right, both of you. I am suddenly glad of the darkness, which hides my blushes."

"I am very glad of your arm, my lord," Susan said timidly to Lord Agerton as they too appeared around the fountain. "I would be quite terrified to be out here unescorted. Is not that foolish when we are on Amberley land?"

"It is quite understandable for a lady to feel that way," Lord Agerton said gallantly.

"It is time to go indoors for supper, I believe," Lord Eden said. "The air is somewhat fresher than fresh."

"I wish my cheeks did not feel so hot," Anna said contritely.

"Serves you right," her cousin said uncharitably.

"I am afraid I grew too accustomed to having my husband's escort everywhere I needed to go," Susan said.

Ellen took Lord Eden's arm and succeeded in lifting her eyes all the way to his chin.

LORD EDEN WAS feeling restless later that night. He could not even think of lying down, let alone sleeping. He took a candle and went downstairs to the conservatory, always a favorite thinking place for him and his sister. And his candle jumped in his hand when it picked up her shadow. She was sitting silently behind a large fern.

"You almost gave me a heart seizure," he said. "This seems quite like old times."

She smiled. "Yes," she said. "I can't tell you how good it feels, Dom, to see you at home again, and to know that you are not off back to the wars in a few days' time. Those were bleak times."

"But all over now," he said, seating himself beside her. "And by hook or by crook, I have come back in one piece. What's troubling you?"

"Does something have to be troubling me?" she asked. "I couldn't sleep, that's all."

"This is your twin," he said, taking her hand in his. "You can tell me if you want. Or we will just sit quietly until we feel sleepy if you don't."

"Allan and I quarreled," she said.

"And it's serious?"

She shrugged. "I don't know," she said. "Maybe it wasn't even a quarrel. I don't know. We didn't yell or throw things as you and I used to do when we fought. But then, you and I always used to forget our rage once we had thrown a few punches. I can't shrug this off."

He sat quietly waiting.

"He went to bed early," she said. "He was tired and in some pain. I know. I recognize the signs. He wouldn't let me help him to his room, though there were two flights of stairs to climb. And he insisted on going in to make his excuses to Alexandra. I went with him to the door of his room anyway."

"It sounds as if your boy is getting some of his spirit back," he said.

"He was thoroughly out of sorts when we got to his room," Madeline said. "And when I mentioned tomorrow, he said I must go riding up the valley with everyone else, and I said that I would prefer to stay with him and read to him. And he was rude about the book we are reading. And . . . Oh, dear, this all sounds so very childish when put into words."

"You said he was tired," he reminded her gently. "He was probably irritable and did not mean half of what he said."

"He did apologize," she said, "when he saw that I was hurt. He said he had not meant it about the book. And he said that the reason he wants me to go riding is that I must enjoy myself and I must have a life separate from his. You see? I said it was not really a quarrel. But it is always happening, Dom. And he is always apologizing to me."

"I think he is recovering, Mad," he said. "I think he needs to feel his independence again. Especially, perhaps, from you, who have tended to his every need even during those weeks when he did not want to live."

"You think he does not want to marry me?" she asked.

"I didn't say that." He squeezed her hand reassuringly. "But he needs to feel that he can do things for himself. And he needs to know that he is not spoiling your life."

"But I have been so happy looking after him," she said. "I have been so in love with him. I know what it is, Dom. I think I need him now more than he needs me. Oh, what a lowering thought. Is it true, do you think?"

"I've no idea," he said. "I have used up my stock of wisdom for one night. But the relationship is changing, Mad. That is clear. Somehow you have to be prepared to change with it."

She sighed. "I suppose you are right," she said. "I wish for once life could be simple and predictable. And then I would probably be screeching with boredom. Should I go riding tomorrow, do you think?"

"Without a doubt, yes," he said.

"Hm," she said. "But I would far prefer to stay with Allan, you know. But enough of me. What is your problem?"

"I don't have any," he said.

"Don't even try it, Dom," she said. "Don't even try it."

He laughed softly. "It's nothing I can discuss," he said. "Not even with you."

"Mrs. Simpson?"

· "Ellen, yes."

"I won't pry, then," she said. "Dom, we must be growing up at long last. We haven't had a decent fight since we both came back to England. How dreary life gets!" She laughed and laid her cheek against his shoulder. "Are you ready for bed yet? I'm not. Shall we just sit?"

"Mhm," he said.

It was his child. He had known it, of course. But she had finally admitted it. It was his child. And Ellen's. There was going to be a child of his own in the world in just six months' time. He closed his eyes and gave himself up to the wonder of it.

And she was not sending him away. He had taken a great gamble, telling her like that that he would go away the next day if she did not want him to stay. He had not planned to say that. The idea had come to his mind unbidden. But she did not want him to go away. She wanted to try to recapture the friendship they had once known.

He had three weeks. Three weeks in which to get to know her again, in which to persuade her to trust him and to like him. To feel comfortable with him.

Three weeks.

And could it be done? Could they be friends? Would they have ever been friends if Charlie had not been there between them? He knew that it was difficult for a man and a woman to be close friends without a physical awareness intruding. Could he and Ellen ever be just friends? Wouldn't there always be something else?

And did it matter if there was something else? Would it

be so disastrous if they loved too? If they wanted each other physically?

Didn't he still love her anyway? Still want her?

But he must close his mind to such thoughts. First and foremost he needed to make a friend of Ellen. He had to do so. It was the only way he could be certain of remaining close to his child. And they could not be friends if she suspected that he still harbored any of those feelings that he had shown her quite freely in Brussels.

His only hope was to quell any love he might still feel for her.

"Sleepy?" he said to his sister. Her head jumped against his shoulder, and he laughed. "Come on, sleepyhead. Let's get you upstairs to bed."

ELLEN WAS SITTING on the window seat in her room, her knees drawn up against her, her cloak drawn about her for warmth. She was staring down at the moonlit formal gardens below, where she had walked just a few hours before.

She had finally admitted the truth to him. And it had, after all, been easy. She felt as if a great load had been lifted from her shoulders. He knew. She had told him.

She had also told him that she did not wish him to go away. She had had a chance to be rid of him. She did not think he would have gone back on his promise to leave the next day if she had said that she wanted him to go. But she had deliberately given up her chance to be rid of him.

She shivered and huddled further inside the cloak. She had said that she would try to allow a friendship to grow between them again. Was it possible? Could they ever be just friends when there had been that other between them? When their child was in her womb?

And did she really want his friendship? Could they be friends and be comfortable and contented again, and Charlie not there to share the friendship with them? Didn't she need to punish herself for the rest of her life for the way in which she had betrayed Charlie with his friend?

Was that what she was doing? Was she punishing herself? But she had forgiven herself and Dominic long ago. Hadn't she? Or had he been right a few hours ago when he had said that the wounds of Waterloo ran a great deal deeper than any of the survivors realized?

If it were not for the guilt, would she still love Dominic? Beneath the guilt, had she stopped loving him?

But no. She did not love him. She must not love him. He wanted to know their child. He wanted to see it as it grew. That was perfectly understandable, and she knew she would not be able to deny him that right. She must not complicate matters by falling in love with him again. That would be far too painful for her, and embarrassing too if he ever suspected.

He wanted them to be friends. And it was desirable that they be so. She wanted it to be so. She would try. For three weeks she would try to let friendship grow and other feelings remain dead.

She shivered again as she heard more than one set of quiet footsteps pass her room. She was not the only person mad enough to be still up, then. But she must get to bed and to sleep if she was to be fit to ride in the morning. Besides, she was half-frozen.

He had kissed her. And she had not been outraged. She had felt enormously comforted by the brief touch of his lips.

A mad thought. One very definitely not to be repeated.

20

ALL THE ADULTS OF THE HOUSE, EXCEPT THE
dowager countess and Allan Penworth, joined the
ride the following morning. Anna and Walter and Lord
Agerton rode over to join them, as did Susan and two of her
brothers. They were to ride inland up the valley in which
Amberley Court was set.

It was a very good thing that they were to ride in a place
where it would be impossible for the horses to move faster
than a walk, Susan said timidly to anyone who was willing
to listen. She was so very afraid to gallop, and she knew that
she spoiled the enjoyment of her companions when she
held them to a walk.

Lord Agerton declared that he would stay at the back of
the group with her, and she could move at whatever pace
she found comfortable.

"You are very obliging, my lord, I am sure," she said, favoring him with a look of melting gratitude from wide
hazel eyes.

They rode out, two abreast, past the formal gardens,
across the stone bridge that spanned the stream, and
turned up the valley, the sounds of the horses' hooves

muted by the masses of fallen and rotting leaves underfoot.

"There is always a very special smell about autumn," the earl said to Ellen, with whom he rode. "I suppose it should be unpleasant, since it is largely the smell of decay, but it is not."

"It is a very English smell," she said. "I had forgotten it. It is strange how smells can bring back vivid memories. My father used to take me walking in the parks when I was a child. We would always walk on the grass during the autumn so that we could crunch leaves underfoot. They were happy times."

"Are you glad to be back in England?" he asked.

"Yes," she said. "I do not regret my ten years as a wanderer, because I learned a great deal about life that I might not otherwise know. And I had my husband for five years. I was happy. He was all the home I needed during those years. Besides, it is foolish to regret anything from one's past. Everything that happens helps to shape us into the people we are. But I am glad to be home again. I would not wish to settle permanently in any other country."

"But you are quite right," he said. "People are really home, are they not? I have always been greatly attached to Amberley Court. If anyone were to take it away from me, I think I would die a little inside. But if ever I had to make the choice between this place and my wife and babies—well, there would be no choice at all."

Lord Eden had Anna prattling at his side, telling him all about the triumphs of her Season during the spring, reminding him of her disappointment that he had not been there to see her or escort her at all, confiding her hope that her father would take her again the following spring.

"Then you can come too, Dominic," she said, "and lead me into the first set of the first ball of my second Season."

"I probably would not be able to fight my way past all the young bucks clustered about you, Anna," he said.

"Oh, but I would send them all away," she said, "so that you could sign my card first. For two sets. I wonder who it was who made the foolish rule that one can dance only twice with the same gentleman in the same evening. Don't you think it silly, Dominic?"

"It depends on how badly I want to dance with one particular lady," he said.

He was watching Ellen riding ahead of them with his brother. They were doing a great deal of talking and smiling. There was a certain satisfaction in knowing that she and Edmund and Alexandra got along well together. She looked happy this morning, and very lovely in her black velvet riding habit. It brought back vivid memories to see her on horseback.

They rode along a valley that was beautiful despite the bareness of the trees. The stream flowed past them on its way to the sea. The tree-covered slopes grew steeper as they proceeded, and the valley floor narrower.

Lord Amberley stopped when they had ridden for more than a mile. "There is a magnificent view back along the valley to Amberley and the sea from the top of this slope," he said to Ellen and the riders behind them. "It is rather a steep climb, I'm afraid, and has to be done on foot, but it is well worth the effort. Is anyone feeling energetic?"

It seemed that everyone was. They all dismounted, the gentlemen tethering the horses to the trees. Lord Eden turned to find Ellen. He wanted to be with her when she saw the view.

"Oh, dear," Susan said at his elbow, while Lord Agerton

was still busy with her horse, "I think I had better stay here, my lord. Climbing up might be possible, but I know I would be terrified to come down again. I have no head for heights. I shall be quite all right down here. I shall take a turn along the bank of the stream and back."

"What, Susan?" Lord Eden said with a grin. "You can never be so chickenhearted. You, who used to climb trees in pursuit of trapped kittens?"

"But I always used to get stuck," she said. "And someone had to come to my rescue."

"I have a sturdy arm," he said. "Will you trust it to keep you from falling? I will not let you slip, I promise."

"Oh, thank you," she said. "You are very kind."

Anna and Jennifer, Walter and Miles Courtney were having a race to the top of the slope, with a great deal of crashing through the trees and shouting and shrieking. The others ascended somewhat more sedately. Susan hung heavily on Lord Eden's arm and forced him to frequent stops, with the result that they were soon far behind the rest.

"I am spoiling your enjoyment," she said.

"Not at all." He smiled down at her. "You were always such a timid little thing, Susan. How is it that you could survive a life of following the drum for three whole years?"

"It was not easy," she said. "I found it very difficult, my lord. But I felt that I must stay close to my husband, you see."

He covered her hand with his. "Of course," he said. "Do you miss him, Susan?"

"Life must go on," she said, accepting the large linen handkerchief that he held out to her. "I would not burden you with my grief, my lord. It is good to be home with my family and friends. That is, if I may take the liberty of calling you my friend, my lord."

"Well," he said in some amusement, "if I am not your friend, Susan, I don't know who is."

By the time they reached the clearing almost at the top of the slope, it seemed that everyone else had already looked his fill. Except for Ellen, who was still gazing downward, back along the valley the way they had ridden to the house and its gardens and outbuildings, and to the distant line of the sea.

"Well, here comes Susan at last," one of her brothers announced.

"You are not to think naughty thoughts," she scolded loudly. "Lord Eden was merely helping me ascend the slope. I am so foolish that I had to rest several times. Nothing else was happening at all."

Howard Courtney flushed, and Lord Amberley exchanged a look with his wife. Madeline paused in her conversation with Lord Agerton and looked closely at Susan. Lord Eden, too, looked down at her, startled, and across to Ellen, who still had her back to him. Susan released his arm and strolled across to join her.

"It is a lovely view, is it not?" she said. "It was very bad of Howard to suggest what he did just now. I am all of a blush, Mrs. Simpson. All because Lord Eden was my beau before I chose my husband instead of him. I am afraid that I hurt him badly at the time, but that was a long time ago. And you and I know that being a widow ousts all thoughts of beaux and romance quite out of one's head. The very idea!"

Ellen smiled. "I don't believe anyone thought any such thing," she said.

"Oh, I am not so sure of that," Susan said. "Just consider what Anna said about you last evening. She was merely being silly, of course, you being in mourning for your husband and in a delicate situation besides. But I felt for you even so. It is painful to be accused of flirting, is it not?"

The younger people were beginning the descent with as much noise and enthusiasm as they had shown on the way up.

"Come, Susan," Lord Eden said from behind the two ladies. "I have enlisted Agerton's support for the descent. With one of us on each side of you, I don't think you could fall even if you tried."

"Oh," she said, "how kind you are. I am such a silly goose, Mrs. Simpson."

Ellen, looking at Lord Eden for the first time that morning, found herself smiling back when he grinned and even winked at her.

When they were all at the bottom of the hill and mounted again, Lord Amberley gave them the choice of continuing on up the valley or returning to the house.

"Oh, do let us continue," Jennifer said eagerly, and immediately clapped a hand to her mouth. "That is, if everyone else wishes to do so, of course, my lord."

But it seemed that everyone did—the most vocal elements of the group, anyway.

"It seems we are not to see anything of our children this morning after all," Lord Amberley said apologetically to his wife.

"Doubtless they will survive," she said. "Mama had promised to paint with Christopher, apparently. What sort of disaster that may lead to, I shudder to think."

They both laughed.

"We will take them for a ride down onto the beach this afternoon, shall we?" he suggested.

"That sounds like heaven, Edmund," she said with a smile.

A mile or so farther upstream, they came to faster-flowing water and a trail of old stepping-stones spanning its width.

"Aha, they are still here," Lord Eden said. "Walter, Howard, are those stones in the center not the very ones we placed there three years or so ago? The old ones had disappeared, I recall."

"Yes, they are," Madeline said, riding up alongside her brother. "I recognize the very flat one in the middle. The very solid and safe one. It does not look near as much fun as the one that used to wobble there when we were children."

"Do you remember the dunking I got once when I fell in?" Lord Eden said with a grin. "What were we doing at that particular time? Crossing backward, or on one leg, or blindfold?"

"We did them all at one time or another," Howard said. "I think it was blindfold and backward when I got wet—and had a thrashing for it when I got home."

"Do let us go across," Anna said. "There are the ruins of an old abbey at the top of the slope opposite, Jennifer. I want to show it to you."

Lord Eden groaned. "Oh, the energy of the young!" he said, dismounting and lifting first his cousin and then Jennifer to the ground. "Away you go, then, children. We older folk will follow at a more sedate pace."

Anna pulled a face and turned toward the stream.

He lifted Madeline to the ground. She stood staring ahead along the bank of the stream.

"It was just along there," she said, "that he kissed me for

the first time. The last time I was here, Dom. It seems like forever ago."

"Purnell?" he said. "So it was. I believe I was walking Susan along the opposite bank—because she was afraid to cross over—and nobly resisting the urge to kiss her. Oh, Lord! Another lifetime, Mad."

Susan, who had been lifted to the ground by the earl, was protesting quite clearly and timidly that she could not possibly set foot on one of the stepping-stones, not if her life depended on it. She looked appealingly at Lord Eden.

"And I have no intention of going across either, Susan," Lord Amberley said. "I have had quite enough violent exercise for one day, I thank you. You and I will stroll along the bank together and tell each other how foolishly all these children are behaving. Shall we?"

"Oh," Susan said, glancing at Lord Agerton, who was helping the countess across the stones, and at Lord Eden, who was tethering Ellen's horse to a tree. "You are very kind, my lord."

"Not at all, Susan," he said. "I will be glad of the company."

"I am sure you do not need my hand," Lord Eden said with a smile at Ellen. "I have watched you cross much worse without assistance. But I must play the gentleman, you see, in case anyone is looking." He stretched out a hand to her.

She placed hers in it and followed his lead across the stones, which were indeed sturdy and safe.

"Do you want to go up?" he asked when they reached the other side. "Or shall we stroll along the bank here? Is it wise for you to have so much exercise?"

"Perhaps not overmuch," she said. "The stroll sounds good. But perhaps you want to stay with the others?"

"I think I will be safe with you," he said with a grin.

She took his arm and they strolled slowly along the bank and among the trees, which grew right to the water's edge on that side of the stream. It was good to have the bitterness behind them, she thought, to be able to think of him, however cautiously, as a friend again. His arm felt strong and reassuring beneath hers. She did feel rather tired from the ride.

"You grew up in a very beautiful place," she said.

"Yes." He looked down at her. It was only just beginning to register on his mind that this was Ellen Simpson and that she was at his childhood home with him and that they were walking together, their arms linked, in quiet harmony with each other. "We had something of an idyllic childhood. Madeline and I were as wild as could be, and always into the most hair-raising scrapes. And Edmund was no better, from what I have heard. Perry Lampman used to be his particular partner in crime. Until Edmund was forced to grow up very fast at the age of nineteen, when our father died."

"That must have been a hard time for you," she said.

"Yes," he agreed, "but our father had always lavished a great deal of affection on us, and that held us together after he was gone." He grinned. "Unfortunately, affection did not lighten his hand when I was into some trouble. My only hope was that Madeline was in it with me. He would never beat her, you see, and could not in all conscience beat me for a shared offense."

She smiled up at him. "I find now," she said, "that I am able to picture the places where several of those stories you told me took place." She remembered suddenly where she had heard those stories and waited for the pain of embarrassment. But he had been right in what he had said the night before. There had been more between them during those days in her rooms than just the physical. She had sat on a chair and he had lain on the bed, hand in hand, getting to know each other.

"Yes," he said. "This in particular was a favorite playground."

"I have reconciled with my father. Did you know?" she asked.

"You did go to visit him, then?" he said. "I am glad, Ellen. I remember stories you told me of your childhood, and I understood that you had been fond of him."

"He still drinks," she said. "Worse than ever, I believe."

"Does that upset you?"

She considered. "Only for his sake," she said. "He is not a happy man. He believes he really is my father, Dominic."

"Does he?" He smiled at her. "Perhaps I should be calling you 'Lady Ellen,' then."

"He wants me to go and live with him when I leave here," she said.

"And are you going to?" he asked. "You are not going to move into your father-in-law's house?"

"No," she said. She stared straight ahead of her along the path. "I told him the truth before I left town. And Dorothy too. I will not be going back to them."

He resisted the urge to draw her more closely against his side. He concentrated every effort of will on being a comfortable, friendly presence for her.

"Well," he said, "I am happy you have found your father again, Ellen. Everyone should have someone he can call his own."

"I always felt safe with him," she said, looking up at him and smiling. "When he held my hand, nothing in the world could harm me."

"That is what fathers are for," he said.

"I always felt that way with Charlie too," she said, looking deliberately into his eyes to dispel instantly any awkward-ness that that name would arouse between them. "All the dirt and the discomfort, the tedium, the danger, mattered not one bit when Charlie was there. The whole of the French army could not have harmed me if his arms were about me. It was only when he was in battle that I was afraid. And then I was always mortally afraid."

"Yes," he said quietly. "War is cruel on wives and mothers."

They strolled in silence for a couple of minutes. He could feel the tension in her and could only walk quietly at her side and hope to bring her reassurance.

"Tell me," she said finally, her voice trembling. "I want to know. I must know. You said you were with him when he died. Tell me how it happened. Tell me about those few days. I have to know."

"I don't think he suffered," he said, curling his fingers be-neath hers as they rested on his arm and holding her hand tightly. She had quickened their pace. "He did not die in agony, as so many poor men did. He just . . . went away, Ellen. I saw he had been hit and went to him. He recognized me, and he said your name and Miss Simpson's name. But I don't think he heard anything I said in reply. He went too quickly. And then I was hit immediately after."

He could see that she was biting hard on her lower lip. "There was a man," she said. "I had him brought to my rooms from outside the cathedral. He was getting wet. He was going to die, but I did not want him to die wet and alone. He was not unconscious, but he was halfway there into death. He was past pain too, like Charlie. I sat with him and held his hand while he died. I wondered if someone else was doing as much for Charlie."

"He knew I was there," he said. "He was not alone."

He could see that her eyes were bright with tears, but she would not give in to them. "Tell me the rest," she said. "Tell me the whole of it. He lived for three days after I last saw him. I want to know about those days."

He began with the tedious hours they had spent at Mont St. Jean waiting for the order to march that had apparently gone astray. And he told her about the march south to Quatre Bras and the battle there and the trudge north the next day through the rain and the mud and with the French coming up on them and peppering them with shot. He told her about the night spent sleeping on the muddy ground and about the part of the Battle of Waterloo that he had seen.

"It was just one battle too many," she said when he had finished. "But I hope it was the last. I hope it is all over now. For Mrs. Byng's sake, and Mrs. Cleary's and Mrs. Slattery's. I'm glad you have told me. I have wanted to know for a long time. And have dreaded knowing. I have had nightmares in which he has been screaming and writhing in agony."

"No," he said. "You need not have them any longer, Ellen. I have told you the truth. I have not covered it up for your comfort."

"That had crossed my mind too," she said, smiling fleetingly. "Thank you, Dominic. I am glad you were there with him. If I could not be with him myself, I am glad it was you. He loved you."

"I think the only thing that kept me going on that ghastly ride back to Brussels," he said, "was my need to bring you the news myself. I didn't want anyone else telling you. Or no one at all."

She nodded and stopped walking suddenly. She was fighting an inner battle, he could see. He took her firmly by the shoulders and drew her against him. He did not kiss her. He laid his cheek against hers and rocked her in his arms.

"I shed all my tears for him long ago," she said. "I am not going to cry all over you. But it is such a relief to know. Such a relief, Dominic. Perhaps I will be able to start letting him go now. A part of me still expects him to walk through every open door."

"I know," he said. "I know." And he closed his eyes and rocked her and wondered at the enormous self-delusion that had ever made him imagine that he had mistaken his feelings for her in Brussels. He held her to him and allowed her to take from him the comfort she needed, and smelled that familiar fragrance from her hair and felt the slim grace of her body. Still slender—she was not yet swollen with their child.

She rested her cheek on his broad shoulder and closed her eyes. And gave herself up to the comfort of his warm and strong body, his circling arms. And was glad that she had asked him, glad that he had told her. And glad that he had come into Charlie's life and into hers more than three years before. He had comforted Charlie as he lay dying, and now he was there for her too.

She raised her head finally and looked up into his eyes. She touched his cheek with her fingertips. "Dominic," she said, "I have never stopped liking you, you know. You were a good friend to Charlie. I am glad we have been able to get back beyond that other again. Thank you for telling me."

He smiled down at her.

"The others will think we are lost," she said, stepping back from him and smiling more brightly. "Though I have not heard any stampede down the hill yet. Have you?"

"You cheated," Lord Amberley called from the opposite bank as Lord Eden was handing Ellen back across the stepping-stones. "You did not climb after all. Susan and I were at least honest about our laziness, were we not, my dear?"

"Ah, but we put our lives in peril by venturing across these stones," Lord Eden said cheerfully. "We did not cower on this side, did we, Ellen?"

"We also risked the danger of being run over by those exuberant children if they had chosen to come back down," Ellen said. "Here they come now. Oh, dear, is that Jennifer shrieking? Or is it Anna? What hoydens! This is very good for Jennifer, my lord, though I fear it is sending her back into childhood. I am very grateful to you for inviting us here."

The earl glanced from her to his brother and back again. "I dare to hope that it is good for both of you, ma'am," he said, turning to lift Susan back into the saddle. "You are looking well. Is that my wife actually running down the slope? Perhaps it is a blessing that I do not have a quizzing glass about me. May I lift you up too?"

"If you will just give me a boost, my lord," Ellen said, "I can mount myself."

"No you won't!" Lord Eden took the two strides that separated them. "I will lift you, Ellen."

Lord Amberley looked in mingled amusement and curiosity at his brother and turned to grin at his wife, who was part of the group crossing noisily over the stepping-stones.

THE EARL AND COUNTESS invited anyone who was interested to join them in a walk on the beach during the afternoon, but they did warn that the outing was intended for the children and would be focused on them.

The dowager countess suggested a drive into the village of Abbotsford—after they had all rested from the exertions of the morning, that was. She had looked with particular significance at Ellen. The shops did not have a great deal to offer, she explained, but it was a pretty place. And they might call upon the Misses Stanhope, who would be delighted to make their acquaintance, or on the rector's wife, if they could extricate her from her rapidly growing brood of hopeful children.

Ellen and Jennifer agreed to the drive.

Allan Penworth too was to rest after luncheon. Madeline walked upstairs with him, careful not to offer him any assistance at all.

"It is a beautiful day," she said. "You will probably enjoy sitting in the churchyard or outside the inn while the rest of us look in the shops. You will like the village."

"I intend to spend the afternoon outside painting," he said. "I had a long talk with your mother this morning, and she has lent me all the necessary equipment."

"Oh, good," she said. "Where are we going to go? Onto the terrace?"

"*We* are not going anywhere," he said. "You are going with the other ladies to enjoy an afternoon in the village. I am going to the other side of the bridge to paint the house."

"You will need someone to carry your easel and your brushes and things," she said. "I will be quite delighted to help you, Allan. I can visit the village anytime."

"There are such people as servants," he said. "All I need to do is ask for help. It is a very simple matter."

"But I want to stay," she said. "I miss those days, Allan, when we were always alone together. Let's do something together this afternoon."

"A few minutes ago," he said, "you were full of enthusiasm for showing off your village to Mrs. Simpson. You don't need to give up that pleasure for me, Madeline. I will be quite happy painting alone. I prefer to be alone when I paint. I can concentrate better."

They came to a stop outside his room.

"You really don't want me with you, do you?" she said. "I am getting on your nerves, Allan?"

He looked exasperated. "No, you don't get on my nerves," he said. "Have I said the wrong thing again? I have, haven't I? I have hurt you again. I don't seem to be able to help doing so these days, though I never mean to do it. Stay with me, then, Madeline, if it is what you really wish to do. I would like that."

"I think we should end our betrothal," she said in a rush, her voice not quite steady. She looked about her hastily to make sure that the corridor was deserted.

"What?" he looked at her, incredulous. "Have I hurt you that badly? I must be a far worse brute than I thought. I merely wanted you to have a pleasant afternoon, free of the necessity of fetching and carrying for me. Come, Madeline, don't overreact. Smile at me and say you forgive me."

"It is not just today," she said. "And it is not your fault. Perhaps this was inevitable, Allan. You are recovering and regaining your independence. You don't need me any longer."

"Yes, I do," he said, reaching out for her hand, which she kept clasped in the other one in front of her. "I wouldn't be alive now if it were not for you. Do you think I can ever forget that?"

"I'm not blaming you," she said. "You did need me, yes. You leaned on me for a long time. And I made the mistake of thinking that you would always need me like that. It was very naive of me. You don't need me now, and I have to be happy for you that you don't."

He tried to laugh to relieve the tension. "Can we not just love each other?" he asked. "Does there have to be any need? Any dependence? Can we not just have a normal, happy marriage?"

She shook her head slowly. "I don't think so," she said. "I don't think we love each other, Allan. Not in that way."

"I love you," he said. "You are very, very special to me. I owe you my life and my sanity."

"I love you dearly too, Allan," she said. "But I don't think we could make a marriage of it. We are too different from each other. We would bicker and bicker and come to thoroughly dislike each other before we had been married a year. I don't want that to happen. I am too fond of you."

He shifted his weight on his crutches and blew out air from puffed cheeks. "I can't quite believe I am having this conversation," he said. "You always seemed so unattainable, you know. Lady Madeline Raine, whom everyone admired. I did not think you had even noticed me. And now I feel as if I am the one who has let you down. I have made you unhappy."

"No, not you," she said. "You really are not to blame for anything, Allan. I am only unhappy with myself. My life seems to have been one string of self-delusions. Yet this time I was so sure. Oh, never mind. We must be thankful that we have come to our senses before it is too late."

"I will make arrangements to leave tomorrow, then," he said.

"Oh, no!" She reached out a hand to touch his arm. "No, Allan. That would cause unbearable pain and embarrassment. Please stay. You like Mama and Edmund and Dominic, don't you? And you are painting and playing the pianoforte. You are gaining more independence here. Stay awhile."

"I don't want to cause you any unpleasantness," he said, frowning. "If you want, I will stay for a few days longer, then. I'm sorry about this, Madeline. More sorry than I can say."

"Well," she said, smiling, "at least we have been able to put an end to a betrothal without hurling things at each other's heads. We are still friends, are we not?"

"You will always be my friend," he said. "I will always love you, Madeline."

"Like a sister," she said. "It will be better that way. You are in some pain, standing there, Allan. Go inside your room now and lie down for an hour. And do it. Don't pace the floor brooding on what has just happened."

"Yes, ma'am," he said, raising one hand in a smart salute and smiling at her rather ruefully.

21

RAIN STARTED AT SOME TIME DURING THE
night and continued to fall for the following two
days. A most miserable sight, Madeline declared to anyone
who was prepared to sympathize, when one had been im-
prisoned in a city for months on end and now had boundless energy to work off. She promised Ellen and Jennifer
that on the next fine day they would ride down onto the
beach and perhaps even climb the steep path up to the
clifftop.

"That way you can see both places during the same outing," she said. "That is, if the rain ever stops and the mist
ever lifts."

But for the time being the mist hung low over the valley
and a fine rain came steadily down. Lord Eden took Jennifer
to visit the Carringtons on one day and the Courtneys the
next. The earl and countess divided their time between
their children and their guests. Madeline and Ellen sat in the
music room a few times, listening to Lieutenant Penworth
play. And the dowager countess spent time with him in the
portrait gallery, the two of them discussing the paintings
there.

Ellen declined the chance to be a part of both visits. She felt a little tired after the day of the ride and the visit to the village, and felt the need to spend some time quietly indoors. Alone, even, if she could be so without appearing rude to her hosts.

She was not actively miserable. Indeed, she felt a certain contentment that she had not felt since Charlie's death. But she needed to live through those last days of his life as Dominic had described them to her. She needed to fill in the gap that had yawned empty and frightening for so long. She had said good-bye to him in their rooms—she could still see him, eager to be on his way, to have done with the pain of parting, his eyes devouring her—and then there had been nothing. Only Dominic, through his pain and his fever, telling her that Charlie was gone. And only her realization weeks later that it was true. And only that walk over the churned-up land south of Waterloo where she knew he was buried with thousands of other men.

She needed to live through in her mind what he had lived during those days. She needed to watch him die. And she needed to accept his death. She needed to let him go.

Charlie had been her husband. Dearly, dearly loved. But "had been" were the key words. He was dead. He was a part of her past. Always to be remembered. Always to be cherished in memory. But in the past.

And at last she could think of him with only a dull ache of longing. At last she could remember and smile at some of the memories. The terrible raw agony of her grief was over.

And she had a future to look ahead to. She had felt her child move in her.

"That climb up the cliffs is really quite dangerous, though very exhilarating," the countess said to her as they sat together in the morning room, stitching. "And it is very strenuous to go up. The first time I did it was in the opposite direction. And Edmund would allow it only after I had promised faithfully to cling to his hand every step of the way. We were betrothed then." She smiled at the memory.

"I am looking forward to seeing the sea again," Ellen said. "It seems strange that we are so close and have not yet seen it."

"English rain!" the countess said. "You know, what I have been trying to say as tactfully as possible is that perhaps you should not tackle that climb. I will stay down on the beach with you if you wish, and we shall stroll along like a couple of respectable matrons."

"Because I am increasing?" Ellen asked.

The countess lowered her head over her work. "We have heard about that, naturally," she said. "Your father-in-law did make a public announcement."

"I am feeling quite well," Ellen said, "and do not get as tired as I did at first. But I think you are right. I shall take the walk on the beach without the climb."

"I am glad for you," the countess said. "You are good with children. You are happy about it, aren't you?"

"Yes." Ellen put down her own work on her lap. "Oh, quite ecstatic. I didn't think it would ever happen to me. I had quite resigned myself to being childless."

"It is the most wonderful feeling in the world, is it not?" Lady Amberley said, smiling warmly at the other. "One feels heavy and uncomfortable and lethargic at the end, and then there is all the pain of the birthing. And when it is over, one feels that one could never ever go through such a dread experience again. But then a few months later, one thinks that perhaps after all one can do it one more time." She laughed. "I am at that last stage at the moment, and very envious of you."

The dowager countess too found the opportunity to advise Ellen not to do anything too strenuous.

"Young people are quite, quite mad, my dear," she said, "and feel that they must ever be squandering their energy. But you must not feel that you have to keep up with them. Edmund and Dominic and Walter will see to it that your stepdaughter is kept safe, you know."

"I have already decided not to climb the cliff, ma'am," Ellen said. "I just wish the rain would stop so that I may at least see the cliff."

They both laughed.

And Ellen marveled again how both ladies could be perfectly aware of her pregnancy and doubtless suspected its paternity, and yet could treat her with such quiet courtesy and even friendliness.

Lord Eden found her on the second afternoon when she had sought out some privacy in the conservatory. She was stitching at her embroidery. She smiled at him and returned her attention to her work.

But of course she was very aware of him, standing tall and straight with his back to her, looking out at rain-soaked lawns and trees. His hands were clasped behind him. They were fidgeting.

She stitched on, his tension conveying itself to her. And yet he did not look tense when he turned to face her. He was smiling.

"I am afraid I frightened Miss Simpson on the way home from the Courtneys' just now," he said. "The roadway down the hill opposite is very steep. I told her not to worry if the carriage slid a little in the mud. The coachman had been with Edmund for almost a year without having an accident. The one before him lasted only six months."

"And I suppose the road is quite safe?" Ellen said.

"Oh, assuredly." He grinned. "And the coachman was my father's before he was Edmund's. But she is made of stern stuff, your stepdaughter. I felt sorry for the deception when she only turned white and clung to the strap and did not scream at all."

"Wretch!" Ellen said, laughing despite herself. "I hope she ripped up at you when she realized the truth."

"She was so brave," he said, "that I did not have the heart to tell her."

There was an awkward little silence after they had both laughed again, and Ellen dipped her head to her embroidery.

"Ellen," he said, "I think we should marry."

She looked up at him, her needle suspended in the air.

"I know that you are not even halfway through your mourning period yet," he said. "I know that you loved Charlie and still love him and always will. And I know that you are able and willing to take care of this child on your own, Ellen. But even so, it will be an illegitimate child. You have chosen not to try to give it the respectability of Charlie's name. Let it have my name, then. Marry me. Will you?"

"No, Dominic," she said. "No, it would not be right."

"Why not?" he asked. He stooped down in front of her so that he could look into her face. "It seems to me the only right thing to do."

"I have been married once," she said. "It was a good marriage. We loved each other. I couldn't contemplate a loveless marriage."

He winced slightly. "I know you don't love me," he said. "I would not expect that, Ellen. But listen to me. There are three of us here, not just two. I can get up and walk away from you and live the life of my choice. You can leave this place and go to your father or find yourself a place in the country and live the life of your choice. But there is someone else who has no choices. Someone who will go through life with the label of bastard. Do you want that?"

"I will use my free choice to love the child every moment for the rest of my life," she said. Her eyes were on his hands, which held her wrists so that she could no longer sew.

"It won't be enough, Ellen," he said. "And all the money and superior schooling I will be able to offer will not alter the fact that in the eyes of the world the child will be my by-blow."

She closed her eyes.

"Marry me, Ellen," he said. "If you love our child, marry me."

"We will grow to hate each other," she said. "There is only one good reason for marriage, Dominic, and in our case it does not exist."

"Then we must make the best of what we have," he said. "We don't hate each other now, Ellen. We like each other. You admitted that to me just the other day. And we both want the best for the child we have created together. There is no reason why we cannot have a perfectly contented marriage."

She bit her lower lip and looked at him, shaking her head. "This is all wrong, Dominic," she said. "It does not feel right."

"Then we'll make it right," he said. His hands had moved from her wrists to clasp her own hands tightly. "Say yes, Ellen. It's the only decent thing we can do."

She clung to his hands and looked into his green eyes, fixed anxiously on her own. And felt trapped. She had had very little choice the first time, except to throw herself on the charity of Charlie's sister in London. So she had begged him to marry her. Now she had even less choice. She must make the baby her main consideration, and that left her with no personal choice at all.

Two forced marriages. The only difference was that the first time she had known that Charlie loved her, that she had a chance of making him happy and therefore of making herself happy too. This time she was being married entirely out of a sense of duty to a person who was only a part of her at the moment, but not really her at all.

He did not know the stresses and strains of marriage. Her love for him would become a hopeless thing and would sour and die. Her love would become a chain about his neck, and he would fight it and come to hate her.

And their child would be caught in the middle, as she had been caught between the jealousies and hatreds of her own parents. And yet without marriage, the child would be called bastard, would never be quite respectable.

There was really no choice at all.

"Yes, then," she said. "I'll marry you, Dominic."

He squeezed her hands so hard they hurt. "You won't be sorry," he said, lifting one of those hands to his lips. "I'll see to it that you will never be sorry, Ellen. Shall I make the announcement tonight?"

"No." She pulled her hands from his and rose to her feet. She turned away from him. "No, not today. Jennifer doesn't know yet. I . . . I haven't found the right moment to tell her. Give me a few days."

He stood behind her, his hands on her shoulders. "As many days as you want," he said. "Don't feel rushed. And, Ellen, don't be unhappy. I don't want to see you unhappy. It will work out for the best, you will see."

She turned toward him, a determined smile on her face.

"For a newly betrothed couple," she said, "we are being rather gloomy, aren't we? We must try to be fond of each other, Dominic. And to share with each other. I have felt the baby move in the last few days. I don't think it is imagination. I have felt it more than once."

"Have you?" His eyes widened and looked deeply into hers. And he smiled, a warm, joyful smile that lit up his whole face.

She nodded.

ON THE THIRD DAY, not only had the mist lifted and the rain stopped, but the clouds had moved off altogether and the sun shone. A brisk, fresh breeze brought with it the salt smell of the sea.

Jennifer wandered out onto the terrace after luncheon, impatient for the arrival of Anna and the others from the Carrington house and Miles Courtney from the other direction. When they came, they would all be able to leave for the long-promised ride to the beach and climb to the clifftop.

Lieutenant Penworth was standing on the terrace, propped up on his crutches.

"What are you planning to do this afternoon?" she asked.

"Paint," he said, "or play the pianoforte or read. My choices are myriad."

"I'm sorry," she said. "It was a perfectly civil question."

He looked across at her and away again. "I am going to wait until you all leave," he said, "and go to the stables to have the fastest horse left there saddled. Perhaps I will not even wait for it to be saddled. And I am going to ride up the hillside and gallop out onto the cliffs."

"I said I'm sorry," she said. "Was my question tactless? But one cannot forever be tiptoeing around you, you know. I am sorry that you cannot ride and walk with us, but the fact is that you cannot. So am I to pretend that I am not going to be doing those things? Am I to pretend that I am not looking forward to them? Am I to pretend afterward that I did not really enjoy myself? That would be nonsense, and you would know that I was patronizing you, and you would be even more annoyed than you are now."

He grinned suddenly and quite unexpectedly. "Little spitfire!" he said. "You remind me of one of my sisters. Never a day passed without our having a good fight."

"She has my profoundest sympathies," Jennifer said.

"I will say one thing," he said. "After I have had the pleasure of conversing with you, I invariably feel angry enough to throw things. And on the whole, I think that is better than the mild irritability I feel with most other people."

"Madeline should be made into a saint," she said, "for putting up with you. I would certainly never do so."

"Ah," he said, "but you have never been asked to."

"That was such a glorious set-down," she said, "that I will not even try to cap it, sir. I see that the Carringtons and Lord Agerton are on the way. I am going to enjoy myself. Good day to you."

LORD EDEN RODE at the head of the group with Anna. He had been somewhat amused to notice her maneuvering to have him as a partner. And yet not entirely amused. She was no longer a little girl to be indulged by an older cousin whom she had chosen to make her hero.

Besides, he was a betrothed man. Soon to be a married man and a father. It amazed him that he had been able to live through almost twenty-four hours without blurting his secret to Edmund or to Madeline. Or to someone. He felt distinctly like a child with a precious new toy.

It didn't matter that she did not love him, that she had agreed to marry him only because he had convinced her that their child would suffer if she did not. The fact was that she *had* agreed to marry him. She was his betrothed. He would bring her to love him by very slow degrees after they were married. In such a way that she would not feel threatened, that she would not feel disloyal to her memories of her first husband.

And in the meantime he would withhold the truth from her. She would never marry him if she suspected that his feelings for her were as powerful as they had been during that week when they had been lovers. A sense of honor would make her draw back.

But no matter. On such a day and in such surroundings, one could feel boundless optimism.

"And Papa keeps saying no, but all the time he winks at Mama," Anna was saying, "so I know he means yes. Oh, it will be so splendid next year, Dominic. I will not be over-awed as I was this year, and I will already know a few people. And you will be there, and everyone will see me with the most handsome gentleman in London. You will be there, won't you? You really must come."

He smiled at her. "I plan to become lord of my own manor immediately after Christmas," he said. "I may well be enjoying myself so much that I will decide to rusticate, Anna. I really can't promise anything."

"Oh," she said, "you could not possibly be so horrid. After you were away all last spring. You know I have had my heart set on it forever, Dominic. Tell me you are only teasing me."

"I wonder," he said, "if your riding skills have improved since I rode with you last. Do you think you can race me to the beach?"

"You are about to play your usual trick of galloping off while I am still replying, aren't you?" she cried, and she shrieked and dug her spurs into her horse's sides.

Lord Eden grinned and watched her go for a few seconds before going in pursuit of her.

"He will overtake her, poor girl," the countess said to Ellen. "No one in living memory has ever raced Dominic on horseback. I was foolish enough to try the first time I rode down onto the beach. He was at the appointed rock and dismounted already before I came up to him. It was a dreadful humiliation." She laughed.

Lord Eden stopped when grass gave way to sand. He reached up to lift his cousin down.

"Anna," he said, "while we have some privacy, my dear, we need to have a little talk."

"Oh, dear," she said. "And you have that serious look. I can guess about what."

"Can you?" he said. "You are my cousin, dear. I am very proud of your beauty and your vivacity. I have been delighted to hear of the success of your first Season, and not at all surprised. And I am very, very fond of you."

She grimaced.

"And that is all, Anna." He kept his voice firm, though his eyes looked gently enough down at her.

"I know that," she said. "I have always known that, Dominic. But old dreams are sometimes hard to let go of."

"Some young man is going to be very fortunate," he said.

She pulled a face. "I had one offer in the spring," she said.

He smiled. "Did you? You did not reject him on account of me, I hope."

"Oh, no," she said. "I found him stuffy."

"Then he certainly would not do," he said.

"Don't make fun of me, Dominic," she said. "I am not a child. I know I frequently behave like one, but I don't feel like a child. And I can be hurt."

He brushed one finger beneath her chin. "I was not making fun," he said. "Whoever you choose, Anna, will have to be very special. I absolutely insist on it. Because you are very special. A ray of sunshine, no less. And I know that you are not a child and that you can be hurt. If you were still a child, I would probably allow this fantasy to continue. And if I did not know you could be hurt, I would not have challenged you to this race so that I might talk privately with you. I don't want you hurt, Anna. This must end now. Understood?"

She sighed and peeped up at him, rather shamefaced. "Yes," she said. "Just assure me of one thing, Dominic. You are not going to marry Susan, are you?"

"Susan?" he said. "Good Lord, no. Whatever gave you that idea?"

"She did," she said. "She is always telling Jennifer and Mrs. Simpson how you used to love her and how she broke your heart by marrying Lieutenant Jennings. And you were kissing her on the hill the other day, were you not?"

"Good Lord!" he said. "No, I was not. And no, I am not about to marry Susan, Anna. I can even make that a promise, if it will make you feel better."

"It will," she said.

"I promise, then," he said. "Now, let's tether these horses so that the stablehands who come to fetch them afterward will not have to search over miles of country to find them. And here come the others."

They all left their horses and walked across the beach for

about a mile to a large black rock that was almost directly at the foot of the narrow pathway that snaked its way up the almost sheer face of the high cliffs.

They were fortunate that the tide had only just started to come in, Lord Amberley explained to Ellen, taking her arm through his. If it were right in, there would be no climbing, as the water came right up to the cliffs.

"Has anyone ever been cut off by the tide?" she asked.

"Perry and I once as lads," he said. "We sat on top of the black rock and dared each other to be the first to leave. By the time each of us realized that the other was just not going to give in, the water was swirling about the base of the rock. Fortunately, it never does reach to the top. Those were long and cold hours while we were there."

"Your parents must have been worried," she said.

"They saw us from the top of the cliffs," he said, his eyes twinkling. "Unfortunately we could see them too, and a knowledge of how much less comfortable we would feel when our fathers' hands got to us did nothing to make the hours pass more pleasantly."

"I suppose you never did it again," she said.

"I can remember having to lie facedown on my bed for at least an hour after my father had finished with me," he said. "No, we did not do it again. We were very inventive Perry and I. We always found new mischief to get ourselves into."

They both chuckled.

"Will your memories make you a more indulgent parent?" she asked.

"Not at all," he said. "I promised Alex before our marriage that I would never lay a violent hand on any children of ours. And I won't. But I am sure I will think of some other perfectly satisfactory punishments. And I will need them. I already recognize the occasional gleam in my son's eyes."

"Oh," Jennifer said when they reached the rock and she gazed up the cliff that towered over them. "We are going up there? Is it possible?"

"You have to cling to the rock by your teeth in places," Walter said. "But it is possible. It is not for the fainthearted, though."

"Well," she said, "my teeth are as strong as the next person's, I suppose."

"I'll scramble up this first cluster of rocks, then," he said, "and haul you up after. Once you are up on the path, it is just a matter of putting one foot in front of the other and not freezing when you are halfway up."

"You are a wonderful builder of confidence," she said, setting her hands on her hips and watching him climb up the first few feet, which the tides had worn sheer and smooth.

"It is really not as bad as it looks," the countess said reassuringly. "The path widens as you get higher, and is really quite firm underfoot."

"You may wish to avoid looking down," the earl said.

"Here you are, then," Walter said, kneeling on the path and reaching down a hand for Jennifer's. "You must keep hold of my hand when you are up here."

Madeline and Lord Agerton, Anna and Miles followed them up.

"You had better go up to see that they all behave themselves," the countess said to her husband, drawing a grin from him in response. "Mrs. Simpson and I are going to walk on the beach."

"Oh, I do wish I could go up too," Ellen said. "This sea air is marvelous. And the view must be lovely from up there."

"We will drive up there tomorrow," the countess said.

Lord Eden smiled down into Ellen's wistful face. "Do you want to go now?" he asked. "We can take it very slowly. We do not have to keep up to the others."

"Dominic!" Lady Amberley said.

"Oh, I would love to," Ellen said. "Do you think I might?"

The countess looked appealingly to her husband. He merely raised his eyebrows to her.

"We'll stop every few feet for you to rest," Lord Eden said. "And you needn't look so cross with us both, Alexandra. This is a lady who has tramped and ridden through mud and searing heat, and forded swollen rivers and crossed the Pyrenees Mountains into France. Ellen is no wilting flower."

"But she has never been pregnant before," his sister-in-law said.

"Alex." The earl held out a hand for hers. "You are merely trying to avoid having to make the climb yourself, aren't you? There has been too much of London and soft living for you, my girl. Come here and I'll lift you up. We'll allow Dominic and Mrs. Simpson to come at their own speed behind us. We will take the gigs home when we get to the top, Dominic, and send one back for you."

"I feel rather like a naughty child," Ellen said to Lord Eden a few minutes later, when she had hold of his hand and was moving slowly upward, "doing the forbidden."

"There is a broad ledge a little higher," he said. "We will stop there for a while."

It was quite magnificent, Ellen decided when they stood on the ledge. They already seemed high up, though they had not come very far. The breeze was a wind up there, and was whipping her cloak against her. The tide was coming in fast. There were several lines of breakers stretched across the miles of the beach, those closest to the sand white with foam. The sun was sparkling on the water.

"There is not a lovelier sight on earth, is there?" she said. "The sea always makes me want to cry."

"It is a lovely sight and yet it makes you want to cry?" he said.

She turned her head to smile at him. "With the wonder of it," she said. "Not from misery."

"We are island people," he said. "The sea is in our blood."

"I suppose so." She set her hands against her abdomen and stood very still.

"You are all right?" His voice was anxious.

"Oh, yes, quite all right," she said. "He moved, Dominic. Oh, and again." She looked at him and smiled in delight. "Feel for yourself."

He stood behind her and put his arms about her, one hand stretched over her ribs beneath her breasts, the other lower. She took that hand in hers, set it flat against her, and waited, very still.

"There. Oh, there," she said. "Did you feel it?" She held up a silencing hand and waited again. "Oh, did you feel it, Dominic? Do you think he is protesting the climb?"

"That bubble?" he said. "Was that it?"

She laid her head back against his shoulder and laughed softly. "Yes, that bubble," she said. "A tiny foot or fist. He is really there, you see, making his presence felt."

He wrapped his arms about her and held her against him. "Was it wise to come up here?" he asked. "Would you prefer to go back down?"

"No, indeed," she said. "Your son and I, sir, are not so chickenhearted. I think he is merely signaling his protest because I have stopped."

"Is he?" he said. "Sooner or later, I am going to have to teach him that he may not give orders to his mother."

"He is wise, you see," she said. "He is doing so while he still may. While you cannot get your hands on him."

He laughed softly, stopped himself just in time from kissing her cheek, and gazed quietly out to sea with her for a few minutes more before releasing her, taking her hand in a firm clasp, and resuming the ascent.

Walter and Jennifer had scarcely paused in their climb, and emerged hot and panting on the clifftop long before anyone else. The two gigs that Lord Amberley had had sent from the house were waiting there, Lieutenant Penworth sitting in one of them.

Jennifer walked across to him, trying to catch her breath. "You came," she said. "What a good idea. Can you see the view?"

"I have seen a lot of sheep," he said. "Do they qualify as a view?"

"No." She laughed. "Oh, I can't talk. I am so breathless."

"You will doubtless be disappointed to know that I drove this gig here myself," he said. "It was not quite as exhilarating as galloping a fast horse, of course. But infinitely preferable to an afternoon spent at a pianoforte keyboard."

"And I am supposed to be disappointed?" she said. "I do not follow your meaning, sir. But I can't argue. No breath. I am going to tell Madeline you are here. She must be close to the top."

She somehow found the energy to walk back to the clifftop while Walter climbed into the gig beside Allan Penworth.

Madeline and Lord Agerton were indeed almost at the top, she saw. So were most of the others. Except for Ellen and Lord Eden, standing on the broad ledge far down, wrapped in each other's arms. She was unable to remove her eyes from them for a few startled moments. Then she turned and half-ran back to the gig, her message undelivered.

"Oh, do look at them, Edmund," the countess said. "Is there nothing you can do to persuade them that they were made for each other?"

"They seem to be doing quite nicely on their own," he said, looking obediently down.

"But they will persist in making difficulties for themselves," she said, "mark my words. And in another two weeks she will go back to London and he will go to Wiltshire, and they will both be miserable."

"If they do anything so foolish," he said, "it will be by their own choice, love. It almost happened to us, if you will remember. But being the sensible people we are, we worked out our own problems without anyone's help, and here we are living happily ever after."

"Is there nothing you can do?" she asked.

"Nothing whatsoever," he said firmly, looking down again at his brother, who had his arms about Ellen Simpson from behind and was gazing with her down to the beach and the breakers below.

22

*M*ADELINE FOLLOWED ALLAN PENWORTH into the green salon when they arrived home i the gig. She clasped her hands behind her and did not hel him to lower himself into a chair even though she could se that he was very tired.

"It was lovely to see you up there on the cliffs," she sai "and to know that you had driven the one gig yourself. I ar very proud of my patient, Allan."

"And so you should be," he said with a smile that sh knew hid pain. "If it were not for your bullying, I woul probably be lying comfortably staring at a ceiling i Brussels now."

She laughed. "I don't think so," she said. "I credit yo with far more spirit than that."

"I am going to go home," he said. "To Devonshire, mean. It is time I faced the music."

"I'm so glad," she said. "Your mother will be happy."

He grimaced. "I can just imagine it," he said. "She wi not be willing for me to lift a spoon for myself."

"I'm quite sure you will soon show them that you ar

perfectly capable of wielding not only a spoon but also a knife and fork," she said.

"I'll be leaving here within a few days, Madeline," he said.

She smiled rather sadly. "Will you?"

"Do you want me to have a word with your brother before I go?" he asked.

"No." She shook her head. "I'll tell him after you have left. Allan, I feel that I want to cry, and yet this is the only way, is it not? Will you write to me at least? I don't want to lose my star patient altogether."

"I'll write," he said.

"I will not offer to help you to your room," she said. "But that is where you must go, Allan. You do not quite know what to do with yourself, do you?"

He smiled. "I'll go, nurse," he said, "without argument."

She walked out into the hallway with him and watched him make his slow progress up the first few stairs. She turned toward the library. Edmund had gone in there after their return with a bundle of letters in his hand. Perhaps there was one for her.

There was one—from Lady Andrea Potts, who was in Paris with the colonel. But Madeline had scarcely broken the seal and read the first paragraph before having her attention effectively diverted by the hurried arrival of her sister-in-law.

"I had just sat down with Christopher on my knee," she said breathlessly, eager eyes directed at her husband, who was leaning against the mantel, smiling indulgently at her. "Where is it, Edmund?"

"Where is what?" he asked, eyebrows raised.

"Oh, don't tease!" she said. "My letter from James. Where is it?"

"Oh, that," he said. "Now, let me see. Where did I put it?"

He looked about him before patting the breast of his coat and withdrawing a letter from an inside pocket. "Is this it? Ah, yes. Addressed to the Countess of Amberley. You, my love. From Mr. James Purnell in Canada."

"Oh, Edmund, give it to me!" she said in exasperation, snatching it from his hand and ignoring his grin. "This is two in one year. How splendid. Do you suppose he is all right?"

"I suppose he is still alive if he can write you a letter," the earl said. "And I suppose you will find out the rest when you have opened and read the letter. How am I expected to know?"

"Oh!" the countess said, turning away from him while Madeline read over again for the seventh time the last sentence of the first paragraph of her own letter.

"He is in Montreal," the countess said. "He has come out of the interior this year and is to work in Montreal for the winter." She read on. "He says it is very strange to be back in Lower Canada after being inland for three years. The people and the buildings and the noises are difficult to get used to. Imagine, Edmund!"

Madeline no longer read the sentence. She merely directed her eyes toward it.

"Oh, Edmund!" The countess spun around to face her smiling, lounging husband, her eyes shining and excited. "He is coming home next summer." She looked back to the letter. "He is bringing the furs to auction. He will be here for a few months. Oh." She looked at him, speechless for a moment. "I am so excited."

"Yes," the earl said, "I had noticed. I imagine Madeline has had her suspicions too. Would you say Alex is looking forward to seeing her brother again, Madeline?"

"What?" Madeline said. "Oh, yes, I think so."

"He has never seen the children," the countess said. "I wonder if he even knows about Caroline yet. Or about Papa. Perhaps he does not even know that."

"The physician only suspected heart trouble, Alex," the earl said. "Your father has seemed quite well since last winter."

"Oh," she said, holding the letter against her and twirling around. "He is coming home at last. I must go and tell your mama. And Dominic if he is back yet."

The Earl of Amberley chuckled as his wife left the room. "I suppose a mere husband will have to take second place for a while next summer," he said. "Do you remember Purnell, Madeline? But of course you do. He was here for a while during the summer of my betrothal to Alex. And who could forget the strange way he left in the middle of the night and the middle of a ball? Rather a strange character, wasn't he? But very fond of Alex and she of him. Did you like him?"

Madeline considered. "He was very quiet," she said. "I did not have a great deal to do with him. I scarcely remember him."

"How is Lady Andrea?" he asked, nodding toward her own letter.

"What?" she said. "Oh, I haven't finished it yet. I was listening to Alexandra. I am very happy for her. I think I'll take this upstairs with me." She smiled and left the room.

He was coming home. Oh, dear God, he was coming home. Or to England, anyway. Probably not to Amberley. His parents, Lord and Lady Beckworth, lived in Yorkshire. He would doubtless go there. Alexandra would travel there to meet him. Edmund and the children would go with her.

It was unlikely that he would come to Amberley.

If he did, she would stay away. She would go to Dom in Wiltshire, perhaps.

She would not have to see him even if he came. She did not want to see him.

Oh, God, he was coming home. Perhaps to Amberley. Perhaps she would see him again.

ELLEN WAS SMILING to herself as she unpinned her hair and shook it loose. She had been given her orders, and she would obey them. She would lie down and rest for an hour.

She would have done so anyway. She really was feeling quite tired. But it had been amusing and rather touching to have Dominic tell her in the gig on the way home that she must promise him to go to her room without delay, or he would carry her there. And to have his mother meet her in the hallway, take her arm through hers, and escort her to her room, scolding her gently along the way.

But she was not sorry she had made that climb. And really, they had done it in such slow stages that there had been very little exertion involved. And then, when they had reached the top and had to wait for one of the gigs to return for them, Dominic had made her lie down on the grass, spreading his coat beneath her in case there was any dampness left in the ground.

"But you will be cold," she had protested. "This is October, Dominic."

He had stretched out on the grass beside her, the dampness notwithstanding, and propped himself up on one elbow.

"I have survived worse," he had said. "So have you."

"Do you remember . . . ?" And they had been off again

into shared reminiscences, so that the arrival of the gig had finally taken them by surprise.

Ellen got into bed beneath the top cover and closed her eyes. She imposed relaxation on her body. They could surely be friends after all. And that would be enough. She would make it enough. It had been a happy afternoon. Blissfully happy.

The door to her room suddenly opened without any knock to herald someone's arrival. Ellen turned her head to find Jennifer standing there, her face white, in obvious distress.

"What is it?" She pushed herself up on an elbow.

Jennifer closed the door and stood against it. "How long has it been going on?" she asked. "Since before Papa died?"

"What?" Ellen frowned.

"You and Lord Eden," the girl said. "Were you lovers even when Papa was still alive? Were you?"

Ellen closed her eyes briefly and swung her legs over the side of the bed. "Jennifer . . ." she said.

The girl's voice was shaking. "I suppose it is his baby you are expecting too," she said, "and not Papa's at all. It is, isn't it?"

"I was never unfaithful to your father," Ellen said. "Never, Jennifer. I loved him."

"He never suspected, did he?" Jennifer said. "And neither did I. Papa thought that Lord Eden was always visiting because they were friends. But it was you and him, wasn't it? And it is hardly surprising. I am only amazed that I was naive enough not to see it. Papa was not a handsome man, and he was much older than you. Lord Eden is the most handsome man I have known. How long has it been going on, Ellen? For years?"

Ellen shook her head. "Listen to me," she said. "I know

you are distraught and that you will not believe anything I say now. But listen, please. And when you have calmed down, you will know that I have told you the truth."

She had never seen Jennifer sneer before. But she saw it now. "Papa believed your lies for years," she said. "And I have always believed them. Let me see if I believe this one. I am listening."

"Lord Eden—Dominic—and I are betrothed," Ellen said. "And you are right. It is his child. I conceived it a month after your father's death. While Dominic was recovering from his wounds in my rooms."

"A remarkable recovery!" Jennifer said.

"There was nothing between us before that," Ellen said. "He was your father's friend. I was his wife. And I was faithful to him entirely from inclination. I loved him. Afterward, when Dominic was with me, we turned to each other for comfort, and this child was conceived. What we did was wrong. We both owed your father's memory better than that. I have lived through terrible pangs of guilt, and even accused myself of infidelity at first. But I was not unfaithful, Jennifer, and I would not have been if your father had lived. Neither would Dominic. He is a man of honor."

"You're a slut and a whore!" Jennifer said quietly.

Ellen got hurriedly to her feet. A shaking hand came up to cover her mouth. "You will know when you have had time to think," she said, "that you are being unfair, Jennifer. I wish you had not found out like this. Did you suspect when we were together this afternoon? I have been trying to find a way to tell you. Your grandfather and your aunt know already, though they do not know the identity of the father. I will talk with Lady Amberley or her mother-in-law. Perhaps they can help you. I know I can't at the moment. I'm so sorry."

"I don't need anyone's help," Jennifer said. "I am not a child to be comforted with a hug. I lost Papa just a few months ago. But I still had you. I loved you as if you really were my mother, though you are young enough to be my sister. I am glad you are neither, Ellen. And I am glad at least that Papa never knew what was going on under his very nose. His wife and his best friend! It would have killed him."

Ellen bent her head and closed her eyes. After a few moments she heard the door of her room open and close again.

Half an hour passed before she felt calm enough to go in search of the dowager Countess of Amberley.

LIEUTENANT PENWORTH FOUND JENNIFER half an hour after that in the music room. She was sitting at the pianoforte depressing keys seemingly at random with one finger.

"You are going right back to basics?" he said. "Wouldn't scales be more productive?"

She put her hands palm-up, one on top of the other, in her lap and looked down at them.

"I must have said something particularly clever," he said, hobbling closer to her on his crutches, "if I have silenced you."

"Go away," she said quietly.

He stopped behind the bench and looked down at the cluster of dark ringlets at the back of her head. "Why do I have the feeling that what you are really saying is 'please help me'?" he said. "What's the matter?"

"Go away," she said.

He sat down slowly and carefully on the edge of the bench. "I have lost some of my body parts," he said. "But I still have two perfectly serviceable shoulders left. Do you want to use one of them?"

She put one hand flat along the keyboard and pressed down all the keys beneath it. Then she slammed the hand down twice more. "Leave me alone," she said. "Just leave me alone!"

He looked at her hand for a few silent moments before positioning his crutches under his arms and starting to get up.

"Don't go!" she said. And she spread both arms along the keyboard and laid her forehead down on her hands. The noise was quite deafening until it faded away.

He set one hand lightly against the curls and sat quietly.

"Ellen's baby is not Papa's," she said. "It is Lord Eden's and they are going to be married. And Papa has not been dead four months yet. And I have no business saying this to a near-stranger."

"That doesn't matter," he said. "Sometimes it is easier to talk to a stranger. You are badly hurt?"

"Papa worshiped her," she said. "I think he loved her more than he loved me. And she pretended to love him. But she deceived him. With his closest friend."

"I saw them together," he said gently. "Your father and your stepmother, I mean. It never seemed like pretense to me. Are you sure this was going on before your father died?"

"She swears it was not," she said. "But she is a liar as well as everything else I called her. I hate her. And him. But her more, because she deceived me too. I loved her."

"Perhaps she is telling the truth," he said. "Eden was with her, wasn't he, after he was wounded? There can be a powerful bond between a wounded man and the woman who nurses him. I know. It happened to me too. Perhaps there was nothing between them until then. I have the greatest respect for Mrs. Simpson. And for Eden. I don't think they would have done that to your father."

"Were you in love with Madeline before you were wounded?" she asked.

"Not really." He moved his hand to her shoulder as she sat up again. "I admired her a great deal. But then, I admired several young ladies, yourself included. I fell in love with her afterward—for a time. We have ended our betrothal now."

She looked sharply around at him.

"We have not quarreled," he said. "We have merely agreed, rather sadly, that what happened in Brussels was not a very real or lasting experience. We would not suit. We realize it now. Strange things can happen in those sorts of circumstances, you know. Perhaps even what has occurred with Eden and your stepmother. Give her a chance to show you that she is not what you called her—I can imagine what that was. But don't assume without further proof that what has happened since your father's death was also happening before then."

"You are being kind to me," she said. "Why? I never lose an opportunity to be rude to you."

"Perhaps that is why," he said with a smile. "Perhaps I have needed someone to be rude to me. Too much kindness has been driving me insane."

He removed his hand from her shoulder as the door to the music room opened behind them. He turned to see the dowager countess enter. She smiled at him and raised her eyebrows significantly.

"I am going to choose a book in the library," he said, pulling his crutches beneath his arms again.

The dowager watched him leave the room, while Jennifer sat with bent head again, examining the palms of her hands.

"Well, my poor child," the dowager said, taking the place on the bench that Allan Penworth had just vacated and putting an arm about the girl's shoulders, "it would seem that my son and your stepmother have been causing you some pain."

THEY WERE ALL INVITED that evening to dine with the Courtneys. Just an informal gathering, Mr. Courtney had assured them genially when he had come over the previous day, in the rain, to issue the invitation, to keep the young people amused. He said nothing about the older people, but everyone knew that Mr. Courtney liked nothing better than a lively social gathering, especially when it was in his own home.

He insisted on calling his home a farmhouse and his drawing room a parlor. In reality, he was a prosperous tenant farmer, a fact that was reflected in the size and grandeur of his home. But Mr. Courtney was not one to put on airs. His only real ambition had ever been to marry his only daughter well, and he had achieved that three years before, when she had married the younger brother of Baron Renfrew.

Even Lieutenant Penworth decided that he would join the party. He shared a carriage with Madeline, Lord Eden, and Ellen. Jennifer, who had neither looked at nor exchanged a word with Ellen since the afternoon, traveled in the other carriage with the earl and his wife and mother.

Lord Eden touched Ellen's hand while a footman was helping the lieutenant into the carriage and Madeline was hovering over him.

"Trouble?" he asked quietly.

She nodded.

"You told her, then?" he asked.

She shook her head. "She guessed. But not quite accurately, I'm afraid."

They did not have a chance to say any more. The other two had settled into their places, and the conversation became general.

The Lampmans had also been invited for dinner. The Mortons, the Cartwrights, the Carringtons, and the Misses Stanhope joined them later in the evening, and Mr. Courtney announced that there would be dancing in the parlor for anyone who cared to indulge in some exertion.

"No offense meant, ma'am," he said in his hearty voice, taking one of Ellen's hands between both his own large ones, "you being in mourning and all. But Susan has been feeling low, and Mrs. Courtney and I thought that a little informal dancing with friends would be showing no disrespect for the dead."

"No offense is taken, sir," she said, smiling at him. "And a little dancing would be very pleasant."

Miss Letitia Stanhope had agreed to play the pianoforte, having quite recovered from her chill. Mr. Colin Courtney was to play the violin, though he had made it clear to his father that he would dance a few times with his young wife.

Lord Eden danced the opening set with Lady Lampman and the second with his sister-in-law. He had taken several uneasy looks at both Ellen and Jennifer and judged it wise to stay away from both for the first part of the evening, anyway.

He led the elder Miss Stanhope into a vigorous country dance, and soon had her blushing and shrieking and assuring him that someone of her years could not be expected to twirl quite as fast as the young girls.

"But you were always a dreadful tease," she said breathlessly during a pause while they made an arch for another couple to twirl down the set. "You and Sir Perry, both."

"Not twirl fast, ma'am?" he said. "Someone of nine-and-twenty not able to twirl fast? I find it hard to believe."

Miss Stanhope shrieked again and called him a rogue.

He was breathless himself by the time the set had come to an end. He stood by the open door of the parlor to benefit from some of the coolness from the hallway beyond. Susan collided with him there on her way out of the room.

"Oh, my lord," she said, looking up at him with large eyes, "I do beg your pardon. I did not see you standing there."

Lord Eden smiled in some amusement. He thought he was too large a target to be invisible. It was amazing the number of times in the past several years that Susan had run into him.

"I was on my way outside," she said.

"Not 'outside' as in 'outdoors,' I hope," he said. "Is it not a mite chilly, Susan?"

"It is warm in here," she said. "Besides, there are three new kittens in the barn, and I don't trust the dogs not to harm them, despite what Papa and Howard say. Poor little things. They are so helpless." Her eyes became suspiciously bright.

"Well, then," he said, "we must simply beat off the brutes with a stick, Susan. And you shall show me the kittens."

"Oh, but you must stay here," she said. "You will want to dance. I would not dream of taking you out into the cold, my lord."

He smiled. "A few minutes will not ruin my enjoyment,"

he said. "Especially when there are new kittens to be admired."

"You are very kind," she said as they left the room and went in search of their cloaks.

"How fortunate you have been," she said with a sigh as they picked their way across the farmyard a few minutes later, Lord Eden holding a lantern aloft, "to have had such a loving family to come home to. And such a distinguished family, too."

"Yes," he said. "It is good to be back."

"My husband was of a distinguished family too," she said. "I miss him so, you know. It is so lonely to be without him."

"Is it, Susan?" Lord Eden hung the lantern carefully on a nail inside the door of the barn and covered her hand with his. "Give it time. It has been less than four months."

"I know," she said, "but I feel so helpless and alone. He was very strong and dependable. He looked after me."

He felt in his pocket for a handkerchief and held it out to her.

"Oh," she said, her voice high and trembling, "I am so unhappy. I pretend, you know, so that no one will know and pity me. But I am so unhappy."

She was in his arms suddenly, her hands spread against his chest, her face hidden against his waistcoat beneath his cloak. Lord Eden wrapped his arms about her and rocked her comfortingly.

"Hush now," he murmured. "No one would blame you for crying, Susan. It is perfectly natural."

"Oh," she said when she could speak around her sobs, "you are so kind. You were always so very kind to me."

When she lifted a tear-stained face to his, Lord Eden kissed it. He kissed the tears from her eyes and cheeks, and he kissed the pouting little mouth that he used to find so enticing.

"Oh," she said, sighing and resting her head against his shoulder, "I always feel so safe with you."

"And so you are," he said, kissing the top of her head. "Come, Susan, you must show me these kittens, and then I will take you back inside. The sound of music will cheer you up again."

"Yes, it will," she said, looking at him with wide-eyed gratitude and stooping into a bed of straw to lift up the kittens one by one and lay them against her cheek. She crooned to them and kissed their fur.

Lord Eden watched her with a smile and reached for the lantern as soon as she had put the last one down again.

"I cannot go indoors yet, my lord," she said. "I must look a perfect mess, and my eyes must be fiery red. I cannot let anyone see me like this. You go on in. I will stay with the kittens for a while. Take the lantern. I can find my way in the darkness."

"How foolish to think I would abandon you, Susan," he said. "But your eyes look perfectly fine to me. I have never known anyone who could cry as you can without getting red eyes as a result. We will walk slowly back to the house, shall we?"

She leaned heavily on his arm as they walked.

"We had better go in," she said with a sigh. "I am sure we will have been missed, and everyone will be wondering what we are doing. If we stay any longer, some of them will be foolish enough to expect some sort of announcement."

"Well, we certainly would not wish to put your reputation in such danger, would we?" he said, smiling at her. "Besides, Susan, everyone knows that you were so devoted to your husband that it will be a long time yet before you can think of choosing another. I think your good name is safe."

"Oh, yes," she said, "I am sure it is, my lord."

"And then," he said, "everyone knows that we were childhood friends, Susan, and will quite understand if we treat each other with greater freedom than strangers would enjoy. You do not need to worry about being forced into a situation in which you will have to receive my addresses. I would not allow you to be so harassed. Never, my dear. I have too much respect for our friendship."

"Oh," she said, darting a glance up at him as they entered the lighted hallway of her father's house, "you are most kind, my lord."

He smiled fondly at her and handed the lantern to a servant. "Think nothing of it," he said. "What are friends for, Susan, but to help and defend each other?"

ELLEN HAD DANCED with Mr. Morton and Lord Agerton and Sir Peregrine. She had even succeeded in smiling and conversing. But every single moment she was aware of a brightly gay Jennifer, and constantly her ears rang with the accusation, "You are a slut and a whore."

She still did not know if it would be wiser to seek out Jennifer and try to talk to her again, or to give the girl time in which to think. She had decided to take the latter course, on the advice of the dowager countess. Her future mother-in-law.

Strangely, she had not found it difficult earlier to pour out the whole story. Perhaps she had still been too distressed over her encounter with Jennifer to feel embarrassment at having to admit the whole truth to Dominic's mother. Or perhaps the fact that that lady had crossed her sitting room and put an arm about her shoulders and called her her poor dear had had something to do with easing the situation.

"How very delighted I am to hear that you and Dominic are to marry, dear," the countess had said, kissing her cheek when the story had all been told. "I was so very afraid that you would each be foolish enough to let the other go."

"You can possibly want me as a daughter-in-law, ma'am?" Ellen had asked.

"I cannot imagine any lady I would want more for Dominic," the other had assured her. "You will be a companion to him, not merely someone to protect. A companion as well as someone to love is what he has always needed, though he has been foolish enough not to realize it for himself until now."

"I do love him," Ellen had assured her. "I am not marrying him just because I am in an awkward situation."

The dowager had clucked her tongue. "Well, of course you love each other," she had said. "Now, I will go in search of your stepdaughter. She is a dear and sensible girl. She will need a little time to adjust to the new facts, that is all. Give her that time, dear. Don't press her. And for now, leave her to me."

So Ellen had left Jennifer to the dowager countess. And was not at all sure that she had not taken the coward's way out.

"Dance with me, Ellen?" Lord Eden asked as Miss Letitia and Colin began to play a waltz.

She had planned to keep away from him for the rest of the evening at least. She did not want to make matters worse as far as her stepdaughter was concerned. But it was a waltz, and he was smiling at her, and she could not help but remember how wonderful the afternoon had been before they had arrived home.

"Yes," she said, placing one hand in his and reaching up the other to rest on his shoulder.

"Is Miss Simpson very upset?" he asked as they began dancing. "From the almost desperate way she seems to be enjoying herself, I would guess that she is."

"She believes that I was unfaithful to Charlie long before his death," she said. "She refuses to listen to reason."

"And if I talk to her, I will only make matters worse, doubtless," he said.

She nodded. "Your mother had a talk with her this afternoon," she said. "I went to her and told her everything, I'm afraid."

"I'm delighted you did," he said. "I am eager to have this thing right out in the open, Ellen. I want to set a wedding date."

"Do you?" she said. "I don't know, Dominic. It still does not seem right."

He held her hand more tightly. "Oh, no," he said. "You are not going to change your mind again now, Ellen. Absolutely not. But listen. Miss Letitia and Colin are making a truly heroic effort to sound like a whole orchestra. Let us enjoy the waltz, shall we?"

She almost wished after a couple of minutes that they had continued the conversation, however awkward it might have been. She did not know of a dance that could make one more aware of the man one was partnered by than a waltz. She remembered the time she had waltzed with him at the Duke of Wellington's ball. The time when she had been pushed against him. When she had become physically aware of him for the first time.

She could smell his cologne again.

"What do you use to wash your hair?" he asked, his smiling green eyes seeming very close. "It must be something quite different from anything used by any other lady of my acquaintance. A very enticing fragrance."

MR. COURTNEY TOOK a hearty farewell of each of his guests several hours later. But he had something more to say to the Earl and Countess of Amberley, in the strictest confidence. Mr. Courtney spoke *sotto voce* when speaking in confidence. But since his normal speaking voice was often compared by his fond neighbors to a soft bellow, it was hardly surprising that even his whispers were heard by every one of the departing guests.

Susan, it seemed, had just accepted the offer of Lord Agerton. Not that there was anything public or official yet, of course, the beaming father added for the edification of all his listeners and the mortification of his daughter. Susan would not be out of mourning until the following summer. But they might all expect a late-summer wedding.

"My daughter to be the Viscountess Agerton!" he said, fairly bursting with pride and goodwill. "Well, my lord, who would have thought it?"

Susan blushed and hung her head and peeped up into the face of her future betrothed.

23

*E*LLEN WAS ROLLING HER HAIR INTO ITS USUAL knot at the nape of her neck. She had not brought Prudence into the country with her. She had been accustomed for years to managing without the services of a maid.

She was dawdling, she realized. It was well past her usual time of going downstairs to breakfast. And the outdoors certainly looked inviting. Despite fallen leaves and bare branches, there was a look of summer about the clear blue sky and brightly shining sun.

But she was dawdling anyway. And her heart made an uncomfortable lurch when there was a sudden knock on the door of her bedchamber.

"Come in," she called, and looked in the mirror to see that it was indeed Jennifer who came inside and closed the door quietly behind her. Ellen put down her comb and turned on her stool.

The girl was looking pale, rather as she had looked when Ellen first came home from Belgium.

"Good morning," she said rather lamely.

"Good morning, Jennifer." Ellen clasped her hands in her lap.

"You were right," the girl said in a rush. "When I thought about it, I knew that you were telling me the truth. And Lady Amberley told me that she knows Lord Eden could not behave so dishonorably, and that she did not think you could either. And Lieutenant Penworth says that such things often happen when a woman nurses an injured man. And besides, I think I would have known. Papa might not have, but I think I would."

She stopped as abruptly as she had begun.

Ellen closed her eyes briefly. "Thank you," she said. "I don't think I could have borne to live with your hatred."

Jennifer crossed the room to the window and stood looking out. "I'm sorry," she said, "but even though I believe you, I cannot forgive you. I will try not to hate you, but I don't believe I can ever love you again."

"I'm sorry too," Ellen said very quietly. "I did love your father, Jennifer. My whole life was focused on making him happy. And I think I succeeded. I still do love him. I always will."

"No," Jennifer said. "You could never have loved him. You are going to marry Lord Eden. And you love him too, don't you?"

"Yes," Ellen said.

"Well, then, all is said." Jennifer turned back toward the room, her eyes bleak. "You cannot love twice in a lifetime. Either you loved Papa or you love Lord Eden. Or you have never loved anyone."

"Oh, Jennifer." Ellen looked at her pleadingly. "You are very young, dear. I suppose every young girl believes that true love can happen only once to each person. Everyone dreams of finding that one person with whom she can live in bliss for the rest of her life. It does not always happen that way. Love is a far greater gift than any of us realize. I don't love your father any the less because I love Dominic. And I don't love Dominic the less because I will always love your father. I can't choose between the two loves and say that one is greater than the other. I can only tell you that I would have remained faithful to your papa and I would have loved him too for the rest of my life if he had not been snatched from me."

"I'm sorry, Ellen." The girl's eyes looked at her in misery. "I want to forgive you. I love you so much more than I love Aunt Dorothy or Uncle Phillip, or even Grandpapa. You have seemed like my very own even though you are not my real mother, because Papa was happy with you. I want things to be as they were until yesterday, but they can't ever be the same again, can they?"

Ellen shook her head. "No," she said. "We can never go back, Jennifer. Only forward. But I am not a different person from the one you loved yesterday morning. And you are not different. Only hurt and bewildered. I think you set me on something of a pedestal, didn't you, and I have come toppling down. I am just human, alas. But I need you. You may think that because I have Dominic and will have my baby, I will have no further need of you. But you are my only link with my first husband, Jennifer. My loss will be doubled if I lose you too."

Jennifer stared at her uncertainly, one hand twisting the fabric of her dress. "You will be living at his home in Wiltshire," she said.

"Probably," Ellen said. "It will be your home too, whenever you want it to be. Dominic knows that I think of you as my daughter."

"You won't want me," the girl said. "You will have your real son or daughter. You won't want me."

"Jennifer!" Ellen rose to her feet for the first time. "Have you not listened to what I have been saying? You are my family. At the moment, you are almost my only family. I am not married yet, and my baby has not been born yet. I have my father, whom I rediscovered in London a few weeks ago, and you. Wherever Dominic chooses to make our home will be yours too. Not because I will consider it a duty to take you in. I will not—your grandfather is quite capable of giving you a home and all the comforts and love to go with it. It will be because I love you and want you as part of my family."

Jennifer continued to twist the fabric of her dress. "I will have to go away and think," she said. "I was so determined not to forgive you. But I can't remember all of the reasons any longer. I'm going now."

"All right," Ellen said.

But when the girl reached the door, she paused with her hand on the knob, turned, whisked herself across the room to hug Ellen very hard, and then rushed from the room without another word.

MADELINE WAS ALONE in the breakfast room with her twin, everyone else having already left the table or not yet arrived. They were laughing.

"Did you see her face, Dom?" Madeline said. "She looked as if she would have dearly liked to stuff a cushion down poor Mr. Courtney's throat."

"She was embarrassed," he said. "Susan is very easily embarrassed."

"Fiddle!" she said. "I do wonder why she objected to the

announcement's being made, though. Because it was the end of the evening, perhaps, and she was not at the very center of an admiring crowd?"

"You are cruel, Mad," he said. "You never have had any patience with Susan."

"I can have all the patience in the world with her," she said, "now that I know she is not going to marry you. I have been a little worried. You have been her first choice, you know."

"A mere baron?" he said. "When Agerton is a viscount? But perhaps you are right. I hate to do her an injustice, but I do believe she was trying to compromise me last night so that I would feel obliged to offer for her."

"To compromise you?" she said, and laughed anew. "Oh, Dom, Susan is a priceless character, is she not? Will she make poor Lord Agerton's life a misery, do you suppose?"

"I think not," he said. "She was reasonably loyal to Jennings while he lived, as far as I know. And this time she will have her title as soon as she leaves the altar. She will be thoroughly happy."

"I am not going to marry Allan," she said. "Have you suspected?"

He looked steadily at her. "I wondered," he said, "when he announced yesterday that he will be leaving tomorrow. Who broke the engagement?"

"I did," she said. "But I think it was a great relief to him. We would not have suited. You were right all along, Dom."

"Are you upset?" he asked, reaching across the table for her hand.

She shrugged. "Not really," she said. "A little sorry, perhaps, for the awkwardness, for I am dearly fond of him. And restless. But no matter. I will contrive somehow to live on and to enjoy life. I always do."

He squeezed her hand.

"And what about you?" she asked. "Dare I ask if the apparent amity between you and Mrs. Simpson in the last few days means anything?"

He grinned. "Yes," he said. "It means that there is an amity between us, Mad."

She pulled a face at him.

He winked at her. "And perhaps a little more. I'm not at liberty to say anything more just yet."

She dropped her napkin on the table and ran around the table to wrap her arms about his neck from behind. "Then I will not by any means tell you how happy I am for you," she said. "I won't say a word." She kissed his cheek. "Did Alexandra tell you that her brother is coming home next summer?"

He rested one hand on her arm. "Is that important to you?" he asked.

"Not at all, silly," she said, straightening up and ruffling his hair. "But it is very important to Alexandra. She is excited."

"Nice of you, then," he said, "to bring it to my attention purely for her sake, Mad."

She laughed. "It was more than three years ago," she said. "I am not foolish enough to think that an old infatuation can be rekindled, Dom. I have grown up a little since that time. And don't look at me like that. I know that I am just deceiving myself, and not you at all. Well, then, I do want to see him again. Just out of curiosity. So there! Are you satisfied, you horrid man?"

"You are probably crossing off days in your diary already," he said, and covered his head with his hands as she tried to beat a tattoo on it with the back of a spoon.

• • •

LIEUTENANT PENWORTH TOLD the dowager countess when she inquired at the luncheon table that no one need concern themselves about him. He intended to spend his final afternoon in the country outdoors painting.

Jennifer was sitting next to him. "Are you good?" she asked while the other occupants of the table began to talk about something else.

"If I say yes," he said, "I will doubtless be accused of conceit. If I say no, you will accuse me of feeling sorry for myself again. I choose to say nothing."

"I see you are in your usual sunny mood," she said. "How are you going to carry everything?"

"I thought of using the easel as one of my crutches," he said, "and grasping everything else in my teeth."

Jennifer laughed. "It was a foolish question," she said. "Doubtless you mean that you do not wish me to offer my help. I was not about to, sir."

"Stupid of me to think such a thing," he said. "Actually I have servants lined up to load the gig for me, and a groom to drive me partway down the valley, from where there is, according to the earl's mother, a particularly lovely view of the house, and to return for me two hours later. You see how I am beginning to be able to organize my life again?"

"I am all admiration," she said. "May I come too?"

"I am not good company when I am painting," he said. "I like to lose myself in what I am doing and am easily distracted by someone trying to chatter to me."

"I will be very quiet," she said, "and not even whisper to you. I declined an invitation to go riding with Anna and Walter and some other people this afternoon. I said I was tired."

"Did you?" He looked more closely at her. "Come if you

must, then. But I do not want to hear any complaints that you are bored. If you are, you may just pick yourself up and walk back to the house. Understood?"

"And to think," she said, "that there was a time when I thought you a gallant and dashing officer. You are not very gracious, are you?"

"If I had two legs," he said, "I would go down on one of them and beg you to accompany me. Under the circumstances, I would look rather foolish, would I not?"

"Decidedly," she agreed.

An hour later the gig bounced its way for perhaps half a mile down the valley before the lieutenant was satisfied that he had the view of the house that the dowager had told him about. Jennifer spread a blanket on the ground and sat on it, her arms wrapped about her knees while he set up his easel and stool a short distance away in such a manner that she would not be able to see his work.

"Did you sort out your problem yesterday?" he asked before seating himself.

"I think so," she said with a sigh. "I was very naive, it seems, expecting that some people in this world are perfect. Ellen is not perfect, after all, but she is not a villain either."

"So all is well between you again?" he asked.

"I think so," she said. "A little strained, but not quite broken."

"I am glad," he said. "Now, you must stop talking to me so that I can concentrate."

"But I did not say the first word," she said indignantly. "You did."

She could have painted too, since painting had always been one of her favorite activities. But she had decided

.merely to watch and be lazy. She felt lethargic after an emotional twenty-four hours.

She was sitting in the same position an hour later, lost in daydreams, when she was recalled to reality with a start by the voice of her companion.

"All right," he said vengefully. He cleaned his brush with furious energy and pushed himself upright with his crutches. "You win."

"I am delighted to hear it," she said. "But what is the prize? And what was the game?"

"You have made quite sure that you have ruined my afternoon," he said.

"I?" She looked at him, all amazement. "I have not made a sound."

"I might have been able to concentrate better if you had been shouting and singing," he said.

"Well." Jennifer glared up at him indignantly. "There is no pleasing you, is there?"

He spent some time sitting down awkwardly on the blanket beside her. Jennifer clasped her knees even more tightly and did not offer her help.

"I wish I had died!" he said unexpectedly.

"But you did not," she said.

"I think I could accept the loss of my leg," he said, rubbing his hip and grimacing. "I think in time I can learn to adjust my way of life to that. It is my face I cannot reconcile myself to."

"You think yourself very ugly?" she asked.

"I know myself very ugly." He spoke through his teeth and continued to rub his hip. "How can I ever . . . ? How can I live anything like a normal life?"

"By becoming unaware of your scars," she said. "If you keep hiding from people, turning your face away so that only the unscarred profile shows, they will continue to notice you. And if you keep on scowling, they will think you ugly."

He laughed. "And will doubtless think me handsome if I smile?"

"No," she said. "You will never be handsome. Intriguing, perhaps. Attractive, perhaps."

"Attractive!" he said scornfully. "I am going home, you will be pleased to know. Before Christmas. I must face my family, even though it will be an ordeal."

"Doubtless," she said. "Are you going to scowl at them too?"

"You are not a very sympathetic person, are you?" he said.

"You once yelled at me not to pity you," she said. "Have you changed your mind?"

"No," he said. "I would a thousand times prefer your taunts to everyone else's pity."

"A compliment!" she said. "We are making progress."

He stared ahead of him. "How one moment of time can change the course of a whole lifetime," he said. "I used to dream of a perfectly normal life. I didn't ask for much. Just my home and family. A wife by the time I was thirty, perhaps. Some children. A quiet life."

"And now you must live the life of a hermit because you are ugly and crippled?" she asked.

He glared at her from his one eye. "It pleases you to make fun of me," he said. "What woman would not recoil in disgust at an advance from me? Do you know why I have not been able to paint this afternoon? Because I have been sitting there wanting to kiss you, that's why. Now, tell me that the idea does not repel you."

She thought for a moment. "The idea does not repel me," she said.

"Ah," he said, "you are brave. Are you relying on the fact that I am a gentleman and will not put the matter to the test?"

She lifted a hand to trace lightly the line of his scar with one finger. "Does it hurt?" she asked.

"Not a light touch like that," he said.

"Does this hurt?" She leaned forward and laid her lips against the scar. She was blushing hotly when she pulled back again.

"No."

"Kiss me, then." Her eyes were on his chin. "Put it to the test."

"You do not have to be kind," he said, his voice quiet with controlled fury. "You of all people."

"Oh!" Jennifer scrambled to her feet and took a few steps away from the blanket. "Oh, how could you! Could you not see how much courage it took to ask to be kissed? I could die of mortification. I hate you, sir, and I hope no woman will ever have you. You deserve to live a solitary life. I have never in my life been so humiliated."

"Jennifer!" His voice finally penetrated her embarrassment. There was a suggestion of laughter in it. "Come back here, please. Look, I cannot come and fetch you. I'm truly sorry. I was too busy feeling my own confusion to recognize your courage. Please sit down again."

"I ought not," she said warily, sitting back down nevertheless on one corner of the blanket and keeping her spine very straight. "I should walk back to the house."

"Will you let me kiss you?" he asked. "I have been wanting to do so all afternoon. And long before this afternoon, if the truth were known."

She could feel herself flush even more deeply as she wriggled closer to him on the blanket again and he put one arm up about her shoulders. The other hand came against her cheek, his thumb pushing up beneath her chin. She felt as if her cheeks were about to burst into flame.

"You are so pretty," he said, "and so spirited. I wish I were quite whole for you, Jennifer."

She was not given a chance to reply. His mouth was on hers, lightly exploring. And lifting away so that she could end the experiment right there if she wanted. But her arm was up about his neck by that time, and her mouth reaching for his again.

Somehow, during the next few minutes or hours they shifted position so that they were lying rather than sitting on the blanket. And somehow, during the same time span Jennifer lost her wits. The only thing she could think of to say when she was finally released was a rather meaningless "Oh!"

He lay down beside her, one arm beneath his head. "Thank you," he said, finding her hand with his. "You are a very kind lady despite the frequently barbed tongue. You will be looking forward to the end of your mourning period and to finding a handsome husband."

"One with two legs and two arms and two eyes," she said. "Oh, yes, sir, my head is filled with nothing else."

"Why is your tone sarcastic?" he asked.

"Strangely," she said, "at the moment you spoke, I was thinking of a one-legged, one-eyed man who is not particularly handsome."

There was a pause.

"I have nothing to offer you, Jennifer," he said.

"No, of course not," she said. "One has only to look at you to see that you are no more than half a man."

"You cannot want me."

Jennifer said nothing. She sat up on the blanket and wrapped her arms about her knees again.

"When my leg—or what is left of it—has healed properly," he said, "I am going to see about having an artificial limb. Perhaps I will never get used to it. And then again, perhaps I will. But I think I am going to try."

She still said nothing.

"Jennifer." He sat up beside her with some difficulty and rubbed his hip again. "Perhaps by next summer I will be in better health. My scars will have faded a little. I will have sorted things out with my family. Your mourning will be over. I could come up to London then."

She did not answer him.

"Would you want me to?" he asked hesitantly.

She shrugged. "Would you?"

"I asked first," he said. "But no matter. Yes, I would." He rested a hand against the back of her neck. "I have liked you since Brussels. Except that there you were dazzled by Eden and I was infatuated with Madeline. And we have not had much chance for anything since then except getting on each other's nerves. But I find that I can say good-bye to everyone in this house tomorrow except you. I like all the others and will miss them. I will ache for you."

"I wish you weren't going," she said.

"So do I." He squeezed the sides of her neck. "But I think it is best. We are not quite ready for each other yet, Jennifer. I have to learn what kind of life it is that I will be living. I have to regain some of my strength—and I am talking not just about physical strength. And you too have to adjust to the changes in your life. It will be best to wait until next summer."

"I suppose so," she said. "I just wish it were not tomorrow. I wish there were a little more time."

"There is a little more," he said. "I don't see the gig coming yet, do you?"

She shaded her eyes and looked toward the house. "No," she said.

"Well, then," he said, collapsing heavily back on the blanket and lifting his arms to her. "Come and kiss me again. And I will tell you that I love you, you little termagant. Shall I?"

"Yes, please," she said, coming down across the upper part of his body and kissing his scarred cheek. "And I will tell you the same thing, Allan. You go first."

"All right," he said. "But the kiss before anything. I can tell you I love you in the gig going home if necessary. But I can't kiss you there. Not without shocking the groom."

He spread his hand over the back of her head and guided her mouth down onto his.

ELLEN WAS KNEELING on the grass of the lawn beside the house, holding on to Caroline's hands as the child bounced on wobbly legs. The Countess of Amberley was standing beside them, watching her husband roll a ball to her shrieking son.

"I hope I have a little girl like you," Ellen said to the child. "But then, perhaps I would be equally delighted with a son."

"You think it matters," the countess said, "until the baby is born and gives its first cry. I wanted Christopher to be a boy, of course, so that Edmund would have his heir. But I wanted Caroline to be a boy too as a companion for her brother. Yet I had to take only one look at her as the doctor told me I had a daughter, and I thought what a fool I had been to have thought I wanted a son. Now the next one can be what it pleases. I just hope it decides to arrive within the next year or so."

"Perhaps it will be twins," Ellen said, "and you will have one of each. There are some in the family, after all."

"Then perhaps yours will be twins too," the countess said with a laugh, and then grimaced and bit her lip and shook her head.

"Don't be embarrassed." Ellen stood up, the baby in her arms. "The thought had crossed my mind too."

"I don't think I am usually quite so gauche," Lady Amberley said. "I will have nightmares about that one."

"Well, you need not," Ellen said, laughing at her. "I am not at all ashamed of the fact that I am expecting Dominic's child—or children. Let's change the subject. Tell me more about your brother."

"James?" The countess smiled. "He was by far the most important person in my life until I met Edmund. I had a very secluded and rather unhappy childhood and girlhood, I'm afraid. I am not complaining, by the way. The years of happiness I have known here have made up a thousandfold for every lonely moment. James was my idol. He could do absolutely nothing wrong in my eyes." She laughed. "He still can't, for that matter. Are you sure you wish me to pursue this line of conversation? You might become dreadfully bored after an hour or so."

"I don't think so." Ellen knelt on the grass again and set down the wriggling child. The countess sat down beside her.

Lord Eden found them there half an hour later. He stooped down on his haunches and smiled at the two ladies. "Hello, little beauty," he said to his niece. "I don't suppose you have a smile for Uncle Dom today, do you?"

Two dark and solemn eyes regarded him unblinkingly.

"I didn't think so," he said, touching her soft dark curls with a gentle hand. "You are going to slay men by the thousands when you grow up. Eyes like that should not be allowed. Whoosh!"

This last exclamation was provoked by the fact that his nephew had just launched himself onto his back.

"Is that my old pal?" he asked. "You just about bowled me right over with that one."

"Old pal," the child said, leaning over his uncle's shoulder and giggling into his face.

"Ellen," Lord Eden said, tousling the boy's hair, "come for a walk?"

She smiled and got to her feet.

"Just don't make her climb any cliffs today, Dominic, please," the countess said, only to look up to find both her husband and her brother-in-law grinning down at her. "Odious pair!"

Caroline had the grace to wait until her uncle was strolling away toward the bridge with Ellen before looking up at her father, smiling that special smile that lit up her whole face, and raising her arms to be picked up.

"Bad little princess," he said, stooping down for her.

"Oh, Edmund—" his wife began, but he held up a staying hand.

"No, Alex," he said. "Absolutely and irrevocably no. I will not interfere. And unless my intuition is quite wide of the mark, I really don't think any interference will be necessary. They are two reasonably sensible adults who have almost worked their way through a problem. If you want a prediction, I would say that we will be hearing an interesting announcement before another week has passed. So forget it. I am not going to do anything."

"How rude you are to interrupt me," she said. "I was merely going to remark that she told me quite openly that the child is Dominic's. And I was about to predict that he is bearing her away to make her an offer. The very idea that I would ask you to interfere in adult affairs!"

Caroline had spotted the ball and wanted to get down again. The earl set her on the grass and turned to smile at his wife.

"It makes one almost envious, does it not?" he said. "Look, Alex, they are turning up the valley. Our valley. We haven't visited our hut since coming home, have we?"

"We have had guests to entertain," she reminded him.

"Soon," he promised her, leaning down, his hands clasped behind his back, to kiss her lingeringly on the lips. "We'll find the time to go up there soon, Alex. Who knows? Perhaps we will start our third child there, as we did our first. Now what are you indignant about?"

"You should not kiss me in public like that," she said, turning pink. "Someone will see."

He raised his eyebrows. "Christopher and Caroline?" he said. "It would be dreadful indeed for them to discover that their papa still fancies their mama at the advanced age of four-and-twenty, would it not? Or is it the servants you are worried about? I imagine they all have the intelligence to have drawn their own conclusions long ago from the fact that we have but one bedchamber between the two of us. Alex, you are poppy red. I really can't resist the urge to discover if there is any brighter color."

He set his hands at her waist and kissed her even more lingeringly.

She made no attempt to fight her way free.

24

"THE BEACH OR THE VALLEY?" LORD EDEN ASKED as they reached the stone bridge across the stream.

"The valley," Ellen said. "It is so very peaceful."

"And the day is very like summer," he said, "despite all the signs of autumn."

He took her hand in his as soon as they were out of sight of his brother and sister-in-law. She did not resist. They walked in companionable silence for a while.

"What has happened with your stepdaughter?" he asked. "You appear to be on reasonably good terms today."

Ellen told him of her morning encounter with Jennifer and of the fact that the girl had made a few stilted attempts at luncheon to address remarks to her, even when it had not been necessary to do so.

"It will take a little time," she said. "But I think our broken relationship can be repaired. I am afraid she has just learned one painful lesson of adulthood—that those adults we have depended upon and loved are also weak and fallible mortals."

"I will have a talk with her," he said, "though she probably does not feel particularly friendly toward me at present. I will assure her that she will always have a home with us."

They walked on.

"At the risk of incurring Alexandra's wrath," he said when they came to the place where they had tethered their horses on another day, "shall we climb up? The view should be lovely on a clear day like this."

They scrambled up the bank and through the trees until they reached the clearing almost at the top of the slope. And they stood side by side, not quite touching, looking back along the valley to the sea.

"I'm glad," Ellen said, "that it all belongs to someone who appreciates it. Your brother does, doesn't he?"

"It is only since I have been away," he said, "that I have stopped thinking of it as my home. I love Amberley. It is my childhood home, and Edmund's home. But for the first time I feel some enthusiasm for going to my own property. It is a lovely place, Ellen, in quite a different way from this. And it is mine. I will be able to establish my family there from the start."

Ellen took a step away and sat down on the grass. Lord Eden joined her there.

"Now that your stepdaughter knows," he said, "there is no further reason for us to delay announcing our betrothal, is there?"

Ellen hugged her knees. "I suppose not," she said.

He laughed softly. "I think it is as plain as the nose on everyone's face anyway," he said.

"Yes."

"I want to set a wedding date, Ellen," he said. "Will this side of Christmas be too soon for you? I thought perhaps we could marry in the chapel beside the house here, with just our families present. Under the circumstances, I don't think it would be appropriate to have a public wedding, would it?"

"Let's talk about it later," she said, turning her face up to the sun and closing her eyes. "Let's just enjoy the day, Dominic."

"And talking about weddings spoils the day?" he said. "Very well, then. Let's enjoy the day." He lay back on the grass and clasped his hands behind his head.

They were silent for a while, and Ellen began to relax in the sunshine that felt almost hot on her face. Had she hurt him, she wondered, by refusing to talk about anything as definite as a wedding date? She would have to talk about it soon. Their betrothal would doubtless be officially announced later that day, and then there would be no avoiding the questions of date and place.

She turned her head to look at him. He was gazing back, his eyes half-closed against the sunlight, his mouth half-smiling.

"Come down here," he said, stretching one arm along the ground.

She lay back, her head on his arm, and closed her eyes. A couple of minutes passed before the light of the sun against her eyelids was blocked out and she felt his mouth on hers, warm and light, his lips slightly parted.

She opened her eyes when the pressure was removed, and looked up into his green eyes. He smiled slowly, and she felt herself smile in response. She did not move.

His tongue explored her lips when his mouth returned to hers, and probed gently between. It was a long and a lazy kiss. Ellen did not move, beyond relaxing her lips and allowing his tongue its will. He felt good. He smelled good. She felt her whole body relax.

She kept her eyes closed when he stopped kissing her

and lay back down beside her again. His hand was caressing her face, his thumb moving lightly over her eyelids and her cheeks. Over her mouth. And the hand moved down to touch her breasts, to trace their outline, to cup their fullness. And down over her waist and abdomen.

"You are losing your waist," he murmured against her ear.

"Yes." She did not open her eyes. She willed the spell not to be broken.

His hand moved over her, touching, exploring, caressing through her clothing. And it felt so very good. She wanted to turn into his arms, to wrap her own about him. But she lay still and seemingly relaxed.

His hand was edging up the skirt of her dress and was finally beneath it, strong and warm against her legs, against her inner thighs. Up over her stomach, over the early swelling of her pregnancy.

She lay still and relaxed, with closed eyes.

And then his mouth was on hers again, light still, but open this time, and his tongue reached deep into her mouth to stroke her slowly and gently. And his hand stripped away undergarments and caressed her unhurriedly, circling and circling the place where he was not ready to touch her yet.

Her hands were flat on the grass beside her.

But she was no longer relaxed. His mouth was at her throat, and his hand was touching her very lightly, and stroking her very lightly in a way that made her throb from the place he touched to her throat.

His hand left her in order to adjust his own clothing. She lay with closed eyes beside him. But she opened them when he spoke to her.

"Come, Ellen," he said softly, and reached across to lift her over him.

She looked into his eyes as he brought her down fully onto him, and then lifted up onto her knees and threw back her head until her face was bathed in the light and warmth of the sun.

And the throbbing turned to a pain and an agony.

And to a tension that was past bearing.

"Dominic!" she called to him.

And to a bursting of ecstasy.

And to a slow, shuddering return to life and happiness and fulfillment.

Strong arms came about her and lowered her to the grass beside him, and held her close. A warm mouth sought out hers and kissed her lingeringly.

"Marriage will not be such a terrible fate, you see," he murmured against her lips.

Her eyes fluttered open and looked into his. But she was in too deep a lethargy to summon a smile. She let herself slip beyond lethargy.

Lord Eden closed his eyes and rested his cheek against the smooth hair on top of her head. He supposed he would sleep. He felt relaxed right down to his toes, and utterly satiated. But he didn't particularly want to sleep. There was just too much physical contentment to be savored.

He had not really intended to make love to her. That had not been his reason for taking her walking or for bringing her up there. He had wanted to be with her, to build on the feeling of friendship that had grown between them since their arrival at Amberley, and to talk to her about their wedding and his plans to take her immediately afterward into Wiltshire.

Even when he had invited her to lie beside him and had

started to kiss her, he had not meant to take the embrace any farther. He had wanted to touch her, to discover the changes in her body that the presence of his child in her was bringing about. He had felt the slight and soft thickening of her waist.

And it had all become suddenly and achingly real to him. She was with child by him. He had known it with his head for some time, had planned a whole lifetime around the fact. But for the first time he felt it with his body. She had taken his seed into her. Their child was gradually swelling her body. The body of the woman he was touching. The woman he loved.

And without any conscious decision on his part, he had started to make love to her, his mouth and his tongue inviting her to physical intimacy, his hand beneath her clothes, against her warm and enticing flesh. And she had made love to him. Though she had not moved or opened her eyes while she was on the ground, and though she had knelt above him, her head thrown back after he had lifted her astride him and joined them, and was thrusting his own need and love into her. She had made love to him too. He had felt her need, her total surrender to him. And she had cried out his name a moment before she had shuddered into release.

He had been right in what he had said to her before she fell asleep. He must convince her of that when she woke up, her defenses firmly in place again. Their marriage would have a chance for success. They were friends. They were good together sexually. He loved her. There was only one ingredient for happiness missing. And that did not have to be disastrous. He would not smother her with his love. He would be content to be her friend day by day, and to pour out his love for her in bed, where perhaps she would not quite recognize it for what it was.

His mind wandered back over the past few months to the disaster that had succeeded Madeline's unexpected arrival in her rooms in Brussels. They had come a long way since that dreadful afternoon. He had much to be thankful for. And a whole lifetime of hope ahead. He was not going to let his mind dwell on the one small source of discontent.

His mind slid into sleep.

ELLEN WAS DISORIENTED for only a moment after she woke up. She was lying against Dominic, her cheek pressed to the lapel of his coat, his one arm beneath her neck, the other hand at her waist. She could tell from his breathing that he was asleep.

Had she become an utter wanton? They were on an open hillside, not quite surrounded by trees, lying asleep in each other's arms. And before they had fallen asleep, they had made love without even a thought to possible discovery. And in a way more erotic than she had ever experienced before.

It was nothing short of scandalous.

It had been wonderful!

She eased her head back to look up into his face, but his eyes opened even as she did so, looked blankly into hers, focused on hers, and smiled in that way that never failed to make her stomach turn a somersault inside her.

"Are you offended?" he asked. "I didn't set out to seduce you, Ellen. It just happened. But you are to be my wife soon anyway." He kissed the tip of her nose.

"Yes," she said.

He drew back his head and looked at her. "Why do your

eyes always turn bleak when I mention our marriage?" he said. "Don't you want to marry me, Ellen? Do you feel coerced?"

She did not answer for a while. "I just wish the baby had not forced it on us," she said.

"Is that what you think?" He frowned. "You think I am marrying you only because of the child?"

"Well, it's true, isn't it?" she said. "And it's the sensible thing to do and the responsible thing to do. And I honor you for being willing to do it, and I am not going to back out, because it would be selfish and irresponsible to do so. I just wish it were not so."

"The baby is not why I am marrying you," he said quietly. "It is just the excuse."

"The excuse?"

"I have been unfair to you, Ellen, and I'm sorry," he said. "I used the argument that I thought would best work with you, and it seems that I have succeeded very well indeed. But it was an argument that came from desperation."

She merely looked at him.

"I didn't think there was any other way of getting you," he said. "But it was not the honorable thing to do. I owed you the truth, especially since I was asking you to be my wife. Married couples should not have any secrets from each other."

"What is the truth?" she asked.

He looked rather shamefaced. "Pure selfishness, I'm afraid," he said. "I love you, and I love the child because it is yours. Ours. I haven't stopped loving you since I discovered you hovering over my bed in Brussels, the only stable being in a world of delirium and pain. In fact, I love you more now than I did then, because we have developed a relationship since then. I'm sorry, Ellen. I know you don't need this when you have just lost Charlie. But I won't burden you with my love, I promise you."

"I did love him," she said carefully. "For those years there was nothing brighter in my life than my feelings for him."

"I know," he said. "I will never make you feel guilty for feeling that way."

"I love him still," she said. "He is a part of me. And I won't ever stop loving him and occasionally crying for him."

"I know, Ellen."

"I will never love you as I loved him," she said.

He nodded.

"But then, I never loved him as I love you."

He looked into her eyes, his expression quite blank.

"I never knew," she said, "that love for two men could be so intense and all-consuming and yet so different. Charlie was my very best friend, my brother, my father, my protector. And, yes, my lover too, for we had a quite normal marriage and I loved the physical part of it because it brought me closer to him than I could be at any other time. I would have been happy with him for the rest of my life, Dominic. I would never have allowed anything more than a vague and unwilling attraction to you."

"I know."

"And you are my consuming passion, my web of love," she said. "I don't think I can ever have enough of you. And yet it is not just physical, either. At one time I thought it was, and that was when I despised and hated myself. But it is not. It is a passion, a hunger, for you, not just for your lovemaking. A hunger to be with you and part of you for a lifetime. I can return your love, Dominic, provided only you accept that a part of me will always be Charlie's."

He laid a finger along the length of her nose. "I would

think the less of you," he said, "if I thought that it might ever be otherwise."

They smiled tentatively at each other.

"So, Ellen Simpson," he said, "do you feel a little better now at the prospect of marrying me?"

She nodded.

"Before Christmas?"

"Tomorrow, if you wish," she said.

"Alas," he said, "there are such things as banns."

"A shame," she said.

"Besides, I have to ride to London, with or without you, to ask the Earl of Harrowby for the hand of his daughter. Do you think he is likely to cut up nasty?"

She smiled slowly at him. "You are going to do that?" she asked. "When I am a widow of five-and-twenty, and perhaps not his daughter anyway? How lovely, Dominic. He will be very pleased."

"Not likely to poke me in the nose because I have caused his daughter to be increasing?" he said.

She shook her head. "I think he will thank you for making it possible for him to become a grandpapa so soon."

"I can have the banns read next Sunday, then?" he asked.

She nodded.

He sat up suddenly and got to his feet. He reached down a hand for hers.

"How indisposed is your condition making you feel?" he asked, pulling her up beside him.

"Not at all," she said. "I have never felt healthier in my life."

"Good," he said, stooping to wrap his arms firmly about her waist and lifting her from the ground to twirl her around and around until she was shrieking with laughter.

"It is so good to hear you laugh, Ellen," he said as he

came to a stop and set her feet back on the ground. "I am going to try to fill your life with laughter."

"I wonder if the world will ever stop spinning wildly about me for as long as I am with you," she said breathlessly.

"Absolutely not, my love," he said against her mouth, before deepening the kiss. "I make you a solemn promise here and now that it never will."

"Then good-bye equilibrium and sanity," she said, wrapping her arms up about his neck. "My love."

About the Author

MARY BALOGH is the *New York Times* bestselling author of *Simply Magic, Simply Love, Simply Unforgettable* and the acclaimed Slightly novels: *Slightly Married, Slightly Wicked, Slightly Scandalous, Slightly Tempted, Slightly Sinful,* and *Slightly Dangerous,* as well as the romances *No Man's Mistress, More Than a Mistress, A Summer to Remember,* and *One Night for Love.* A former teacher, she grew up in Wales and now lives in Canada.

Read on for a sneak peek
at the next enchanting novel in
Mary Balogh's series
featuring the teachers at
Miss Martin's School for Girls.

Simply Perfect

CLAUDIA MARTIN'S STORY

Coming in spring 2008
from Delacorte Press

Simply Perfect

on sale spring 2008

CLAUDIA MARTIN HAD ALREADY HAD A HARD day at school.

First Mademoiselle Pierre, one of the nonresident teachers, had sent a messenger just before breakfast with the news that she was indisposed with a migraine headache and would be unable to come to school. Claudia, as both owner and headmistress, had been obliged to conduct most of the French and music classes in addition to her own subjects. French was no great problem; music was more of a challenge. Worse, the account books, which she had intended to bring up-to-date during her spare classes today, remained undone, with days fast running out in which to get accomplished all the myriad tasks that needed doing.

Then just before the noonday meal, when classes were over for the morning and discipline was at its slackest, Paula Hern had decided that she objected to the way Molly Wiggins *looked* at her, and voiced her displeasure publicly and eloquently. And since Paula's father was a successful businessman and as rich as Croesus and Paula put on airs accordingly, while Molly was the youngest—and most timid—of the charity girls and did not even know who her father was, then *of course* Agnes Ryde had felt obliged to jump into the fray in vigorous defense of the downtrodden, her Cockney accent returning with ear-jarring clarity. Claudia had been forced to deal with the matter and extract more-or-less sincere apologies from all sides and mete out suitable punishments to all except the more-or-less innocent Molly.

Then, an hour later, just when Miss Walton had been about to step outdoors with the junior class en route to Bath Abbey, where she had intended to give an informal lesson in art and architecture, the heavens had opened in a downpour to end downpours and there had been all the fuss of finding the girls somewhere else to go within the school and something else to do. Not that that had been Claudia's problem, but she *had* been made annoyingly aware of the girls' loud disappointment beyond her class-room door as she struggled to teach French irregular verbs. She had finally gone out there to inform them that if they had any complaint about the untimely arrival of the rain, then they must take it up privately with God during their evening prayers but that in the meantime they would be *silent* until Miss Walton had closed a classroom door behind them.

Then, just after classes were finished for the afternoon and the girls had gone upstairs to comb their hair and wash their hands for tea, something had gone wrong with the doorknob on one of the dormitories, and eight of the girls, trapped inside until Mr. Keeble, the elderly school porter, had creaked his way up there to release them before mending the knob, had screeched and giggled and rattled the door. Miss Thompson had dealt with the crisis by reading them a lecture on patience and decorum, though circumstances had forced her to speak in a voice that could be heard from within—and therefore through much of the rest of the school too, including Claudia's office.

It had *not* been the best of days, as Claudia had just been remarking—without contradiction—to Eleanor Thompson and Lila Walton over tea in her private sitting room a short while after the prisoners had been freed. She could do with far fewer such days.

And yet now!

Now, to cap everything off and make an already trying day more so, there was a marquess awaiting her pleasure in the visitors' parlor downstairs.

A *marquess,* for the love of all that was wonderful!

That was what the silver-edged visiting card she held between two fingers said—the *Marquess of Attingsborough.* The porter had just delivered it into her hands, looking sour and disapproving as he did so—not an unusual expression for him, especially when any male who was not a teacher invaded his domain.

"A *marquess,*" she said, looking up from the card to frown at her fellow teachers. "Whatever can he want? Did he say, Mr. Keeble?"

"He did not say and I did not ask, miss," the porter replied. "But if you was to ask me, he is up to no good. He *smiled* at me."

"Ha! A cardinal sin indeed," Claudia said dryly while Eleanor laughed.

"Perhaps," Lila suggested, "he has a daughter he wishes to place at the school."

"A *marquess*?" Claudia raised her eyebrows and Lila looked suitably quelled.

"Perhaps, Claudia," Eleanor said, a twinkle in her eye, "he has *two* daughters."

Claudia snorted and then sighed, took one more sip of her tea, and got reluctantly to her feet.

"I suppose I had better go and see what he wants," she said. "It will be more productive than sitting here guessing. But of all things to happen, today of all days. A *marquess*."

Eleanor laughed again. "Poor man," she said. "I pity him."

Claudia had never had much use for the aristocracy—idle, arrogant, coldhearted, nasty lot—though the marriage of two of her teachers and closest friends to titled gentlemen had forced her to admit during the past few years that perhaps *some* of them might be agreeable and even worthy individuals. But it did not amuse her to have one of their number, a stranger, intrude into her own world without a by-your-leave, especially at the end of a difficult day.

She did not believe for a single moment that this marquess wished to place any daughter of his at her school.

She preceded Mr. Keeble down the stairs, since she did not wish to move at his slow pace. She ought, she supposed, to have gone into her bedchamber first to see that she was looking respectable, which she was quite possibly not doing after a hard day at school. She usually made sure that she presented a neat appearance to visitors. But she scorned to make such an effort for a *marquess* and risk appearing obsequious in her own eyes.

By the time she opened the door into the visitors' parlor, she was bristling with a quite unjustified indignation. How dared he come here to disturb her on her own property, whatever his business might be?

She looked down at the visiting card still in her hand.

"The Marquess of Attingsborough?" she said in a voice not unlike the one she had used on Paula Hern earlier in the day—the one that said she was not going to be at all impressed by any pretension of grandeur.

"At your service, ma'am. Miss Martin, I presume?" He

was standing across the room, close to the window. He bowed elegantly.

Claudia's indignation soared. One steady glance at him was not sufficient upon which to make any informed judgment of his character, of course, but, *really*, if the man had any imperfection of form or feature or taste in apparel, it was by no means apparent. He was tall, and broad of shoulder and chest, and slim of waist and hips. His legs were long and well shaped. His hair was dark and thick and shining, his face handsome, his eyes and mouth good-humored. He was dressed with impeccable elegance but without a trace of ostentation. His Hessian boots alone were probably worth a fortune, and Claudia guessed that if she were to stand directly over them and look down, she would see her own face reflected in them—and probably her flat, untidy hair and limp dress collar as well.

She clasped her hands at her waist lest she test her theory by touching the collar points. She held his card pinched between one thumb and forefinger.

"What may I do for you, sir?" she asked, deliberately avoiding calling him *my lord*—a ridiculous affectation, in her opinion.

He smiled at her, and if perfection could be improved upon, it had just happened—he had good teeth. Claudia steeled herself to resist the charm she was sure he possessed in aces.

"I come as a messenger, ma'am," he said, "from Lady Whitleaf."

He reached into an inner pocket of his coat and withdrew a sealed paper.

"From Susanna?" Claudia took one step farther into the room.

Susanna Osbourne had been a teacher at the school until her marriage last year to Viscount Whitleaf. Claudia had always rejoiced at Susanna's good fortune in making both an eligible marriage and a love match, and yet she still mourned her own loss of a dear friend and colleague *and* good teacher. She had lost three such friends—all in the same cause—over the course of four years. Sometimes it was hard not to be selfishly depressed by it all.

"When she knew I was coming to Bath to spend a few days with my mother and my father, who is taking the waters," the marquess said, "she asked me to call here and pay my respects to you. And she gave me this letter, perhaps to convince you that I am no impostor."

His eyes smiled again as he came across the room and placed the letter in her hand. And, as if at least his eyes could not have been mud-colored or something equally nondescript, she could see that they were a clear blue, almost like a summer sky.

Susanna had asked him to come and pay his respects? *Why?*

"Whitleaf is the cousin of a cousin of mine," the marquess explained. "Or an *almost* cousin of mine, anyway. It is complicated, as family relationships often are. Lauren Butler, Viscountess Ravensberg, is a cousin by virtue of the fact that her mother married my aunt's brother-in-law. We have been close since childhood. And Whitleaf is Lauren's first cousin. And so in a sense both he and his lady have a strong familial claim on me."

If he was a marquess, Claudia thought with sudden suspicion, and his father was still alive, *what did that make his father?* But he was here at Susanna's behest and it behooved her to be a little better than just icily polite.

"Thank you," she said, "for coming in person to deliver the letter. I am much obliged to you, sir. May I offer you a cup of tea?" She willed him to say no.

"I will not put you to that trouble, ma'am," he said, smiling again. "I understand you are to leave for London in two days' time?"

Ah. Susanna must have told him that. Mr. Hatchard, her man of business in London, had found employment for two of her senior girls, both charity pupils, but he had been unusually evasive about the identity of the prospective employers, even when she had asked quite specifically in her last letter to him. The paying girls at the school had families to look after their interests, of course. Claudia had appointed herself family to the rest and never released any girl who had no employment to which to go or any about whose expected employment she felt any strong misgiving.

At Eleanor's suggestion, Claudia was going to go to London with Flora Bains and Edna Wood so that she could find out exactly where they were to be placed as governesses, and withdraw her consent if she was not satisfied. There were still a few weeks of the school year left, but Eleanor had assured her that she was perfectly willing and able to take charge of affairs during Claudia's absence, which would surely be no longer than a week or ten days. Claudia had agreed to go, partly because there was another matter upon which she wished to speak with Mr. Hatchard in person.

"I am," she told the marquess.

"Whiteleaf intended to send a carriage for your convenience," the marquess told her, "but I was able to inform him that it would be quite unnecessary to put himself to the trouble."

"Of course it would," Claudia agreed. "I have already hired a carriage."

"I will see about *un*-hiring it for you, if I may be permitted, ma'am," he said. "I plan to return to town on the same day and will be pleased to offer you the comfort of my own carriage and my protection for the journey."

Oh, goodness, heaven forbid!

"That will be quite unnecessary, sir," she said firmly. "I have already made the arrangements."

"Hired carriages are notorious for their lack of springs and all other comforts," he said. "I beg you will reconsider."

"Perhaps you do not fully understand, sir," she said. "I am to be accompanied by two schoolgirls on the journey."

"Yes," he said, "so Lady Whitleaf informed me. Do they prattle? Or, worse, do they giggle? Very young ladies have an atrocious tendency to do both."

"My girls are taught how to behave appropriately in company, Lord Attingsborough," she said stiffly. Too late she saw the twinkle in his eyes and understood that he had been joking.

"I do not doubt it, ma'am," he said, "and feel quite confident in trusting your word. Allow me, if you will, to escort all three of you ladies to Lady Whitleaf's door. She will be vastly impressed with my gallantry and will be bound to spread the word among my family and friends."

Now he was talking utter nonsense. But how could she decently refuse? She desperately searched around in her head for some irrefutable argument that would dissuade him. Nothing came to mind, however, that did not seem ungracious, even downright rude. But she would rather travel a thousand miles in a springless carriage than to London in his company.

Why?

Was she overawed by his title and magnificence? She bristled at the very idea.

At his . . . *maleness,* then? She was uncomfortably aware that he possessed that in abundance.

But how ridiculous that would be. He was simply a gentleman offering a courtesy to an aging spinster, who happened to be a friend of his almost-cousin's cousin's wife—goodness, it *was* a tenuous connection. But she held a letter from Susanna in her hand. Susanna obviously trusted him.

An *aging spinster*? When it came to any consideration of age, she thought, there was probably not much difference between the two of them. Now *there* was a thought. Here was this man, obviously at the very pinnacle of his masculine appeal in his middle thirties, and then there was she.

He was looking at her with raised eyebrows and smiling eyes.

"Oh, very well," she said briskly. "But you may live to regret your offer."

His smile broadened and it seemed to an indignant Claudia that there was no end to this man's appeal. As she had suspected, he had charm oozing from every pore and was therefore *not* to be trusted one inch farther than she could see him. She would keep a *very* careful eye upon her two girls during the journey to London.

"I do hope not, ma'am," he said. "Shall we make an early start?"

"It is what I intended," she told him. She added grudgingly, "Thank you, Lord Attingsborough. You are most kind."

"It will be my pleasure, Miss Martin." He bowed deeply again. "May I ask a small favor in return? May I be given a tour of the school? I must confess that the idea of an institution that actually provides an *education* to girls fascinates me. Lady Whitleaf has spoken with enthusiasm about your establishment. She taught here, I understand."

Claudia drew a slow, deep breath through flared nostrils. Whatever reason could this man have for touring a girls' school except idle curiosity—or worse? Her instinct was to say a very firm no. But she had just accepted a favor from him, and it was admittedly a large one—she did not doubt that his carriage would be far more comfortable than the one she had hired or that they would be treated with greater respect at every toll gate they passed and at every inn where they stopped for a change of horses. And he was a friend of Susanna's.

But really!

She had not thought her day could possibly get any worse. She had been wrong.

"Certainly. I will show you around myself," she said curtly, turning to the door. She would have opened it herself, but he reached around her, engulfing her for a startled moment in the scent of some enticing and doubtless indecently expensive male cologne, opened the door, and indicated with a smile that she should precede him into the hall.

At least, she thought, classes were over for the day and all the girls would be safely in the dining hall, having tea.

She was wrong about that, of course, she remembered as soon as she opened the door into the art room. The final assembly of the school year was not far off and all sorts of preparations and rehearsals were in progress, as they had been every day for the past week or so.

A few of the girls were working with Mr. Upton on the stage backdrop. They all turned to see who had come in and then proceeded to gawk at the grand visitor. Claudia was obliged to introduce the two men. They shook hands, and the marquess strolled closer to inspect the artwork and ask a few intelligent questions. Mr. Upton beamed at him when he left the room with her a few minutes later, and all the girls gazed worshipfully after him.

And then in the music room they came upon the madrigal choir, which was practicing, in the absence of Mademoiselle Pierre, under the supervision of Miss Wilding.

They hit an ear-shattering discord at full volume just as Claudia opened the door, and then they dissolved into self-conscious giggles while Miss Wilding blushed and looked dismayed.

Claudia, raising her eyebrows, introduced the teacher to the marquess and explained that the regular choirmistress was indisposed today. Though even as she spoke she was annoyed with herself for feeling that any explanation was necessary.

"Madrigal singing," he said, smiling at the girls, "can be the most satisfying but the most frustrating thing, can it not? There is perhaps one other person out of the group singing the same part as oneself and six or eight others all bellowing out something quite different. If one's lone ally falters one is lost without hope of recovery. I never mastered the art when I was at school, I must confess. During my very first practice someone suggested to me that I try out for the cricket team—which just happened to practice at the same time."

The girls laughed, and all of them visibly relaxed.

"I will wager," he said, "that there is something in your repertoire that you can sing to perfection. May I be honored to hear it?" He turned his smile upon Miss Wilding.

" 'The Cuckoo,' miss," Sylvia Hetheridge suggested to a murmur of approval from the rest of the group.

And they sang in five parts without once faltering or hitting a sour note, a glorious shower of "cuckoos" echoing about the room every time they reached the chorus of the song.

When they were finished, they all turned as one to the Marquess of Attingsborough, just as if he were visiting royalty, and he applauded and smiled.

"Bravo!" he said. "Your skill overwhelms me, not to

mention the loveliness of your voices. I am more than ever convinced that I was wise to stick to cricket."

The girls were all laughing and gazing worshipfully after him when he left with Claudia.

Mr. Huckerby was in the dancing hall, putting a group of girls through their paces in a particularly intricate dance that they would perform during the assembly. The marquess shook his hand and smiled at the girls and admired their performance and charmed them all until they were all smiling and—of course—*gazing worshipfully at him.*

He asked intelligent and perceptive questions of Claudia as she showed him some of the empty classrooms and the library. He was in no hurry as he looked about each room and read the titles on the spines of many of the books.

"There was a pianoforte in the music room," he said as they made their way to the sewing room, "and other instruments too. I noticed a violin and a flute in particular. Do you offer individual music lessons here, Miss Martin?"

"Indeed we do," she said. "We offer everything necessary to make accomplished young ladies of our pupils, as well as persons with a sound academic education."

He looked around the sewing room from just inside the door but did not walk farther into it.

"And do you teach other skills here in addition to sewing and embroidery?" he asked. "Knitting, perhaps? Tatting? Crochet?"

"All three," she said as he closed the door and she led the way to the assembly hall. It had been a ballroom once upon a time, when the building was a private home.

"It is a pleasingly designed room," he said, standing in the middle of the gleaming wood floor and turning all about before looking up at the high, coved ceiling. "Indeed, I like the whole school, Miss Martin. There are windows and light everywhere and a pleasant atmosphere. Thank you for giving me a guided tour."

He turned his most charming smile on her, and Claudia, still holding both his visiting card and Susanna's letter, clasped her free hand about her wrist and looked back with deliberate severity.

"I am delighted you approve," she said.

His smile was arrested for a moment until he chuckled softly.

"I do beg your pardon," he said. "I have taken enough of your time."

He indicated the door with one arm, and Claudia led the way back to the entrance hall, feeling—and resenting the feeling—that she had somehow been unmannerly, for those last words she had spoken had been meant ironically and he had known it.

But before they reached the hall they were forced to pause for a few moments while the junior class filed out of the dining hall in good order, on their way from tea to study hall, where they would catch up on any work not completed during the day or else read or write letters or stitch at some needlework.

They all turned their heads to gaze at the grand visitor, and the Marquess of Attingsborough smiled genially back at them, setting them all to giggling and preening as they hurried along.

All of which went to prove, Claudia thought, that even eleven- and twelve-year-olds could not resist the charms of a handsome man. It boded ill—or *continued* to bode ill—for the future of the female half of the human race.

Mr. Keeble, frowning ferociously, bless his heart, was holding the marquess's hat and cane and was standing close to the front door as if to dare the visitor to try prolonging his visit further.

"I will see you early two mornings from now, then, Miss Martin?" the marquess said, taking his hat and cane and turning to her as Mr. Keeble opened the door and stood to one side, ready to close it behind him at the earliest opportunity.

"We will be ready."